ARROGANT MONSTER

VLASOV BRATVA
BOOK 1

NICOLE FOX

Copyright © 2022 by Nicole Fox

All rights reserved.

No part of this book may be reproduced in any form or by any electronic or mechanical means, including information storage and retrieval systems, without written permission from the author, except for the use of brief quotations in a book review.

❦ Created with Vellum

MAILING LIST

Sign up to my mailing list!
New subscribers receive a FREE steamy bad boy romance novel.

Click the link below to join.
https://sendfox.com/nicolefox

ALSO BY NICOLE FOX

Zhukova Bratva

Tarnished Tyrant

Tarnished Queen

Stepanov Bratva

Satin Sinner

Satin Princess

Makarova Bratva

Shattered Altar

Shattered Cradle

Solovev Bratva

Ravaged Crown

Ravaged Throne

Vorobev Bratva

Velvet Devil

Velvet Angel

Romanoff Bratva

Immaculate Deception

Immaculate Corruption

Kovalyov Bratva

Gilded Cage

Gilded Tears

Jaded Soul

Jaded Devil

Ripped Veil

Ripped Lace

Mazzeo Mafia Duet

Liar's Lullaby (Book 1)

Sinner's Lullaby (Book 2)

Bratva Crime Syndicate

Can be read in any order!

Lies He Told Me

Scars He Gave Me

Sins He Taught Me

Belluci Mafia Trilogy

Corrupted Angel (Book 1)

Corrupted Queen (Book 2)

Corrupted Empire (Book 3)

De Maggio Mafia Duet

Devil in a Suit (Book 1)

Devil at the Altar (Book 2)

Kornilov Bratva Duet

Married to the Don (Book 1)

Til Death Do Us Part (Book 2)

Heirs to the Bratva Empire

Can be read in any order!

Kostya

Maksim

Andrei

Princes of Ravenlake Academy (Bully Romance)

Can be read as standalones!

Cruel Prep

Cruel Academy

Cruel Elite

Tsezar Bratva

Nightfall (Book 1)

Daybreak (Book 2)

Russian Crime Brotherhood

Can be read in any order!

Owned by the Mob Boss

Unprotected with the Mob Boss

Knocked Up by the Mob Boss

Sold to the Mob Boss

Stolen by the Mob Boss

Trapped with the Mob Boss

Volkov Bratva

Broken Vows (Book 1)

Broken Hope (Book 2)

Broken Sins *(standalone)*

Other Standalones

Vin: A Mafia Romance

Box Sets

Bratva Mob Bosses (Russian Crime Brotherhood Books 1-6)

Tsezar Bratva (Tsezar Bratva Duet Books 1-2)

Heirs to the Bratva Empire

The Mafia Dons Collection

The Don's Corruption

ARROGANT MONSTER
VLASOV BRATVA BOOK 1

How did I end up playing fake fiancée to a runaway criminal?

Well, let me start on the day of my wedding.

I was supposed to get married today—but that's a whole 'nother story.

The part that matters is that I took the car and ran, still in my wedding dress.

I promptly crash said car into a bridge, and when I get out to check the damage…

I trip and fall right into the river below.

That should've been it for little old me.

Goodnight. Close the curtains. Roll the credits.

Drowned by my own wedding dress—how morbidly appropriate.

But then someone saves me.

Not just any someone, but the most gorgeous someone I've ever seen.

As it turns out, though, my someone isn't just a random Good Samaritan.

He's a fugitive on the run.

And he wants me to be his alibi.

That's how I wind up lying to the cops, posing as newlyweds—Mr. and Mrs. Someone, on our way to happily-ever-after.

That's how I wind up spending the night in the woods with an escaped convict.

And then, in the morning…

He's gone.

Or so I thought.

But ten years later, there he is again: my husband for a night.

And—although he doesn't know it yet…

The father of my baby.

***Arrogant Monster* is Book 1 of the Vlasov Bratva duet. The story continues in Book 2, *Arrogant Mistake*.**

1

KINSLEY

I'm learning something new today: running from your wedding is *hard*.

The movies always make it look easy. Carefree, slow motion, big dramatic music swelling in the background. But in reality, it's none of that. It's messy. It's ugly. It's hard.

It's hard to sprint down the steps of the place you were supposed to exchange vows with your partner for life.

It's hard to climb into the honeymoon car you were supposed to share with him as you drove off to start your new lives together.

It's hard—because of your heels and your skirts—to reach the gas pedal to put as much distance between you and him as possible, and it's hard to see the road through your veil of tears, and it's hard to find the tissues in the glove box to wipe off the blood and sweat and running makeup from your face so you don't stain the white lace that once held so much hope for you and now holds nothing but nightmares.

But this runaway bride didn't have a choice.

So I ran down the steps.

I got in the car.

And I drove.

Now, I'm chewing up highway. One hundred, one ten, one hundred twenty miles per hour. The lines on the asphalt blur behind fresh tears.

When I glance in the mirror, I cringe. The woman looking back at me is horrifying.

Black eyeliner and red rouge streak my cheeks like war paint, mixed in with the crumbling grit of my foundation. My hair is falling from its intricate braids and frizzing around my head in some twisted kind of halo.

It's tough not to hate myself for ending up here. If I'd been a little more self-aware, just a little bit sooner, I wouldn't be hurtling down this lonely stretch of road, looking back over my shoulder every few seconds. All this could have been avoided. If only I'd—

Another long honk and the blinding flash of oncoming headlights force my attention back in front of me. My hands are shaking on the wheel. This is the third time in as many minutes that someone's had to remind me that I'm driving and I need to be paying attention. Eyes forward, not back.

But I can't stop checking my rearview mirror. If I slow down, there's a possibility he can catch up.

And if he catches up…

Once this last car passes, the highway goes back to looking deserted. Dusk is coming soon. There's nothing but pine trees and tall elms on either side. Road ahead and road behind. Nothing living and breathing except for the last gasps of the roadkill piled up on the shoulder, every bit as black and red and bruised as I am.

There's probably a very poignant metaphor in there somewhere, but I'm too trauma-struck to get it.

BRRRING. My phone starts screeching, and I jump in my seat. I glance at the screen on instinct, but I already know who it is. Even the thought of answering his call is making my stomach turn.

When I turn my eyes back up to the windshield, I realize I'm once again drifting onto the opposite side of the road. There's no oncoming traffic, but there is a bridge ahead. I'm currently on course to smash right into the steel I-beams supporting it.

I gasp, slam the brakes, and swerve hard to the right.

Too hard.

As I'm whipping hand over hand to correct course, my bracelet gets caught in the folds of my skirts. The wheel spins out of control. Tires scream. Engines scream. I scream.

I see the side of the bridge looming like a monster in a dream. The screech of the brakes feels like it's coming from inside me, and the stench of burning rubber smells like something out of hell itself.

This is it, I think. *This is how this whole stupid day ends. It's almost fitting.*

There's a crunch of metal and the tortured scream of the smoking wheels. But by some miracle, the car stops.

I'm okay.

After all that noise, it's eerie how fast it gets silent. The forest on either side swallows up every drop of sound.

"Shit," I whisper into all that silence. "Shit. Shit. Shit."

I close my eyes and rest my forehead on the steering wheel, though even that little contact stings and aches. *Just breathe, Kinsley,* I coach myself. *Everything is going to be fine if you can just—*

BRRRING! BRRRING!

I grab my phone as it starts going off again and slam it hard against the dashboard. It bounces off and lands right back where it was in the passenger's seat, a little latticework of cracks spreading across the front.

But at least it stops screaming at me. Thank God for small mercies.

I lean back in my seat and sob until I can't inhale. I've moved from *Just breathe* to *Just cry* and I'm about to step up to *Just curl into a little ball and die* when I decide that one more second spent in this car is a second too long.

I push open the door and step out onto the cracked tarmac of the bridge, pulling my train of fabric along with me.

Outside, I suck in huge gusts of air, but it doesn't really help. Nothing helps, nothing reduces the weight of this concrete slab of shame on my chest, and nothing seems to erase those last few moments from my mind. The moments that made me run from my own happily-ever-after.

The shattering glass.

The wild fury in his eyes.

I hear something from beyond the bridge, somewhere out in the thicket of trees, and I get the feeling that whatever made that noise is staring back at me. Paranoia, I tell myself. Just my mind conjuring up irrational fears.

There's no one else here. Just sky and bridge and the river coursing twelve feet below.

I look over the edge. The water looks calm from where I'm standing. But the rush of the current tips me off to the forces surging beneath its surface.

The echoes in my head are still reverberating. *You dumb bitch!* he'd screamed. *Why the fuck can't you smile on your fucking wedding day?*

I tried. I really did. But I was never very good at playing pretend. That was more of my parents' game, not mine.

I dig my fingers into the front folds of the bodice, but it doesn't alleviate the pressure there. It's too damn tight. There's too much fabric. I feel like the dress is trying to swallow me whole.

Dizziness ripples through my vision for a moment, and the water seems to twist into a whirlpool.

Step back, Kinsley. You're too close to the edge.

I do step back. At least, I think I do. But somewhere along the way, I mess that up, too—*Can't you do anything right, you stupid whore?!*—and I guess I trip or stumble or something, I'm not sure, it all happens so fast, but then I feel the scream of wind in my face, and I know I'm falling, falling, falling.

A second later, I feel the cold embrace of the river.

When I open my mouth to scream, water rushes in. The currents I suspected from above are here now and they're real and they're strong. They grab hold of my dress and drag me down.

This can't be how it ends, I think miserably to myself. *I was supposed to have a better life than she did.*

I kick my legs out beneath me, but they just get entangled in the thick, unforgiving fabric of my skirt. The dress is weighing me down. It's pulling me under. How morbidly fitting—killed by my own wedding dress. What a way to go.

I see my mother taking shape in the murky underworld of the water, or maybe it's just my oxygen-starved brain playing tricks on me. It doesn't really matter whether it's real or a hallucination, though, because my reaction would be the same either way.

No. Hell no.

I kick up as hard as I can, and I'll be damned, I break through the surface. I suck in one huge, gasping breath. It's the sweetest air I've ever tasted.

Then the frigid fingers of the river lock around my ankle and reel me back down.

My dress is too heavy now that it's soaked with water, and the river is too deep and too rapid. It's getting harder to kick, to move, to fight.

Most of all, it's getting harder to care.

I see another mirage take shape in front of me. Now, I'm sure I'm hallucinating, because it's a man who's way too gorgeous to be real. Dark hair flows around the sharp lines of his face. He reaches for me and my eyes close. The sharp pain is still there, but I'm not worried anymore. He's got me.

And then we're kicking up together, and there's air again, and I'm throwing up water and my eyes sting with tears.

2

KINSLEY

Dying, as far as I can tell, really sucks. Not that I'd expected to fade gracefully away on a bed of roses or anything quite that fairy-tale-esque. But shouldn't there be at least a little bit more dignity involved? Puking your guts out with dirt caked beneath your fingernails hardly seems like the way to go.

"Get it all out."

I can feel something at my back. A strong hand holding me upright while more murky river water spews out of me. When I stop hacking up fluid, I glance to the side.

The man is crouched next to me, eyes furrowed in a permanent brood. There's something about his gaze that keeps me still, and it's not just the intense cobalt blue of his irises, glowing like they're lit from within.

It's an unblinking confidence, bordering on arrogance. It's a look that says, *Stay there.* I obey without thinking.

"Are you alright?" he asks in a voice that's deep, gravelly, harsh. It's as if he hasn't spoken in weeks and he dislikes the sound of his own words.

"The car…" I whisper, looking up at the bridge overhead. I can see the headlights slicing through the shadows, and when the wind blows, I hear the clink and rustle of the cans that my best friend Emma tied to the back, right underneath the hand-painted banner that says *Just Married*.

"The car is fine. You, not so much."

"I'm fine," I say breathlessly. But it's force of habit. Repeat a lie to yourself long enough and it starts to feel true. Either that or you just get too numb to keep seeing the difference.

"Are you, though?"

"I… I don't know how I am," I stammer.

I sound weak. I sound like the very thing I swore I would never become: a victim.

The man's eyes run over my body. I haven't gotten to the part yet where I ask him where the hell he came from and what on earth he's doing in the middle of an unremarkable stretch of woods on the outskirts of Hartford, Connecticut. He could be a vicious axe murderer, an alien, a mirage. Maybe all three.

But there's nothing in those blue eyes but curiosity. It's a removed kind of curiosity, though. His gaze doesn't make me feel uncomfortable. Not the way I've felt when other men look at me, at least. Like I'm a prize to be claimed. A meal to be eaten. Like I'm no better than a means to an end.

"You need to breathe," he observes suddenly.

Or maybe it's not sudden at all. But it feels like everything from the last few hours has been happening in horrifying slow motion, and it's just now catching up to normal speed again. The effect is like being abruptly slapped in the face.

I blink. "What?"

He leans a little closer. His eyes really are extraordinary. It's such a pure shade of blue. Nothing to muddy it. Just open sky, deep ocean, the very heart of a sapphire.

"You need to breathe," he says again.

There's a snap in his voice that carries natural command. But it's not unkind. Though I suspect it would only take a little effort on his part to change that.

"You're in shock. Open your mouth."

I frown. "What?"

He repeats it again. I watch his lips move in a sort of haunted detachment. I'm floating above all this, watching it happen from afar.

"Open," he says, raising his finger to my lips, "Your. Mouth."

The moment his fingertip touches my bottom lip, my mouth parts. It feels as though he's put a spell on me. I don't remember deciding to listen to him. I just *do*.

"Good girl. Now, breathe," he murmurs.

Air fills my lungs. I feel my chest expand and the world rush in with it. I can smell the woodsy scents of earth and musk and asphalt and animal.

Oh, sweet, sweet baby Jesus, I can breathe.

He drops his finger to his side. I feel a spark of disappointment at the absence of his touch, which doesn't make the slightest bit of sense.

"Who are you?" I ask quietly.

"I think the bloodstained woman in the wet wedding dress should answer that question first."

I frown, wondering for one wild moment what the hell he's talking about. Then I look down and see the cascades of flowing white silk. Now with a generous layer of river dirt caked into the bottom hemline.

Shattering glass.

Wild fury in his eyes.

The memory lunges at me out of nowhere. I try to back away from it in my head, but Tom's furious eyes keep getting bigger and bigger and the sound of shattering glass keeps getting louder and louder.

I force myself to my feet, determined not to lie in the dirt forever. That would just be confirmation of what I suspect I've always been: a broken thing. But as I try to get to my feet, I stumble.

"Careful there."

The man moves faster than I thought possible, grabs my arm, and just like that, I'm not stumbling anymore.

Just like that, he's holding me.

Just like that, I'm doomed.

He pulls me upright. There's no distance between us now. No foot of space to keep me comfortable. There's just my body against his and his eyes looking into mine.

When was the last time a man held me like this? Tom had, when we first started dating. But his body felt different. Insubstantial, in a weird sort of way. This man is made of muscle. Of presence. He radiates strength.

The way he holds me is different, too. Tom had been looking for something every time he touched me. This man is asking for nothing.

Instead, he's giving me everything I never knew I needed.

"I'm Kinsley," I say.

"Pleasure's all mine, Kinsley."

"Do you have a name?"

"Everyone has a name."

I frown. "That's not an answer."

He doesn't smile. And I can understand why. His features are uniquely suited to broodiness. His nose is so straight, I want to place my finger at the top and run it down the bridge.

"You're hurt," he observes.

He lifts his hand again. This time, he brushes the backs of his fingers against my right cheek. All I can feel is a tingly warmth spreading across my face.

"Someone hit you," he says again in that voice that sounds like rocks on steel. "It left a mark."

Whatever spell he had me under, it breaks against those words. I recoil from him, and he drops his hands instantly. As if to prove that he was touching me because I needed the support, not because he actually wanted to do it.

My heart leaps into my throat. I feel trapped and skittish, like it only just occurred to me that nothing that has happened today feels real and I need to get the hell out of Dodge so I can wake up from this nightmare.

"No one hit me," I say automatically.

I have no idea why I'm denying it. But I do know it's not about protecting Tom. Maybe it's about protecting myself.

People used to look at my mother the way this man is looking at me, and I always despised it. I swore I'd be different, and even though fate has dragged me right back into the exact same place she suffered in, I'm still stubbornly defiant. *Not me!* I'm screaming at the universe. *You won't do to me what you did to her!*

"No one hit me."

"You already said that." Just like that, his tone shifts. It turns dark, fierce. It fractures into a dozen different pieces, and every single one of those shards is aimed right at vulnerable old me.

"I... I fell," I stammer stupidly.

His expression doesn't change. I don't know why I feel the need to explain anything to this man. He's a stranger. A stranger who walked out of the woods like some apparition from a dream. But his eyes demand explanation, and God help me, I'm giving it to him.

"I was... walking down the stairs," I continue. "And I tripped. I fell."

I glance down, my face burning scarlet red. I can see him at the edge of my vision still gazing at me impassively.

"Anyway," I add, "I have to go."

"Late for a wedding?" he asks, deadpan.

It takes me a long moment to realize he's making a joke. It then occurs to me—way, way too late—that this whole interaction is bizarre beyond words. "Where did you come from? Were you... camping, or something?"

He shakes his head, but offers me nothing else.

"You never told me your name," I remind him.

"No, I didn't." He glances up towards the bridge. "I'm going to go take a look at your car. See if it's repairable."

He starts hiking up the sloped, rocky curve that leads to the bridge. I hesitate for only a second before I start to follow. My dress is so heavy that it takes all my energy to keep moving, and the muddy ground does me no favors. By the time I reach the car, he's already shutting the hood.

"It'll drive. No lasting damage." He chooses his words carefully, as though there's only a finite amount left and he doesn't want to use them all up in one go.

"So... I can get in and go?"

He glances towards me. "Are you asking permission?"

I laugh bitterly. "No. Just, sometimes, I think my life would be easier if someone just told me what to do and how to do it."

I wait for him to look at me as though I'm insane—more likely concussed, but insane would also work as a plausible explanation—but his expression doesn't change.

"That... that was a strange thing to say... wasn't it?" I mumble awkwardly.

"If it's how you feel, it's not strange."

"No one ever says how they really feel. Not to a complete stranger."

"Maybe they should start."

I try looking at him the way he's looking at me. Unblinkingly. Unapologetically. The eye contact intensifies, but I still refuse to break it.

The sirens do that for me.

I gasp when the first wail sings through the air. I turn my gaze out towards the empty road behind us. "Ambulance," I guess.

He shakes his head. "No. Police."

He nods once, crisply as if reaching a decision, then opens the passenger side door and gestures for me to get in.

"Time to go," he says casually.

I look at the passenger seat and then back at him. "You're driving?"

"Yes. You're in no fit state to drive, and I'm not interested in taking another plunge into the next river we find. But if you'd like to stay, be my guest."

There's plenty in there that I could argue with. Plenty in there that I *should* argue with. But I make the mistake of looking at his cobalt blue eyes, and that's what seals the deal.

I get into the car, and we drive.

3

DANIIL

It's been fourteen months since I've seen a woman.

This one was worth the wait.

She's slumped limply against her seat, skin ghostly, stare vacant. She looks almost lifeless. A china doll who would move anywhere I put her. Her hair is plastered down the sides of her face and water droplets still sparkle across the tops of her breasts. She's soaking the seat through, but she doesn't seem to notice.

"Seatbelt," I say.

She turns, looking through me more than at me. "Huh?"

I lean over to grab the seatbelt and put it on for her. She smells of lilacs and champagne, and my dick stiffens in my pants almost instantaneously.

It'd be easy to say that this would happen for any female I saw today. Over a year of captivity reduces a man to his most animalistic instincts. But I know in my marrow that that's not true.

It isn't because she's *a* woman.

It's because she's *this* one.

Pink lips, soft as a cloud. Blushing cheeks. Pale green eyes like the highest leaf on a tree right when the dawn begins to break.

The latch of the belt clicks into place. My hand brushes her chest as I withdraw it. She's cinched up in too many layers of lace and fabric for it to be sexual in the least, but something about that faint contact makes me shiver regardless.

The whole time, she just watches me blankly.

I'm lucky to have found her in this state. Panicked, vulnerable, broken. She's as much on the run as I am, albeit in very, very different ways. I have to capitalize on this moment as much as I can before she starts waking up.

Before she starts fighting back.

So I pull the car out and resume driving, heading in the same direction she'd been going in. The vehicle groans and shudders at first, but it evens out as we pick up speed. The sirens grow louder.

It takes a few miles, but the girl slowly regains her senses. She sees my eyes flitting between the rearview mirror and the road ahead, and eventually, she makes the connection.

"Are those sirens for you?" she asks quietly. The only other sound is the hum of the highway.

I keep my eyes forward. "Yes."

I can feel her looking at me. Not the way she did when we first met, in that stunned, cautiously hopeful way that a sleeping person looks around at the contents of their dream. This time, her eyes are sharp and critical. Cynical, even. They've seen things that broke her, and now, they're always primed and ready to see more of the same.

"What did you do?" she asks. Softer this time. More cautious.

"I disobeyed a man who didn't like being disobeyed."

Behind us, I see the first flickers of red and blue lights casting up against the canopy. They're a long way back, but closing in fast. The sirens get louder and louder with every passing second. I have to make a move. Quickly.

I slow the car down, I'm searching, I'm searching—*perfect*.

A barely-there little offshoot of dirt-packed path leads into the woods. The mouth of the path, marked by two oaks as thick around as my waist, is just wide enough to let this beaten-to-death car through.

I whip the wheel smoothly to the right. Kinsley screams, but I ignore it. I'm perfectly in control. One tire bumps off the road, then two, three, four, then we're bumping along and leaving the lights of the highway behind us. The forest swallows us up.

I get us about a quarter-mile in, hopefully deep enough that no passing headlights will reflect off the car. I kill the engine and sit in silence. I can hear Kinsley swallow.

"What are we doing?" she gulps.

"Be quiet." I look up again at the rearview mirror. Just barely visible through row after row of looming pines, I see a caravan of cop cars scream past. When they're gone, it's silent again.

I feel Kinsley's eyes on me and I turn to regard her. In the moonlight filtering down through the treetops, she's ethereally beautiful. Her eyes glow and the soft whisper of her breathing is erotic in a way I didn't know such a thing could be.

What's strangest of all is that she isn't as terrified as I expected. Or maybe she is, but she just doesn't have the capacity to feel that level of fear anymore. Rest your hand on a hot stove for too long and you'll lose all sensation in it. I get the feeling that she's fleeing serious pain.

"What do they want with you?" she asks.

"They want to put me back in a cell."

The green in her eyes shimmers. I'm half-tempted to reach out and clean the scabbed blood from the corner of her lip, but I keep my hands tucked in my lap.

"You… you mean… you were in prison?"

"I was. Not anymore. And I'm not going back."

She looks down at my clothes. Dark, crusted, and anonymous, they've seen better days, though to call them "mine" is a stretch. They were in the duffel bag that was waiting for me at the first contact point after I broke out. I had just enough time to unearth it before that plan went to shit and I ended up tromping through the woods in search of a new way to freedom.

Fucking Petro. My best friend could've picked out a change of clothes that looked a little less like a potato sack. I'm sure he thought it was hilarious.

"You don't have to be afraid of me," I tell Kinsley. "You just have to cooperate."

The blunted fear in her face recedes for a moment before it's replaced with indignation. "Meaning what?" she asks. "If I don't cooperate, then I have every reason to be afraid of you? That's a threat, not a reassurance."

"You're not wrong."

She stiffens and leans away from me. I'm not sure what she was expecting—she got in the car with a man from the woods twice her size. She's lucky she's still breathing.

Her eyes flicker to the handle of the door where the lock is.

"I wouldn't run if I were you," I advise her.

"Because you'd come after me?"

"Because you'd trip. Again."

"I'm better at running than you realize," she snaps.

"I think that's truer than even *you* realize, princess."

Her mouth clasps shut. The black makeup rimming her eyes has run into angry streaks down her face. It's beautiful in its own way. I've always been drawn to broken things.

"All I need is to get to my next pickup point," I explain. "Once I get there, you won't have to see or hear from me ever again."

"Why do you need me at all?" she asks.

"You're going to be my alibi."

BRRRING.

Our heads snap in unison to her phone. I hadn't even noticed it underneath all that wet fabric. She reaches for it, but I grab it before she can.

"I'm afraid I can't let you answer that."

I see a dark flame light up her eyes. She'd seemed docile when she'd first gotten into the car. But then again, she was still bathing in the after-effects of shock.

So maybe she's not as tame as I'd thought. Which only makes my aching cock harder to ignore.

She stares at me, her lips parting ever-so-slightly. Is she doing that on purpose? Does she know how distracting that is? My dick twitches erratically, like a starving man smelling meat for the first time in fourteen endless months.

"They'll be looking for me," she says in a small voice. "The search will lead them right to you. Let me answer."

"So you can give me away? I think not."

"So I can throw them off."

"I'll be long gone before then," I assure her. "But if it means that much to you, fine—I'll let you take the call."

I press "ACCEPT" and put it on speaker, then place the phone on the dashboard between us.

A man's voice fills the car. "Kinsley?" he screeches. "Kinsley!"

"Tom," she replies softly. "I'm here."

"Here?" he repeats. "No, you are not. You're clearly *not* fucking here."

"I meant—"

"Where the fuck are you?" he demands.

She throws a tentative glance my way. "I just needed… some space."

"So you took the fuckin' wedding car and ran? What the hell were you thinking?"

"I wasn't thinking!" she snaps. Strangely enough, I'm glad to hear her voice rise in her own defense. "I was scared, Tom."

"Oh, for Christ's sake. It was a little goddamn spat. It happens all the time. You're just being overdramatic, as per usual."

The sound of his voice alone is setting off a cascade of reactions in her. Her chest is rising and falling fast. Her eyes are flushed with anger. Her fingers tremble as she stares at the black screen. She seems to have forgotten that I'm here at all.

"You… you—" She looks up and catches my eyes. Her cheeks bloom with color. "You scared me today," she says at last. "The way you behaved, the way you reacted—

"Yeah, yeah, I've heard the sob story. But I'm not your damn father, Kinsley. So stop putting that on me."

"This is not about him."

"This is *all* about him!" he retorts. "You assume that we'll end up like your parents did. Lord knows you dragged me to enough fuckin' couples therapy sessions to make all that shit perfectly clear."

I watch as she fidgets in her seat. Her knee is bouncing up and down, up and down, and the moonlight catches the dried blood on her face.

But she doesn't cry.

I admire that.

"I'm hanging up now," she says at last.

"Yeah?" he scoffs. "And then what, Kinsley? Where're you gonna go?"

"I don't know. Somewhere new. Somewhere far. It doesn't matter."

"Right, because you'll do so well on your own. Who do you have, Kinsley?" he asks viciously. "No friends, no family. I'm it. I'm your whole world. Without me, you're nothing."

That bit, I admire less.

Time to intervene.

I scoop the phone up and hold it close to my mouth. I want to make sure this son of a bitch really hears me. Kinsley gasps and makes a flailing grab for the phone, but the attempt is half-hearted. All it takes is one withering glare for her to retreat back into her seat.

"Tom, from one man to another, let me say: go fuck yourself."

I hear him splutter into a stunned silence. It stretches on for a few long breaths before he finally sacks up enough to talk again.

"Who the hell is this?" he spits.

"Don't you worry about Kinsley. I've got her now."

"What the fuck? Who are you?"

I smirk. "The man Kinsley is moving on with."

Then I hang up and place the phone delicately back between us. She stares at it for a while before she moves her gaze to me.

"I… I can't believe you just did that. He's… he's my fiancé."

"I believe 'Thank you' is the phrase you're looking for. And he isn't your fiancé; he's your ex-fiancé. You ran out on him, remember? Because he hit you. Or is it that you fell? I can't remember where we ended that discussion."

She frowns and shudders all at once. It looks like the timelapse of a flower wilting. Chin falls, face falls, shoulder falls, all of her crumpling in on herself.

"Things got heated," she whispers down towards the floorboards. "He didn't mean to do it. It was the first time—"

"Today a liar, tomorrow a thief," I intone mercilessly. "Today an abuser, tomorrow a killer. If you start justifying it now, you'll spend the rest of your life justifying everything he ever does to you. Every scar, every curse, every bruise that no one else can see. You made the right choice in leaving."

She sighs deeply. Tension whistles out of every pore. "I know I did."

I hear the wail of another siren. Time is growing short, and we can't stay here forever. They'll be combing the woods soon.

I look at Kinsley. "You can get out if you want."

"Do I really have a choice?"

"You always have a choice."

"If I come with you, I'll be aiding and abetting a criminal, won't I?"

I nod. "Among other things. But every good story starts with a leap of faith, princess. Care to jump?"

She swallows hard. That seals it. When she looks up at me, I see the determination in her eyes. "Fuck it. Let's go."

I start to reverse the car down the dirt path. "That's the spirit."

"What will you say if they catch us?" she muses.

"Simple," I reply. "Every bride needs a groom. And you're in the market for a new one. So… 'til death do us part, princess."

4

KINSLEY

"You don't exactly look like a groom," I remark, surveying him from head to toe.

My eyes catch on his hands. They're huge, matching the rest of him. Rough, too. Callused and veiny, covered in grit and small scars like shooting stars. Tattoos spiderweb across the backs of his knuckles.

"What do I look like?" he asks.

"A man on the run."

He rolls his eyes. "Fucking Petro…"

"Huh?"

"Nothing. I look like what I am. That's fine."

"There's a suitcase in the trunk," I blurt. "This was… It was supposed to be the car we were driving to our honeymoon. We were supposed to leave after the ceremony. Anyway, we packed a bag for the trip. Tom probably has some clothes that might fit you."

He regards me for a long moment. Those cool blue eyes pass over me like they're seeing stuff I never meant to show him. Then he nods, stops the car just before we've re-entered the highway, and gets out.

I watch in the side mirror as he walks around and opens the trunk. I hear the double pop of the suitcase latches unclasping, then the rustle of clothing.

There's a weird sort of anxiety churning around in my gut as he starts to unbutton his shirt. The first slices of his chest appear. Two abs, four, six. A smattering of dark chest hair.

He shrugs out of it and tosses it into the woods, revealing biceps with a thick green vein winding through. He undoes the buckle of his pants, starts to shrug them down his hips—and then he glances right into the mirror.

I blush stop-sign red and drop my gaze quickly. I could swear I hear an amused chuckle, although that might be just my overactive imagination.

I keep my eyes fixed in my lap, even when I hear the trunk slam closed, the crunch of boots on gravel, and then the driver's door opening again. Only when the still-nameless man clears his throat do I look up.

He's got the too-short pants cuffed over his ankles and the sleeves of Tom's too-small shirt rolled up in a way that is somehow inexplicably stylish. The fabric clings to him like a second skin. I can trace every curve in his abs, the path of every vein in his forearms. He's a walking anatomy chart.

"It fits," I mumble unnecessarily.

"Not quite," he says as he slides behind the wheel. "But it'll do for now."

"Now what?" I ask.

"Now," he says ominously, "we decide what we're going to do with you."

My eyes go wide with panic. "You… you said you wouldn't hurt me."

"Don't be so dramatic. I was talking about your face."

I pull down the sunshade and slide open the pocket mirror on the surface. My face stares back at me, unrecognizable and broken.

I tried to clean up when I first hit the road, though you wouldn't know it by looking at me. Sweat, makeup, tears, and flecks of blood have caked together to form a grotesque picture of a wedding day gone wrong. I look like something out of a nightmare.

And just like that, I'm ashamed. Not just because of how I look. But also because the outsides match the insides. This stranger from the woods is seeing me at the lowest point in my life.

Well, one of them, anyway. Though it's more of a "take your pick" kind of deal. There are plenty of low points to choose from.

"I look terrible."

I turn my face side to side. Each angle is worse than the one before it. I'm so wrapped up in self-pity that I don't see him reach for me until he's touching the bottom of my chin.

I gasp and flinch away. He just sighs, grips my chin again, and draws me forward.

"Hold still."

He rummages around in the glove compartment and pulls out a box of wet wipes. Then he brings one to my face and starts drawing it along my skin. I smell the tang of alcohol and the lemon fragrance.

I find myself wanting to explain. To tell him that this isn't how I normally look, how I normally act. This is the result of a series of harsh realizations and bad choices. This is the face of a desperate woman who decided she had to make a drastic change to keep herself from becoming the very thing she always feared she would turn into.

"I don't usually wear so much makeup," I say before I can bite my tongue. He makes no sign to show that he's heard me, but the silence is so loud it's starting to hurt, so I keep talking just to hold it at bay. "Tom's mother is the one who insisted on a makeup artist for today. So I just went along with it to make her happy. I do a lot of that, I think. Too much. I'm always trying to—"

"Stop talking."

I clamp my lips shut. More shame burns my cheeks. It's bad enough to be falling to pieces on your wedding day. It's worse to do it in front of a man like this.

He turns me this way and that, then nods. "Good enough."

I look in the mirror again. My skin is mostly bare now, though if I peer close, I can still see where the tears and the blood ran together into a single winding track.

"Thank you," I mumble.

He nods again. A man of few words, this one. Then he cranks the engine to life and pulls us back onto the highway. We drive for another ten minutes in a barren silence, until we round a wide bend...

And see cops waiting at a roadblock ahead.

My heart jumps into my throat and tries to choke me out. I'm ready for anything—for him to take us off-road again, for him to drive right through the blockade and smear Hartford County's finest all over the windshield. Hell, I'd be ready for him to sprout wings and take off like an eagle. That's how unreal this day has been.

But none of that happens. He just cruises to a stop where the officer is signaling and rolls his window down. I hear the clack of boots on asphalt as the officer walks up to the car.

And then, right before he reaches us, I witness the craziest transformation. The man's hand finds my thigh, cupping me like he's been doing it our whole lives. His shoulders melt into an easy posture, his face relaxes into a warm smile, and the ever-present brooding tension in his forehead eases away.

It's un-fucking-canny. In the space of a breath, he goes from monster-in-the-woods to happily-just-married.

"Evenin', Officer," he says in a casual drawl with a faint folksy twang. "I wasn't speeding, was I?"

The policeman doesn't answer the question as he crouches down to scrutinize both of us. "Just married, eh?" he grunts. His mustache twitches.

My savior grins broadly, an unmistakable pride radiating from him. "Still got the newlywed glow, huh? It's only been a few hours, so I s'pose we'll see how long that lasts."

The officer nods. His face is dour, but that mustache is still twitching. I can't decide whether that's a good sign or a bad one. I'm also more than slightly distracted by his hand on my thigh. Huge and hot and heavy.

"Well, congratulations to you both," the officer says shortly. "To answer your question, no, you weren't speeding. We're doing routine checks along this stretch of road."

"What seems to be the issue, officer?" His tone is flawless. His expression is all concern. He's playing his part to perfection.

"There's an escaped convict on the loose," he informs us. "He's supposed to be armed and extremely dangerous, with a trail of bodies in his wake. So needless to say, if you see anything weird, report it. We don't want you folks running into some kind of monstrous killer."

And just like that, everything gets much, much more serious.

5

DANIIL

I feel her tense up beneath my palm. I resist looking over at her, because I already know what I'll see—fear etched clear as day in those pretty green eyes.

I squeeze her thigh. Subtly enough that the cop won't see, but hard enough so that Kinsley will get the message.

Don't you dare fuck this up.

"Ma'am," the officer says suddenly, "are you alright?"

Kinsley jerks her head towards the dash to look up at him as though she's just noticed we're not alone. Her smile is unconvincing. My grip on her tightens.

"I'm fine," she croaks.

The officer's expression downshifts slightly. Just one subtle tick in the wrong direction. "Are you looking forward to your honeymoon?"

It's obvious what he's doing: testing the waters, looking for weak points. Trying to draw Kinsley into a conversation that will either make or break the little charade we're playing.

"Ma'am?"

"Sorry," Kinsley stammers, "what was that?"

"I asked if you were looking forward to your honeymoon."

"Oh, yeah. Totally. Of course, I can't wait."

But she's too weak and uncertain. I can see the officer—McPherson, I read off his badge—grow increasingly suspicious.

"Do me a favor and sit tight, folks." McPherson backs away and starts whispering into the radio strapped on his shoulder.

"I'm sorry," Kinsley says quickly, as though she's afraid I'm going to pounce on her. "I'm… not used to this."

"Get used to it," I snarl through gritted teeth. "Quickly."

She quivers beneath my touch as McPherson saunters back up and leans down against the car again.

"Looks like you've knocked the front bumper of your car," he notes.

"You can blame my little brother for that," I laugh, rolling my eyes in fake exasperation. "He decided to take a joyride around the hotel before the ceremony. Figured no one would notice. Kid got into Yale last month, but you'd think he was more suited to picking up trash on the side of the highway, maturity-wise."

"Yeah, well, they do say boys grow up slow."

I laugh good-naturedly. Kinsley, meanwhile, is staring blankly at me like she's trying to solve a complex math problem. McPherson shifts his gaze from me to her.

"How was the wedding, ma'am?" he asks.

I wonder if he's already called for backup. That would make things significantly more difficult. But not impossible.

"It was..." Kinsley stops short and sighs deeply. "I'm sorry—I know I must seem a little off for a woman who just got married."

I'm white-knuckling her thigh at this point. Where the fuck is she going with this?

"I'm just a little preoccupied," Kinsley continues. "My mother passed away a few years ago. And I keep thinking about her. She would have loved to have been there. I was fine during the ceremony. I guess it's just all hitting me at once now."

For one pregnant pause, I wonder if she oversold the delivery. McPherson's face hidden behind that bushy mustache is close to unreadable.

Then he eases up. "Alright, folks. Enjoy your trip. Keep your eyes open, like I told ya." That mustache keeps wriggling back and forth.

"Will do. Thanks, officer," I say.

I roll up the window and restart the engine. Kinsley looks straight ahead as she runs her hands over her silk skirts. Another cop waves us through the blockade and we start picking up speed again. A silent minute passes before we round a curve in the road and they disappear from sight.

"Is it true?" Kinsley blurts suddenly.

"Is what true?"

Her eyes snap to me. "The part where I'm apparently in the car with a killer."

She stares at me, waiting for an answer. But I know I won't be able to give her a satisfactory one. Certainly not a short one.

"That's not what I was put in jail for," I say at last.

She frowns. "You really hate answering questions, don't you?"

"A smart woman would stop asking them."

"Guess I'm not that smart."

"What are you then, Kinsley?"

"I'm trying to figure that out." Her voice gains strength as she speaks. "I may not know who I am, but I know who I'm not. And I'm not a bad person."

"It feels like you're saying that I am."

"You're on the run from the cops. So the evidence isn't looking great."

"I was wrongfully accused."

"Yeah, well, who isn't?"

I roll my eyes and regrip the steering wheel. "I'm not playing these games with you. Believe me or don't; it's your call. I don't care either way."

Out of the corner of my eyes, I see hers narrowing. "You're not about to try and convince me of anything, are you?"

"I find that to be a waste of time."

"Because you don't care what I think?"

"Don't take it personally," I tell her coldly. "I don't care what anyone thinks."

"Figures," she mutters.

I shouldn't engage. It would be better if this quasi-hostage situation were a silent one. But I've spent the last year and a half in a dank jail cell, surrounded by ugly, violent brutes. In comparison, Kinsley feels like a breath of fresh air. I can't help but inhale her.

"What figures?" I ask.

She's locked and loaded with her answer. "If you cared what people think, then you wouldn't do horrible things. Not caring gives you the license to do whatever the hell you want and not have to feel guilty about it."

"I wasted away a lot of my life feeling guilty. I'm done with that now."

She looks at me curiously. "What were you guilty about?"

I glance back at her. "Answering people's questions, for one."

She rolls her eyes, and I turn the car into another pathway that leads into the forest. "Where are we going?" she bleats nervously.

"Right here."

I drive in as far as I can go before the road tapers off into branching footpaths that can't be accessed with a vehicle.

"But why?"

"What did I just say about asking too many questions?"

She crosses her arms over her chest. I don't miss how it pushes her breasts up high in that unlaced corset. "I think I have a right to know what we're doing and why."

I sigh and slump back in the seat. "We're stopping here because every pompous motherfucker with a badge is lined up on the highway from here to California looking for a man like me. We got lucky back there. It won't happen again. So we spend the night here, and in the morning, we find a new way out."

She harrumphs, but she seems mostly satisfied with that explanation. I grimace and rub my throat. It's the most words I've spoken in the last six months combined.

Her phone starts to ring again. "It's not him," she says quietly, reading my dark expression. "It's my best friend."

I see the name **EMMA** and a picture of a smiling brunette flash across her screen. To my surprise, Kinsley silences it without answering.

She gazes into the middle distance just beyond the windshield. I follow her line of sight, but there's nothing to be seen out there. Just acres and acres of dark forest.

"The officer said you were armed," she murmurs.

I spread my hands wide. "You shouldn't believe everything you hear."

She sighs, then starts to pick uncomfortably at the few bands of the corset that are still wound tight around her chest.

"Go change," I tell her. "There's a suitcase in the trunk."

She almost laughs before she stifles it. Throwing open the door, she lurches out unsteadily and limps around the car to the trunk. I keep an eye on her through the rearview mirror, just like she did to me, as she sorts through the suitcase and pulls out a pair of jeans and a black shirt. The only difference is that, when she glances up to see if I'm watching, I make no secret of that fact. I just stare back.

Even from here and in the dark, I can see her cheeks glowing red.

She starts fussing with her dress. A zipper goes down, a tie gets loosed. But when she gets to the back section, she can't quite reach.

Don't get involved, Daniil, I growl at myself internally. *It's a bad idea, a really fucking bad—*

But I'm already up and moving.

I circle around to the back of the vehicle. "Stop," I rasp. She freezes at once, a deer in the headlights.

I grab her hips and twist her around. Then I take her wrists in my hands and plant each of them on the roof of the car. "Stay." My voice is breathy. It fogs up in the cool forest air.

I unlace the ties one at a time. With every release, she sighs deeper. When the ties are done, I start on the buttons. When those are done, too, I begin to pry the heavy fabric away from her pale skin.

I don't get far before she jerks away. "I can do this part myself, thanks."

I smirk and back away. But I keep watching. I can't stop myself.

She keeps her back to me as she peels the dress down her torso. Beneath it, she's wearing a thin white camisole that's still partially transparent from her sweat and her impromptu river plunge. I can see the soft lines of her body, screaming to be touched and caressed.

I feel a guttural sound building up at the back of my throat. The caged beast inside me roars to be set free. I'm hard as stone, but I ball my hands into fists and stop myself from touching her.

Nothing good can come of that.

She turns, and I expect her to reach for the outfit she pulled out of the suitcase. Instead, she just looks at me. Neither of us says a word. But the tension is thick enough to choke me.

In all my life, she might be the most fragile thing I've ever seen. One strong puff of wind will dash her heart to pieces.

One kiss might do the same.

6

KINSLEY

If I didn't know it before, I know it for certain now: I'm broken.

Because only a broken woman would look a killer in the eye and wish for more.

He cocks his head to the side. "Who let you down?" he ponders. "Besides the bastard you left at the altar. I don't think you're dumb enough to let him hurt you. Not in any way that truly matters."

I shake my head. "It doesn't matter now. They're all gone."

"What you told the police officer… it was true, wasn't it? About your mother."

I nod. "Yeah. Except for the part where I said I wished she'd been here today. I'm not sure seeing her daughter as a runaway bride would have been high on her bucket list." I fidget in place for a moment before I blurt out the latest in an ongoing line of stupid questions. "What would you have done if the cops stopped us?"

"Killed them all, ditched you by the side of the road, and taken off."

His cold, detached casualness makes me literally shiver. The fact that I'm still wearing just a sweaty, waterlogged camisole doesn't help.

"You're not joking, are you?"

"Again with the questions. You don't always want the answers, you know. Even if you think you do."

"You're good at this, aren't you?"

"Yes. Which part in particular are you referring to?"

"Charming people," I say, waving a hand through the air. "Manipulating them. Convincing them to do things they would never in a million years think of doing."

"Like convincing you to get into the car with me?" he asks.

"Yeah," I say, narrowing my eyes at him. "Like that."

"I didn't really have to try very hard."

I tense, my fists balling up tight. "I'd just run out on my own wedding. To a man I thought I was going to spend the rest of my life with. I was scared and confused. I was vulnerable. Choosing to come along… it had nothing to do with you."

"I never said it did."

His tone is sharp. It takes him just a word or two per sentence to cut me down to size. And he does it all while remaining so aloof, so effortless. I didn't know men like him existed, to be honest. Men who ride so high above the world that everyone else just looks like ants to them.

"I lied for you back there," I point out.

"I'm aware. Well-done. We'll make a killer of you yet."

"Not funny." I cross my arms. "The least you could do is tell me your name."

"I could give you a name," he says. "What makes you think it'll be the real one?"

"I suppose I'll just have to trust you."

At that, to my surprise, he smiles at me. For the first time since he dove into a raging river and dragged me out of it and saved my life, the corners of his mouth turn up in a grin. A real grin, not a fake one or a smirk, but the authentic warmth of one human being connecting with another. I was starting to wonder if he knew how to do that.

I'm also realizing something else, as the heat from that grin warms up everywhere on my body that his cold, brooding rage has shivered down to ice: I'm fucked.

"Daniil," he says. The smile disappears and the gravel comes back in his voice. "My name is Daniil."

"Daniil," I repeat. It's the kind of name that bears repeating. "Nice to meet you."

I've always been one of those silly, naive little girls who believes in fate. I saged the house whenever Tom was away on business and I looked for hope every morning in my horoscope. I knew it was illogical, but I couldn't let it go. The idea of God felt too far-fetched and godlessness felt too bleak. So I split the difference and put my trust in the stars and hoped it would be enough.

I'm still not sure if it is.

"Wait here."

I frown. "I'm not a dog."

"No," he agrees. "But you will listen."

He walks away, and despite my determination, I stay. Not like a dog. But a woman who's never come across a man like him before.

A man who's commanding without being condescending. A man who knows what he wants and how to get it. A man who has an ass that could make a nun forsake her vows.

I watch him until he disappears behind trees. Then I finish changing and turn my attention to the car. That's when I notice that my phone is lighting up yet again. I check the screen, nervous that it might be Tom calling me back.

But it's Emma. I drop into the seat and answer quickly before she gives up.

"Jesus, Kinz!" she gasps as soon as she hears my breathing. 'Are you okay?"

"I'm fine," I reassure her. "I'm safe." I glance through the window of the car, but I can't see Daniil anymore. Just unbroken darkness. "Thank you for helping me get out of there."

"Of course," Emma says. "What are maids of honor for, if not to help the bride escape?"

"You're an amazing friend."

"A more amazing friend would have convinced you to break up with that fucking asswipe before the wedding day."

"I wouldn't have listened."

"I should have tried anyway."

"It doesn't really matter now. I did it. I left. What's… what's happening over there?"

"Oh, you know," she tosses off. "Just general chaos. Tom punched one of the waiters. Not sure why. I just know he lost his shit once he realized you were gone."

"He called me."

She sucks in a sharp breath. "And you actually answered?"

"He needed to know that I wasn't coming back."

"You're too damn nice."

I take a deep breath to steady my nerves. "When the coast is clear, I'm going back to my apartment to get my stuff. Would it be okay if I spent a few days with you?"

"Of course. You're welcome for as long as you need, babe. You know that."

"You're the best."

"And you're my fucking hero. Not only did you run out on the asshole, but you took the wedding car! Legendary."

"That was your idea!" I remind her with a laugh.

"Sure, but I didn't think you'd actually listen. Maybe now, you'll start listening to my good ideas more. I've got lots of them."

I smile. "Listen, I'll call you later, okay?"

"Wait, where are you now?"

I glance up at the still-silent forest all around me. "It's... a long story."

"Ooh, I'm intrigued. Lemme make some popcorn real quick."

"I have to—"

Before I can finish the sentence, the phone is snatched from my hand. "Hey!" I cry out, but he's already cut the line.

Daniil stares down at me, his cobalt blue eyes roiling with icy fire. "Did you give away our location?"

"No, of course not!"

He looks through my call log before switching off the phone. "If the cops are on their way—"

"No one is on their way," I snap, raising my voice loud enough to create an eerie echo beneath the canopy. "I didn't say anything."

"How can I be sure?"

"I guess you'll just have to trust me," I hiss. "Like I trusted you."

His eyes are narrowed dubiously. He says nothing.

"Not good at that, are you?" I press. "Trust."

"I don't rely on trust."

"Sometimes, you don't have a choice."

"I make my own choices, princess."

"Oh yeah? Well, what are you gonna choose now?" I demand. "Leave me here?"

He strokes his beard. "I could."

"But you won't," I say confidently, even though I'm running on fumes and relying on hope and neither one of those is a good way to get where you want to go.

"Is that right?" he asks. "And how did you come to that conclusion?"

"Trust," I fire back. "It's all some of us have to go on."

7

KINSLEY

"You're turning out to be extremely naïve," he says as he gets into the car and slams the door shut.

"And you're turning out to be a raging asshole," I fire back, feeling suddenly much feistier than I have since the moment he pulled me from the river. "Bet you were a regular ol' Mr. Congeniality in prison."

Stop talking, Kinsley. I probably should. But it's funny how easy it is to ignore the voice in my head, even when it's right. Maybe even *especially* when it's right. Matter of fact, that's actually a great explanation for why I ended up in a blood-soaked wedding dress today.

He adjusts in his seat, and when his arm moves to the side, I tense up immediately, expecting to see the black mouth of a revolver aimed right at me.

"Something wrong, princess?" he asks.

"I thought… Never mind."

"You thought I was going to pull a gun on you."

"The cop said you were armed."

He puffs out a derisive breath of air. "They're just grasping at straws. Not that I need a gun. I've done worse with less. Much worse."

He stares out into the canopy of darkness like he's reliving some long-buried memory. I want to know what's behind those dark, masked eyes. A world of secrets that I haven't even begun to scratch the surface of.

Nor should you want to.

That's the broken part of me talking. The part I'm most inclined to listen to, as of late.

I don't make a peep, but he whips around suddenly to stare at me. Almost as if he can hear my thoughts.

Don't be ridiculous, Kinz. Don't be so paranoid.

Too late on both counts.

His gaze rakes over me once, quickly, but it doesn't linger. When he looks away, though, I feel the strangest sense of loss in its absence.

"What did your friend say?" he asks. "On the phone."

"She was just calling to check up on me. She wanted to know if I was alright."

"And what did you tell her?"

"What happened to trusting each other?"

He says nothing. Just a stoic, brooding ball of increasingly irritating silence.

I roll my eyes. "If you must know, she called to tell me that she was proud of me. For running."

"She wasn't a fan of your fiancé's, I'm guessing."

"No, she wasn't a fan," I admit.

"She'll learn to love him, I'm sure."

I suck in a sharp breath. "What are you trying to imply?"

"I think you know."

"I'm not going to go crawling back to the man who hit me." My voice is sharp and crackling, but almost too much so. Overcompensation, maybe.

Daniil shrugs. "So you say. That is how most abusive relationships work."

"First of all, I'm not ever going back to him. And second of all, it wasn't an abusive relationship."

Daniil's eyes glide over to mine. He holds the contact for two seconds and turns away once again, as if he's bored. Again, I can't help feeling like he took something from me, and I want it back.

"He's never hit me before," I add quietly. Almost shamefully.

He laughs cruelly. "So because he only did it the one time, he's off the hook?"

"I didn't say—"

"If I killed a man, do I get a free pass until the second time I kill? The third? How high do the numbers go?"

"Stop!" I cry out. My fists are knotted tight at my sides. "All I meant is that there are nuances to every situation. We were both running high on emotions, we were fighting—"

"If you get into the habit of making excuses for him now, you'll find an excuse to go back to him, too."

"I'm not going back to him," I say firmly.

To my surprise, he seems to accept that. "Good. I'll hold you to it."

I wait a tense breath before I ask a question that's been burning in my head since we started down this road of interrogation. "Why do you even care?"

He reclines his seat down a little and places one hand behind his head. "I don't." His eyes flutter closed like he truly couldn't care less either way. It's crazy how such a small gesture can feel like a literal slap in the face.

I stiffen up, feeling stupid for doing it even as I do. "You have some nerve, lecturing me about this shit when you've literally killed people."

He doesn't seem in the least bit concerned. "The people I kill deserve to die."

"Oh, sure," I say sarcastically. "That makes all the difference. You're a hero. Let the world erect statues in your honor."

He turns his head to the side and glances at me. Those blue eyes should be criminal. I guess they are, literally speaking, but—I digress.

"Who are you?" I croak into the tense silence.

He laughs, a sound like concrete smashing glass. "Trust me, princess: you don't want to know."

"Considering I'm hiding out with you—from the cops, no less—I think I *do* want to know, actually."

"You're going to come through this alive. Isn't that enough?"

"You would think," I say softly. "You told me that you were in jail because you disobeyed someone?"

"Yes."

"This man was... your boss?"

"You could say that."

"What would *you* say?" I ask impatiently.

"Asshole," he says promptly. "I would say he was an asshole."

"That doesn't really tell me much."

"That is not by accident."

I glare at him, but it doesn't do me any good. He's got his eyes shut again and his face tilted up to the roof of the car.

Stay in the silence, Kinsley. The silence can't hurt you. It's good advice from the voice in my head once again. But as it turns out, it's awfully hard to listen to your instincts when you've spent half a lifetime ignoring them.

"How did you disobey him?" I press.

"I stepped in when I should have stood by."

"You're a real poet, aren't you?" I say sarcastically.

"Not the worst thing I've been called," he remarks. "But not the nicest, either."

"What have you got against poets?"

"Poets are people who spend so much time feeling that they never actually experience anything in life."

"And you know this because of all the poets you've met?" I ask, a little flustered by how readily and brutally that answer came out.

"There were a few in prison." One eye flickers open a beat later. I see a hint of amusement there. "That was a joke, by the way."

"Oh. Didn't realize you made those."

"There are many things you do not and will never realize about me, *sladkaya*."

"You're not exactly giving me much to work with," I shoot back. "You did kind of take me hostage."

"That's not how I remember it."

"Tell me then: how do you remember it?"

"I remember jumping into freezing fucking water to save you from death at the hands of your own wedding dress."

I find myself blushing at the memory. My skin is still partly blue from the experience, like my body is still clinging to its brush with extinction. "Sure, okay, fine. You did do that. Just for the record, though, I can swim."

"Of course you can. You looked like a great swimmer. I only jumped in because I needed a good wash after my stint in prison."

His eyes are open again. They stare at me with razor-sharp focus.

Unblinking.

Hypnotizing.

Incredibly freaking frustrating.

"That was another joke," he adds.

"You're a regular court jester, you know that?"

"I was the class clown on my cell block."

"Really?" I ask stupidly.

His blue eyes turn dark. "No."

I blush and turn to the windshield. Darkness blinks back at me. The canopy overhead blots out the moon and most of the stars, and the car's headlights are turned off, so the only light is the tiny bits of it that can make it down from the night sky.

Stay in the silence, Kinsley. The silence can't—

"So is it fair to assume your boss is a powerful man?"

Guess I'm an idiot.

He sighs. "Are we still on that? Yes, my boss is a powerful man."

"How powerful are we talking?" I ask. "Like, hardened gangster? Narco kingpin? Crooked business mogul?"

He raises one thick eyebrow. "You watch too many movies."

I groan. "Not only did I get slapped by my fiancé and run out on my wedding, but I also crashed my car, fell off a bridge, and almost drowned in a river. If that weren't enough for one day, I am now stuck in the middle of the woods in the black of night with a rather rude and wanted felon. Who, may I add, I recently lied to the cops on behalf of, making me an accomplice to jailbreak at the very least. Can't you cut me some slack and answer a few questions?"

He mutters something in a harsh language I can't decipher—Russian, maybe?—then adds in English, "I should've stayed in fucking prison."

"So yes? To one of those? Gangster, kingpin, mogul?"

"Let's call it all of the above."

I nod. "Makes sense. And you're one of his minions?"

He gives me a furious glare that makes me shrink back in my seat. "I'm no man's minion. I did my job. Until the day I decided doing my job wasn't worth the consequences."

His words from earlier float through my memory. *I stepped in when I should have stood by...*

"He was hurting someone," he says softly, coaxing goosebumps to life up and down my arms and legs. "She was defenseless and screaming. And I—"

"Stepped in," I murmur, taking the words from his mouth.

"Yes. I stepped in."

My voice is hushed and somber now. "So you know a thing about abusive relationships then?"

"More than I'd care to. It's not an easy cycle to break."

I gulp and nod. "I watched my father hit my mother. Over and over again. She ran away a few times. But she always ended up back in that house. Back with him."

I feel that moment again. The moment when I'd looked into Tom's eyes and seen my father looking back at me. The slap he'd given me had barely hurt. But it parted the fracture inside me. It split me down the middle, and the kind of black, clotted, rotten blood that I've spent years damming up came pouring right out. There wasn't a thing I could do to stop it.

All I could do was try to outrun it.

"I'm not like my mother, though," I protest. But it's sort of feeble, and I think he can sense that.

"Time will tell."

My eyes flash to his. I want him to see the fight in me, the fire. I want him to see that I'm not just another defenseless damsel who needs protecting.

"Did you save her?" I ask abruptly.

"No. I did not."

The curt, clipped words send a shiver down my spine. I search his face for emotion, for some semblance of pain or regret. But he's too composed. Too practiced in secrecy. It's like waiting for a stone to start crying. You'll be waiting forever.

"I'm sorry."

"For what?" he asks sharply.

"You shouldn't have been put in prison for trying to save someone who needed saving. You're a good—"

"Stop." Pinpricks of a threatening sort of light shine out of his irises. I might have been terrified if I wasn't starting to feel a different kind of emotion entirely. "You don't know me."

I swallow hard. "What if I do? Partly, at least. Does that scare you? That maybe, just maybe, I might know how it feels to be you. Worse yet, that I might *understand* you?"

His laughter comes out in a thick, guttural bark laced with disbelief and condescension. "You don't understand shit, princess," he seethes. "I've done things that would make you piss yourself with fear."

He's trying to make me recoil by attacking. But I see it for what it is—because I've seen that same exact thing in myself.

"You don't scare me," I say proudly.

He straightens up in his reclined seat. He looks me dead in the eye, the blue of his irises hardening to chipped ice. "I've spent the last fourteen months in prison, Kinsley," he says. My skin hums with pleasure from the mere sound of my name on his lips. "For most of those months, I was in solitary confinement. That's weeks—endless fucking weeks—without seeing or hearing from another living thing. Not a man, not a mouse. And definitely not a woman."

His eyes dip down to the straps of my dress, to my breasts. He doesn't look away. Not this time.

"So tell me: what do you think a man in my position would do with a girl in yours?"

I swallow again. It's an almost deafening sound in the dense quiet of the car, of the forest. I can't deny that my skin is flushed and my heartbeat is hammering hard against my ribcage.

I also can't deny all the heat churning between my legs.

"Scared now?" he asks.

"Yes," I whisper.

Because I *am* scared.

But not in the way he thinks.

I'm mostly scared of what I'm about to do.

I push myself out of my seat and hoist my leg over the gear shift. It's not as smooth or as confident as I would have liked, but I get where I was going in the end.

I straddle his lap. My thighs grip his waist and I can feel his body heat scorching the air as it comes for me. He smells like river and musk.

"Careful," he warns in a deep growl that I feel more than I hear. "You know what they say about playing with fire."

"Maybe I'm the fire."

He smiles. It's a ghostly one. Faint, practically nonexistent.

But it's enough to strike the match.

My fingers land on Daniil's neck, brushing against the thin tendrils of a tattoo creeping its way out of the collar of my ex-fiancé's shirt.

When I kiss him, I feel something hot and sharp and powerful buzz from my lips all the way down through my core.

His hands land on my back and run all the way down my spine until they reach my ass. He squeezes hard, making me yelp. But then his touch melts from aggressive to gentle.

He kisses me back hard. Passionate, but not demanding. He parts my lips with only the slightest of nudges, his tongue winding in with mine seamlessly. As though we've done this countless times before and we're just finding our rhythm again.

He places the fingers of one hand on my throat. I can feel all five points trace lines down my skin until he reaches my breast. He strokes there gently, turning my nipples to granite underneath his palm.

I can sense his hunger, his need to be inside me. But he's holding back. He's trying to give me the release *I* need first.

When his fingers push past my panties and slip inside me, I gasp, jerking my face away from his and breaking our kiss.

But he doesn't let me go far. His other hand clasps my jaw to force me to stare back at him. He holds me in place as he fucks me with his fingers. "Don't look away," he snarls.

"Oh God..." I gasp. "Don't stop."

My voice sounds alien to my own ears. Who is that woman who just spoke? I sure as hell don't recognize her. She sounds like someone who *wants* this. Who's willing to risk everything for it. She sounds like the kind of woman who's brave enough to give herself up in the front seat of a car... in the middle of the woods... to an escaped convict... on the day she was supposed to marry another man.

Details, shmetails.

Daniil's tongue glides along my collarbone. His fingers push me upwards, long enough for him to unbuckle his pants and release his cock.

It's jaw-droppingly massive. But I don't have time to wonder if it will fit inside me before he's withdrawing his fingers, lining himself up at my entrance, and then with a shuddering groan, pulling me down onto him.

The first thrust takes my breath away. His, too, by the looks of it. A low, throaty exhale escapes past his gritted teeth. He starts to pick up tempo. I want to say something—to beg him to go slow, maybe, or perhaps the exact opposite, actually, to beg him to go as fast and as hard as he can so I can let myself fall apart while I pretend for precisely the length of one orgasm that everything I've done today is okay—but I can't get a single word out.

It's too much.

It's all too fucking much.

His tongue laps around one nipple, then the other, as he coaxes me with his hands to bounce up and down on him faster and faster. And then faster and faster, and faster and faster, until we're sweating and it's a blur of motion and grunting and mingled breath and then—

"Oh God... oh God!"

He touches my clit, just the barest graze, but that's enough. I come with my forehead against his, bucking so hard on his cock that I feel as though I'm in real danger of splitting apart.

"Fuck," he growls. It's a masterclass in self-restraint that that's all he says.

I feel his teeth scrape the skin of my neck. Then I feel heat—his heat—fill me up. Two hard pumps. One gasping, finishing thrust.

And then he goes still.

I kiss his brow, even though I recognize that we haven't quite reached that level of intimacy yet and I cringe as soon as I pull my lips away. I tell myself that at least this happened at night. In the morning, I'll be able to pretend none of it was real.

He's silent as I slide off him and make my way back to the passenger's seat.

"Sleep," is all he says as he tucks himself away and leans back in his seat.

I almost bark out an incredulous laugh. Sleep feels impossible. But when I lie back and close my eyes, body still thrumming from head to toe, I feel it creep up on me. Turns out that running out on your wedding, crashing your car, and almost drowning is more draining than I would have thought.

The next thing I know, I'm waking up to a sore back and the dawn spotlight breaking through the trees. There's daylight.

And Daniil is gone.

8

DANIIL
TEN YEARS LATER

"You like my earrings?"

I glance at the dark red rubies hanging off Alisha's ears. They're shaped like teardrops and surrounded by diamonds. Utterly predictable. Women like her love to scream *Look at me* in every way but with their words.

"They're fine."

"'Fine'?" She frowns. "You mean you don't remember them?"

This is what comes of asking Petro to buy gifts on my behalf. Not that he chose poorly—my second-in-command has good taste. Even tonight, she's dressed to showcase those rubies. A low-cut dress the color of fine wine and black stilettos that lend another five inches to her already statuesque figure. All courtesy of yours truly—in a manner of speaking.

"Alisha," I say with a sigh, "relax. Have another glass of wine."

"That's your strategy, isn't it?" she demands. "Ply me with wine until I forget that I'm wasting my time with you?"

I cock my head to the side. "Is that how you feel?"

"Yes," she says, flipping her strawberry blonde hair over her shoulder. "Well, sometimes."

"I certainly don't want you to feel that way."

Her eyes soften immediately. She lunges forward and places her hand over mine. "Dani, I just want to be closer to you. I want to feel like we're moving forward."

My eyes stare unblinkingly into hers. I've become less and less capable of sympathy recently. Not that I was ever particularly good at it to begin with. "If you feel like you're wasting your time with me, then feel free to move on. Maybe that'd be best for both of us."

She freezes, her hand tightening over mine before she plucks it away. "What?"

I flag down one of the roaming waistcoats. "We'll take the check now," I tell him.

"Right away, sir."

When I turn back to Alisha, her jaw is wide open. "How can you be so… cruel?" she whispers.

"I never pretended to be anything else."

"But… but you sent me gifts this morning," she says with watery eyes. "Silk lingerie. Louis Vuitton perfumes. Chopard diamonds."

"That was generous of me," I drawl.

Her eyes turn flat as the realization hits. "Petro," she spits. "Petro sent me those gifts, didn't he?"

"I paid for them. Surely that counts for something."

She looks away for a moment. Her cheekbones really are beautiful. They were the first thing I'd noticed about her. It's a flawless profile in a flawless setting.

But there's no matching the sight that's been seared into my mind's eye for ten long years—a bride's cheeks flushed red with lust as our breath steamed up a car lost deep in the woods.

"You always introduce me by name," she blurts suddenly.

I raise an eyebrow. "That is usually how introductions work."

"What I mean is, you never introduce me as your girlfriend," she clarifies. "I'm always just Alisha Diego. Period."

I sigh and say nothing. There's no point. She's getting herself worked up, which is fine if that's what she wants. But I want no part in it.

As I watch, a single diamond tear unravels itself down her cheek.

"Don't waste tears on me," I remind her. It's not the first time in the last decade that I've told a woman those words. It probably won't be the last.

"You—you made me believe…"

"No," I interrupt harshly. Her mouth snaps shut and I snare her in my gaze. "I didn't make you believe a single fucking thing. I was honest with you from the beginning. I never lied about who I am or what I wanted. You chose to believe in something I never offered."

The waiter appears with the check and hands it to me. I don't bother looking, just hand him my Amex Black and wave him off without ever once taking my eyes off Alisha. She's crumbling right before me.

"I think it's time I took you home. You're distraught."

I stand up, but she remains seated, looking shell-shocked. When she finally looks up at me, I see the desperate threat of realization there.

"Alisha," I say firmly. "Come."

She gets up numbly and follows me through the restaurant. I step out into the cool autumn breeze. The valet pulls up right then in my Rolls Royce. I let him open the door for her, tip him, and then get behind the wheel. The moment Alisha's door shuts, I rev the engine and speed out of Le Grand's obnoxiously gaudy parking lot. Fucking topiary shaped like jungle animals as far as the eye can see. It irritates me.

"Is there someone else?" Alisha blurts at the first traffic light we come to.

"No. There's no one else."

No one I've seen in ten years, at least.

"What is it then?" she demands. "Don't tell me you're afraid of commitment like every other man out there. That would be so… boring."

"Maybe it's just you."

Her head snaps to gawk straight at me in disbelief. She waits for me to take it back. When I don't, she wriggles around in her seat like she wants to jump right out of the car. "You're an asshole!"

"As I've told you multiple times, I never pretended otherwise."

With exquisite timing, I come to a stop outside her apartment building. It looks nice. Overpriced, but nice. Not that I've been inside long enough to form an opinion. I don't do sleepovers.

"Goodnight, Alisha. Good luck out there."

It doesn't look like she's heard me. I suppress a sigh. Sometimes, a guy just wants a little fucking alone time. A nice glass of brandy and—

A broken girl in a wedding dress.

No. Fuck no.

Back in the present, Alisha is looking at me with a desperate gleam in her eyes. "Will you come inside?" she asks, her chest rising and falling hard.

"No."

It's strange how one night can consume a lifetime while ten years can go by in a flash. I feel like those scant few hours in the woods lasted longer than the decade that's followed.

Point being, two years may feel like something to Alisha. But to me, it's just the length of time that passed between Kinsley's breaths and her moans.

The sparkle of Alisha's rubies catch my eye again. They look like drops of frozen blood.

She takes her hand off mine, but places it over my crotch instead. "Everyone needs something," she says, changing her tone. It's meant to be alluring, but it just comes off as forced and grotesque. "Tell me what you want and I'll give it to you."

"You can't give me what I want."

She should know now. Maybe it's my fault for not making her understand sooner. I have nothing to give her but expensive gifts and orgasms when I can spare the time. Perhaps that's why she's clinging so tightly, even at the expense of her dignity.

"Try me," she says, squeezing between my legs. "I know you want children. Let me have your baby. Let me give you a son."

I stare back at her listlessly, waiting for her to wise up and remove her hand. She doesn't. She just gets more and more desperate as she tries to cajole my dick to life.

"Let me—"

"Alisha," I say, peeling her hand off of time, "it's time to say goodnight."

Her eyes split with disappointment. She wrenches her hand away like I burned her and stares at the windshield. "Will I see you again?" she asks without looking at me.

"Probably not."

"So these last two years... did they mean anything to you?"

"It was a nice distraction."

I hear her gasp and the rustle of her motion at the same time. I sigh wearily. I was hoping she wouldn't be so predictable. Guess I was wrong.

Sure enough, her hand is hurtling across the car on a collision course with my face. I reach out and stop it dead in its tracks before she can land the blow. My fingers squeeze her wrist hard enough to dam up the flow of her circulation.

"You don't want to do that, Alisha."

"You're hurting me," she wheezes.

"I'll hurt you a lot more if we stay together," I promise. Then I let her go.

She rips her hand away again and grapples with the handle of the car door. It takes her a moment, but she gets it open and storms off towards her building. Her heels click furiously on the pavement.

The doorman standing at attention beneath the awning says something to her, but she ignores him and turns back towards the car instead. I don't bother waiting for her no-doubt-scathing final words; I just drive away. It probably wasn't going to be clever, anyway.

I exhale as the engine growls beneath me and carries me away from the wreckage of yet another relationship I barely wanted to begin with.

First thing tomorrow morning, I'm going to have a talk with Petro about his freedom with my fucking credit cards. Silk lingerie, perfumes, *and* diamonds? He's lost his damn mind.

I take the exit onto the highway. It's a long way home, a windy one, and a dark one, especially with the thunderstorm just starting to roll in. But all of those things suit my mood right now. I turn on the sound system and the crunch of aggressive metal music snarls from the speakers to shake my bones.

I let myself settle into the speed of the car. I lean with the turns and press the pedal harder. The road unfolds like a black ribbon in the night. No lights. No other living soul.

Until I take a bend too sharp, and see the glare of oncoming headlights...

On *my* side of the road.

Everything happens so fast. The other driver seems to realize just how far off-course he is, because he panics and swings the car back to the right. But he overcorrects. One tire, then two, then all four leave the road, and there's no recovering from that. I whip aside just in time to avoid his fishtailing bumper. In my rearview mirror, I watch as the car slams nose-first into one of the unlit light posts that stand sentinel along the highway.

I stomp the brakes and glide to a stop a hundred yards down the road. "Fucking moron," I mutter impatiently as I get out of my car and trek towards the lamppost.

Lightning flashes through the sky. Before I reach the car, the driver's door is thrown open, and I see the thick heel of a black boot hit the gravel of the road.

"What the fuck were you—"

The woman emerging from the car stops short, her eyes going wide with disbelief. I freeze, taking in her features slowly, making sure I've got it right this time.

I've come across hundreds of brunettes in the last ten years. A few of them with skin pale like milk. Fewer still with eyes the right shade of green.

None of them have been her.

But there's always been a moment, a tiny split second of searching, when I've thought it might be. It's inevitably a disappointment, one that I bury deep inside along with all the rest.

Until now.

"Oh my God…" she breathes.

And I know instantly.

It's her.

9

KINSLEY
ONE HOUR EARLIER

BFFFEAEAE EMMA: *How's it going?*

I make sure my date is still preoccupied with checking out the girl with the butterfly tramp stamp at the next table over before I quickly fire back a reply to Emma's text with my phone held in my lap out of sight.

KINSLEY: *im coming home soon. everything OK?*

EMMA: *Oh no. What's wrong with him?*

I glance up. Liam is smiling at the waitress now. The one with the big boobs and the two open top buttons. That is not a coincidence by any stretch of the imagination—it's almost like anyone with a B cup or smaller is invisible to him.

KINSLEY: *he's gross. staring like super pervy at everyone who passes by with a uterus.*

EMMA: *Is he aware that he's on a date with the finest uterus owner in all the land? Maybe you're just not engaging him in that scintillating Kinsley banter we all know and love.*

KINSLEY: are you trying to be annoying, or does it just come naturally?

She just sends me two emojis, one with a halo and one winking. I laugh at my irrepressibly sassy best friend, swipe out of our conversation thread, and turn my attention back to Mr. Wandering Stare.

"Should we keep the party going at the bar next door?" Liam suggests.

I cringe. "Oh, um, thanks, Liam, but I really should be getting home. I've got an early start in the morning."

"And to think I was about to invite you back to my place." He grins wolfishly in a manner I'm liking less and less as the night passes. I didn't like it very much in the first place.

I give him a tight smile that I'm hoping he'll interpret as a polite brushoff. "Sorry, not tonight."

"Ah, I see what you're getting at," he says with a waggle of his too-bushy eyebrows. "Another night then."

So much for a polite brushoff. "Oh, wow, is that the time?" I exclaim, avoiding his question altogether. "I've really gotta get going." The delivery is a little over the top, but I have a feeling Googly Eyes here isn't the most discerning customer on the block.

"It's not that late." He scowls. "Don't be a party pooper."

"I'm usually in bed by nine," I say, getting to my feet and shouldering my purse. "So this is a late night for me."

"Slow your horses. We ain't even paid up yet, partner."

I force a smile at the bad mixed metaphors and the worse country accent as I sink back into my seat. "Oh. Yeah. Sorry."

He snaps at the waiter, who's busy taking another table's order, and imperiously calls for the "cheque." I know that's how he spells it in his head because he says it with two syllables like that. Strike number bazillion for the night for Mr. Liam Griffith, life insurance salesman, amateur DJ, all-around loser. Strike number quadrillion for my dating career.

The waiter sighs and goes to get the bill, presumably so he can get us out of sight sooner rather than later. Then Liam looks back at me and grins like a loon. You know a date is bad when you find yourself hoping that he'll start checking out other women again.

"Has anyone ever told you that you have extraordinarily striking eyes?" he says, leaning in close enough for me to smell the ketchup on his breath.

The tables at this restaurant are small. They leave plenty of room for tons of elbow and knee bumping, which has happened with enough frequency that I'm starting to think he finds bruise-worthy appendage contact to be arousing. I turn my body to the side so that my legs are pointed out, towards the doors. As in, the place I'd really like to be walking towards.

"You did, actually," I remind him. "When we first met."

"That's right. That's how I got you to agree to go on a date with me."

More like the growing realization that I haven't been on a date in over two years. I don't bother correcting him.

"I haven't really seen you at the gym since that day, though," he points out.

"It's my friend who has a membership at Toned. They were offering free spin sessions for friends of members and Emma thought I might enjoy it."

"And did you?"

"I prefer running."

"You run often?"

"As often as I can." *Matter of fact,* I think to myself, *I'd love to run out of here right now. I'd be good at it, too.*

But also in a larger, cosmic kind of sense. Running from my past. Running from my demons. I'm not quite as good at that, though not for lack of trying.

"Well, you're in great shape," he says as his eyes snake over my body with approval. "I figured you pretty much lived at the gym. Me, too."

He brings his hand back behind his head and honest-to-God flexes at me. I have to reach for my glass of water just to hide for a few seconds so I don't laugh right in his face.

"Where is that waiter?" I murmur.

"You're in a rush," he says, the smile sliding off his face.

"Am I? I just, uh… I don't like driving in the dark."

That's not a lie. But I'm certainly not about to explain to this guy why cars at night frighten me. Why they've frightened me for ten years, actually.

"I could have picked you up," he scolds. "But you insisted you'd meet me here. I get it, I get it—Miss Independent. You and every other woman out there these days."

"Well, it is a first date," I say with a shaky laugh.

He frowns. "Is it 'cause you're paranoid or 'cause you're conservative?" he asks.

In your case, I'm just not interested. "A little bit of both, maybe."

His eyebrows knit together, but he manages to hide his disappointment behind a smile. I prefer it when he doesn't smile. Much less creepy.

"Here you go, sir," the waiter says at last, dropping the bill in the center of the table.

I reach for it at the same time that Liam does, but he manages to wrestle it out of my hand. "No way, Jose," he says firmly. "I've got this."

"Please," I insist. "Let's split it."

"Not a chance, buckaroo," he says, resorting back to that abominable cowboy voice he likes so much. "This one's on me."

He pops in his credit card—which, I note, has his father's name on it—and hands it over to the waiter with a self-satisfied smile. "Thank you, my good man."

I have to resist the urge to roll my eyes.

"Nice restaurant, huh?" he remarks. His eyes follow a busty blonde as she sashays from the table to the bathroom.

"Very nice," I agree. I'm finding my fork suddenly fascinating.

"It's on the pricey side," Liam blathers on, "but I knew you were worth it."

I have my eyes fixed on the waiter. He's at the counter now, swiping Liam's card. "Did you now?" I ask distractedly.

"I've been going to that gym for years. I've never met a woman half as pretty as you. And trust me, I looked."

"Oh yeah? What else were you looking for?"

"Sorry?" he asks, looking confused.

"I'm sure there were other things you were looking for in a woman, apart from attractiveness?"

"Oh," he laughs. "Nothing as important." His smile withers when he realizes I'm not laughing with him. "That was a joke."

I nod grimly. "I laughed. Oh, look, here's the waiter."

I'm out of my seat before Liam has signed across the dotted line. I know I'm being overly critical—after all, he did pay for the meal, and it was a nice meal, and he wasn't even that much of an asshole, just sort of cringy and annoying.

But there's no escaping the fact that I felt pressured into this date from the start. Also, as bad as I wish it were true, we're not quite at the finish line yet.

As a matter of fact, I can already see his lips puckering. I swallow back that acrid, *you're-about-to-vomit* taste in my mouth.

He rests his hand on the small of my back as we make our way out of the restaurant like we're moving through a crowded club, although there's ten feet of space in either direction. When we get outside, I'm glad to see that I've parked on the opposite end of the lot from him.

"There I am," I tell him, pointing to my blue Mini Cooper. "Guess the fun's over."

"Let me walk you to your car."

"You really don't have to do that."

"It'd be my pleasure."

He's saying all the right things. He's doing all the right things. So why the hell can't I jump on board and just enjoy myself?

He throws me that leering smile of his, and I feel my skin recoil.

Oh yeah. That's why.

"Cute car," he comments.

I take a step back out of kissing range. "Thank you so much for dinner, Liam."

He pursues me. His hand paws at my hip as he breathes into my face, "I know this part of the night can be a little awkward…"

"It doesn't have to be!" I yelp, a little too desperately.

He laughs, a little too loud. "Great minds think alike, Kelsey."

That's not my name, but I'd rather get out of the blast zone than correct him. "Mhmm, they sure do. Well, goodni—"

Uh-oh. The lips are imminent. They're dry and puckered up and aimed right for me like the asteroid that killed the dinosaurs. His eyes are closed, too, which is good in the sense that he can't see the horror on my face and bad in the sense that he's really not gonna like what he finds in about *three, two, one—*

I jump out of the way. He misses me altogether, thrusts his tongue into empty air, and then promptly stumbles forward a few steps until he runs into the back of a pickup truck parked in the handicap spot.

"Goodnight, Liam!" I call from where I'm standing, a yard to the right.

He opens his eyes. I almost laugh out loud at the pure, unadulterated shock on his face. In all his wildest dreams, he never saw this end result coming.

I don't know what to say, so I do what I do best—I run.

I leap into my car and start the engine. Shifting into drive, I give him an awkward salute and haul ass out of the parking lot. "Jesus," I mutter as I see his short, chubby frame fade blue into the darkness. "You really made a mess out of that one, Kinz."

The further away I get from Liam and the restaurant, the more I can finally start to breathe again. Then I remember that there's a pint of half-baked cookie dough ice scream in the fridge, and my mood perks up considerably.

The only bummer is that the drive home from this part of town sucks. The whole strip of high-wattage lights along the side of the road is burned out and the county is too broke or too stubborn to fix them, so it's like driving through an unlit cave. I always crank the music up higher when I go through the dark part.

"Let's see," I say to myself, trying to find a station to settle on. "Golden Oldies—no. Classical music—not tonight. Heavy metal—not any night."

I'm still flicking through stations when a peal of lightning zig-zags across the sky. At the same time, I look up and realize something—

I've drifted all the way into the other lane.

And there's someone else headed right for me.

I've always been a pretty terrible driver, but this is bad, even for someone with my track record. I'm fully aimed at the oncoming car. That being said, he's gotta be doing at least a hundred and fifty miles an hour. It feels like his headlights are screaming at me. The station is still blaring thunderous heavy metal, another bolt of lightning and the accompanying clap of thunder make my head spin, and I'm freaking out, clamming up like I always do, and then I close my eyes, the other thing I always do, because if I don't see it then it can't hurt me and so—

WHAM.

My hands are smarter than I am. At the last second, I slam the brakes and twist the wheel just enough to go screeching past the other driver. Less fortunately, I promptly impale my car on one of those aforementioned broken light poles. The vibration of impact shakes my whole skeleton. My brain rattles around in my skull.

When I've come back to my senses, I kill the engine. The sound of smoke escaping from under the hood is like nails on a chalkboard. In the rearview mirror, I see that the other driver has pulled over to the side of the road a hundred yards away.

I also see his silhouette, striding toward me. Another shock of lightning illuminates him briefly. Tall, chiseled, as dark-haired and dark-eyed as the night around him.

I swallow hard, suddenly nervous, and then gear myself up and out of the car. He's already shouting, "What the fuck were you—"

Then I stop short. He gets close. More lightning. This time, I'm close enough to see it set his face aglow.

My memory's playing tricks on me again. It has to be.

Because I *know* that face. I know that man. He's different now, but then, ten years have passed. Of course he would be different. I'm sure I am, too.

It's everything that has stayed the same that convinces me of who he is. Those broad shoulders, that confident walk. Those cobalt blue eyes.

"Oh my God…"

He takes a step towards me, his brow wrinkling with the same haunting recognition that's got its claws in me. His black jacket billows in the sudden rush of wind.

"Well, well," he says. "Nice to see you again, princess. Missed me?"

My jaw is hanging somewhere around my knees. "You…" I mumble stupidly.

"You're still a pretty shit driver," he observes.

I wish I could say something back, but I'm frazzled beyond belief by the most unlikely crossing of paths in the history of paths crossing. Unfortunately, it doesn't seem like it's having the same effect on him.

Finally, I find my voice. "You—I—You were driving like a maniac!"

He frowns. The broodiness… I remember that very well. It makes me shiver now the way it did when I first saw it. "I was on my side of the road."

"Sure, doing like ten times the speed limit! You could have killed me!"

"You look fairly alive."

"No thanks to you!"

He just stands there, with calm detachment as his weapon of choice. It's obnoxiously effective. I want to run at him head-on and shove him to the ground.

He glances over at my car. "Your car, on the other hand, has seen better days."

"It's new," I snap. "Or at least, it was. Christ, this is going to cost me a fortune."

"You need to breathe," he advises.

"What I need is for men like you to stop driving as though they own the whole damn road."

"Is there a reason you're so angry?" His shrewd eyes swipe over my body as though he's clocked everything new about me in a matter of moments.

"Oh, I don't know. I guess I get kinda pissed when some rich asshole in a fancy car runs me off the road!"

I turn on my heel and stomp back to my car.

"Where are you going?" he calls.

"Away from you!" I feel a drop of rain land on my cheek, but I barely register the unfurling crop of storm clouds overhead.

I've got bigger fish to fry than a few cracks of lightning.

"You can't just leave, Kinsley."

I stop, shudder, and swallow. The sound of my name on his lips… It does something powerful to me.

"Why can't I?" I ask, whirling around to face him again. The various iterations of speeches I've prepared in my head over the last decade disappear altogether. Probably because I'd never imagined I'd actually have the opportunity to use them. "You left without a goodbye. Why shouldn't I?"

10

DANIIL

Her dark hair is longer than I remember. Straighter, too. Her green eyes are rimmed with coal, but the makeup she's wearing is composed and understated.

Unlike the last time, when it ran in muddied streaks of blood and mascara and river water down her face.

"Did I hurt you?" I ask quietly.

Her brow scrunches together, trying to deny what she's already admitted with everything but her words. "Don't flatter yourself."

"I thought it would be easier that way. For you to wake up and find me gone."

"Bullshit," she snaps. "It was easier for you to just get lost before I woke up. Don't pretend like your decision had anything to do with me."

"I assumed you'd forget about me and move on with your life."

"I did," she snaps. "I have."

I raise my eyebrows, but say nothing. She's busy gnashing her teeth and failing miserably at keeping her emotions caged up. If it weren't for the rolling thunder overhead, I would have been able to hear her molars grind. Huffing, she turns and makes another attempt to get back into her car.

"This time, it's not drivable," I tell her, walking over. "You need help."

"I don't want any help from you," she says, glaring at me through her open window. "I've had enough of your 'help' for a lifetime."

"Then you're gonna be stuck here for a while."

Shrugging, I start the trek back to my car. I'm hardly twenty yards away before I hear her car door slam again. When I glance back over my shoulder, she's staring at the busted fender and the thin trickle of smoke rising from the cracked hood.

She looks up at me, and at the exact same moment that we make eye contact, it starts raining. Hard.

"Fuck," she groans. The clatter of rain on asphalt almost drowns out her soft whimper. "What the hell do we do now?"

"Get into my car."

"Like hell I will," she snaps. She turns and starts yanking on her car door again. But the metal must've crumbled in a way that keeps it shut this time, because she gets nowhere with it.

"Don't be a child," I retort. "Get in."

I grab her by the arm and reel her, kicking and struggling the whole time, down to where my car is pulled over on the shoulder. Halfway through, she gives up the fight and just lets me drag her like a lifeless doll.

I throw her into the passenger seat and walk around to the driver's side. The moment I pull my door shut, the sound of the rain is cut in half. The radio is still burbling quietly inside.

Her eyes narrow when I twist the key in the ignition. "Where are we going?" she demands.

"We can't stay here. We're in the middle of the highway. We'll ride out the storm somewhere comfortable."

"Oh, so a car isn't good enough for you anymore?"

I glance at her and suppress a chuckle. "I've come up in the world."

She eyes my Tom Ford suit jacket. "Clearly."

"I never pegged you for the judgmental type."

"Yeah, well, a lot can change in ten years," she says harshly, looking determinedly out her window. I don't look anywhere but at her. "I'm not going anyplace far. Pick the first place you see with a roof and we stop there."

"You've gotten a lot better at barking orders, too," I note.

She doesn't answer with anything but a glare. I pull back onto the road and we slice a couple miles through the rain.

"There," she says, pointing towards a neon-glowing bar nestled at the corner of the road. "You can stop there."

It looks like a decent-enough place, so I pull the car to a stop right outside the premises. From here, it's a short run to the awning hanging over the saloon doors.

I have an umbrella in the back, but Kinsley doesn't wait for me to offer it. She opens the door the moment I've stopped and makes a run for cover. I sigh and follow her.

By the time I get inside, she's sitting at the bar and poking at her phone.

"Hello?" she says, pressing the phone to her ear. "Hello? ... Goddammit."

"The reception out here ain't worth a damn, ma'am," the bartender tells her sympathetically. "Especially in this storm."

She ignores me when I take the stool next to hers. "Is there a landline here I can use?"

The bartender jerks his head over to a passageway in the far side of the bar. "You'll find a payphone just before the ladies' restroom. Not sure it'll work, either, though. Thing's been on the fritz for years."

She jumps off the stool and heads off in search of the payphone. I shake my head. Still stubborn. Some things never change.

"Brandy," I tell the bartender.

The man nods and picks a bottle off the top shelf as he hums along to the jukebox. He's a beefy guy, big in every direction, with the beard to match.

"Anything for your lady friend?"

"I'll let her choose her own drink or there'll be hell to pay."

"Smart thinking," he chuckles, sliding the brandy over the counter towards me. "I'm Chester."

I drain the drink in one gulp, then set the glass back down. "Another."

Kinsley emerges from the passageway. It's obvious from her sour expression that she didn't have much luck with the in-house phone.

"Tow truck on its way?" I ask pleasantly.

She throws me a glare that could peel paint just as Chester puts my second glass of brandy down in front of me. "What's that?" she asks, reaching for the glass before I can answer.

"Brandy," Chester answers for me. "Best in the house. Your man here looked like he wasn't much of one for the cheap stuff."

She rolls her eyes. "Oh, heaven forbid he gets anything less than the best. I'll just take a coffee, please. Black. We can't all go from prison to prince in a decade."

I raise one eyebrow. "It didn't even take me a quarter of a decade, actually."

Chester wisely decides to shuffle off to the back in search of coffee instead of sticking around to eavesdrop.

"How's Tom?" I ask casually.

"Is that supposed to be a test or something?"

"I did say I would hold you to it. I'm a man of my word. Are you a woman of yours?"

She places both her elbows on the countertop. "I didn't go back to him. I met him once, to return the ring and the car. That was it."

"Impressive."

"If you were there, you probably wouldn't think so," she says dryly.

She's changed. I can hear the years in her voice. I wonder if I added to the aged timbre of it. "Why do you say that?"

"I was hoping for an apology from him."

"Ah. Unsuccessful, I bet."

"You gonna tell me off?" she asks cautiously.

"For being optimistic?"

"I think the word you're looking for is 'naïve.'" She keeps her gaze averted, but I notice that her shoulders tense. Her wet hair clings to the sides of her face, turning the tips from dark brown to dusky black. "I made a lot of mistakes that day."

"Do you think leaving your fiancé at the altar was one of them?"

Her eyes snap to mine. "Of course not."

"Good."

"Good news, ma'am," Chester says, materializing from the kitchen door. "There's a hot cup of coffee heading your way."

"It's Kinsley," she says. "And thank you."

He nods pleasantly, but I notice the way his eyes linger on her face. He appreciates a pretty woman. Problem is, this particular woman is here with me.

He seems to realize that the second my gaze locks onto him. It's a primal kind of communication. Man to man. Beast to beast. He gets it, and promptly tucks his tail between his legs.

Bobbing his head again, he turns and busies himself cleaning a set of already-clean glasses. "Lemme know if I can get you folks anything," he mumbles without looking up.

Kinsley presses her forehead to the cool wooden surface of the bar top. "All I want is strong enough cell reception so I can call Triple A and get my car towed." She glances through the blacked-out windows. It's a torrential downpour outside. "Doesn't look like that's going to happen anytime soon, though."

Chester might not be as smart as I gave him credit for, because he turns back to us and grins. He's missing a fair few teeth. "Got a rugrat at home waiting for the two of you?" he asks.

Kinsley tenses right up. Her spine straightens into a harsh line. "We're not together."

Chester raises his eyebrows. "Oh?"

She shakes her head. "This is the guy who nearly barreled into my car and forced me off the road. He's the reason I need a tow truck in the first place."

Chester runs a hand through his hair. "Huh. How 'bout that? I just assumed the two of you knew each other. You've got a way about ya, y'know? Like, chemistry. Sparks."

I've always enjoyed an awkward silence. You can tell so much about people when you make them uncomfortable. Kinsley, for instance. She keeps checking her phone compulsively. She doesn't want to make eye contact with me, but she can't help glancing my way every few seconds, too. It's like she's worried I'll disappear on her again.

"There's no—"

"It's been ten years since we last saw each other," I cut in smoothly. "Kinsley here is a little upset about how we left things."

She's glaring a hole into the side of my face.

"We went to high school together," I say, crafting a story on the spot just to amuse myself. I take a sip of brandy. "Kinsley was infatuated with me."

Her eyes flash with green fire. "Ha! Mr. Prom King always did have the biggest ego of any boy in school. Glad to see some things don't change."

"Some things don't need changing."

She rolls her eyes. "Right, of course not. Why improve on perfection?" she asks sarcastically. Kinsley turns to Chester. "Christ on a cracker. I should have ordered alcohol instead of coffee."

The kitchen door sweeps open. "Speak of the devil!" Chester cackles as a greasy young man in a white apron appears with a steaming mug in hand. "Thanks, Duffy. There you are, Kinsley. I can drop in a splash of something if you decide you want an extra kick."

"I'm good for now, thanks," she sighs.

Chester leans over the bar on his flabby, tattooed elbows. "So what happened, kids?" he probes. "I'm invested now. The two of you had some hot-'n'-heavy fling that ended in tears and broken hearts?"

"A broken heart would imply my heart was ever involved," she snaps. "And as for Daniil… well, he doesn't have a heart to break in the first place."

Chester turns to me with raised eyebrows and a look that reads, *You'll have your hands full with this one.*

I smirk. "Guilty."

"Every man's got one," Chester says. He's talking more to Kinsley than to me.

"Not this man," she says, her eyes drifting over to me for a moment. "I know him."

"Do you, Kinsley?" I ask. "Do you know me?"

She takes a sip of her coffee and winces at its bitterness. Her green eyes are sharp with accusation. "It's honestly so unoriginal. The confident jock who gets away with literal freaking murder just because he's got a nice jawline." She turns to Chester. "It's all just smoke and mirrors. To confuse the weak and the vulnerable."

Chester is starting to realize he's wandered into a hornet's nest. "Seems like the two of you have some issues to resolve," he says uncomfortably, topping up my brandy again.

"The only issue I want to resolve is the one involving my car," Kinsley says firmly. "I have no interest in fixing anything else."

"Okaaay," he says, moving away from the two of us. "I think I'm going to slide over to the other end of the bar. Before the sexual tension between the two of you combusts and takes me down with you, heh heh."

He ambles on over to the lonely man sitting at the opposite end of the bar with a half-full beer cradled between his hands.

When we're alone, she squirms in her seat. It's entertaining, watching her wage a war inside her own head. Somehow, both sides are losing.

She glances over at me and her eyes narrow. "You're enjoying this, aren't you?"

"I never expected to find you touchier than you were ten years ago."

"A lot can change in a decade." Her eyes flicker over my clothes. "Who'd you murder for that coat?"

"No one who didn't deserve to die."

"Right," she drawls sarcastically. "The noble criminal. The killer with an ironclad moral code."

"I never claimed to have morals. But I do have a code that I follow."

"I'd ask you to explain, but you'll probably say something cliché and predictable."

"Take a guess."

"If you tell me, you'll have to kill me? she suggests.

"You're right. Too cliché."

"What happens in Vegas stays in Vegas?"

"Too commercial."

"No one needs to know where the bodies are buried?"

I shake my head. "Actually, I find it helpful to share that information. I can't possibly be expected to remember where *all* the bodies are buried."

She goes through about a half-dozen different expressions in the blink of an eye. A laugh, a frown, a raised eyebrow, a parted lip.

"Still can't tell if I'm joking or not?"

She settles on the frown. "I'll get it eventually."

"Best not," I say.

"Why?" she asks. "Because knowing puts my life in danger?"

"No. Because if you know, all the mystery you love so much will disappear."

She rolls her eyes. "Believe me, I swore off the mysterious, broody types a long time ago." She takes another big gulp of her coffee. "Right around the time you left me alone in the woods without an explanation or a goodbye." Then she gets to her feet. "Pardon me. I'm going to go try Triple A again."

She strides off towards the alcove near the bathroom. I glance towards the windows. We've been sitting here twenty minutes and the rain has finally slowed.

Chester appears and clears the empty brandy glass in front of me. "Fuckin' hell, man," he says in a low voice, glancing after where Kinsley just went. "You gonna do something about that or what?"

Oh, I'm gonna do something about that.

I just don't know what yet.

11

KINSLEY

The water I'm splashing onto my face is cold enough to sting, but instead of helping, it's pulling me back into the throes of nostalgia.

Nostalgia. Is that even the right word? Can you long for something that you never really had in the first place?

I remember that dizzying feeling right before I fell from the bridge. The drop in my stomach when I realized I was hurtling towards the water. The wedding dress, shrouding me and choking me and dragging me down. It's a memory chock full of metaphors I'm unwilling to parse. The bottom line is that I am way in over my head here.

Shit. That's a metaphor, too, isn't it?

I look up at the faded oval mirror resting over the sink. My expression is wary, but my eyes look heart-wrenchingly alive. Like he just pulled me from the water all over again.

"Stop it," I snap at my reflection.

"Stop what?"

One of the stall doors behind me opens and a woman approaches the sink next to me. She's wearing a business suit, weirdly enough, with bright caramel eyes peering curiously at my reflection.

"Sorry," I mumble. "I didn't realize anyone was in here."

She arches one perfectly shaped eyebrow at me. "You alright, hon?" she asks. "You seem a little on edge."

On edge. Again, with the metaphors. *Jesus Christ, universe—give it a rest already.*

"Yeah, you could say that."

"Does it have something to do with that tall drink of water you're sitting with at the bar?"

I smile painfully. "Is it that obvious?"

"Mhmm. My mama used to say to me all the time: pretty men come with a boatload of problems. She was a smart lady."

Great. If that's the case, then I'm screwed.

"There are exceptions to every rule, aren't there?"

She laughs musically. "Oh, bless your heart, dear. You're one of the naïve ones."

I wince. "I'd rather think of myself as optimistic."

"More power to you then," she remarks as she pops out a stick of mocha-colored lipstick from her stylish black clutch. "I don't blame you for wanting to be optimistic where that one is concerned though," she says, talking between coats of lipstick. "That jawline is enough to make me consider switching teams."

"I wouldn't," I tell her. "Your mom was probably right about the whole boatload-of-problems thing."

"She usually was. Have a nice night, doll."

She gives me a little wink and leaves the restroom. I take a deep breath and turn back to my reflection. I don't look any more composed than when I first walked in here.

Ping. Ping. Ping. I almost do a happy dance when I hear my phone start to vibrate. Reception must've come back online. My home screen shows three texts: one from Emma, two from Liam. I open Emma's first.

EMMA: *The puppy's sleeping and I'm sipping wine on your couch. I'm guessing since you still haven't got home, you're getting laid? For the love of God, I sincerely hope so. Remember to use condoms!*

I roll my eyes and switch threads.

LIAM: *Hey sexy. I haven't been able to stop thinking about you since I got home.*

LIAM: *A woman like you deserves to be kissed. Often. And everywhere. Give me a chance to show you how much I appreciate your gorgeous body.*

There's a picture attached, which no amount of money in the galaxy could get me to open. "Ugh," I mutter, swiping out without replying and immediately purging that from my memory.

I dial in the number for Triple-A and wait nervously for an operator. It rings and rings, and then—

"Triple A. How may I help you?"

Sweet baby Jesus, thank you, I pray silently. Into the phone, I say, "Hi, my name is Kinsley Whitlow. I had an accident on Route 320 near Big Horn Bar, and my car needs to be towed."

I can hear the sound of the operator pursing her lips. "We can send a tow truck in the next twenty minutes. It'll cost you approximately… five hundred and seventy-three dollars to get you from there to the nearest mechanic shop."

I cringe at the number. "And that's just for the tow?"

"Yes, ma'am. The mechanic will have to assess the damage when the car is brought in. He'll provide you with an estimate then."

"Okay," I grimace. "Five hundred and seventy-three dollars it is."

I hang up, put my phone away, and dab my face clean with a paper towel. Then I make sure my makeup isn't too badly smeared before I leave the restroom.

Daniil is still sitting by the bar, leaning back casually in his black suit and his unwavering confidence. He looks even more in control now, if that's even possible.

"Managed to call Triple A?"

I turn to Chester, who's sticking to the opposite end of the bar now. "Uh, yeah," I say uncomfortably. "Gonna cost an arm and a leg, but they're taking care of it."

"Tell them not to. I will."

"You'll take care of it?"

He nods. "Leave it to me."

"Leave it to you?"

He takes a sip of his brandy. "If you're going to repeat everything I say, we might be here a long time."

"Considering our past experience, I think I'd rather handle this myself."

He shrugs like he doesn't give a damn one way or another. "Suit yourself."

"You don't have to stay here with me, you know," I tell him. "You can leave whenever. Like now, for instance. Or now. Or now."

"I'm not staying here for you."

I can feel the heated flush on my skin, but I ignore it and return to my coffee. I have no desire to finish it, though. I just want to keep my hands busy.

"What are you staying for then?"

He lifts his glass up. "I'm not one to waste alcohol."

"You just waste my time then?"

I expect some sharp comeback. But instead, he leans forward. This close, the blue of his eyes is hypnotic.

"I don't think I'm wasting your time at all," he says softly. "As a matter of fact, I get the feeling you've been waiting for me all these years."

I rear back and scoff. "Is that the vibe I'm giving off, Daniil? Are you really so egotistical that you think I've spent the last decade pining for you?"

"Tell me I'm wrong."

He's probably setting some kind of trap for me, but I'm too infuriated to see it. "Yes, you're freaking wrong," I snap. "I haven't been pining for you. More like I've been cursing your name."

He raises an eyebrow. Still thick and confident. Still able to express so much with so little.

I grind my teeth together, suddenly craving the strongest drink possible. A Long Island iced tea, or maybe just isopropyl straight from the bottle. "You appeared at a vulnerable moment in my life," I finish. "That's all it was."

He still says nothing, and goddammit, that's the most infuriating thing he could've said.

I survey him despite my better instincts, trying to suss out some clue as to how the criminal in borrowed rags had turned it all around. The suit alone must've cost a small fortune and the watch on his wrist is worth more than I'll make in a lifetime. The watchface is black, but in place of numbers…

"Are those emeralds?"

He follows my gaze and observes his watch for a moment. "Yes."

"Diamonds were too showy for you, huh?" I ask sarcastically.

"I'm partial to the color green." He smirks. "Since about… ten years ago, give or take."

My heart does this strange little jump that I haven't felt in… oh, I dunno—ten years, give or take.

Oh no. Oh no. Oh no. Not happening. This cannot be happening.

"I should get going," I blurt, jumping off the stool. My elbow knocks over my half-empty coffee mug and it splashes sideways on the bar. "Shit!"

I start to hunt for napkins to mop up the mess, but my brain is in the midst of a full-on, five-red-chili-pepper meltdown. *ABORT! LEAVE! ESCAPE NOW! RUN WHILE YOU STILL CAN!*

He hasn't budged from his stool and he doesn't look like he's about to move anytime soon. Which doesn't matter to me. In fact, it's better for me.

Best if he doesn't try to follow me. Because I've moved on.

I repeat that to myself: *I have moved on.* It doesn't sound much better the second time around.

"How do you plan on getting home?"

"It's this great invention called a cab."

"No," he says simply.

I arch an incredulous eyebrow. "No?"

"No, you're not taking a cab. I'll drive you."

"Don't bother," I say. "You've done enough for one night. Enough for a lifetime, actually." I pull up my rideshare app and hail an Uber immediately. "My driver will be here in four minutes," I announce.

A silent thirty seconds ticks past. Daniil doesn't look away from me even once.

Funny how four minutes can feel like a lifetime when there's a pair of icy blue eyes watching your every move.

Chester comes over while I'm studiously avoiding Daniil's gaze. "You folks headed out?" he asks.

I stand up and shoulder my purse. "I am. Can't speak for him." I start to fumble for my wallet, but Daniil pulls out his faster than me and drops two hundred dollars on the coffee-stained counter like it's nothing.

I think about telling him to stick his generosity up his own ass, but then again, he did abandon me in the forest on the worst day of my life, so maybe buying my coffee is the least he can do now. I turn and head for the door.

"I'm not about to thank you," I warn him as he trails me like a ghost.

He laughs. "I would have been surprised if you did."

I see the headlights of a Toyota Camry pulling into the parking lot. "That's my ride." I look over at him, leaning stoically against one pillar of the awning. "I'm never gonna see you again after tonight. So goodbye, or whatever."

"You never know, princess. It's a small world."

I ignore the shiver those words send surging over my skin and give the driver a cheery wave. When he pulls to a stop in front of me, I walk to the back door of the sedan and pull it open. *Just go*, screams the voice in my head. *Get in the car and go.*

But I can't resist the question that's been on the back of my mind since we entered this bar.

"Whatever happened to your boss?" I call over to Daniil, who hasn't moved. "The one who put you away?"

"He's around. But he's not my boss anymore."

"You're your own boss now."

He nods. "I always was. I just had to remind myself of that."

"Goodbye, Daniil."

"Goodnight, Kinsley."

⁓

"This your place, lady?" the driver asks half an hour later.

I glance out the window and see the faded white façade of my one-story house. I'm using the term "my" loosely, considering the house is rented, not owned.

"Oh. Sorry. Yeah, it is," I stutter. "Thank you."

I get out and head to the front door. The light is on in the living room, which means Emma has probably fallen asleep in front of the television. But when I let myself in, she's awake after all, flicking idly through a gossip magazine on the couch.

"There you are!" Emma yawns, pulling back the blanket she's got over her knees. "I was beginning to worry."

"Sorry," I say, sitting down on the sofa beside Emma's outstretched legs. "Long night."

She pushes herself upright. "Everything alright? Did something happen on your date?"

"Date?"

"Um, yeah. The date you went on tonight. With that guy from the gym...?"

"Shit. Liam. Right."

"Okay, I'm definitely worried now," Emma proclaims, grabbing my arm. "Jesus, are those goosebumps? Is Liam, like—"

"Oh, God no," I interrupt hurriedly, wrinkling my nose. "The date was a nightmare. He's not for me."

"I didn't think he was. But I thought he might be good practice."

"He wasn't good for anything but ogling other women." I sigh and let my head flop back on the couch. "I got into a little accident on my way home."

Emma's eyebrows leap up on her forehead. "What?!" Her little button nose is twitching, too. It's always weirdly expressive. I call her Bugs Bunny when she's being extra dramatic.

"Don't be such a worrywart," I scold playfully. "I'm right here. It all turned out okay in the end."

"Then why do you look like you've just seen a ghost?"

"I... knew the guy in the other car. The one that I nearly drove into."

Her warm brown eyes are laced with worry. "Who was it?"

"It was... It was him."

"Him?" she repeats in confusion. Then it hits her. "Wait. As in *him, him*?"

I just nod.

Emma crosses herself. "Lord have mercy on us all."

"Shh!" I reprimand as I glance toward the closed door at the end of the hall.

"Never mind that!" Emma snaps. "Tell me what happened. I want every detail. Did you recognize him immediately? Did he recognize you? What did he say? How did he look? Did you tell him—"

"Em, slow down. I'm still processing."

"Fine. Lame, but fine. Can I get you anything?" she asks. "Glass of water? Glass of wine? Whole bottle of wine?"

I take a deep breath, the first good inhale I've gotten since Daniil materialized out of the shadows. "Chocolate?"

"Way ahead of you," Emma says, snatching up the half-eaten chocolate bar on the coffee table and handing it to me.

"Bless you."

"I don't need blessings. I need information."

I take a huge bite out of the candy and sigh again. "I recognized him right away. He recognized me, too. It all happened so fast. I got out of my car, still a little shook-up, and… boom. Him."

"Looking…?"

"Looking so damn good that it should be criminal," I finish. Then I roll my eyes at my own unintended double entendre. "Knowing him, it probably was."

"And what about Isla?" Emma asks. "Did you tell him that he has a daughter?"

"No," I say firmly. "And I don't plan to, either."

12

DANIIL

"Fuck, this is good," Petro says, stuffing his face with a cut of ribeye dripping truffle butter. He looks up at me for the first time since the food hit the table. "Not hungry?"

"You're hungry enough for the both of us."

Petro's dark curls bob as he reaches for his beer. "You haven't even touched your drink."

"Don't even think about it. Did you run the license plate I gave you?"

My right-hand man offers me a shit-eating grin. "Ah, I see the problem. The reason you're not being very conversational. I knew you had her on the brain."

I roll my eyes. "I forgot that you expect my undivided attention when we're together."

"Our time together is sacred, amigo. Never forget that."

"You're about to get hit in the head with a chicken wing," I warn him, dangling one at him.

He just smiles, as implacable as ever. "Would you actually throw it, though?" he ponders. "Seems wasteful. Looks juicy."

"Get it yourself."

Petro gets out of his chair and lunges for the chicken like he hasn't seen food in years. You'd think he was a three-hundred pound offensive lineman, not the skin-and-bones pain in my ass he actually is.

"You're so damn moody when you don't get laid, man," he remarks as he starts happily ripping meat off the bone.

"What makes you think I didn't get laid?"

"Because you dumped Alisha, and I'm guessing she wasn't in the mood to put out after that. Although, knowing you, you could've talked her into it, ya silver-tongued devil."

"That's why I keep you around," I drawl. "You know me well."

Petro gives me a wink. "Well enough to know that this girl means something to you, even if you refuse to admit it."

"What girl?"

He sighs mournfully at me even as he bites into the chicken leg again. "'What girl.' *What girl,* he says. Little Miss Runaway Bride, of course."

I eye him coldly. "You forget who you're talking to, Petro."

My best friend shakes his head. "No, you're the one forgetting. I've been around a long time, brother. Long enough to know that this girl, this Kinsley? She's not nothing."

"Never said she was. The last time, she was just a convenient alibi."

"And this time?"

"A pain in the ass, mostly. Not unlike yourself."

Petro smirks. "How'd she look?"

"Pissed."

He shrugs like that makes sense. "You did disappear on her without a word. Can't blame the broad."

I roll my eyes and swirl my liquor around in the glass without sipping it. I'm suddenly not in the mood to eat or drink. "You sound like her."

"She actually admitted it? I'll be damned. You must've made an impression, big guy. Which is a surprise, if you ask me."

"I didn't—"

"Because," he continues as if I hadn't spoken, "you're the moodiest son of a bitch I've ever met. I'll be honest, it was a turn-off for me the first time we met."

"We were twelve," I remind him.

"And you wouldn't share your lunch with me," he says solemnly. "I've never forgotten that."

"I think I've more than made up for that by sharing everything else in my life with you since then."

He smiles roguishly. "Does that sharing policy extend to Lady Whitlow?"

My eyes flash to his with the promise of pain. "You want to keep your dick attached?"

He crosses his arms triumphantly. I curse myself for falling into his trap so easily. "Tell me again how she doesn't mean anything to you," he jabs. "Go on, say it."

"She was the first woman I fucked after jail. Yeah, I remember her. Sue me."

"So romantic," Petro says with a mock dreamy expression on his face. "So basically, what you're telling me is that you lost your prison virginity to her. I get it, though, I get it. I've been there."

I roll my eyes yet again. They're getting quite the workout tonight. Petro is in rare form. "You spent one night in jail for unpaid parking tickets, idiot."

"Because my best friend conveniently 'forgot' to post bail," he retorts. "A tattooed skinhead almost chewed my leg off."

"I wish he had. I have a feeling you'd be much less chatty."

"Perish the thought." He spears another bite of steak and shovels it in the second after he's swallowed the chicken. Then he grabs his beer, washes it all down with a huge glug, and leans back in his seat to exhale contentedly and rub his belly. "I'm stuffed. We should eat in the dining room more often."

The dining room of my mansion is a long, rectangular hall flanked along the walls with portraits, priceless pottery, and medieval weapons. Some I inherited. Some I bought myself. Some are gifts, given to me by old friends looking to make new alliances.

"There is no 'we' here," I growl irritably. "There is only me. My house, my dining room—"

"Your runaway bride," Petro finishes. "Yeah, yeah, yeah. I got it. You know, you're all big and bad and well-dressed now, but deep down, you're still the mean twelve-year old who wouldn't give me a bite of his sandwich."

"Remind me why I keep you around again?"

Petro smirks. "For my good looks."

"That's not it."

"For my sense of humor?"

"Try again."

He sighs. "Because I'm useful."

"Prove it."

"Asshole," he mutters, just loud enough so that I can hear. Then he pulls out his phone and scrolls through it. "Yes, Don Vlasov, sir, I tracked the license plate number you gave me."

"And?"

He reads off his phone. "License plate KNX482, registered to a Ms. Kinsley Jane Whitlow. Currently being held in a privately-owned auto body shop in Hartford called Milson's Spare Parts. The car was towed in late last night."

"'Bout time you started doing your job," I say, getting to my feet.

"Wait," Petro protests, "where are you going?"

"Where do you think?"

Petro snatches up his beer and hustles out of the dining room behind me. "You're going there *now*?"

"It would appear so."

"But why? It's not like she's going to be there."

"You are woefully shortsighted, my friend."

"Using words like 'woefully' doesn't make you smarter than me, dickhead."

I chuckle as we make our way outside to the circular gravel driveway where my favorite blue Mercedes is parked, ready and waiting. Petro is still talking up a storm.

"So you're going to… wait, don't say it, lemme guess: steal her car and then leave her a series of clues that'll lead her right to your doorstep?" he suggests.

"One of your worst ideas to date, my friend. And that's saying something." I get in the car.

Petro is still talking, so I roll down the window. He'll be an endless irritant if I don't let him get the last word. "… can see why she's so pissed at you," he complains. "You're annoying."

"Try not to bother me for the next couple of hours," I advise him.

"Two hours? You have a meeting with the Greeks in two hours!" he says, panicked.

"If I'm late, stall."

"Get real. Daniil, you're gonna blow off the Greek mob for a woman you barely know? Daniil? Daniil!"

I laugh and cruise out of the gates. By the time I reach the highway, I have the body shop plugged into my navigation system. The roads are empty; the sky is clear.

Everything is happening just the way I intended it.

Milson's Spare Parts is every bit the crude, rundown shithole I was expecting. Two large sheds of corrugated tin with the doors rolled up, revealing an absolute disaster of oily car parts and the shells of wrecked vehicles hoisted up on platforms. I recognize Kinsley's car immediately.

The moment I pull to a stop, all eyes are on me. Or rather, all eyes are on my Mercedes. It wasn't my most understated choice, but this is one of those instances where throwing weight around is worthwhile.

"That's a beaut, man," one of the mechanics remarks as he saunters over. The grease on his dull gray tee pales in comparison to the grease in his hair and beard. He's a walking fire hazard. "Doesn't belong in this dump, though. We'd only do it damage."

"This car is not the reason I'm here," I say. "I'm actually looking for another car. That one."

He turns in the direction of my finger. "The Mini?"

"That's the one."

He looks shocked by that. "Well, shit. My dad's the one who accepted the call to tow it down here," he says. "Maybe I should go fetch him?"

"You do that."

Greasy returns a few seconds later, followed by an older version of himself.

"Hiya," the older man says, offering me his hand. "I'm Gregory Milson. This is my son, Peyton."

I give them both a nod and point behind them. "I'm here about the Mini Cooper."

The old man looks at the car as if he's not sure which one I'm talking about. *"That* one?" He clears his throat gruffly. "What's that car got to do with you, if you don't mind me askin'? The owner was here this morning. She didn't mention anything about sending over a guy."

"She's on a whole independent kick," I say smoothly. It's not quite a lie. "But she's not so good with cars." That's not quite a lie, either.

Gregory exchanges a glance with his son. "What exactly do you want from me, sir?"

"I want you to hand the car over to me."

"H… hand it over?"

"My team will be here momentarily to pick it up."

"I'm… well, I'm afraid I can't do that, sir," Milson stammers. "Not without authorization from the owner."

"The owner is stubborn," I say. "I would know. I'm her husband."

"Husband?" Greasy interjects. "I didn't see no ring on her finger."

I turn to him, making sure he catches the full force of my glare. "Spent a lot of time looking at her, did you?"

Greasy goes pale, and he actually takes a step back. He must be older than me. Closer to forty than thirty. But he looks like a scared child who knows he's in trouble.

"I, uh… that… well…"

"Jesus," Milson snaps at his son. "Get it together, Peyton."

"It ain't a crime to look," he protests.

I take a step forward without ever breaking eye contact. "That depends on whose woman you're looking at."

My tone is pleasant.

My intention is anything but.

"I didn't m-mean any d-disrespect," Greasy stutters.

"Glad to hear it. Now, be a good boy and run along while I speak to your father."

It's an insulting dismissal for a grown man, but he's smart enough to walk away instead of attempting to salvage his pride.

The elder Milson looks less than thrilled, though. That pinched, disappointed expression on his face hits too close to home.

He looks like my own father.

"I oughta call the owner and check with her first," he mumbles.

"No."

He falters a little, his eyes slipping to my Mercedes. "Can you prove you're her husband?"

"Also no."

He pauses, still unsure which way to swing. I decide to make it easy for him. I open my wallet and ruffle through the stack of green cash in there. His eyes light up, but then I snap it shut and draw his attention back to me.

He swallows hard. "What about the law, sir? I could get in trouble for somethin' like this."

I scoff. "Do I strike you as the kind of man who's concerned about the law?"

His gaze flickers once more to my Mercedes. "Four hundred dollars," he says. "And I'll hand her over. No questions asked."

I fork over the bills, watching his face the whole time.

"He didn't touch her, you know," Milson says quickly. "My son, I mean. He didn't touch your wife. If that's what you're thinking."

"If that's what I was thinking, your son would be bleeding face-down in the dirt, drawing his last breaths," I inform him, just as my boys pull up in a shiny yellow tow truck. Kostya, one of my lieutenants, salutes me from the driver's seat as he rolls the window down.

"Sir," he greets coolly.

I point to Kinsley's car. "That one. Take it to the garage and fix it."

"Yes, sir."

Him and three other Bratva men hop out of the tow truck and get to work. Milson stares at them as they walk into his garage, claiming the space as though they own it. No one puts up a fight.

"Who the hell are you?" Milson asks in awe.

I smirk. "It's not important for you to know."

With that, my business here is done. I turn and head back towards my car. Halfway there, I hear Gregory pipe up. "Sir, one more question."

I sigh and halt in place without turning around. "I thought we agreed to none of those."

I hear him fidget nervously in the dirt. "What do I say to the lady when she comes looking for her car?"

I turn and face him. I'm quiet for a long time. "Tell her to go back to the beginning," I say at last. "She'll find her car there."

Then I spin around once more and finish the walk to my car. I'm laughing to myself as I gun it, sending a rooster tail of dirt and gravel flying over the shellshocked Milson men behind me.

Back to the beginning.

Yeah, that'll definitely piss her off.

13

KINSLEY

"I'm sorry; I don't understand," I say in disbelief, staring the shop owner in the face. "What do you mean, 'My car isn't here'?"

He looks over both shoulders like he's expecting backup. None is forthcoming. "Um, your, uh… your husband came and took it." He shifts uncomfortably from one foot to the other.

"My… my… my what?"

The man, stout and hairy, blinks like a stoned ape. "Your husband, ma'am."

It all clicks suddenly, as if my ears popped on an airplane and suddenly I can hear again. "Was he tall? Good-looking? Kind of had 'rich asshole' vibes?"

"So you do know him," he chuckles.

"Unfortunately." I gnash my teeth. "Did he say where he was taking my car?"

"No, ma'am. Well, not precisely. He did leave a message, though. He said, uh…" He glances down at a Post-It Note stuck behind the desk. "He said, *'Go back to the beginning. You'll find your car there.'*"

The blood thrumming in my ears is deafeningly loud. "Say that again."

"*'Go back to the beginning. You'll find your car there,'*" he repeats with a little more confidence the second time around.

"Oh my God," I whimper. "You gotta be fucking kidding me."

I'd called him a poet once. Sarcastically, of course. Seems he's intent on living up to the title now.

I pull out my phone and attempt to flag down another Uber when an incoming call starts to vibrate.

"Hi," I grit out.

"Whoa, something wrong? Did they fuck up your car? Is the Blue Stallion okay?" Emma asks without pausing for a breath. "I told you that place seemed dodgy. How badly did they screw up?"

"Well, they lost my car. So I'd say, pretty damn bad."

"Okay, um… okay. Wow. Well, we can sue. Or, like, commit arson. Mr. FBI Agent, if you're listening to this call, I'm just joking." In a stage whisper, she adds, "*I'm not joking.*"

That's what I love about Emma—she adopts my problems instantaneously like she doesn't have enough of her own. It's never a "me" problem, always a "we" problem. Whether or not it actually has anything to do with her.

"No, put down the matches, Em. It's only sort of the garage's fault."

I can hear her purse her lips. "Okay, well, I'm clearly missing some part of the story. Fill a girl in."

I exhale and squeeze the bridge of my nose to ward off the looming migraine. "They handed my car over yesterday to a man who claimed to be my husband."

"Unless you got married without telling me... then they're lying?"

"No," I sigh, "the man who claimed to be my husband did the lying. Not surprising, really. He's obviously good at it."

"Wait... you don't think—"

"Of course it's him," I say. "Who else could it be?"

"He... he wouldn't. Would he? He wouldn't. No, he wouldn't."

"*'Go back to the beginning. That's where you'll find it.'*"

"Pardon?"

"It's the message he left me. Apparently, he's trying to draw me into a scavenger hunt or something."

"Aww. Adorable!"

"Emma!"

"Right, right," she corrects quickly. "We hate him. Grr. Do you know where the 'beginning' is?"

"I have an idea."

"Fabulous. Where are you right now?"

"Still at the body shop. I'll have to call another ride. I let the first one go."

"Don't bother. I'll swing by and get you."

"What about work?"

"Work, shmork," she dismisses. "I'm a waitress with a boss who wants in my pants, like, stupid bad. I'll be there in ten."

I let loose a weary breath. "You're an angel."

"Guilty as charged."

I hang up and turn to find that the shop owner is still hovering behind me, looking nervous and sweaty. "Out of curiosity," I ask, "how much did he pay you?"

He freezes in place. "Ma'am…"

"Relax. I'm not going to do anything. I'm just interested."

The man sighs, sounding every bit as weary as I do. "Four hundred dollars," he says, directing his answer toward his feet.

I laugh bitterly. "You could have gotten ten times that."

With that, I'm out of things to say. I push through the door, stride away, and go wait by the corner of the road for Emma. I pace back and forth, anxious and exhausted at the same time.

Back to the beginning. God, that's cruel.

The beginning is the thing I've wanted to put behind me since the moment I woke up to an empty car and a silent forest.

The beginning is the thing I've been running from for ten years.

The beginning is the last place on Earth I want to be.

∽

Emma arrives ten minutes later, with her windows rolled down and music blaring from inside the car. Bon Jovi, *It's My Life.*

"Perfect soundtrack for this little scavenger hunt, huh?" she asks, flashing me an enthusiastic grin.

"Wrong attitude," I scowl as I walk around to the passenger seat. "You're supposed to be feeling fury and resentment. Not… whatever this is."

"Excitement?" She clocks my grimace and pushes me in the shoulder. "Oh, come on. You're not even a little bit excited?"

"Which part should I be excited about?"

"About seeing him again, duh."

My body betrays me with shooting tingles that run from my head right down to my toes. At least it's invisible to the naked eye. Easy to deny. Even to Emma.

"No," I reply. "Definitely not."

"Very emphatic. Very believable."

"Would you believe me if I was tentative?"

She flips her hair out of her face. "I'm just saying, no man has ever gotten you this riled up before."

"Because no man has been this infuriating before."

"Really?" Emma asks skeptically. "What about the mouth breather with the collection of porcelain dolls?"

I turn to her with a frown. "You dated that guy, not me."

"Yeah, well, I couldn't think of any weirdos you dated. In fact, it's hard to think of anyone you've dated."

"Liam."

"Liam was three days ago, and that's making the word 'dated' do a whole lotta work there, babe. I had to force you to go out with him and you're not planning on seeing him again. So no, that doesn't count."

"What's your point?" I ask miserably.

"My point is that you really haven't put yourself out there, Kinz. And I think this guy might be the reason why."

"Please—"

"You forget, I was there with you in The Dark Times."

The Dark Times. That's what we call the days after the wedding, before I found out I was pregnant. It's not a period of my life I ever want to go back to.

"Don't remind me."

"You need to be reminded," Emma says gently. "You were so—"

"Don't say it."

"… heartbroken," she finishes. I glare at her, but she just shrugs defiantly. "I haven't brought it up in forever and a half. I always figured, why bring up something that you'd never be able to resolve? But now's your chance!"

"My chance for what?"

"To resolve this. To get closure. To get some answers."

"It's been ten years, Emma. He's changed. So have I."

"What about Isla?"

I stiffen defensively. "Isla has me. And you."

"Sure, I'm her cool, fun, hip, and incredibly sexy aunt," Emma agrees, flashing me a grin. "But I'm definitely not her daddy. Neither are you."

I slump back against the headrest. "You don't understand. I can't let him into my life. Into *our* lives."

"Why not?"

"Because… because he will consume us." I take a breath to try to stop my downward spiral, but I'm not sure it's doing any good. "He's dangerous. I'm not sure I fully realized it at the time. Or at least, I wasn't in the right frame of mind to properly realize it. But I get it now. He's dangerous. He's a bad guy and he's done bad stuff in the past and he'll do bad stuff in the future. If I let him, he'll do bad stuff to me."

Emma rests a hand on my thigh. "Look, I hear you, I really do. But you said it yourself a billion times—something weird happened that night. Maybe he's a bad guy; I wouldn't know him from Adam. But you sure didn't think so back then." She grimaces in frustration. "I'm making a huge mess of this, but I guess what I'm trying to say is, what if he's not dangerous *to you?*"

I glance at her, ashamed of the way my eyes are tearing up while all this emotion gets the better of me. But if there's one person I don't mind sharing my tears with, it's her.

"I'm not the naïve girl who agreed to marry Tom anymore, Em," I whisper. "I left that version of Kinsley behind a long time ago. And I'm not about to go falling backwards just because he decided to show up again."

"What about Isla? Don't you think she deserves to know who her father is?"

"Of course she does. And if he were any other man, I might have considered telling him about her," I insist. "But he's not just any man. He's... he's..."

I struggle to find the words I'm looking for. When I glance up, Emma's looking at me sympathetically.

"He's the one man you actually felt something for," she guesses softly.

I take a deep breath. My tears taste bitter where they pass my lips. "Who knows what I was feeling? It's all jumbled together now. I was so scared that day. And confused, and unhappy, and a trillion other things all at once. I constructed a fantasy and I lived in it for way longer than I should have. Everything that happened was only because he held a mirror up to me and forced me to look at myself. At my life, my mistakes, all that stuff." I clear my throat. "At the end of the day, though, he was just a stranger who fished me out of a river. I attached more meaning to it than I should have."

We're quiet for a while. Then Emma reaches out and pats my hand just once. That's all she needs to do or say. We've been friends for so long at this point that words are mostly unnecessary. A pat of the hand is plenty.

Sighing, she regrips the wheel. "Okay, hon. We still need to get your car back. Do you know where the 'beginning' is?"

"Yeah," I say. "I think."

"Off we go then," Emma says cheerily, pulling the car back onto the road. "You'll have to direct me, though. The navigator's not going to understand 'the spot where Kinsley banged a convict.'"

⁓

I tense up when I see the dirt path diverge from the highway. Was that vine there before? That bush, that rock? I can't remember. But that mouth of darkness ready to swallow us up into the guts of the forest—that hasn't changed one bit.

"Slow down," I tell Emma. "Right over there. That's it."

She directs the car where I'm pointing, parks, and turns to me. "Now what?"

I smile as warmly as I can, which isn't that convincing. "Thanks for the ride, Em."

She doubles back, startled. "You want me to leave?"

"I can take it from here."

"Like hell you can! You literally just told me this guy is dangerous. You had a whole speech about it and everything."

"And you just told me that he's not dangerous to me."

"I said it's a possibility, not a fact."

"Well, I can't keep up. I'm getting emotional whiplash here."

"Kinz—"

"I'll be fine. I swear. The moment I spot my car, I'll let you know."

"I'd be the worst BFFAEAEAE if I let you go traipsing into the woods alone."

I reach out and grip her hand. "I just... I need to do this alone, Emma. I know that sounds dumb and maybe it is. But... please?"

She eyes me warily for a long time before she sighs. "Fine. I don't like it, but fine. Promise you'll call me as soon as you get the car back?"

"Promise."

She gives me a terse nod. "Okay, best of luck to you. If he gets handsy..."

"I'll kick him in the nuts and run away."

"Sure, that's fine," she shrugs. "Or you can have your way with him. Whichever seems more appropriate."

I shove her away from me. "You're sending some real mixed messages today."

She laughs. "Text me, okay?"

"Yeah. I will."

I get out of the car and watch her drive off, checking her side mirrors the entire time. Then I head into the forest.

Right back to the beginning.

14

DANIIL

I hear her before I see her. Her footsteps mix in with the skittering animals and the swish of wind through trees. It's daytime, but down here, it feels like dusk. The trees are clustered thick enough to blot out most of the light.

But there's enough of it left to cast shadows. I notice her silhouette fall against the bed of fallen leaves on the forest floor.

And just like that, I'm transported ten years into the past.

"I take it you got my message," I rumble, ignoring how my chest clenches tight with her smell, her proximity.

"Yeah," she scoffs. "Cracked the case. Excuse me for not celebrating. Now, where are my car keys?"

"Right here." I lift my hand and shimmy the keychain. "Come and get 'em, princess."

"You always did talk to me like I was a dog," she scowls. "'*Stay. Come. No.*'" She snorts and flicks her hair over her shoulder. "Throw me the keys. I'm not coming over there."

"I don't bite."

Kinsley snorts again. "I doubt that very, very much."

"So much for all that trust we built," I remark casually. "You know, *sladkaya*, I'm starting to sense some unresolved issues between us."

"The only thing left to resolve between us is the transfer of those car keys into my hands," she retorts.

I glance down at the worn keychain. "Who's this supposed to be?" I ask, poking at the little figurine hanging there. "Wonder Woman? You never struck me as a superhero fan."

"I'm not really a fan. But Isl—"

She stops short, freezing on a word that doesn't manage to make it out of her still-plump, still-pink, still-inviting lips.

"But…?" I prompt.

She takes a deep breath. "You didn't drag me into the woods just to catch up on the last decade, Daniil. So then why are we here? Why would you even take my car in the first place?"

"You saw the shithole you took it to. I would have thought the answer was obvious."

"Is that your version of an apology?" she asks incredulously. Behind her, a woodpecker is hammering away at the trunk of a tree. *Rap-tat-tap-rap*, over and over again.

"I don't make apologies."

"Imagine my surprise. You don't give explanations, either, I'll bet. Must be nice," she says, scanning my Brioni suit slowly. "To live your life that way. Us normal folks don't have that luxury."

"Something tells me you weren't in a hurry to explain what happened between us to anyone."

She frowns and taps a finger against her lips. "You're talking about the morning I woke up in an empty car in the middle of the woods the day after I was supposed to get married? I guess not." She toes the ground. A cloud of dry dust rises into the air. "After I figured out you weren't coming back, I drove to my apartment and packed a bag. Then I moved into my friend's place so that I wouldn't have to deal with exactly those kinds of explanations."

"Emma's a good friend."

"Yes, she—" She breaks off and stares at me in disbelief. "Are you stalking me? How do you know about Emma? I didn't mention her at all."

"Not this time, no," I agree. "But last time, you did. She called to check on you after you'd taken the car and ran from your wedding."

Her face goes slack with realization, but the shock lingers. "You… you remember her name."

"I remember a lot of things."

She swallows back her surprise. "So you haven't been stalking me?"

I smile. "I'm a busy man now, Kinsley. I don't have time to follow you from morning to night. Riveting though your schedule may be." I saunter closer to her. "Does that disappoint you?"

"What you're seeing is relief, not disappointment."

"I'm not so sure you're telling me the truth, *sladkaya*."

What she says next takes me by surprise. *"Perestan' nazyvat menya tak."*

Stop calling me that.

I feel a jolt of some inexplicable carnal need at the sound of those words on her lips. In my mother tongue, no less. The accent is atrocious, but I understand every bit.

"You speak Russian."

"I didn't back then," she says calmly. "And I don't claim to speak it properly now. Just enough to get me through a simple conversation. You called me that word a few times. *Sladkaya.* I wanted to know what it meant, so I looked it up. Learned a few things in the process. Anyway," she finishes, shaking her head to clear the thoughts, "I'm done bickering with you. Give me my keys."

"No, I don't think I will."

She grits her teeth. "I forgot how damn infuriating you are."

"And arrogant. Don't forget that."

"Believe me, I haven't. That part is sealed into my brain." Her gaze rakes up and down my clothes, my posture, the Hublot watch glistening on my wrist. "How'd you do all this, anyway? Do you send off for a 'Rich Douche' outfit from some mail order catalog?"

"I was always rich," I inform her.

She cackles. "If that were true, you'd never have been imprisoned in the first place. Rich men never see the inside of a jail cell."

I don't miss the note of bitterness in her voice. The little dove has learned some more things about the world since we last crossed paths. Not nice things, either.

"The man I pissed off was even richer than me."

She considers that for a moment. "Your boss?"

"That's right."

"Did he try to come after you?"

"In a manner of speaking."

She rolls her eyes. "I forgot how much you love speaking in riddles. Is that a subconscious thing or is it purely for my benefit?"

"You decide."

She rolls her eyes yet again. At this point, she might as well leave them up there.

"My boss was never interested in putting me away for good," I explain. "He wanted to ensure that he'd have my loyalty without the insubordination after I was released."

She snorts. "I could have told him that you were a lost cause."

"You didn't need to."

She squints at me, trying to decipher how all these puzzle pieces fit together. "So you broke out. You went back to him for seconds. And you…?"

"I built my own empire. My own legacy. Challenging him was just icing."

"What about the woman you stepped in to defend?" she asks hesitantly, like she knows it's a bad idea to venture down this rabbit hole but she just can't stop herself. "Who was she?"

"She was his wife."

"Oh," Kinsley breathes. Her gaze shifts unconsciously to the exact spot we'd parked the last time we were in this neck of the woods. As if there's evidence of that night still entwined in the trees.

"You chose that, then," she decides, returning her eyes to mine. "You could've done nothing. Most people would've done nothing."

"Most people are cowards."

She nods and bites at her lower lip. "Tell me something I don't know. There were plenty of people who knew my mother was being abused, even before I told them. They didn't do a damn thing. It was just more convenient not to. To pretend everything was fine."

Her eyes have softened considerably. Their green hue is warm under the canopy, and they catch the autumn colors. She glances at her car, and this time, she really looks at it. "You had the bumper fixed," she notes with surprise. "What's the catch?"

"No catch."

"There's always a catch. Men like you never do anything without a reason," she says firmly. She checks the time on her simple black wristwatch. "Well, this has been predictably harrowing. But I have to get back to my life."

"Good luck with that."

She blinks at me expectantly. "I'm going to need my car keys to do so," she says, her tone as brittle as the dry leaves under our feet.

"Here they are," I say, holding them up again. She starts to reach for them, but then I raise my hand too high for her to get to. "Although, now that I think of it, there is one more thing we need to take care of first."

"Nope," she retorts, "I think we're all good."

"Your vehicle was uninsured," I tell her.

"Gee, thanks, Dad," she seethes. "Are you gonna show me how to change a flat tire, too? Teach me to throw a baseball?"

I ignore her jabs. "I took care of it for you."

She stops short, her eyes going wide. "Excuse me?"

I nod. "You'll need to pick up the papers when they're ready. Shouldn't be more than a few days."

She stares at me with her mouth hanging open. Out of nowhere, I find myself wondering how she'd react if I were to slip my finger between her lips. Part of me thinks she'd suck instinctively. The other, wiser part of me thinks that she'd probably try to take a bite.

"Who the hell are you?" she whispers in shock and awe.

It's not really a question for me to answer, though. It's just her trying to figure out how her map of the world needs to change now that she's seen my true place in it.

I can see the tease of her nipples through the tight blue t-shirt she's wearing. It's either the chill in the air or it's me. I'm willing to put money on the latter.

"I'm your husband, remember?" I say with a wink.

Kinsley scowls, grabs the keys out of my hand, and retreats.

15

KINSLEY

"Ms. Whitlow? I thought I gave you the day off."

I turn towards Principal Bridges and offer him a smile I hope is convincing. "You did. I finished my errands earlier than expected, and Isla's not gonna be done for another half hour, so I thought I'd come grab some papers to grade at home."

"All work and no play makes Jack a dull boy," he recites in a sing-song voice, winking. Then he switches to the low, concerned voice he uses on the students when he thinks they're going through something at home and asks, "Are you okay, Kinsley?"

"Of course," I lie as I try to hide my wince. "Why wouldn't I be?"

I hate how I sound. False and cheery, when my insides are a churning mess of emotions that don't have a name.

"Have you spoken to Ms. Roe?" Bridges asks.

I tense up immediately. "I thought Isla's problems in class were… resolved?"

"I'm not sure it's the kind of thing that can be resolved with a conversation and a couple of days away from school, Kinsley," he says gently. "Isla is… struggling."

"She's fine."

She's not.

"On the surface, perhaps," Bridges concedes sympathetically. "But something seems to be bothering her lately. She's restless, unfocused. I think you'd benefit from talking to Ms. Roe again about her progress in class."

I nod and gulp. "Thank you, Mr. Bridges. I'll do that."

"Please do, Kinsley." He eyes me over the rims of his glasses. "We all want what's best for you and your daughter."

His words hang in the air for a moment. Then he nods like he's satisfied, turns, and walks away.

As he disappears around the corner, I duck into the teachers' lounge to grab a couple of things from my locker. Since second period is in session, the lounge is practically deserted. The only other person in here is Martha Levinson, the ever-present substitute teacher who looks older than time itself.

"Hi, Mrs. Levinson," I say, giving her a wave. I make sure to speak extra loud. She doesn't hear very well.

She looks up at me through her unbelievably massive, unbelievably thick glasses. "Oh, hello, dear. Kelly, isn't it?"

"Kinsley. Close enough."

"That's right. I'm sorry, I'm not good with names. I get so many of them daily. Occupational hazard of substituting."

I grin pleasantly, then I step over to my locker, open it, and cling to the door as though it's the only thing keeping me standing. With my face hidden from view, I close my eyes and try to breathe.

Deep breaths, Kinsley. In and out. Nice, deep breaths. Everything is going to be fine.

"Are you okay, honey?" Mrs. Levison asks, noticing that I've been staring at a half-empty locker for an uncomfortable amount of time.

"Of course," I say as brightly as I can. I slam my locker shut. "All good."

My legs are still a little wobbly, so I take a chair to Mrs. Levinson's right and pretend like I didn't just have this alarmingly unsettling conversation with my daughter's father. Whom I haven't seen in ten years. Who also has no idea he has a daughter in the first place.

Breathe, I repeat to myself.

Simple advice in theory. Very difficult to do in practice.

"You have a daughter in the school, don't you?"

I nod. "Isla. She's in fifth grade. Ms. Roe's class."

"Ms. Roe," Mrs. Levinson says, rolling her eyes. She sees me stifling a laugh and winks. "You seem like a sensible girl. You know what I'm talking about."

"I'm stuck here full-time, Mrs. Levinson. It's dangerous to offer up my honest opinions about my colleagues. Makes for trouble, you know?"

She laughs, a sound like a wheezy old couch belching up dust. "Oh, I understand. Used to be the same for me before I retired. How long have you worked at Crestmore Academy?"

"Well, back in the day, I was a student here, actually. But I've been working here ever since I enrolled Isla," I reply. "Four years now."

"Oh, I see. A family affair. It's a nice school."

"Yeah," I say softly. "It is. Most of the time."

In my head, I add, *It was nicer for me when Louisa was here.*

But she's long gone. You'd think I would have grown used to that by now. Some wounds just never finish healing, I guess. The scars on my wrists are proof of that, among other things.

My gaze strays to a bulletin board behind Mrs. Levinson's head. It's a colorful mess, wallpapered over with flyers and notices. Bake sales and PTA meetings and the like. But when I see one flamingo-colored sheet, my heart double-clutches in my chest.

"They're having a dance soon," I mumble.

"Sorry?"

I get up and walk over to the board. The design of the poster is simple. Just the silhouette of a little girl dancing on her father's legs. But it hurts like a knife to the gut.

"Father-Daughter Dance," I read out in a weird, croaking rasp.

"Oh! How wonderful. Your little one must be so excited."

"Somehow, I doubt that," I drawl under my breath.

"Oh?"

I glance over and realize suddenly that Mrs. Levinson isn't quite as dusty and old as I used to assume. There's a sharp, perceptive glow behind those glasses. She sees a lot more than she lets on.

"She doesn't… That is to say, I'm not married."

"Another young divorcée," Mrs. Levinson says regretfully. "It seems divorce is quite the trend these days."

"No, actually, I was never married."

"Ah, the other trend," she says. "And Isla's father?"

"He's not in the picture. He never was."

Something starts humming in my pocket. I reach for my vibrating phone and glance at the screen. It's a text message from Emma.

Well???? What happened!??? Tell me everything! Did you get your car back???

"You'll have to excuse me," I say to Mrs. Levinson. "I have to go pick up Isla."

Before she can answer, I grab my sling bag, hoist it over one shoulder, and hustle out of the teachers' lounge. I make my way through the still-quiet corridors, and outside to the main courtyard where the kids run through at the end of the day.

I pull out my phone again and tap out a quick text to Emma. *i got my car back. he was there.*

Her response is immediate. *Of course he was there. What did he say? What did you say? How did it end? Did he fix the car?*

The bell rings just then with a deafening clang. I hear the growing tide of children laughing and screaming, feet stomping, backpacks zipping open and closed. The doors burst open to release the flood. I search through the faces for my daughter, but I don't see her yet.

I glance down at my phone when it buzzes again and realize that I accidentally sent a string of meaningless emojis.

EMMA: *EGGPLANT EMOJI!? YOU HAD SEX WITH HIM!?*

"Jesus," I mutter before I start texting rapidly. *of course not! i didn't even realize i sent it. butt text.*

She sends me a rolling-eyes emoji. *Text responsibly, dammit.*

Five minutes since the bell tolled and I'm still waiting on her. Other kids filter out in their little mini-flocks, but I can't find my daughter in any of them. Slowly, the flow of kids trickles to nothing. Still no Isla.

Frowning, I go to her classroom. When I stick my head in the door, I see her. She's sitting in the far corner, doodling in a sketchbook with an enviable degree of focus.

A voice from behind the desk startles me.

"Hi, Ms. Whitlow," Ms. Roe says dourly. "I was hoping you'd come by today."

"What's going on?" I ask, looking towards Isla, who still doesn't seem to have noticed that I'm here.

"Isla needed some quiet time," Heather explains, looking at me with a somber expression. "She wanted to spend it in the classroom while you finished up."

I glance towards my daughter. Her head is bent down so far over her desk that it looks like she's napping on the table. Like she wants to curl up and disappear from this world.

"How was she today?"

"Still not very cooperative," Heather sighs. "She refuses to participate in group activities. She prefers to sit in a corner and daydream."

"She just needs some time. That's all."

Another expression I don't particularly like glides across Heather's face. She chooses her words carefully. "Listen, Kinsley… Mr. Bridges talked to me about going easy on Isla, but I'm not sure that's the right approach."

I feel my hackles rise. "And what do you think would be the right approach?"

"Kids get bullied all the time," Heather says with a shrug. "They don't usually get this much special treatment because of it. Isla just needs to develop a thicker skin. I don't think we're doing her any favors by mollycoddling her."

I swallow back my anger, reminding myself that Heather Roe is going to be Isla's teacher for six more months. I can't afford to get on her bad side. "Heather, she's nine. And she's also a very sensitive kid—"

"All kids are sensitive," she says, interrupting me.

"Really?" I ask. "What about the girl who pushed Isla down a few months ago and called her an 'ugly piece of shit'? That one is sensitive, too?"

"It doesn't help anyone for you to get upset, Kinsley."

"She's my child, Heather! And she's getting bullied. Which is something you, as her teacher, should have prevented."

"Now, hold on—"

"Mom?"

I turn towards Isla, who has finally realized I'm here. I rip away from Heather and take the desk beside Isla's. "Hey, hon. What have you got there?"

She pushes the sketchbook towards me. She's drawn a silhouette. The silhouette of a little girl dancing on her father's feet. The same one I saw in the teachers' lounge.

Just like that, I feel my heart plunge right into my stomach acid.

"Honey…"

"Can we go home now?" she blurts. "I don't wanna be at school anymore."

I nod in defeat. "Of course. Let's go."

I help Isla gather up her things and then we duck out of the classroom. On our way out, I throw Heather a glare that she can't misinterpret.

I know I'm not handling this well, but it's been an emotionally wrought few days, and it's harder to be mature when you're already trying so hard just to keep it together.

"The car's back!" Isla says when she sees the Blue Stallion parked in my designated spot on the teacher's lot.

"The car's back," I say with a conflicted smile. "As good as new."

As much as I begrudge him for the unwelcome intrusion into my life, Daniil did a good job repairing it. The fender sparkles in the afternoon sun. We pile in and I start driving, wracking my brain for things to say to her that'll make her smile.

"How about we bake some cupcakes tonight?" I suggest. That used to be a surefire way of cheering her up.

"No, thanks."

I glance at my somber little girl. She's tried to slick back her curly brown hair into a ponytail. But her hair's gathered at the corners of the rubber band, creating knots that I know she'll pay for later.

"You should keep your hair loose, sweetheart," I say.

"It's too curly. I don't like it."

I suppress a sigh. I'm not sure when she got so judgmental about her appearance. I'd expected it at sixteen. But nine? It feels heartbreakingly early.

"Your hair's beautiful."

She frowns. "No, it's not. And for the record, it doesn't help to lie to me."

"Isla!"

She shrugs, stiffens her upper lip, and goes back to staring out her window. We pull up to the house without another word. The silence feels especially heavy today.

The moment I've got the front door open, Isla arrows straight to her room. She practically lives there now. The only times she can be coaxed out is when Aunt Emma comes over.

"What about a snack?" I call after her before she can close her bedroom door.

"Not hungry."

"Isla, you have to eat some—"

SLAM. No response.

I exhale noisily. Everything's become a struggle with her lately. Every decision ends up in a negotiation. Every conversation ends up in tears.

On my end more often than hers.

She might not be hungry, but I'm starving. I cut up carrots and potatoes and put them in a pot to boil. Then I roll out some puff pastry and put it in the oven to blind bake.

The kitchen has always been my favorite space in this house. It's the largest room, which isn't saying much, but it's bright and airy. I like to keep the doors to the garden open to let in any spare breeze. Today, there's none to be found. Shocker.

I grab some orange juice from the fridge. When the door swings closed, I stop and look at it, feeling my heart keep making its way down. It'll be swimming in my shoes by bedtime at this rate.

The refrigerator door is papered with Isla's drawings and old pictures that I've collected over the years. Little snapshots of our lives. Isla's first crawl. Isla's first day at kindergarten. Isla's first day at the beach. The day she lost her first tooth. The day she put in her—

I stare at the fridge, realizing that the picture of Isla with her first set of braces is gone.

I abandon the orange juice, go down the hall, and rap quietly on Isla's door. I nudge it open a moment later to see her bent over her desk with her sketchbook and pencils. She seems to prefer their company to mine lately. Doesn't mean I'm going to stop trying to break through, though.

"Isla, what happened to the picture that was on the fridge?" I ask. "The one with your braces?"

"I took it down," she says, without looking up.

"Why?"

"Because I hate my braces."

That's a new thing, too. She seems to hate everything these days. The new dress I bought her from a flea market. Flea markets. Dresses.

I wonder how long until "Mom" joins her list.

I take a seat next to her and put my hand over hers. She looks up in alarm at the touch, as if I haven't made that very same gesture for, oh, I don't know… her entire life.

"Kiddo," I say softly, "what's going on with you?"

Her eyebrows pull together and her lip quivers slightly. It's obvious that my question is unraveling her, but she fights to hold herself together. Like she doesn't want to show the world—not even me—an ounce of weakness.

Where does she get that pride from?

I think I know the answer. I just don't want to say it out loud.

"I just want to draw," she says softly.

I swallow and charge forward anyway. "Honey, I know you've gone through a tough time in school lately. And I have no good explanation for you, except to say—well, kids are mean sometimes. But it has nothing to do with you."

"That's not how it feels," she mumbles.

I have to bite my tongue to keep my own tears from spilling loose. "I know. It's not fair."

She pulls her hand out from under mine. "Are you going to see that man again?" she asks suddenly.

For one shocking moment, I think she's talking about Daniil. I haven't told her anything about him, for very good reason. "What man?"

Isla blinks. "The man you went out on a date with."

"Oh. Him."

"You didn't like him?"

"It's not that. He was... fine."

"But...?"

I give her a smile. "We just weren't right for each other."

"You say that about every man."

I frown. "Do I?"

Isla nods. "Aunt Emma says it's because you're waiting for someone else."

I feel the shock congeal on my face. Isla just goes back to her sketchpad, and I'm left sitting there feeling strangely unsettled.

Am I waiting for someone else? It doesn't feel right, doesn't sit right in my head.

I shake the thoughts away. Isla goes right back to drawing, as if I don't exist anymore. Grimacing, I retreat to the kitchen to take the pie out of the oven and pour in the boiled vegetables. I drag some rosemary through, add the puff pastry cover over the vegetable mix, and pop it back in the oven.

With that done, I step out into the garden with my phone and pull up Liam's conversation thread. He's sent me two more messages since our date. I've left both unanswered. The last one is asking me out again.

I take a deep breath and start to reply.

Hey Liam, sorry that I've been a bit MIA. It's been a busy few days. As for dinner on Saturday… I'd love to.

I stare at the words on the screen for a few seconds. Then I delete the last three, change it to **that would be nice**, and hit send before I lose my nerve.

Because I'm not waiting for someone else.

I'm *not*.

And I'm gonna prove it.

16

DANIIL

"Oh, hell yeah. Lemme get at those cigars."

I snap the box closed right on Petro's hand. He yelps and recoils, cupping his bruised fingers to his lips to nurse the pain away.

"You look like a ten-year-old girl drying her nail polish," I inform him.

"You nearly severed my fingertips, asshat."

"If I was going to sever anything, it wouldn't be your fingertips."

Petro drops into the seat next to me and throws his feet up onto the thick wooden coffee table in front of us. "If I've said it once, I've said it a hundred times: you need to get laid."

"Sex is your answer to everything."

"Because it solves everything," he insists. "Well, most things anyway."

"That's the first time I've heard that particular caveat from you. I sense a story."

He sighs bitterly. "Morgan walked in on me with Stephanie."

I snort with laughter. "Let me guess: it didn't end up in a threesome?"

"I did float the idea," Petro admits with a boyish grin. "They may or may not have responded with violence."

"Good on them. You deserve it."

"I'm innocent," he protests. "Pure as the driven snow."

I chuckle and lean back in my armchair. "I hope you told them that."

"I'd already gotten slapped once," Petro says, glaring at me. "I may be a horny bastard, but I'm not stupid. Now, are you going to keep being an asshole, or can I have a cigar?"

"Depends."

"On what?" he asks with a tired sigh.

"On whether or not you did the search I asked you to do."

Petro pouts instantly. "Jesus, you're obsessed with this girl," he says. "I'm starting to think you might like her more than me."

"You're only just now starting to think that?"

"Asshole," he mutters. "Yes, Your Holiness, I did the search you asked for. Now, can I have a cigar, please and thank you?"

I roll my eyes and open the box back up. He grabs a cigar as though he's worried I'll change my mind and snap the lid closed on his fingers again. In his defense, I'm considering it.

He lights it up, takes a long drag, and exhales with a satisfied sigh. "Fuck yeah, that's the stuff. Do we have some good gin lying around?"

"You're pushing it now."

He once again mutters something that sounds suspiciously like "asshole." I ignore it pointedly. "I suppose you want to know what I found out?" he says.

"You're a perceptive one, aren't you?"

He smirks. "Well, what I found is… nothing."

"Nothing," I repeat dubiously. "Nothing?"

"Not a damn thing. She's a good girl through and through. Not getting car insurance was probably the riskiest thing she's done all her life." He pauses for a moment before adding, "Aside from sleeping with you, obviously."

"I hope you're not too attached to your fingertips," I drawl, "because you're about to be unattached to them."

Petro carefully tucks his hand behind a pillow, as if that would stop me. "She lives in a rented house in the suburbs. She works at Crestmore Academy as a teacher. As far as a personal life goes, she doesn't seem to have one. No social media, no social clubs, nothing. The girl's a ghost."

Hm. I stroke my chin and consider what that might mean.

Petro sees me thinking and leans forward. "What is it about this girl?" he asks with genuine curiosity.

If only I knew myself.

"She's a distraction," I say aloud.

Petro narrows his eyes, not buying my bullshit for a second. "You know, I've seen you with women over the years. I know when that's true and I know when it's not."

"Save the psychoanalysis for someone who really needs it, Petro. I don't pay you to be Freud."

"Maybe you should," he says. "You could use a therapist."

"Please. I would break a therapist before they got to the bottom of my issues."

"So you admit you have issues?"

"My main issue is you."

"Please. I'm the love of your life," Petro laughs. "Let's face it, brother: women will come and go. Neither one of us are poster boys for commitment, you know?"

I turn my unlit cigar over and over in my hands. "You think you know me so well."

"I do," Petro asserts confidently. "This girl stands out because you only had her that one night. If you'd hung on longer, she would have turned into every other woman you've fucked and forgotten: ancient history."

"Thanks, Doc. I'll keep that in mind." I roll my eyes and toss the cigar onto the coffee table. "Send me her address," I tell him. "Oh, and did you finalize the insurance papers for her car?"

"I'll send you everything within the hour," he says. "You want me to put Vlad or Kon on the job?"

"What job?"

"Tailing her…?" he says slowly, like I'm so dim I've already forgotten.

I shake my head. "No. I'm handling that part myself."

"Even now?" Petro asks, straightening up. He seems to have forgotten the still-burning cigar dangling from his fingers. "With the wolves at our gates?"

"You know I hate it when you get dramatic."

But Petro barrels ahead, keeping the urgency in his tone. "We got another message from the Semenovs."

"Burn it."

"Daniil!"

"Burn it and bury the ashes," I snarl. "I'm not entertaining any kind of correspondence with that outfit of fucking goons."

"So you've said—"

"Then why are you making me repeat myself, *sobrat?*"

"Because this time..." He produces a letter from his back pocket. "... he wrote it himself."

That gives me pause. I take the letter from Petro and frown at the handwriting slashed across the back of the envelope. Gregor used his own personal stationery for this one. The Semenov crest glares from the flap in green and red.

I turn the letter over in my hands. "How long were you planning on sitting on this?"

"It only came in an hour ago, just before I walked in here looking for you. The plan was to get you in a good mood before I handed it over."

"Meaning what?" I demand. "You think I should accept his request for a meeting?"

Petro releases a tired sigh. "I think you should at least read the letter, Daniil."

I run my thumb over the seal, feeling the raised embossing. It makes my hackles rise, just the sight of it alone. Too many memories etched into that cursed fucking symbol.

I snatch the lighter off the table and spark a flame that dances blue.

Petro tenses up. "Daniil, easy there. C'mon, man. Think about this."

"There's nothing to think about. The motherfucker put me in jail."

"He wants to kiss and make up," Petro says, eyeing the open flame warily. "Isn't that worth something?"

"He wants my men, my connections, my empire," I snap. "He's not trying to make up; he's trying to take what I have built."

"You won't know that until you open that letter," he says, knowing full well that I'm capable of burning the letter to a crisp without even cracking the seal. "He wrote to you himself."

I snort. "It only took him ten years."

"He's bending."

"No, he's bullshitting."

"The fact that he wrote—"

"Is proof that he's getting old and desperate," I interject. "We defied him, Petro. We betrayed him. He's not going to just forget that."

"He might," Petro says pointedly. "If—"

"No. Final answer."

Petro knows me well enough to fall silent immediately. I put the flame to paper and watch as the fire curls around the edges of the letter before devouring it whole.

I throw the blackened scraps on the table and lean back against the cushions. "Set up meetings with the new dealers. We're finishing what we started the day I broke out of that fucking cell."

"We've come pretty far, brother. Don't you think—"

"I've got farther still left to go. And I'll do it all on my own."

Petro drops his head into his hands, dismayed by my stubbornness. It's not the first time, and it won't be the last. "Always the path of most resistance with you, isn't it?"

I smirk. "Where's the fun in doing it any other way?"

17

KINSLEY

I wrinkle my nose in disgust at the reflection in the mirror.

It's too much cleavage. I do want to make an effort tonight. But I don't want Liam getting the wrong idea, and the red dress I'm wearing is a little too *va-va-voom* for my taste.

"Damn, girl!"

I flinch in surprise as Emma invites herself into my room. She proceeds to collapse onto her side on my bed, a bag of sour gummy worms clutched in her hand as per usual.

"That dress is fire," she adds. "Drooly emoji, eggplant emoji, et cetera."

"That's the problem," I say grimly, peeling down the zip that starts where the scooped V neckline ends. "It sends the wrong message."

"That you're young and vibrant and sexy?" Emma asks, stuffing a long gummy worm into her mouth. "God forbid."

"That I'm easy," I amend.

"Gimme a break," Emma says, rolling her eyes. "No one could ever accuse you of being 'easy.'"

I throw her a glare as I shimmy out of the red dress and toss it in the 'no' pile. "I just don't want him making assumptions about tonight."

"People have sex on the first date all the damn time, Kinz," Emma retorts. "Just the other night, I slept with this guy and I didn't even get his name."

"That's not a date; that's a hook-up. Totally different ball game."

"So maybe that's what you need, too. A nice, fun, no-strings-attached 'hook-up'," she says, wagging her eyebrows at me.

I turn to my closet and riffle through the rest of the hangers. But it's slim pickings. I've got sweatpants, work clothes, and very little in between. Grimacing, I drop down onto the ottoman I use like a hamper and put my head in my hands.

"This is a disaster in the making," I mutter.

"Hey! None of that negativity in here," Emma says. I hear the bed squeaks as she pushes herself upright and pads over to where I'm sitting. Taking my hands in hers, she says, "Look at yourself, Kinz. You're gorgeous. You want a guy? Boom, you've got him. It's that easy. You're pretty and you're smart and you're brave and you're special. And, not to get too lewd here or anything, but your tits are fantastic."

I stifle a laugh and roll my eyes. "All thanks go to Victoria," I mumble.

"That bitch and her secrets, I swear," cackles Emma. She squeezes my hands again. "I mean it, though. Any man you want. So if Liam is that man…"

I stiffen, pull my hands out of her grasp, and start rustling through the closet again, hoping that something suitable has miraculously appeared in the last few minutes.

Emma watches me from her seat on the carpet. "Yeah," she remarks, "I didn't think so. So why did you agree on a second date with him again?"

"You're the one who convinced me to go out with him in the first place," I remind her.

"Because I wanted you to put yourself out there! He was only ever meant to be a practice date. You weren't supposed to keep punishing yourself if you weren't interested."

"Well, you didn't make that clear," I say, feigning ignorance as I slip on the blue dress I've tried on twice already. "Anyway, you're right—I do need to put myself out there more."

"And I'm happy about that. But Liam? You said he was creepy."

"Or maybe I was just being overly judgmental?" I suggest, trying to convince myself as much as her. "Maybe I'd written off the date before even going on it. Maybe I need to give him a second chance."

Emma considers that with that puppy-dog-head-to-the-side expression she always uses when she's suspicious of me. "That's a lot of maybes, but fine, it does make some sense."

"See? I'm growing. Learning. Evolving."

"Hm."

I swing around, barely catching the vanishing expression on her face. "What was that?" I demand.

"What was what?" she asks innocently.

"That look you just gave," I accuse. "And that sound you just made. 'Hm.' What kind of 'hm' was that?"

"It was no kind of 'hm' at all."

"B.S.," I snap. "Spill."

Emma offers me a sheepish smile. "I just think the timing is a little suspicious. I'm not sure if this second date with Liam isn't more about... someone else."

I narrow my eyes angrily, but Emma just raises her hands in self-defense. "Don't look at me like that! I didn't say a word about him. No names were named."

"You didn't have to. You're about as subtle as a three-year-old with their hand in the cookie jar."

Emma giggles and sighs fondly. "Oh, man, attack of the memories. It was so cute when Isla did that. I still have those pictures stashed somewhere."

"I am not going out with Liam to prove anything," I say definitively. "To anyone."

"Hm. Okay," Emma says with an annoying smile. "If you say so."

I take a deep breath and pull up the zipper on the side of the blue dress. "Well?" I ask. "What about this one?"

Emma squints hard at the outfit. "Is that your dress?" she asks. "Or your grandma's?"

I purse my lips. "A simple 'no' would have sufficed."

"Where's the fun in that?" Emma says with a wink. She flops onto her back and pops another gummy worm in her mouth. "Sweet baby Jesus, these are addictive."

"How'd you find my stash?"

Emma cackles. "Isla gave away the hiding place."

"Isla knows where it is?"

"Of course," Emma laughs. "She's a smart cookie. She's aware of everything."

"Yeah," I mutter, unzipping the dress and sliding it down my body. "That's what I'm afraid of."

"What was that?"

"Nothing," I say, discarding the blue dress and turning back towards my closet. "Maybe I should try on the pants again?"

"No!" Emma yelps. "No pants. Not again. I know The Gap appreciates your loyal patronage over the years, but if you try wearing those mom jeans out of the house one more time, I'm going to scream or commit arson. Probably both."

"Alright, alright already," I grumble. "Geez. We need to work on your bedside manner."

Emma sighs, leaves her gummy worms on the floor, and stomps over to my closet. "Okay, move aside. I think you need my expertise for this."

"Have at it," I say, relinquishing control and going to collapse in the spot on my bed that Emma just vacated.

I stare at the popcorn ceiling and try to pretend I can't hear her muttering under her breath as she flicks through my closet. "No… no… oh, for the love of God, *hell* no…" After a minute, she announces, "We seriously need to go shopping."

I groan and close my eyes. "It cannot possibly be that bad."

"Yes, it is. I just found a t-shirt you used to wear in high school."

I feel a little blip of sadness. "Is it white with orange stripes?"

"Like Tigger from *Winnie the Pooh*, yeah. And it's way too big for you."

"It was Mom's."

"Oh, shit." Emma blanches and turns to me with a horrified look on her face. "That's right, I can't believe I forgot. I'm so sorry."

I shrug. "I don't blame you. It was a long time ago."

"Kinz—"

I shake my head. "It's okay. I promise." I point back to the closet. "Just… decide my life for me, please and thank you. I can't go to dinner in my underwear."

She arches a devilish brow. "Well…"

"That's a hard no," I say, suppressing a laugh.

"So boring," Emma mutters as she goes back to perusing my clothes. "Ah-ha! What about this one?" She pulls out a strapless white dress with a fitted bodice and a flared skirt that's just short enough to give the pretty little number some edge.

"I don't think so," I say, wrinkling my nose.

"Why not?"

"It was meant to be my prom dress, remember?" I remind her.

"Riiight. But we didn't end up going to prom."

"No, we certainly did not."

"Wait, so you've never actually worn it?"

"No. I always meant to give it away, actually. But I just… never got around to it."

"Meaning you didn't really want to get rid of it," Emma says confidently. "I think tonight's the night, Kinz."

"I don't think so."

Emma marches over to me and shoves the dress into my face. "It's either this, or you squeeze your tatas back into that sexy red number. Your choice." When I don't answer, she nods triumphantly. "That's what I thought. Now, quit yapping and start dressing."

Unwilling to prolong the battle, I slip on the dress. Emma zips me up from behind. It fits remarkably well, considering I've acquired thirteen years and one daughter since I first bought it.

"You're sure it's not too much?" I ask nervously, trying and failing to stuff my breasts back down beneath the neckline. "Not too booby?"

"It's the perfect amount of booby. He's gonna be drooling on the check."

I laugh. "I think I'm gonna offer to pay for this one."

"Of course you are," Emma grumbles. "Just let him pay, Kinsley. If it really means that much to you, the next time we go out to dinner, you can pay for me."

I snort. "What a brilliant suggestion."

"I'm full of easy solutions."

"That don't actually solve the problem, but okay. I just don't want to take advantage of anyone, Em."

Emma waves her hand in my face. "You're not taking advantage. He wants to date you. He definitely wants to bang you. And so if he wants to pay? I say let him. You'll insult his male honor if you don't. The Y chromosomes get very up-in-arms about that sort of thing."

I run a brush through my hair and squint into the little standing mirror I have on my dressing table. "We'll see."

"Just out of curiosity, when was the last time you had sex?"

I nearly choke on my lipstick at the unexpected question.

"Kinz?" Emma persists. She's never been one to let anything go. Like a dog with a bone when it comes to... well, everything.

I drop the bright red tube back into the drawer, wipe off the remnants, and go fishing for another color. "What do you think about this one?" I ask, pulling out a nice taupe. "Too understated?"

"You're ignoring my question."

"Studiously," I say with an impish smile. "Or this one? It's called caramel rose. Sounds so seductive. The marketing team really knocked it out of the park with that one."

Emma crosses her arms and fixes me with an *I-know-damn-well-what-you're-doing* glare. "Go with the caramel rose, and then answer the damn question."

"What does it matter?" I protest.

"I vaguely remember this blonde guy with a sweet smile. Tad or Ted or something stupid like that. But he can't possibly have been your most recent sexperience because that was a few years ago at the very least."

I sigh. "It was Thad. And it was five years ago."

"Wait," Emma says, her eyes going wide. "Are you telling me that Thadley was in fact the last time? Jesus Christ, Kinsley!"

"It's not like I've missed it."

That's a whopper of a lie. I have a well-worn vibrator and a half-empty family-sized pack of backup batteries that can attest to that. Of course, Emma sees right through it. "Okay, my bullshit meter is pinging off the charts. There is no way that's true."

"I just... I can't, Em. I can't do it unless I... feel something."

Emma stops short, and I know immediately, based on the look on her face, that I'm going to regret that statement any second.

"So there was a connection?" she infers. "Between you and broody Prince Not-So-Charming?"

Yup, there it is. Regret by the bucketful. That didn't take long.

"I, well... the thing is—"

"No takesies backsies."

I roll my eyes. "Yes, okay, fine. We had a connection. But it was clearly one-sided, because I woke up the next morning and he was gone. And then all this stuff now. So… yeah. One-sided."

"Maybe he came back later?" she suggests.

"And expected to find me sitting there, waiting for him?" I laugh out loud, sounding a little unhinged as I do it. "Fat chance of that."

"Men can be a little obtuse, to say the least."

"This one is anything but stupid, Em," I assure her.

"Oh, heavens. He gets yummier all the time."

I shake my head at her. "You are hopeless."

"Why?" she asks. "Because I believe in true love?"

"True love?" I balk. "Trust me—this is the farthest thing from that."

"You've spent the last ten years comparing every guy you meet to him. 'Infatuation' doesn't quite cut it. You're obsessed."

"I—"

She holds up a hand to cut me off. "Don't even start. I know you, Kinsley. I was there for all of it. The Dark Times. You lived with me for six weeks after the whole debacle, remember?"

I sigh. "I wish I did. It's mostly a blur."

"Because you were distraught. And not about your failed wedding or your abusive shithead of a fiancé," Emma asserts firmly. "You were distraught because you didn't think you would see Daniil ever again."

I frown. "I don't remember ever saying that."

"You didn't have to. I could see it on your face, the way you described those hours with him, the way you spoke about him. The fact that, when you dreamed, you called out his name."

"I did?" I gasp, aghast that I'd given myself away so freely.

"You did," Emma confirms. "He meant more to you than you were willing to admit back then. And more than you're willing to admit right now. But that doesn't change the fact that he does in fact mean something to you."

I have to plant my hands on the bathroom counter to stop from keeling over. "He… he found me at one of the most vulnerable points in my life," I whisper. "And I suppose without even knowing it, I was looking for something… more." I raise my eyes to meet hers in the mirror over the sink. "But when I woke up the next morning and he was gone… I guess it reminded me of all the times someone important to me just left. And it made me feel—"

"Like an abandoned kid all over again?"

I nod and swallow past the lump in my throat. "I believe in fate," I say. "Everything happens for a reason and all that. So I do believe he was sent to me for a reason. But he was never mine to keep. I get that now."

Emma looks like she wants to disagree. But in the end, she only gives me a sad smile. "You look beautiful, by the way. I'll let you finish getting ready."

Then she turns and slips out.

I face the mirror again and apply a coat of lipstick. Emma was right—the caramel rose was a good pick. "There," I say to myself. "Done."

When I step out of the bathroom, I find my bedroom empty. But there's a pair of strappy black heels and a cerulean shawl laid out neatly on top of the duvet for me. I can't help but smile. She's feisty and thorny and loves to push my buttons. But Emma is the best friend I could ask for.

I'm buckling up the shoes when Isla slips into my room. She's already in her pajamas. "You look really pretty, Mommy."

"Thanks, love," I say, standing to give her a very princess-y twirl and a giggle.

Isla's eyes run up and down the dress with appreciation. They land on my face, and I notice the sadness seep back into her eyes.

"I wish I were as pretty as you."

I freeze immediately. People always say "my blood ran cold," but it's a crazy thing to actually experience exactly that. It's like I'm shivering deep down in my bones, though the air in the room is warm.

Isla lingers at the doorway for a moment longer with that melancholy distance in her eyes. I wobble over and sink onto the bed, not trusting my legs all of the sudden. Every cell in my body is screaming at me to go after her, but I know she needs time to decompress. Chasing her down and forcing her to talk to me will just build resentment that might last forever.

So I sit, useless and agitated. I'm quiet for a while as I try to steady my breathing. Then I hear a rustle at the door. I look up to see Emma standing at the threshold with a gold necklace dangling from her fingertips.

"I was just seeing if you wanted to wear this," she says quietly.

I nod. "Thanks. You heard?"

"Yeah," she sighs. "I heard."

"I'm failing her, Em," I whisper. "I don't even know what to say. She told me she thinks she's ugly the other day. How do I tell her that the things that hurt her now are the most beautiful things about her?"

"You say exactly that," Emma insists as she comes over and sits next to me. "You're not failing anyone, Kinsley. That little girl adores you. Just… keep trying. Keep loving her back. That's all you have to do. Everything else will fix itself in time."

I sigh. That feels so inadequate. There's a little girl one room over who's hurting in a way that breaks my heart, and she won't let me close enough to help. I know Emma is right—one way or another, we'll get through this. But when you're trapped in the middle of a storm, every stroke of lightning feels like the end of the world.

A loud *DING* pulls me from my thoughts. Emma clutches my hand tight. "He's here," she announces, a little unnecessarily.

I stand up, toss the shawl over my shoulders, and grab my purse. "Wish me luck," I mumble.

"Good luck! Remember to use condoms."

I roll my eyes and go down the hallway. When I open the front door, Liam is standing there with a wild bunch of half-wilted peonies in hand.

"Hi," I say self-consciously.

He does a double take and gives me a shameless up-down. "Hot damn," he whistles, his eyes bugging out of their sockets. "You look sexy as fuck."

"Oh." Any points he earned with the flowers go whooshing down the toilet. It's a struggle to keep the smile on my face. "Thanks. You look nice, too."

"Here." He shoves the flowers in my face.

"I'll just go set these inside real quick," I say. I take them from him and hustle into the kitchen to drop them in the first container I see, which turns out to be a tumbler with my sophomore year homecoming date printed on the side.

When I go back to the front door, I find Liam right where I left him. "Ready to go!" I announce as brightly as I can fake it.

But his back is to me, and he doesn't turn around.

"Liam?"

Then I realize he's looking at something out in the distance. A dark, sleek silhouette. It's a car. A nice car, I can tell, though I don't know the first thing about them, as my experience at the body shop can attest to.

But this one screams luxury. It screams power. It screams *Do not even THINK of fucking with me.*

And the man who opens the driver's door and steps out of it screams all of those exact same things.

18

DANIIL

I've been sitting in the dark for twenty minutes, observing the greasy-haired fucker in the Lexus browsing porn on his phone, before the appointed time arrives and he shuffles up to Kinsley's house with a collection of sad flowers in his hand like he just ripped them out of some unsuspecting grandmother's backyard.

I'm growling with distaste. Then her door opens, and I forget all about that hapless idiot.

Because Kinsley looks like a fucking angel.

She's wearing a white mini dress with a flared skirt and a plunging neckline that takes it from sweet to sexy. Her hair flows and the light from the living room behind her glows around her head like a halo. Even from here, I can see the brightness in her eyes. The life. The fire.

The douchebag forks over the flowers, like a cat bringing its owner a dead bird as an offering.

She takes them reluctantly, then steps into the house for a moment and ditches them out of sight. I see her silhouette casting out onto the stoop as she re-emerges.

That's my cue.

I open the door and step out into the night. Both Kinsley and the slimy fuck clutching onto her stare at me, mouths agape.

Her expression is incredulous.

His is idiotic.

"D-Daniil," Kinsley stammers, recovering a lot faster than her dimwitted date. "Wh… what are you doing here?"

She keeps her tone calm, but I can hear the strain underneath it. She's nervous. Very nervous. No prizes for guessing why.

"Just came to deliver your insurance papers," I say, pulling them from the inside of my coat pocket.

"Insurance papers?" the douche asks, stepping forward with his chest held high. "What kind of insurance guy makes home deliveries at eight on a Saturday, eh, pal?"

Jesus. Calling this clown an idiot is an insult to idiots everywhere.

"Do I look like an insurance salesman to you?" I ask.

Kinsley tenses. "I told you before, I can handle my own affairs. And I'll get my own insurance, too."

"Take the papers, Kinsley."

I watch her throat bob as she swallows. Her fear is palpable. I want to lick my lips to savor it.

Despite her reluctance, she reaches out and takes the sheaf of papers from my hand.

"Good girl," I tell her. "I believe 'Thank you, Daniil' is the phrase you're looking for."

"I'm sorry," the douchebag bleats, still fidgeting around in front of me like he's not sure whether to fight or run. "Am I missing something here? Who the hell are you?"

"No one," Kinsley says quickly. "He's just—"

"A friend," I interject. She glares at me and shakes her head, but I just grin back at her. "Kinsley and I are old friends. She needed some help getting an insurance policy for her car."

He frowns. "Doesn't seem like she wants your help, bud."

"Kinsley may not want my help," I agree, my gaze veering from his face to hers. "But she'll take it regardless."

"We really should get going, Liam," she insists, trying to end the conversation before it gets out of hand.

Too late for that, though. It got out of hand ten years ago. It's not going to improve in the immediate future.

"Yeah," her date crows with a self-satisfied smirk. "We should get going. We have an 8:30 rez at Conte tonight."

I arch an eyebrow. "Is that so? Small world. So do I."

Kinsley isn't buying it for a second. "Do you?" she seethes. "How funny."

"I do. A funny coincidence."

"There's no such thing as coincidences."

"For once," I say, "you and I agree."

"Uh, Kinsley, babe?" the douche says, wrapping his meaty hand around her elbow. "Let's go."

It takes all my self-control not to break every finger in that fucking hand.

"Liam, would you mind waiting for me in the car, please?" Kinsley asks, her voice straining with tension.

"What?" he snaps.

She turns to him and blinks, like she's just now consciously processing the fact of his existence. "Just give me a sec, Liam," she says softly. "Please."

His expression sours as he checks his watch. "It's already 8:15," he grunts, his voice unnaturally gruff. "Make it quick. Conte is a bitch to get a table at."

He walks to his Lexus and gets in. I can see the twin points of his eyes staring furiously at me from inside his big-boy car. I turn my back on him.

"Oh, he's a gem," I remark.

She ignores that. "So much for not stalking me, huh?"

"I had to give you the papers."

"I didn't want the papers to begin with."

"You need insurance."

"And I'll get it. But not from you." She huffs a bang out of her face. "This is not your problem, Daniil. So why are you making it your problem?"

I studiously ignore the scent of her perfume dancing on the gentle night breeze. "Let's just say I'm invested."

"In what, exactly?" she demands. "There's really nothing to invest in. I have my own life now. I've moved on."

I snort. "You need to raise your standards then."

Her eyes slide to the Lexus, then back to me, as if I wouldn't notice her hesitation. "He's not a bad guy."

"But is he a good one?"

She snorts derisively. "Oh, and you are?"

"Of course not. But we're not talking about me."

She shakes her head in confusion. "I don't know what you want from me. Is this guilt? Is that what this is? You feel guilty for how you left that morning and you're trying to make amends? Or is it just pity?"

"If I say yes, will you stop being stubborn?"

"I'd rather you say it because it's the truth."

I scowl at her. "The truth is that I don't want you bleeding out on the side of the road while some hack rep for whichever shitty insurance company you decide you can afford hems and haws about whether you get to live or die. That's the truth. Do with it what you please."

There's a long, pregnant pause. "So you do care," she says softly. She grits her teeth. "You make me crazy, you know that?"

"Really?" I drawl sarcastically. "You hide it so well."

"I'm leaving." She turns towards the car, but I can tell she's reluctant to leave me here in front of her house. She glances towards her windows.

"Someone home?" I inquire.

She's definitely uneasy. "Emma," she answers. "She spends the night sometimes."

"The two of you need men."

"Why?" she scoffs. "In my experience, men are mostly good for cumming too soon, leaving the toilet seat up, and disappearing in the morning."

Her words are scathing, though her delivery is anything but. She sounds too tired to muster up the appropriate level of anger.

"And the asshole sitting in the Lexus over there is the one you want to hang around?" I ask.

I despise how I'm sounding right now. Bitter, jaded in ways I can't explain. But I can't control the fierce sense of protectiveness that overwhelms me every time I'm around her. The thought of that motherfucker's hand on Kinsley's wrist is still making me see red.

"Goodnight, Daniil," she says icily.

Then she turns and marches off without waiting for my reply. She gets in the car and they pull out past me, the douchebag's eyes locked on mine the whole time. I stand in place until the taillights disappear around the corner.

When they're gone, I take my phone out of my pocket and dial a number I haven't called in a while.

"Busy?" I ask when the line picks up.

"For you, handsome? Never."

"Good. Meet me at Conte. Fifteen minutes."

19

KINSLEY

"Who the fuck was that guy?" Liam wheezes in disbelief.

I wrap the shawl tightly around my shoulders as the darkness swallows up Daniil behind us. "Just… someone I used to know."

"Seems like you still know him."

"We ran into each other recently," I admit. "And he's decided to help me out with this insurance thingamajig."

Liam scoffs. "He's not here to help you, babe," he says, continuing this recent and alarming trend of calling me a pet name I never, ever asked for. "He's here because he wants to *bang* you. The insurance thing is an excuse. He just wants to get into your—"

"I get it, Liam," I snap. "No need to rephrase. But I really don't think that is what this is."

"Listen, sweetheart, I know guys, okay? This one—"

"Just because a man wants to get in my pants doesn't mean he gets to," I say angrily. "I decide who gets in my pants. Me. No one else."

I'm hoping he'll give it a rest, but after a minute of silence, he continues like a bull in a china shop. He really can't help himself. "So nothing's ever happened between the two of you?"

Too many things happened between the two of us, I want to say. Instead, all I say is, "I really don't want to talk about it. Let's just have a nice night, okay?"

But he keeps blathering on like I hadn't even spoken. "Big guy. Nice car. It'd make sense, that's all I'm saying."

I grit my teeth. "What would make sense, Liam?"

"I'm just sayin', chicks always go for that whole deal."

"I hope you don't think I'm that shallow. Or that easy."

A wise man would have left it there. Liam, it's becoming more and more obvious, is not very wise.

"So… you're not?"

I swallow back my annoyance. "When I met Daniil the first time, he was wearing borrowed clothes and he didn't even have a car."

"Made something of himself since then, did he?"

"Hell if I know. I don't really know what he did in the last ten years. And to be completely honest, I don't really care. I'm not interested in continuing a relationship with him. In any capacity."

Liam grunts, but mercifully, he doesn't say anything else until we pull up to the restaurant ten minutes later.

I try really hard not to scan the place as we walk in, but every now and again, I feel my eyes sliding around. Searching. It's not hard to guess what for.

The moment we're seated, Liam orders wine without asking for my input. I know he's trying to impress me with his knowledge, but I'm barely listening as he berates the waiter over their "shamefully inadequate" list of reds.

A man in a suit goes by and I nearly choke on my water. But it's not Daniil. Just another smartly dressed somebody with cash aplenty to burn.

"Got us a nice Merlot," Liam announces once he's finally stopped harassing the poor server.

"Sounds great," I say. I'm trying to smile, but I'm pretty sure it's coming across as more of a grimace, so I turn my head down and focus on the menu.

But that doesn't go much better. I read the same line fifteen or twenty times in a row without getting any further along. *Cauliflower steak. Cauliflower steak. Cauliflower steak.* After a while, it starts to sound like gibberish.

"What're you thinkin'?" Liam asks.

I look up at him. The wine is already staining his lips, tongue, and teeth a stomach-churning purple. "The, uh… the cauliflower steak, I guess."

He wrinkles his nose. "Gross."

I force a laugh. "So I shouldn't offer you a taste of my dish?"

"Oh, I'd definitely like a taste of your dish," he says, wagging his eyebrows suggestively.

Ick. I'd almost forgotten this side of him. Or made myself forget it, at least.

Every time the doors swing open, my eyes go straight to it. It's pathetic—even I know that. Just as pathetic as how I can still feel the corner of the sheaf of insurance papers Daniil handed me, tickling at my bare thigh from where I folded them up and stuffed them in my purse.

"So… what was it you do again?" he asks as he pours himself a second glass of wine already.

"I'm a teacher, remember?"

"Oh. Huh. Yeah."

He nods, and I can see from the glazed expression in his eyes that he has about as much interest in my job as I do in his gym routine or his thoughts on the merits of Sangiovese versus Cabernet Sauvignon.

"That friend of yours, the one who goes to my gym… You two are close?"

"Emma. Yeah, very. She's my oldest friend. After my parents died, she was my only family."

"Both parents are toast, huh?" he says. "That's tough."

I really hadn't meant for this to pivot into a conversation about my parents or my childhood. I hate talking about both things. Especially with strangers.

"It is what it is."

"How did they die?"

I reach for my glass of water and take a sip. "Um, I'd really rather not talk about it, if that's okay."

He shrugs and starts blabbing again about his super-special biceps workout, which we'd discussed ad nauseum last time around. I look at the ceiling, the other patrons, the stitching on the napkin in my lap—anywhere but at the door. Trying to convince myself that I'm not waiting on pins and needles to see if Daniil was just bullshitting me or not.

"You okay?" Liam asks, and I realize I haven't been listening for ten straight minutes.

"Of course. Sorry. Just a little… tired."

"Tough day at school?"

I'm on the verge of reminding him that it's Saturday when the door chimes.

And this time, I'm not disappointed.

He's at least a foot taller than every other man in this restaurant. He takes up space with all the confidence of a man who knows he's the most important person in the place. His watch glitters on his wrist as he removes his coat and throws it over his shoulder, then turns around. I follow the direction of his half-smile…

To see a woman walk in after him.

"Woman" feels like I'm selling her short, though. She's a goddess, plain and simple. Runway model tall with an Instagram model body, a dazzling copper dress, and acres of tanned skin. Waves of luxurious, strawberry blonde hair flow down her back. The pearls draped around her neck and dangling from her ears seem to glow with their own light.

"What are you—?" Liam twists around in his seat to figure out what's caught my attention. He stops short when he sees Daniil.

That makes two of us.

"Well," Liam says, turning back to me, "he has good taste, I'll give him that."

I don't bother responding. What's there to say? Liam isn't even wrong.

What makes the whole situation worse is that Daniil never once looks this way. I'm sure he knows that I've seen him—he doesn't miss anything. But he doesn't make any indication that he cares to see me.

In the very center of the restaurant, the best seat in the house, the maître d' is seating Daniil and his date. He pulls out the chair for her, which is surprising in and of itself. What's more surprising is how, before he sits down, she places her hand on his arm. It's a small gesture, but it feels intimate.

It really shouldn't matter either way.

It doesn't.

It can't.

20

DANIIL

"You're lucky I hadn't eaten yet."

Kinsley is positioned at the table behind us, a mere two inches to the right of Charlize's face from my vantage point. Every time the little *kiska* so much as flinches this way, I'll know it.

"I'm surprised to hear you eat at all," I reply to Charlize with a smirk. "I figured you subsisted on spite and money."

She gives me a flattered smile. "Business is busy, but a queenpin must always find time to indulge."

"I take it that things are going well."

"People like drugs, my darling," purrs Charlize. "They sell themselves."

She's an impressive woman. And not because she's the human equivalent of a hyena—all smiles until she rips your throat out. Once her father died, she challenged her half-brother for the throne and left the poor bastard gibbering to himself in a mental hospital.

Even after that, no one thought that a woman would be able to take over the infamous Rodrigo Alcanzara's cartel empire and have it flourish. No one but me, that is.

As usual, I was right. And as it turns out, the word "flourish" is doing Charlize's work a disservice—the shit took off like a wildfire. She's got the profits and the dead enemies to prove it.

Like I said: hyena.

"I remember a time when you wanted to run away from it all," I muse.

"That was back when I thought my father would live forever," she laughs with comfortable detachment. "When I was only ever going to be his trophy daughter."

"He'd be proud of what you've done."

"Proud?" she scoffs. "No, he'd be rolling in his grave. 'Trophy daughter' isn't a figure of speech; it's exactly what he wanted. The entire point of a trophy is to be displayed, not to be used. He would have hated that I am now the face of his legacy."

I sip from my glass of wine. "Well, you knew him better than I did."

"That I did," she says. "And I enjoy thinking about him rolling in his grave. Sometimes, I visit him just to tell him things that I know will piss him off."

I shake my head as I chuckle. "You are one of one, Charlize Alcanzara."

I glance over her shoulder to check on Kinsley. The little *sladkaya* averts her eyes immediately, but I see the blush snaking up her cheeks.

She really does look like a wet dream tonight. It's infuriating to know that she's dressed up for that asshole.

She should only look like that for *me*.

"Are you ready to order, ma'am?" the waiter asks, materializing between us and blocking Kinsley from view. I fist my knife and try to contain my temptation to use it on him.

We place our orders and he disappears as quickly as he arrived.

"I'm surprised you picked this restaurant, darling," Charlize says when he's gone, picking up her wine glass and swirling the contents with a practiced hand. "It's not exactly your style."

"No," I agree. "It's not."

"I mean, don't get me wrong, it's nice," she says, looking around. "But since when has 'nice' ever been good enough for Daniil Vlasov?"

"I thought I'd slum it with the riff-raff tonight," I tell her. "Are you always so suspicious?"

"A girl can never be too cautious."

"I agree," I say. "Speaking of being cautious… How is Harwin?"

She bursts out laughing. "My better half is the farthest thing from cautious."

"He looks scared for his life every time I see him. But then again, he's dating you."

She rolls her eyes. "He's a good man. And what's more, I can trust him."

"That is a rare commodity these days."

"He's not part of this world," she admits in a different tone, a more vulnerable one. "As far as I'm concerned, that's his best quality."

I find myself looking once again past Charlize's head at Kinsley. She's trying desperately to look interested in what her idiot date has to say. But her smile isn't convincing in the slightest.

"I can understand that," I murmur. *Not a part of this world.* I used to think that was a mark against her. Now, I'm not so sure.

"Can you?" she asks, still skeptical.

I refocus my attention on Charlize. "Why not?"

"You just don't strike me as the kind of man who would be interested in anyone out of the life."

"In or out doesn't matter to me. I want simple."

"Good luck with that," she snorts. "Relationships are complicated no matter who's involved."

"Which is why I avoid them altogether."

Charlize fixes me with a searching gaze, hunting for answers. "I can't seem to figure out what you're playing at tonight, Daniil. Men are usually blindingly obvious. But you, Mr. Vlasov, are one of one, to steal a phrase."

I laugh. Out of the corner of my eye, I notice Kinsley noticing me. She promptly drops her spoon right into her soup and stifles a mortified yelp.

"Here you go, sir, ma'am," the waiter interrupts, setting our plates down in front of us. "Enjoy your meal."

He walks away and Charlize turns her eagle eyes on me. "Now, why don't you tell me who that pretty little brunette is behind me? And why I'm here in the first place?"

I grin at her. "You really are an amazing woman, you know that?"

She grins right back at me, flashing those flawlessly white teeth. "The moment you start with the flattery, I know I have to keep my guard up."

I press a hand to my chest in mock offense. "You wound me."

"And you're dreaming if you think I'm going to let you leave this restaurant without an explanation. I came when you called, didn't I? You owe me the story."

I take a sip of my wine and sigh. "Her name is Kinsley," I concede. "And you're here because she is."

"I figured as much. Who's the creep she's sitting with?"

"If someone told me his name, I've already forgotten," I say. "He's her date."

"Then I have to question her taste."

"Don't worry. She's not really interested in him. She's only with him because she's trying to deny her feelings for me."

Charlize's eyebrows disappear into her forehead. "Well, well," she chuckles, leaning back in her seat. "I'm certainly glad I came tonight. Dinner and a show, indeed. You like this girl."

"I wouldn't go that far."

"Of course you wouldn't," Charlize says, her tone crackling gleefully. "Because you've never copped to having feelings for anyone or anything in your entire adult life. Which is why this is so thrilling. You're trying to make her jealous. I'll be damned."

"I'm trying to piss her off," I clarify. "If I make her jealous in the process… well, that's just a bonus."

"And why are you trying to piss her off?"

"Because she's extremely fucking stubborn," I growl.

"You mean, she doesn't follow your orders like some trained poodle?" Charlize's eyes twinkle. "Is that what makes this one so special? Or is it something else?"

I grimace inwardly. This is turning into too much of a share-your-feelings session. Not the kind of dinner date I usually go for.

"I can't tell you," I admit. "I met her unexpectedly. She started out as a chance encounter and a convenient alibi."

"And she became…?"

"That remains to be seen."

"Fascinating." Charlize shifts her body to the side in such a way that she can take another look at Kinsley without being obvious about it. "She is pretty," she acknowledges generously. "In that girl-next door-kind of way." That's less generous, but I'm willing to let it slide.

"I'll be sure to let her know you said so," I drawl.

Charlize's eyes flash again. Hyena's eyes in a flawless, symmetrical face. "How did you meet her?" she inquires. "And what alibi would you need that she could provide?"

"It's a long story."

She laughs musically. "You need me, baby. So spill."

I give her the story begrudgingly. The jailbreak, the near-drowning, the night in the woods. When it's all over, the brightness in Charlize's eyes has doubled in intensity.

"That is a rom-com if I ever saw one," she pronounces.

"It was a mistake," I correct. "I had no place in my life for someone like her."

"And now?" Charlize asks pointedly.

I glance once more towards Kinsley. She's staring at her plate like it has something more interesting to say than the man sitting opposite her. Her whole body is stiff with discomfort. She's a caged animal, waiting for the chance to flee.

"Now… nothing has changed."

"And yet here you sit, staring at a woman you claim not to have feelings for, pretending to talk to me while you fantasize about her instead. You talk a big talk, Don Vlasov," Charlize tuts. "But I don't believe you for a second. I see this for what it is: the impossible has happened. The king has fallen for the commoner."

I roll my eyes. "Is being overly dramatic part of being the queenpin?"

"It can be," she says with a delicate shrug of her shoulders. "And you know what this queenpin is going to do now?"

"I'm all ears."

"I'm going to help you." She leans in and starts running her fingers along my arm. Slowly. Seductively. Convincingly. "Is she watching?"

I peer over Charlize's shoulder yet again and confirm what I already knew deep down in my bones.

"She can barely look away."

21

KINSLEY

I must've pissed off someone celestial today. Because the universe is being unnecessarily cruel.

As I watch, the goddess leans in and whispers something in Daniil's ear. Her fingers stroke casually against his arm. It's not a possessive gesture. But then again, it doesn't need to be.

She's got no competition.

He picked that table on purpose, I'm sure of it now. I have a bird's-eye-view, and it's impossible for me not to gawk at them.

I've never seen a couple so perfect for each other. His dark hair against her shiny blonde locks. His tall, stormy broodiness against her lithe, willowy confidence.

Adonis and Aphrodite, in the flesh.

It makes me wonder what he saw in me ten years ago. The answer is obvious, of course: he was slumming it. Taking advantage of the first woman he'd seen in over a year.

"You okay?" Liam asks, his tone turning surly.

This is the second time he's caught me staring off in their general direction. I've become quieter and quieter throughout the meal. I'm surprised he noticed, actually. Somewhere between the biceps routine and the stories of his college drinking days, I lost the thread of the conversation.

"I'm fine. It's just been a long week."

"Has it?" he grumbles. "It seems every time we have a date, you've had a bad day or a long week."

I cringe. "I'm sorry."

"More wine?"

"I better not."

"A little more alcohol might help you loosen up."

"I'm not a very loose person these days," I mumble. "With or without alcohol."

He doesn't even bother to hide his disappointment, and at this point, I can't blame him. Despite my intentions, I haven't exactly been a great date tonight.

Not that he's been a charmer, either. But that's beside the point.

"No," he agrees. "You're not. But you know what? You could always… make it up to me."

He's giving me these sly Pepé Le Pew eyes that make my skin crawl. I'm honestly stunned that he's not actively licking his chops.

I'm about to nip this cringe-inducing detour in the bud, but then the goddess laughs and it takes me right out of the moment. My eyes slide over to their table like they're steering without my control. She's moved even closer to him. Practically on his lap.

I check myself immediately. Daniil isn't anyone to me.

Except the father of your child.

I've been great at pushing that little detail out of my head in the last several years. But now that he's here, in glaring Technicolor, it's harder to ignore. Harder to avoid.

And he isn't exactly making it easy for me.

"You want to go join them?" Liam spits suddenly. His thin veil of tolerance has well and truly dropped. "Because you're clearly not interested in being here with me."

"I… I'm just—"

"Come on, Kinsley. Don't play me for a fool. You've obviously got the hots for that douchebag."

"I—I don't—I just—" I'm spluttering stupidly, lying so blatantly that even the busboy scrubbing dishes in the kitchen can probably tell, but I just can't bring myself to admit it. It's a can of worms I've spent ten years sealing shut. I don't dare open it now.

"No?" he challenges snidely. "Because you look pretty freaking bothered that he's sitting there with another woman. In fact, you look downright jealous."

"Listen, he just took me off guard tonight, okay?" I say, trying to stop this from spiraling into a whole scene. "I didn't expect to see him ever again, much less tonight."

"Okay, and…?"

"And… you were right. Earlier, I mean. We do have history. But it's not what you think. It's in the past, and I definitely don't want a future with him."

"That's not how it looks from where I'm sitting."

I let my chin fall to my chest. It's weirdly hard to breathe all of the sudden. Like the air got thick when I wasn't paying attention. What's that thing they say about feeling like an elephant is sitting on your chest?

"Will you excuse me for a second?" I mumble. "I, uh… need to use the restroom."

Liam rolls his eyes. "Be my guest."

I have to walk right past them on the way to the restroom. My skin tingles with nerves as I pass their table, but neither one even glances at me.

The restroom is mercifully empty when I walk in. I pee first, then I stand in front of the sink and stare at my dejected expression. I look like Eeyore.

"What's wrong with you?" I whisper to my reflection. "Who cares who he's here with? Who cares about him at all?"

I hear the confident *click-click-click* of approaching heels, so I hurriedly turn on the tap to pretend like I wasn't just talking to myself in a public restroom.

The door swings open, and I feel myself go ghostly pale as I catch a glimpse of long strawberry blonde hair and a glistening dress that makes me suck in my gut.

The goddess doesn't go into one of the stalls. She takes the sink next to me and pulls out a tube of lipstick from her stylish Gucci clutch.

Her eyes slide to mine in the mirror. That's when I realize I'm staring.

I can't control the blush that rushes up to my face, so I turn determinedly to my sink. But I'm too late by a long shot.

"You okay, hon?" she asks.

"Fine. I'm fine. Thanks."

"You look a little pale."

All I can think is, *She's going to go back out there and tell Daniil about this and he's going to think he's gotten to me.* I'm pinning all my hopes on the ground opening up beneath my feet and swallowing me whole.

"Oh… I just got my period and I don't have a tampon on me. That's all. Bad timing."

Smooth, says the approving voice in my head. *Very nonchalant. Well-done.*

"Oh, I hate when that happens in the wild," the goddess murmurs. She rifles around in her sleek little clutch and pulls out a tampon. "Here you go. I always carry extras."

Daniil's date is offering me a tampon. "Bizarre" doesn't even begin to cover it.

"Oh, uh, thank you," I say, taking it from her. "That's very sweet."

"Anytime."

She goes back to her reflection and touches up her lips. I stand in place, toying with the tampon like it's a marching band baton as my thoughts pinwheel wildly out of control. I should just step right on out of here. But something has my feet rooted to the ground. A knack for self-destruction, maybe. Or, if that's too melodramatic, maybe just a fetish for embarrassing myself.

The goddess touches up her lipstick and looks at me again. "I like your dress," she says pleasantly. No trace of sarcasm in her voice.

"Thanks," I reply, blushing like a wallflower. "I like your… everything."

She laughs. "Thanks, hon. You enjoy your night now."

I give her an awkward nod and an even worse smile and head back into the restaurant. My table is empty. Liam must have paid and gone outside. That's fine. Great, actually. Damn near fantastic.

All I have to do is stride through the restaurant and out the door, and this nightmare will come to a merciful conclusion. I don't even have to look at Daniil or the goddess. I can just put one foot in front of the other, keep my eyes up, and—

Goddammit. I looked.

"Enjoying your date?"

I freeze. He's a couple yards away, seated alone at his table, but his voice is soft and intimate like he's purring right in my ear.

"Are you enjoying yours?" I retort.

He smirks and shrugs like the answer is self-evident. "You've seen Charlize."

Charlize. Set up for life with a name like that. Plus the body to match.

"Yeah, I've seen her," I say ungraciously. "Does she turn into a pumpkin at midnight?"

I wince as soon as the words are out of my mouth. What has Charlize done to me? Not a damn thing but smile and be helpful with a fake emergency.

His smirk, though… I want so badly to wipe it off his face.

But I'm all out of things to say. Truth be told, I was out of things to say ten years ago, and I haven't restocked since.

So I revert to Plan A and do my best to sweep out of the restaurant without looking too obviously like I'm fleeing in a blind panic.

The street is empty when I walk out. I look around in bewilderment for Liam. Honestly, it would serve me right if he left me here to find my own way home. I've been disinterested at best and downright rude at worst. And yet, would it be the worst thing if he ditched me…?

I'm torn between relief and extreme indignation when—

"Hey, sexy."

I swing around and catch sight of Liam slouching in the broad, cobblestoned alleyway between the restaurant and the building next door. He's leaning against the wall, with one leg bent, dangling a cigarette from his lips. I didn't even know he smoked.

"Sorry," I mumble. "Didn't see you there."

"Did you think I'd left you?" He sees my face and barks out a laugh. "You totally did."

I sigh. "Okay, yes. For a second, I did."

"Would you have blamed me?"

"No, I guess not," I admit. "Thanks for dinner by the way. I really intended to pay tonight, I swear."

"Don't bother," he says lazily, offering me his cigarette. "Want a drag?"

I shake my head. "No thanks. I don't smoke."

"Me neither," he guffaws. "More of a guilty pleasure."

Something in his tone makes me tense up immediately. "Liam—"

"It's okay," he cuts in before I can finish. "I've decided it's okay. I don't mind being used."

The bite of anger in his voice is starting to make me nervous. So is the hungry look in his eyes.

"I didn't mean to use you, Liam," I say carefully. "That was definitely not my intention."

"Intentions don't count for shit," he says darkly. He pushes off the wall and paws my hip before I can dance my way out of reach. "That guy plows through women. But if you want to make him jealous, I'm down for that."

"What are you—"

His fingers tighten against my hip and he pulls me into him, hard.

"Liam!"

His lips come for me. I turn my face to the side just in time to avoid them. "Stop!" I cry out, trying to push him off me.

"Oh, come on," he growls. "Don't be so damn uptight."

He's strong. Too strong. I push at him with all my strength, but it doesn't seem to make a bit of difference. He grabs my hand and pins it behind my back.

That's when my indignation turns to fear.

The kind of fear that puts you back in a bad memory and freezes you there. When one moment collapses into another one that you thought you left behind you, but it turns out it's been lurking in the background the whole time, waiting to show you that life doesn't really change, it doesn't ever really change, it just stays the same, the worst moments repeating themselves over and over and over again…

The shattering glass.

The wild fury in his eyes.

"Stop it, Liam," I plead, hating how weak and frightened my voice sounds. "Get off me! Please… please…"

"You really think I sprung for another fucking meal for *nothing?*" he growls in my ear. "You're such a cocktease. I'm getting what I paid for tonight."

I writhe uselessly, too terrified for words now.

"If it helps," he offers sickeningly, "just close your eyes and imagine I'm him."

22

DANIIL

"She's cute," Charlize remarks, settling back into her seat. "I understand your fascination." I narrow my eyes at her. She just smiles back. "We had a little chat in the ladies' room."

Goddammit. That's what I was worried about.

"She told you how transformative it was, fucking me?" I drawl.

"Bingo," Charlize teases. "She told me they should erect statues of your penis so women everywhere can pay homage. They'd be massive statues, of course."

"Are you done? I paid. We can leave."

"Charming as usual, Daniil." She rises back up with effortless grace. Every man in the restaurant is fixated on her. "Our work here is done, I suppose?"

I stand to join her. "Something like that."

"Did you accomplish everything you came for?"

"She's thinking of me tonight. So yeah, mission accomplished."

She shakes her head while I hold the door open for her. "You're a cruel bastard, but a smart one."

I give her a wink and follow her out onto the street. "Let me go get the—"

"No! Get off me, you bastard!"

Her terrified voice hits me like jumper cables clamped to my balls. I whirl around and catch sight of two shadows writhing in the depths of the alleyway next to the restaurant. Before I've even consciously processed what's happening, I'm in motion.

He's got his lips to her neck. Biting, gnashing. Like she's a piece of meat, not a person. I grab him by the back of his collar and rip him off her. Adrenaline and anger course through me like a hit of heroin. I feel alive with it. Every inch of me burning up with violent fury.

I pull him back long enough to aim. Then my fist makes contact with his face and I hear the satisfying crunch of snapping cartilage. There might be a scream, but I'm too incensed to care.

The fucker stumbles back, clutching his face with both hands in some grotesque tableau of prayer. His eyes are wild with shock, pain, confusion.

Then they land on me, and I see what I was looking for.

Fear.

I punch him again, just to make sure that his nose is in fact broken. Another snap, this one grittier. Good. I want to beat him into fucking rubble.

He collapses at my feet, wailing something unholy. I stand over him, fully intending to deliver him to his maker. I raise one boot high over his pitiful skull. Poised. Coiled. An executioner at the ready.

Then: "No!"

Her hands wrap around my raised arm. I turn to those wild green eyes and stop.

"Don't, Daniil," Kinsley begs, her voice trembling. "He's not worth it."

"He deserves to die."

A shiver passes over her face. She knows I mean it. She knows that if she were to stand back now, I would kill him without remorse.

"Please," she says. "Please don't. That's enough."

"It's not nearly enough. He would have raped you if I hadn't stopped him."

"I know—but I don't want this. I don't want his death on my hands, Daniil."

"Fine. Put it on mine."

"I don't want that for you, either."

I grit my teeth. She doesn't understand. If I killed him, I would face no consequences. His body would disappear, just another missing person lost to the sands of time. If he had anyone who loved him, they'd search for him for a little while. Then they'd mourn him. Then they'd forget.

And meanwhile, the world would be better off because he wasn't in it.

"Kinsley—"

"Daniil."

I turn towards the second voice. Charlize. I'd forgotten she was here at all. Her expression is calm, practical. I expect nothing less.

"Not in front of her," she advises quietly.

"No!" Kinsley yelps immediately. "Not anywhere. Not at all."

Then she does something I don't expect. She raises her hand and places it against my cheek. She draws my eyes with that small, intimate gesture.

"Daniil," she whispers. "Promise me. Not at all."

I have never once been persuaded to show mercy when death had been decided on. Never once.

But in the face of her soft green eyes… I relent.

And for that one singular moment, the relief in her eyes is worth it.

Then she drops her hand from my face, and the grit and nastiness of my world comes rushing back in. Fine—he'll live. But he won't like it.

I squat down beside the squirming piece of shit. At the sight of my face, he lets out a sound that's half-shriek, half-whimper.

I grab his bleeding face hard. "The woman you tried to rape just saved you," I hiss. "You owe her your life. However little that's worth."

I dig my fingers in a little harder. The blood runs thick and hot from his ruined nose. Then, disgusted, I push him away, and he puddles against the cobblestones like a ragdoll.

I get to my feet, grab Kinsley's hand, and spin her towards the road.

The sharp *click-clack* of Charlize's heels follows us to the parking lot. I open the passenger door for Kinsley, whose eyes veer to Charlize for a moment. Almost like she's asking for permission.

"Get in," I growl.

For once, she doesn't argue.

Charlize gets in the back. I slam Kinsley's door, then walk around and climb into the driver's seat. I rip fast through the streets, paying no attention to traffic lights or speed limits. Kinsley's arms are rippling with goosebumps, but tonight, I doubt it has anything to do with my driving.

"What the fuck were you thinking going out with a fucking pig like that?" I growl.

"Daniil," Charlize chimes softly.

That's all she says. A gentle reminder that Kinsley may not be able to handle what I'm about to dole out.

Yeah? Well, fuck that.

"You sure know to pick 'em, don't you?" I snap. "First, an abuser, now a fucking rapist."

"Go easy, Daniil—"

"*Go easy*?" I echo furiously. "Would he have 'gone easy' on her?"

"You think I intentionally pick assholes?" Kinsley explodes suddenly. "You think I walk around looking for men who'll hurt me?"

"It seems that way to me."

"Well, of course it does. Because you don't actually know me. You just think you do."

"Yeah, keep telling yourself that, Kinsley. Maybe one day, you'll actually convince yourself of it."

"You know what, actually? You're right! I do pick assholes. You most of all."

I notice her fingers are trembling, and for a moment—just one tiny moment—I feel bad. Then I think about what that motherfucker would have done to her if I hadn't been around and my conscience clears right up.

"It's cute that you think you picked me."

"Right, of course. Because nothing happens outside of your control, does it, Daniil? Must be nice to make the rules. To be the big swinging dick, the head honcho. No one tells you what to do, do they? You're perfect. Untouchable."

"Perfection is boring, Kinsley," Charlize intercedes with a soft little laugh. "It's much more interesting to be flawed."

"Well, then I guess I'm really fucking interesting."

"At least you're aware of it," I growl.

Her eyes snap to mine. "What do you want from me, Daniil?"

"I want you to start paying attention, or one of these days you're going to end up dead. At the hands of a man, or an automobile, or God knows what else."

"And? Who cares?"

"Excuse me?"

"Are you trying to tell me that you would actually care if I live or die?"

My hands tighten around the wheel. "That's a dumb fucking question," I spit. In my head, though, all I'm thinking is, *Of course I'd care.*

I screech to a stop in front of Kinsley's house. She looks around in surprise, as though she has no idea how we got here in the first place.

There's a light on at the front window. Slowly, she swivels toward me. I notice there's still a tremor in her fingers.

I lean forward and unlatch her seatbelt for her. It snaps back across her chest, and the pop seems to knock her out of her daze.

"Thank you," Kinsley whispers softly. Her gaze flits to me for a moment, and then she grabs her bag and gets out of the car quickly.

I watch her all the way up the door. Her curves in that dress. Her hair in the light leaking through the window. The way she puts one foot carefully in front of the other, aware on some level that she's so dangerously close to falling over an edge she will never be able to climb back up again.

"Am I allowed in the front seat now?" Charlize quips when she's gone.

I shoot her a silent glare and get out of the car. "Kinsley," I call before she can make it to her front door.

She freezes on the spot and turns warily to me. I hear the double clap of the car's doors as Charlize moves up to the passenger's seat.

"You should go," Kinsley bites out. "She's waiting for you."

"She'll keep waiting."

Her eyes narrow a fraction. "Goodnight, Daniil."

"Kinsley," I say sharply. "That was… Christ, fuck me." I growl wordlessly in my chest, then pull out a business card and hand it to her. "Next time you need saving, just call me. Save us both the trouble. And the shitty food."

She stares down at the shiny black card with my number printed in silver in the center.

"There's no name on here." Her expression turns curious. "Who are you?"

"I can't believe it's taken you this long to ask that question."

"I believe I tried asking you earlier. You never answered."

"So why break tradition?"

She sighs. "The whole mystery man thing is getting old, Daniil."

I ignore her. "Just promise me you'll use that number when you need to."

"Why?"

I stare at her soft, innocent features. So beautiful and she's not even aware of it. She thinks her fragility is a weakness.

She's so, so wrong.

"Because whether you know it or not, you need me, Kinsley. And one day, you're going to shoot your pride in the face and admit it."

Silence thumps like a heartbeat around us. The night is pressing in on all sides, pushing her close to me and me close to her. It feels like we're cooped up in a snow globe of darkness, just her and me. It's oddly comforting.

I let loose a long sigh. "Goodnight, Kinsley."

She nods like she's barely holding back words or tears or both, then pivots on her heel and goes up the steps. I watch as she approaches her door. As she unlocks it. As she turns the knob.

But before she opens it, she turns to me one more time. "Daniil?"

"Yes?"

"Thank you."

She holds my gaze for a second longer. Then she slips inside. The door snaps shut. Only then do I glance towards the movement I saw at the right window.

The moment my gaze shifts, the curtains are tugged closed quickly, concealing the person spying on our little exchange.

"Well…" Charlize says when I get back to the car, a ghostly smile playing on her lips. Her eyes are heavy with thoughts, and I know from experience that they're not going to stay hidden for very much longer.

But I'm not in the mood for banter. I swing the car back onto the road and start driving.

"I must say, that turned out to be a much more exciting night than I anticipated."

"I'm insulted," I mutter.

"Don't be." She opens up the mirror and checks her reflection, though we both know there's nothing that needs fixing. "So," she asks, "are you going to keep your word about the miserable bastard you left whimpering in the alley?"

"What do you think?"

"Yesterday, I would have said fuck no. Daniil Vlasov will not let a target go free, promise or not. But certain events in the interim have made me see you in a new light."

"Great," I spit. "Mission accomplished."

"That fucker deserves to die," she intones. "You and I both know that." Her voice drops into the deeper register she uses when we're discussing business. "But you aren't going to kill him, are you?"

I sigh and squeeze the living shit out of the steering wheel. "No, I'm not."

And it boils me up from the inside out.

Charlize laughs. "I never expected to be jealous of another woman," she admits. "Ever."

"You're not jealous of Kinsley."

"I am, actually," she says. "Not because I'm into you—don't flatter yourself like that—but only because I've never been in the presence of a connection like that before. I wasn't even sure it existed."

"You and Harwin—"

"I love the man, spineless and subservient as he may be," she says. "But I'm realistic about matters of the heart. Ours is a comfortable love. It's not a great love."

"This is not love," I say coldly.

She laughs. "Keep telling yourself that, darling. Maybe one day, you'll actually convince yourself of it."

23

KINSLEY

The moment I step into the living room, Emma is there in my face, her eyes wild with excitement. She grabs hold of my shoulders and shakes me.

I felt oddly numb when I walked through the door. But the pressure of her hands on me is bringing the feeling back to my limbs.

"Oh. My. God!" she says again and again. "Please tell me that was Daniil?"

"You saw him?" I ask, wincing.

"I heard the car pull up and I decided to spy on you," she admits shamelessly. "I assumed I'd be watching some awkward goodnight tonsil hockey with Liam or Leo or whatever his name is. But that was, like, a trillion times better."

I roll my eyes and look past her towards Isla's room. "Is she sleeping?"

"Of course she's sleeping. It's past midnight, and I'm a responsible babysitter. Why are you changing the topic?"

"Inquiring about my daughter is changing the topic?"

"Yes!" she practically hisses at me. "Was that Daniil—yes or no?"

"Yes."

I walk into the kitchen. Emma tails me, chomping at the bit. "Why are you acting so casual?" she asks. "Something clearly went down tonight. You got picked up by one guy and dropped off by another. Who, I might add, may just be the most beautiful man I have ever laid eyes on."

"Did you finish another bag of gummy worms by yourself?"

"Why are we talking about gummy worms?"

"Because you are clearly high on something. Since I don't have pot in the house, I'm assuming it's a sugar high."

Emma's eyes flatten into slits. "Har-de-har-har."

"Am I wrong?"

"I may or may not have eaten another bag of gummy worms," she says dismissively. "But that is neither here nor there, and it is certainly not what's driving my excitement right now."

"Daniil, is it?"

"Bingo. He's gorgeous."

"He's a lot more than that," I mutter sarcastically.

Emma's eyes bug out of their sockets. "You mean there's *more*?"

I give her the first half of the story. Daniil showing up outside the house, the insurance papers, the drama with the dinner reservations.

She shakes her head. "This shit is better than a soap opera."

"Not sure you'll feel that way once I finish."

Emma frowns. "Okay, I'll reserve judgment until the end. What happened at the restaurant?"

"Let's just say I couldn't concentrate on Liam because I knew Daniil would show up. And he did—with the most beautiful woman I've ever seen."

"Oh God," Emma gasps. "Plot twist!"

"Obviously, they were seated right next to us. And obviously, I couldn't stop looking over at them. And *extra obviously,* she kept touching his arm and laughing like he's the funniest thing walking."

"What about him? How was he acting?"

"Same as always. Broody, too cool for school, let-her-come-to-me kind of deal."

"So sexy."

"Stop it, I beg you." I dig the heel of my hand into my aching eyes. "Anyway, I kinda spent the entirety of the date obsessing about the two of them and then Liam finally called me out on it."

"Yeah, well, he's a douche. Who cares what he thinks?"

"Me, apparently. I apologized—"

"Oh, for the love of God. You're too damn nice, Kinz."

"Yeah, yeah, yeah. Point is, I was kinda freaking out inside, so I went to the bathroom to pull myself together. And then, of course, who should walk in but the woman herself?"

"The other woman?!"

I laugh, even though it hurts. "She's not the other woman, Emma," I point out. "I am."

"Bullshit," Emma says indignantly. "He is the father of your child!"

My eyes snap in the direction of Isla's room. "Keep your voice down!"

"That kiddo is knocked out for the night. Don't worry," she says with a wave of her hand. "So did you actually speak to her?"

"I was trying to calm down when she walked in. Clearly, I wasn't doing so hot at it because she asked if I was okay."

Emma laughs with disbelief. "And you said...?"

"I panicked and claimed I'd just gotten my period. She gave me one of her tampons. I stumbled through a cringy thank you and then I got the hell out of there. Found Liam having a cigarette in the alleyway beside the restaurant. And... that's when it went from a bad date to a real actual nightmare."

Emma goes still, the glee dissipating from her face. "What do you mean? Did he hurt you?"

The next words are hard to say. "He tried to... to force himself on me."

"WHAT?!"

"Shush! Isla's sleeping."

Emma is clinging hard to my wrist with both hands. "Kinsley, he tried to *rape* you?"

"I... I don't know if he'd have actually gone all the way—"

"Kinsley Jane Whitlow."

I sigh and bury my face against Emma's shoulder. "It was traumatic, and those gym muscles turned out to be effective. I tried to get him off me, but he just kept saying horrible things."

I cringe at the memory, his words snaking their way into my head and leaving little scars where they land. A thousand showers won't clean the stink of his breath off of me.

You're such a cocktease.

Just close your eyes and imagine I'm him.

"I'd rather not repeat any of it," I say at last, sitting upright. "But it didn't happen in the end. Because... because of Daniil."

Emma's jaw literally drops. "You're joking."

I shake my head. "It was so real it became surreal, you know what I mean? He pulled Liam off me and rearranged his face."

"I'm liking this guy more and more by the minute."

"I don't know, Emma," I say softly, realizing I haven't even begun to process what happened tonight. "It was… scary."

"Of course it was—"

"No, I mean, watching Daniil beat the shit out of Liam was scary."

"Hold up. Please don't tell me you felt sorry for that piece of shit?"

"No, not for Liam," I admit. "I just… There was a moment when it seemed like Daniil was actually going to kill him. I saw his face. I heard what he said."

"People say wild stuff in the heat of the moment, Kinsley."

"I've never wished death on anyone, and I'm not about to start now," I say firmly. "But I was worried about Daniil at that moment. I didn't want him to make this colossal mistake that would haunt him for the rest of his life."

Emma is still holding my hand and she squeezes it gently. "I'm so sorry you had to go through that."

"Maybe it's my own fault."

"What the hell are you talking about?"

"I've got a bad track record, that's all I'm saying."

Emma makes a scoffing sound from the depths of her throat. "Screw that. Women choose the wrong men all the time. Me included. That doesn't mean we deserve to get hurt for choosing them. That's bullshit logic, Kinz."

I sigh. "I know."

"Where was the glammy girlfriend while all this was happening?"

"She was there. Standing behind us, watching the whole thing."

"Wait—she didn't call the cops?" Emma asks. "911?"

"No. In fact, she seemed completely unfazed by the whole thing."

"Unfazed?" Emma repeats. "What do you mean?"

"She was just so composed. Kinda like she sees situations like that all the time. She watched Daniil beat the shit out of Liam and she didn't say a word."

"Huh. That's something."

I comb through the memory, picking up on little details that seem glaring now. "When I was trying to convince Daniil to back down, she said something. But she didn't ask him to stop. She said, 'Not in front of her.'"

"'Not in front of her'?" Emma repeats. "As in, not in front of *you*?"

I nod. "It sounded like she was okay with the murder part; she was just trying to prevent him from doing it where I could see."

"Whoa. Who is this chick?"

"It's not just her. It's both of them. Whoever they are, they live in the same world."

"What world do you think that is?"

"Beats the hell out of me," I sigh. "A world where a rich white man can get away with anything."

"Um, I hate to break it to you, sport, but we live in that world, too," Emma snorts. "So then what? Daniil is beating the bejeezus out of Liam, psycho cyborg woman doesn't even bat an eyelash, you intervene, and then…?"

"I guess I managed to convince him to leave it alone. Or maybe she did. I'm not even sure. He just grabbed me and pulled me into his car. And drove me here."

"He also followed you out of the car," Emma says pointedly.

"To give me his card."

Emma picks up the sleek black card and turns it over in her hand. "There's no name on here."

"Nope."

"Just his number?"

"Yup."

She sighs dreamily. "So damn cool."

"It's not cool; it's scary. I always knew he was dangerous," I admit. "But I just thought it was a different kind of dangerous. Like, tax-fraud-plus-a-slap-on-the-wrist-jail-sentence kind of dangerous. Not beat-a-stranger-to-death-with-his-bare-hands kind of dangerous."

I take a deep breath and pluck the card from Emma's hand. "Anyway. I told him I'd accept his stupid insurance policy so long as I can reimburse him for it. I don't want charity."

"Jesus. Kinsley, it's not charity. You have raised his child single-handedly for nine freaking years. Why shouldn't you take something from him?"

"Because that's not how I want to live my life."

"You realize you can't afford to be this proud, right? You have bills to pay. Mouths to feed. Like mine, for instance. With gummy worms."

"I'm painfully aware," I say. "But I don't want his money or his help. Especially if he's dangerous."

"But he's not dangerous to you," Emma says emphatically. "That's the second time now he's saved your life."

That hits me strangely. Goosebumps erupt over my body for the second time tonight. I can't even deny it—because Emma's right.

"This is all so overwhelming," I sigh, dropping my face into my palms.

"Hey now..." Emma wraps her arm around my shoulders. "You need to get some rest."

"I doubt I'll be able to sleep tonight."

Emma nods. "Well, then we can stay up together."

"You don't have to do that."

"I have no place to be. We can sleep in and do something fun tomorrow. Something that will help take your mind off everything." Emma gives me a bracing smile. "Can I ask you a question, though? Do you want to see Daniil again?"

The million dollar question.

"I have to pay him back."

"That's not what I asked."

I sigh. "He has his own life and I have mine," I point out, painfully aware that it's just another way of evading her question.

"Kinz. C'mon. Be real with me. I'm your best friend."

I swallow back the bitter taste of fear in my throat. "It's not even about him. I keep thinking about Isla. I feel like she's missing something in her life. What if this is it? What if *he's* it?"

"Is this because of that father-daughter dance thingy?"

"She mentioned it to you?" I ask, because I know for sure that I haven't.

Emma nods reluctantly. "It might've come up."

"So she is feeling bad about it?"

"Isla would never admit that much, even to me. But if I had to guess, I'd say I think it's another thing she feels left out of."

"See?" I say. "This is what I'm talking about. Do I have the right to deprive Isla of her father? Do I have the right to deprive Daniil of his daughter? It was different before, when I didn't know where he was or how to contact him. But now? Now, there's no excuse."

"No," Emma says with grim finality, holding the card up like a smoking gun. "The ball's in your court now."

24

DANIIL

"We want to do business with you, Don Vlasov."

The man sitting opposite me, Ribisi, is bone-thin with wispy facial hair like a badly weeded garden. His spindly body is hunched over my table, and his eyes keep sliding to the bar in the corner of the sparse conference room where I tend to host men who are desperate to worm their way into my good graces.

"Everyone wants to do business with Don Vlasov," Petro says with a self-satisfied smirk. "Doesn't mean everyone gets to."

Ribisi nods and swallows. He's so thin that I see every bit of the motion in his throat. That Adam's apple bobbing up and slurping down. It's repulsive.

"I think we will make great partners," Ribisi says, addressing only me.

That's a mistake. The surest way to get Petro's undivided attention is to ignore him. I can already see his eyes zinging with devilry.

"Why do you think that?" I ask, bored.

"Because we share a common enemy," Ribisi says.

Ping. My phone vibrates on the table.

"It's no secret that you refuse to work with anyone associated with the Semenovs," the man continues. "And rightly so, considering what the old bastard did to you—"

He stops short when my eyes land on him. It's a silent warning. *Don't pretend you know my past. Don't pretend you understand a single fucking thing.*

I pick up my phone and read the message.

KINSLEY WHITLOW: First off, I just want to say thank you for helping me out the other night.

It's been three days since I dropped her off at her decrepit little hovel. Three days of self-imposed silence. I refuse to make the next move. She will have to do it.

It'd be easy to dismiss the text as simple politeness. But I can see the desperation screaming from between the lines. The grammar, the stilted phrasing—I know damn well she spent hours on end typing and deleting and re-typing this shit, trying to strike the perfect balance of nonchalance and *don't-fuck-with-me*-ness.

My attention turns to her display picture. She's standing on a bridge—ironically enough, given her spotty track record in that department. She's looking off in the distance, but it's clear she knows there's a camera on her, because her smile is a little shy, a little self-conscious.

The angle of the picture is what snares my attention. It's off-center. Awkward in a way I can't quite explain. The angle is shot from low looking up at her. Almost like it was taken by…

I shrug and set aside my suspicions. Hers is a pretty face no matter which way you capture it. My dick certainly agrees.

Ping. Another text message.

KINSLEY WHITLOW: *I appreciate you trying to help me out with the insurance policy. But it's really expensive and I just can't make the numbers work. Is there any way I can cancel it?*

I'm aware that the silence in the room is stretching on uncomfortably and all eyes are on me, but I couldn't give less of a shit as I type back.

DANIIL: *You don't have to afford it. I've taken care of everything.*

KINSLEY: *I thought I made it clear I don't accept charity.*

DANIIL: *Pretend it's an apology.*

The bubbles of her actively typing appear and disappear a few times. I glance up from my phone to find Petro smirking at me.

"Something more important taking up your attention, boss?" he inquires.

I roll my eyes and ignore him. It's best not to feed into him when he's feeling irritating. If you give a mouse a cookie, or whatever the fuck the expression is.

"Ribisi," I growl, "my sources say that you have worked for the Semenovs in the past. Moving weapons for them. Brokering deals for them. Cleaning up after them. The list goes on and on, it seems."

"All true," he says, his eyes tensing immediately. "I don't deny it."

"You didn't exactly volunteer the information, though, did you?"

Ping. I manage to keep my eyes on Ribisi. Just barely.

"Perhaps I wasn't as forthcoming as I should have been, but I never lied, Don Vlasov. I'm just not in the habit of offering information that could reflect poorly on the prospects of a fruitful relationship between our organizations. I'm sure you understand."

I eye him carefully. His words are reasonable enough—you can never trust a man who doesn't operate with a healthy dose of self-interest.

But there's something ineffably snaky about him. A sliminess I don't trust.

"The point is I no longer have anything to do with the Semenovs," Ribisi insists.

"Does Gregor know that?"

"I walked out on our last meeting, so yes, I'm fairly certain he knows where I stand."

"You walked out on him and he let you go?" I ask. "In my experience, turning your back on Gregor Semenov is the best way to guarantee a knife buried in your spine."

"I have men on my side, too," Ribisi says pridefully.

"You didn't walk out of shit, did you? He kicked your sorry ass to the curb."

Ribisi stiffens, and I know I've hit the nail on the head. "I worked with him for nine years, and that whole time, I was loyal. He chose not to appreciate that loyalty. So I decided to find someone who would."

"And now, you're here," I remark apathetically. "Because you wanted to work for me, or because you knew I would be the easiest way to get back at Gregor?"

He raises his eyebrows, but when he realizes I'm serious, his expression flattens. "The latter."

I give him a shark's smile. "I like an honest man. In words, if not deeds."

"For the record, Don Vlasov, your reputation precedes you."

I glance at Petro, who's scrutinizing Ribisi with a studious gaze. I can see his thoughts churning, the gears in his head whirring and grinding.

"So what do you want exactly?" I ask bluntly.

"I am no fool," he says. "I don't intend to seek revenge on Gregor Semenov. The man is still formidable. Going head-to-head with him would be suicide."

I look down at my phone and open Kinsley's latest message. ***You and I both know that you're not the kind of man who apologizes.***

I have to stifle an amused laugh.

"So you came here to use Don Vlasov to fight your battles for you?" Petro asks, playing the worse cop to my bad cop. "No fucking dice. You should've never shown up here in the first place. What a waste of time this has been. My disappointment is immeasurable and my day is ruined."

"I did not come here to be insulted by a lackey!" roars Ribisi.

I look up in time to see him catapult himself out of his seat, his wiry muscles clenched tight and ready for action. Petro stands up, too, but there's much less urgency in his movements. He's lazy, unconcerned, knowing full well he has the upper hand.

Cocky bastard.

"Sit down, both of you," I say calmly. The men begrudgingly sink back into their seats. "Ribisi, when you asked for this meeting, you asked for a fair hearing. And I'm prepared to give it to you."

Ping. I keep my eyes fixed on the scrawny man across the table.

"Accepting you into the fold will be interpreted by the Semenovs as a slap in the face," I continue. "I want to be sure you're worth the trouble."

Ribisi's eyes narrow into slits. "I'm well worth the trouble, I promise you that much."

"I'm the only one worth any goddamn trouble in this Bratva, Ribisi," Petro hisses.

Ribisi's eyes turn to me. "Do you have a muzzle for the dog?"

Petro bursts out laughing. It's one of the reasons I keep him around. He may have all the swagger of the man in charge, but insults don't burn his skin the same way. They just fuel his fire.

"Muzzles don't work on him," I admit sadly. "I've tried."

Petro gives Ribisi a wink. "You're welcome to come find out for yourself how the bite compares to the bark."

"You are a—"

"We're going to do this in stages," I interrupt. "I'm willing to give you a trial period, Ribisi. Trust is earned, one piece at a time."

Ribisi looks at me carefully for a moment. "I hope you don't mind me saying so, Don Vlasov, but you're a lot like Gregor."

"He was my mentor. I learned a lot from him."

"A little too much, in my opinion," Petro mutters under his breath.

"He gets a daily report of you, you know," Ribisi says abruptly.

That gets my attention.

Ribisi nods, sensing my interest. "He has men keeping track of your moves. Not spies, as such. Just… onlookers. If you strike a new business deal or acquire a new piece of land, it's reported to him. He's followed you diligently for years. You frustrate and anger him frequently, but I think a part of him is proud. He feels he can take credit for the don you are now."

The urge to remind him of who is responsible for whom crackles hot in my chest, but I repress it. "You've given me a lot to think about, Ribisi," I say instead. "I'll be in touch soon."

The man nods and rises to his feet, understanding the dismissal. He inclines his head towards me, and even manages a quasi-respectful twitch of the chin in Petro's direction. Then he walks out with his two silent bodyguards at his back.

As soon as the door shuts, Petro shifts his swivel chair towards me.

"Show me the texts, *pendejo*," he says, holding out his hand.

I look at my phone. **KINSLEY: Please. *There's an address on the policy, so I'll go there tomorrow. Just tell me who to speak to and I'll sort this out myself. You don't even have to get involved.***

"Nobody," I say to Petro.

"Don't bullshit a bullshitter, D. It was somebody alright. Somebody pretty and sexy and… brunette? I'll take 'Who is Kinsley Whitlow?' for $1000, Alex."

I ignore him and reply to her. ***Very well. I'll inform them that you're coming. The manager will sort things out to your satisfaction.***

When that's sent, I close the conversation and put my phone back on the table. I look up to see Petro staring at me with an all-knowing smile.

"Oh, it's definitely her. You've got the dopey, hearts-in-your-eyes expression I'm coming to associate with that curvaceous little irritant."

I sigh, lean back in my chair, and run a hand through my hair. "She wants to cancel the insurance policy I got for her. It's apparently too expensive."

He wrinkles his nose up. "She's not the one paying for it."

"She wants to be."

"Huh. Weird. She realizes you have money, doesn't she?"

"I'd say that's been made abundantly clear."

"And she still wants to pay herself?"

"So it would seem."

"Wow. A chick with pride, dignity, principles. I can see why you're fixated," he says, looking thoughtful suddenly. "I can't remember the last time a woman refused to let me pay for something."

"That's because the women you associate with are used to cash changing hands."

"Oh," Petro scoffs imperiously, "so now, you're discriminating against sex workers? Shame on you, Daniil Vlasov. This is a progressive era we're living in. Get with the times."

"Spare me the cultural commentary," I drawl.

He grins. "Does the little minx know what she's getting herself into?"

"Of course not."

Petro laughs. "You're having fun, aren't you? I've never seen you look so animated in a business meeting." He frowns and adds, "Speaking of which, are you really going to give Ribisi a shot?"

"I'm going to vet him first. He's not just going to earn the mark overnight."

"He'll have two marks," Petro points out in a warning tone.

I raise my eyebrows and pull up my shirt sleeve. "We can hardly find fault with him for that," I say, revealing the brand of the Semenovs that rests on my forearm next to the crest of the Vlasov Bratva.

Petro shifts in his seat uncomfortably. "We had good reason to leave."

"Everyone has their reasons," I point out. "Ribisi included."

"This is going to piss off the old bastard. No one this high up has ever defected. Except for us, obviously."

"Which is why I'm accepting him. With conditions."

"Is there a reason you're antagonizing the old man now?"

"The whole of the last ten years has been about antagonizing him," I reply. "But I didn't have the strength or the manpower to go head-to-head with him. Now, I do."

"Ribisi is right, you know. Sometimes, you do remind me of ol' Greggy."

I check my phone again, but there are no new messages. Petro clears his throat pointedly, forcing me to look up at him.

"Just out of curiosity, what is your endgame where this girl is concerned? I mean, you've already banged her."

"Ten years ago."

"Ah. So one more fuck for old time's sake? Is that it?"

No, that's not it. Not by a long shot.

But to Petro, I say, "Pretty much."

Sometimes, it's easier to lie.

25

KINSLEY

My phone sits in my hand with Daniil's last text still pulled up on the screen.

The manager will sort things out to your satisfaction.

That was easier than I thought it would be. Which is making me slightly suspicious—but then again, don't look a gift horse in the mouth, right?

His display picture is—predictably—a pure black backdrop. No images, no text. Just more mystery. Typical.

"Mom, I can't reach the chocolate chips."

I put my phone away and walk over to Isla, who's on her knees on the counter as she stretches for the top cabinet. My sugar stash.

I can't even keep *that* secret.

I get on the stepstool and pull out the bag of chocolate chips. We used to bake together a lot when Isla was younger. But somewhere down the line, the tradition fell by the wayside.

But I've decided today to revive it. The best part? Isla was enthusiastic about it. She's rarely enthusiastic about anything anymore, so I'll take what I can get. Don't look a gift daughter in the mouth, or whatever.

Isla starts pouring chocolate chips into our thick cookie batter, which I already know is delicious, because I've had a little too much before we've even baked it.

"Is that enough?" Isla asks.

The batter has disappeared beneath a sea of chocolate chips. But I wave my hand. "Oh, go on. You only live once."

Isla smiles and adds a few more chips. "This is fun."

"Yeah?" I say excitedly. "You're right. It is fun. We should do this more often."

She nods and I feel lighter instantly.

"Drawing anything new lately?" I ask as she starts stirring the chocolate in.

"A few things," she says shyly, her eyes flickering over to her sketchbook.

"Mind if I take a peek?"

She gives me a timid nod, and I help myself to the sketchbook. The first few pictures, I've already seen. It's the last set that's new to me.

"Honey, you're so talented."

She blushes. "Thanks."

Everyone thinks their child is special, gifted, unique. But I could swear that there is a maturity to my baby girl's art that far surpasses her few years on this planet. It's imaginative and colorful and makes my heart melt every time, because I can see how much of herself she pours into it.

Then I turn the page and freeze.

This one is different than the others. Somber, in a way I can't quite put my finger on. It's a detailed sketch of a young girl who looks almost exactly like Isla. The nose and the eyes are the same, as are the bow-shaped lips and the curve of her eyebrows.

But her hair isn't curly; it's straight.

Her skin isn't freckly; it's clear.

No glasses or braces, none of the auburn tinge that I love in her locks. It's like she erased all the parts of herself that she hates.

And just like that, I feel nauseous.

"Honey…" I say, looking up at her as I pen back the tears threatening to spill loose.

"You don't like it?" she asks, her face falling.

"No, it's not that. Of course it's not that." I'm struggling to figure out what to say to her without completely wrecking her self-confidence. What's left of it, anyway. "It's a gorgeous picture. I'm just worried about… what it means."

She shrugs. "It's just how I would look if I were pretty."

What hurts the most is how matter-of-fact she sounds. Like it's a fact that no one can deny. *The sky is blue. Grass is green. The way I am is ugly.*

"Isla, you are beautiful."

Her eyes narrow. "No, I'm not. It's not nice to lie."

"I'm not lying, baby. I would never lie to you." I swallow back my heartbreak and frustration. "Who told you that you weren't pretty?"

She shrugs again, but she makes the mistake of looking away at the same time. Dead giveaway that we're veering dangerously close to somewhere she's been badly hurt. "Just a bunch of girls in school. They're stupid most of the time. It doesn't matter."

This is the most she's ever admitted aloud. I don't want to break the cone of trust we're in. But I want to press. I need to press.

"It sounds like they're stupid all of the time."

She almost smiles at that. "Maybe."

"Isla, honey—"

"I'm not going to tell you who they are," she interrupts abruptly. "The last time, you spoke to Principal Bridges and it just made things worse."

I stop short. "It did?"

She nods. "Now, they're really nice to me in front of Ms. Roe, but they're really mean when no one's paying attention. Which is most of the time."

"Those little bitches."

"Mom!"

"I'm not taking it back."

She stares at me with her big brown eyes for a moment. Then she smiles. A real smile. A big one. And I want to scream obscenities and cry all at the same time.

I take a deep breath and then grab the ice cream scooper. I make a scoop of cookie dough and push it out onto the bread board between us.

"Go to town."

"Really?"

"It'll be worth the stomachache," I say. "And I think this moment calls for some raw cookie dough, don't you?"

She hesitates for a moment, and that right there—that timidness, that fear, that uncertainty—that shatters my heart all over again.

Then she sighs and smiles and I can breathe again. It still hurts, though. I wonder if it'll ever not hurt to see my baby in pain.

I watch her chewing thoughtfully, her face all bright with the high of sugar. Some days, it's unfathomable to me that she's nine years old, because she could just as easily be a thousand. Then there are the moments when I look at her, and see a scared little girl who still needs her mother.

Except for when it feels like she needs something more.

Like a father.

"So they're still ragging on you?" I say after a few minutes of quiet eating.

"Some days, yes. Some days, no," she admits. "But recently…" She trails off and concentrates on her cookie dough.

"It's gotten worse?" I prod, hoping that she doesn't shut down on me.

"Yeah. Because of the… the dance."

I almost drop the ice cream scooper on the floor. "The father-daughter dance?" I say through a choked throat.

"They make fun of me for not having one. Like, a dad, I mean. They say my dad left because I was so ugly."

My body goes cold with fury. All I want to do is march down to the school and get the names of every single girl in Isla's class. Then I want to shake each and every one of them down until I find the culprits. Then… well, then I might ask Daniil for some pointers on what to do next.

It's a good thing my daughter needs me more right now. Because what I'm feeling, this violence, this rage… it wouldn't be good if I was close enough to them to let it all out.

"They sound like a bunch of scared, miserable little demons," I say, my voice vibrating with the effort of staying calm. "Who lash out to make themselves feel better."

Isla shrugs again. "At least they all have dads."

My heart drops once more. I didn't know it could plummet this low. Fear and sadness, nausea and rage—it's all there in spades. "I didn't realize how much you missed that presence in your life."

"Don't you miss your dad?" she asks, raising those doe eyes to mine.

"My dad was… a different kind of man."

"What does that mean?"

"It means he wasn't very nice."

"Was my dad not a very nice man?" she inquires.

I'm stumped for a moment. Daniil is certainly a confident man. He's a powerful man. He's confident and broody. He can be arrogant, borderline possessive.

But he can also be kind. Thoughtful. Perceptive.

"He—I don't… I mean, I didn't know your father all that well," I admit. If she's opening up to me, it's only fair that I open up to her.

She frowns. "You mean you had a one-night-stand?"

My eyes go wide with alarm. "How do you know about that?"

"I heard some of the older kids talking about it. I know it means sex. That's how babies are born."

I have to breathe through the shock, but I manage to hold my own pretty well. At least, I think so. "I wouldn't call it that," I say, even though it technically ticks all the boxes. "Your father and I didn't know each other very long, but we had a… connection. We understood each other. Not right off the bat, but it was easy to talk to him. I guess I was looking for a friend."

"Where was Aunt Emma?"

"Um, well, she was back at the wedding."

"Whose wedding?"

I smile. "It's a very long story."

"I'd still like to hear it."

I stare at my little girl, faced with the stunning realization that she's not so little anymore. Somewhere along the way, she transformed into a young lady, and I barely noticed.

"Alright. I guess you're getting close to old enough. Well, once upon a time, I was engaged to be married."

Isla's eyes bulge. "You were?"

I nod. "It was a bad decision, honey. The man I was going to marry… He was definitely not a nice guy. And I didn't realize it until the very, very last minute."

I decide to spare her the gory details. *The shattering glass. The wild fury in his eyes.* As wizened as she seems sometimes, I still want to preserve what's left of the innocence in her.

"So Aunt Emma created a distraction and I took the wedding car and drove off."

"Whoa!"

I smile at the fascinated expression on her face. It's like she's seeing me differently, too. More like a badass, and less like her stodgy old mother. And through her eyes, I'm seeing myself differently.

What I did was brave, wasn't it? It was stupid and reckless and it changed everything forever, but it was still brave. One of the few truly brave things I've ever done.

"The thing was, I was really emotional. And very scared. I had a little accident on a bridge on the outskirts of the city and when I got out of the car, I stumbled and fell. Right into a river."

"No way!"

I nod. "I was wearing this huge wedding dress and it was pulling me down. And then… someone saved me."

Her jaw drops. "Was it my dad?"

I nod. "It was your dad. He jumped in the river and pulled me out. And then we talked for a long time. Way into the night."

"Then what happened?"

"Then I woke up the next morning and he was just… gone."

"Gone?"

"He had to leave. But he never knew you existed, Isla. If he had, I'm sure he would have stuck around."

Isla's bottom lip puckers out just a little. "He should have stuck around anyway," she murmurs.

I swallow down a decade's worth of bitterness. "Yeah," I croak. "Maybe. But… well, he had a life to get back to. And I had to sort out my own life. We didn't make each other any promises. It wasn't easy, but knowing you were coming made everything a little brighter."

"So he really doesn't know that I was even born?"

"I'm afraid not."

I feel that annoying little prick of guilt as my conscience starts acting up again. It was one thing when I had no idea where Daniil was. But now? Now, it's a lie, plain and simple.

"What was he like?" Isla asks.

"He was… a very interesting man."

It's a conservative answer. Incredibly safe. But that's all I can allow myself to be right now. The insurance policy he gave me the other night is burning a hole in my purse, and first, I need to sort that out. I need to sever all the ties before he can reel me back into his world.

I can't afford to let that happen.

"Anyhow, storytime is over," I announce. "Let's put these in the oven to bake. You've got swim practice in an hour."

Isla nods, but she makes no move to help me. "If he did know I existed, do you think he would come with me to the father-daughter dance?"

I turn to her in surprise. "Sweetheart…"

She shrugs, but I can tell she's been thinking about this a lot. "It would just be nice to feel like everyone else sometimes. Kinda like I was… normal."

"You *are* normal, sweetheart. Lots of kids don't have daddies."

"But they have stepdads," Isla points out. "And if they don't have daddies at all, they at least have pictures. They have memories. They have a story."

She's fidgeting back and forth in place. I wonder if some emotions are just too big for children. They aren't equipped to handle grief or loss or the soul-sucking absence where a father should be. I want so badly to take some of that away from her so she doesn't have to carry it anymore.

But the older she gets, the less I know how to do that.

"I have an idea," I say suddenly, trying to compensate for my poor life decisions. "How about I go to the dance with you?"

Isla frowns. "But you're not my daddy."

"I'll be like a stand-in."

"You can't stand in for him for someone who's not coming."

"Oh, sweetheart—"

"It's okay," she says, jumping off her seat. "It's probably better if I don't go."

"Why do you say that?"

Her brown eyes swivel away from me. "All the girls are going to Geraldi's to get their dresses. They'll just make fun of everyone who's wearing something different."

"Who are these girls?" I snarl.

"It doesn't matter."

"What if I got you a dress from Geraldi's?" I offer. "Then they won't be able to make fun of you."

She shakes her head. "It's a waste of money."

But I know what she really means. *We can't afford it.*

I take a breath and drop a kiss on her forehead. "Why don't you go pack your bag for swim practice? I'll finish the cookies up and then we can leave."

Isla nods and slinks off to her room. I immediately get on my laptop and search for Geraldi's online. The store pops up and I scroll through the children's formal dresses they have for sale.

"Jesus," I breathe. The price tags are astronomical.

My eyes wander to the sheaf of insurance papers sticking out of my purse. If I was even a fraction uncertain before, I'm not now. I'm deadset on canceling this.

Who needs insurance, anyway? I'll take the highways at snail speed for the rest of my life, I'll forget the left lane even exists, I'll drive everywhere with my caution lights blinking. Whatever it takes to give my daughter what she needs to be happy.

I've done it.

I'll do it.

I'll never stop trying.

∼

After I've dropped Isla off at her swim class, I head for the address listed on the policy. The sign over the building reads *GLOBAL INSURANCE* in bright blue neon. Weirdly anonymous name for a company, but okay.

The receptionist inside is a stunning redhead in a smart green pantsuit. Her hair is slicked back into a tight knot at the back of her head and her dark blue eyes regard me through fashionable round frames.

"Can I help you, ma'am?"

"Yes, my name is Kinsley Whitlow. I was sent here to speak to… Actually, I don't know who."

"One second, I'll check for you," she says politely. She skims through something on her computer, then picks up her phone and dials. I watch as she listens to someone on the other end of the line. "Mhmm. Mhmm. Yes, sir. I'll send her in." She hangs up and stands. "Right this way, Ms. Whitlow."

I follow her down a gleaming glass corridor. It feels like we're walking through a spaceship. At the end of the hall is a giant elevator secured with a keypad. The receptionist punches in a code and the elevator doors slide open. She steps aside to let me in first.

When I turn around, though, she's still on the other side of the doors. "The elevator will take you up to the thirtieth floor," she explains. "There will be someone to assist you there. Thank you for visiting us!"

A chime sounds and the elevator closes. I fidget nervously in place as it whisks me up, so smooth and silent that I barely realize it's moving at all.

When I get to the thirtieth floor, I have to open my mouth wide and work my jaw to get my ears to pop. The doors open to reveal what I could swear is the exact same woman from downstairs. Same blue eyes, same shockingly red hair.

But whereas the one on the ground level had a name tag that said RAQUEL, this one's says RACHEL. Twins with twin names. Spooky.

"Hi," I say. "I'm here to meet, uh… someone. He's expecting me. Or she. I'm not quite sure what's happening, to be honest."

Rachel smiles. It's every bit as dazzling as her sister's. "Right this way, ma'am," she says with the exact same intonation. I follow her confident stride to a set of mahogany doors. With all this shining glass everywhere, it looks like the mouth of an Arctic cave.

I wait for her to open the doors—something tells me that's the proper protocol in this situation—but Rachel just stands there with her hands folded behind her back.

"You are welcome to enter whenever you're ready, ma'am," she says.

I swallow, suddenly nervous. There's a weird crackle in the air. "Oh. Thanks."

I take one more deep breath, then grab the metal handle. It's bizarrely cold to the touch. Rachel's eyes are fixed on me as I pull it open with effort, then slide through the skinny gap.

It slams shut behind me with a resounding clang. The office within is as dark as the outside was bright. Mahogany wood paneling everywhere swallows up the light. The only furniture is a dark metal desk and two dark metal chairs.

And behind that desk…

"Oh God," I gasp.

Daniil smiles. "Hello, *sladkaya*."

26

DANIIL

It's a marvel how much those eyes can convey. Shock, disbelief, anger, fear—it's all there. A riptide of emotion painted in infinite shades of green.

"Daniil."

"I thought you'd have figured it out by now."

"That you own the insurance company?" she asks. "I'll be honest, it wasn't high on my list of hypotheses."

I chuckle. "Sit."

"I don't want to sit," she snaps.

"Suit yourself. Can I get you anything?" I ask. "Coffee, tea, or something stronger?"

"This isn't a social call, Daniil."

I shrug. "You came to discuss business with me. This is how I start my business meetings."

"No, I came to discuss business with the person in charge of my insurance policy."

My grin broadens. "Present and accounted for."

"Jesus," she spits, rolling her eyes. "You are unreal. And before you say something snarky, no, that's not a compliment."

"You look stressed, *sladkaya*."

"I told you to stop calling me that." Her fists are balled up tight at her sides and she's quivering from head to toe.

"What about our history makes you think I'll listen?"

She grimaces. Then she stomps over to one of the chairs facing my desk and drops down. But she stays perched on the edge, like she might get fed up at any moment and try to punch my lights out instead.

She's wearing a tight white tank top tucked into a high-waisted army green skirt. Her boots are a sober beige and she keeps tapping her right heel against the wooden floors.

"This place…" she says, looking around.

"Do you like it?"

"Not really."

I smile. "Why not?"

"There's no color," she says. "No personality. No character. It's just wood and metal and not much else. Where's the life? Where's the art?"

"There's a painting right over there," I say, pointing to the wall behind her.

She laughs out loud when she twists in her seat to see it. "It's a picture of a big black dot against a white background."

"It's minimalistic."

"It's boring," she retorts. "Which I would never have expected from you."

I cock my head to the side. "I'm thrilled to know you find me interesting."

She turns up her nose. "Daniil…" Then her eyes meet mine and her sentence trails off limply. "You already know what I'm about to say."

"I have a pretty good guess."

"I'm serious," she insists. "I want to cancel the policy."

"Because you can't afford it."

"That's right."

"But I can."

She sighs. "I'm uncomfortable accepting this kind of thing from you. It's too much. And it's also unnecessary."

"You've made that clear."

Kinsley throws her hands up in frustration. "You're impossible, you know that?"

"I have been told that, on occasion."

"What does your girlfriend think about this?" she asks.

I have to stifle a louder laugh. *My girlfriend.* The poor little *kiska* in front of me is mortally threatened by a woman she didn't know existed until a few days ago.

I could tell her the truth: that Charlize is nothing of the sort.

But it's more fun to watch her squirm.

"You've seen Charlize," I say. "Does she strike you as the kind of woman who's easily threatened?"

It happens again: her face drops. But this time, she has to struggle harder to pick it back up. It makes me want to kick the desk away so that I can take the quickest route to her and slide my fingers over her lips.

"I... I'm not here to talk about Charlize," she says at last, mustering up as much resolve as she has left.

"Why not?" I ask. "Jealous?"

She frowns. "I'm a lot of things, Daniil. Stubborn, sometimes. Naïve, definitely. Scared, most days. But I am not stupid. So don't try to play me for a fool."

I smile, feeling my cock rise with my respect for her. She has fire aplenty. I like that.

"Fair enough," I say. "It might interest you to know that Charlize and I aren't together. Never have been. Truth be told, I don't think we'd last a single night in the same bed. We'd rip each other's throats out long before we ripped each other's clothes off."

Kinsley blinks rapidly as she struggles to process everything I'm saying. "Um, wow... Okay. I don't really know what to say to that."

"You're not required to say anything. I just thought I'd give you the truth, in good faith."

"But... you wanted me to believe she was your girlfriend."

"I thought it'd be more amusing that way."

"Right," she snaps acidly, her tone once again clipped and resentful. "Turned out to be a real 'amusing' night. Dinner and a rape. Classic."

"He didn't rape you, Kinsley," I remind her softly. "I wouldn't let that happen."

She nods and looks down at her palms. "No, I know. I don't know why I said that." She forces herself to look back up at me. "I did thank you for that, didn't I?"

"You said enough."

I let the silence extend for a moment. She looks like she needs it. Finally, she glances up. A little startled, a little uncertain, a little lost.

But she's not lost. She's in exactly the right place.

"Why did I come here, Daniil?" she asks. "More to the point, why did you bring me here? Am I really so pathetic? Am I such a loser in your eyes that you feel this need to… to be my savior?"

"I've never tried to be anyone's savior." I fold my hands in front of me and look at her in the soft gloom of the office. "It seems to me like you're holding onto some anger, Kinsley. Is this still about Charlize, or is there something more going on with you?"

"Who taught you to be such a dick? Your boss? Who was he, exactly?" she demands. "Some asshole businessman who ripped people off for a living and beat his wife up on the side?"

"No," I say quietly. "He wasn't involved in this company."

"Then what was he involved in?"

"Bad things."

She shudders. "But you're not?"

"I never said that."

"See?" she says. "Never a straight answer. You talk in riddles. You behave in riddles, too."

I know what she's doing. We've had this conversation before and she knows these answers already. But she's deflecting, retreating behind the safe and the comfortable. Because the only other option is to charge headlong into the dark, swirling future. She can't bring herself to do that.

Not yet, at least.

"So this is about what happened ten years ago," I infer softly. She stiffens instantly, a physical confirmation. "You're still mad at me for leaving."

"I realize you never promised me anything," she whispers. "But that day, that night… We talked. I opened up to you in a way that I've never opened up to a complete stranger before. I never talk about my parents to anyone, even people I've known for years. But I opened up to you. I told you about my father. My mother. I trusted you enough to tell you my most vulnerable secrets. And the thing is, I thought you understood. It felt like you could relate somehow. Maybe those conversations didn't mean shit to you, but they did to me."

More silence. This time, it feels cloying. Oppressive. Like it's forcing its way down our throats, both of us at the same time. My dick is painfully hard, uncomfortably so, but the tightness in my chest is even worse.

"What did you want from me, Kinsley?"

She sighs. "I wanted your respect, Daniil. I get it now—it was just about sex for you. But for me, it meant something more."

Her eyes fall back to her lap. I hate that. I'm consumed again with the desire to hurl this desk through the fucking window, to pull her up and show her that her head belongs high, her chest proud. She hates herself for being vulnerable.

But if there's anything I've learned in this world, it's that it's easy to be hard. It's easy to be violent.

It's much harder to offer yourself up to the wolves.

"You know what? It doesn't matter anymore," she says, shaking her head. "You're right—it was a long time ago. And I was just your alibi. Like I said, I can be naïve sometimes. More so ten years ago than now, though. I'm learning."

"Kinsley—"

"My point is, I don't want your insurance, Daniil. I don't want anything from you. Not anymore. So I'm asking you—begging you, really—please just let me out of this."

She stands and turns to leave, but I lunge up and snag her arm before she can go. I pull her forward, back to me, and her eyes meet mine. We stand there, barely an inch of space between us.

Tension builds.

Heat builds.

Things that don't have names build, and build, and build.

"*Sladkaya*, you—"

BRIIIIINGGG. An ear-splitting screech slices through the air. Kinsley yelps and fishes her phone out of her purse.

"Hello? Speaking. Yes… yes… Oh my God…" Her face cracks. I can see the panic and worry ripple through her like shockwaves. "No, of course. Is she hurt? I'll be there soon. Thanks for calling."

She hangs up and rushes right for the door. Just before she reaches it, she stops short and turns to me. "I… I have to go."

"What happened?"

Her eyes twist with secrecy. "Emma's had an accident. I need to go make sure she's okay."

Lie. I can sniff it out a mile away. I don't say anything as she turns and scampers out. But I know one thing for damn sure: whoever Kinsley just rushed out of here for, it definitely wasn't Emma.

27

KINSLEY

It takes me twenty minutes to get to the swimming pool where Isla practices. Which is twenty minutes too long, as far as I'm concerned.

I'm rushing towards the pool when someone calls my name. I whirl around and spot Coach Gracie sitting with Isla in the corner. She's got a big blue towel wrapped around her shoulders.

"Isla, honey! Are you okay? Are you sick? What happened? Is everything alright?"

I know I'm going a mile a minute, but I had way too much time to work myself up during the car ride over here. So much for my solemn vow to drive like a grandma, too. I averaged about forty over the speed limit the whole way, and I side-swiped my mirror on a dense hedge to boot.

Good thing I have expensive insurance.

"She's alright," Gracie assures me. "She just gave us a scare."

I keep my eyes trained on my daughter. Isla hasn't looked up once. The other kids are still splashing around in the pool with the other coaches. The sound of their cheering is giving me a headache.

"What happened?" I'm calmer now, though I still feel the prickly surge of anxiety beneath my skin.

"The kids were practicing their diving, and Isla dived in. But she didn't come back up again. I could see the struggling at the bottom of the pool. So I jumped in and got her. She didn't need CPR or anything. Nothing that serious. But she did ask for you."

I take a deep breath and nod. "Thank you, Coach. I'll take it from here."

Gracie gives me a bracing smile and gets back to her class in the pool. I sit down beside Isla. Still, she doesn't raise her head. Her swimming cap is on, but her goggles are sitting next to her on the wet bench.

"Sweetheart, you wanna talk to me?"

"No."

"Just tell me this: are you okay?"

"I'm fine."

I purse my lips. She's not giving me much, and prying will do more harm than good right now. So I put the talking to rest and wrap an arm around her.

"I'm wet," she warns me.

"Then I'll get wet, too."

She glances at me and sighs. "I want to go home."

"That's a good idea. Why don't you grab your bag and go change? I'll wait out here for you."

While she heads into one of the dressing rooms, Gracie walks back over to me. I've never seen a woman more comfortable in a swimsuit before. She wears it like I wear my shorts at home.

"How is she?" she asks, brow furrowed with concern.

"Couldn't get much out of her," I admit. "She seems a little shaken."

Gracie glances towards the dressing room. "To be honest, she's been distracted for the last couple of weeks, Kinsley."

"She's going through a tough time at school. Some of the other girls have been bullying her."

Gracie's eyebrows fly up on her forehead. I appreciate her surprise. "Really? God, kids can be such little bastards sometimes."

I laugh and sniffle. "I wholeheartedly concur."

"But it does happen," Gracie acknowledges. "Even here. It's important the teachers know how to nip that kind of thing in the bud."

"Not so sure Isla's teacher at school shares the same mindset."

Gracie rolls her eyes. "I hate her already."

"Did Isla say anything to you, by any chance?"

"No, I'm afraid not. She's always pretty quiet in class, even on the best of days. She used to engage with the other kids, but lately... I don't know. It's like she's receding further and further into herself. I hope that doesn't sound too melodramatic."

It does, though. It sends a bolt of fear coursing right through me. It feels like Gracie is describing my mother. Withering away like a flower starved of love. How did this even happen? When did it start? How do I stop it?

"I'm going to take her home now, Gracie." My pulse is shallow and rapid, and I don't like the feeling one bit.

"Of course. You'll let me know how she's doing?"

"Definitely."

We say goodbye and a few minutes later, Isla walks out of the dressing room in a pair of shorts and a t-shirt that's a few sizes too big for her.

"I'm ready to go," she mumbles.

I comb my fingers through her wet hair. For once, she doesn't seem to mind. We walk out together as I rack my brain to think up the best way to get her to open up to me. You can only make so many batches of cookies. Although…

"How about we go get some ice cream?" I suggest. "We haven't been to Carino's in a long time. We could stop by for a scoop before going home."

If she vetoes this idea, I don't know what my fallback plan will be. Luckily for me, she nods. "Okay."

"Awesome. I'm thinking strawberry swirl or peanut butter cup."

She doesn't smile, though she does mumble, "I haven't decided yet."

"Take your time, sweetheart."

We drive silently to Carino's. It's always been our go-to ice cream parlor. Emma, Isla, and I used to come religiously every single week. Sundays were for swims and picnics and ice cream before dinner. I can't remember when that stopped.

Somewhere around the same time Isla started losing her smile, probably.

It's freakishly nostalgic walking into the store. The colors are all the same, just a little faded. The booths are right where we left them, just a little worse for the wear.

Isla meanders away from me, her hair soaking into the back of her baggy shirt.

"Hello, ma'am," the teenage girl behind the counter greets cheerfully. "What can I get you two?"

"Strawberry swirl for me. Isla, what are you thinking?"

"Chocolate chip cookie dough."

I smile. "All about the cookie dough these days, huh? We'll take two scoops of each."

"Coming right up."

Once we've got our ice cream, I lead Isla to a table by the window. She sits opposite me and digs into her ice cream without once looking up.

I let her eat. My gaze flits between the world walking past us and the somber little girl in front of me.

"Is it good?" I ask after a full ten minutes of silence.

She just nods.

When she's done with her ice cream, she pushes it away from her and reaches for a napkin. I offer her my cup. "Want a taste?"

"No, thank you."

"Sunshine…"

"I don't want to talk about it."

I want to swallow my frustration, but it's getting harder and harder to do that. "Okay then," I say. "How about you choose something you would like to talk about? Anything you want, anything at all."

She thinks about it for a little while. "Why don't you ever talk about your parents?"

I wince. She went right for the jugular. "Oh, wow. I gotta say, that's not what I expected."

"You never talk about them. I want to know why."

"Because they lived sad lives, honey," I say, trying to be as delicate as I can. "And I guess talking about them makes me sad, too."

"I've never even seen a picture of them."

I know she hasn't. When we'd moved last, I'd taken my box of memorabilia from my childhood and chucked it. It was meant to be a powerful step. A cleansing, if you will.

Turns out, junking old stuff doesn't remove the memories. The past isn't nearly that easy to get rid of.

"Well, your grandmother was a beautiful woman," I begin. "She was tall and she had long brown hair."

"Like yours?"

"It was the same color, but hers was dead straight. And it was much longer. It went all the way down her back. She used to let me brush it out for her every now and then."

"Like you used to let me do for you."

I smile at the memory of a toddler Isla running a brush through my hair. She used to sit on the bathroom counter and watch me do my makeup in the mornings, too, her chubby little feet swinging back and forth in the air. Sometimes, we'd sing together.

Just thinking about those days makes my heart hurt.

"Maybe it's my turn to brush your hair?" I suggest. "We haven't done that in a while."

She shakes her head. "My hair's too curly," she says. "You'd only catch knots."

I leave it there. I don't want to repeat conversations we've already had. I know as well as anyone that some pains don't get better with attention—they just hurt that much more every time you poke at them.

"What else was she like?" Isla asks. "Grandma, I mean."

"She was very… quiet. She liked to sew and draw—"

"Draw?" Isla gasps, her eyes going wide with excitement.

I nod. "She was quite a good artist. I never actually saw her draw, but I saw her sketchbooks. She had a whole pile of them."

"Why didn't she let you watch her?"

I fidget with the bracelet on my wrist. "I was… well, we weren't that close," I say softly. "It was hard to connect with my mother. She was so quiet. She lived in her own head most of the time."

"Maybe she lived in her sketchbook, too. Like me."

I smile tightly. "You're probably right. I bet the two of you would have gotten along great."

Isla nods. "I think so, too. I wish I could have met her." She taps her fingers against the table. "Mom, how did she die?"

If the first question caught me off-guard, this one floors me. I stammer stupidly for way too long. A lie would be so easy. Just say something sad and simple: cancer or a car accident or a shark attack. Swift. Brutal. But simple.

But the truth? The truth is a beast with a mind of its own.

And today, it wants out.

"You said we could talk about anything I wanted," Isla accuses when I stall for a little too long. "This is what I want to talk about. I'm not a baby anymore."

I sigh. "I'm just not sure you'll understand."

"I'm smarter than you think."

I raise my eyebrows. "I think you're incredibly smart. It has nothing to do with your intelligence."

"Then tell me."

I take a deep breath. Here goes.

"She committed suicide, sweetheart," I say softly. "She took a lot of pills to go to sleep and she never woke up again."

An older couple passes by just as I say the words aloud, and I'm pretty sure I get a few dubious looks. What kind of mom tells her nine-year-old about suicide? A bad one, apparently, in their eyes. I'm not even sure they're wrong.

Isla looks stunned for a moment. "Why did she do it?"

I've been asking myself that question for years, sweetheart. I offer up the only answer I've ever thought of.

"I suppose because she felt she had no way out."

"Out of what?"

"Of her life," I say. "My father was not a good man. He didn't treat your grandmother well. In fact, he hurt her. A lot."

Her face drops. "That's why you don't talk about him."

"Right. And your grandma… She was the victim, but there are times I get so angry at her, too."

"For leaving you?"

I smile, if only to hold back the tears in my eyes. "You really are smart, kiddo."

"Sometimes, I get mad at my dad, too," she says softly. "For not being there for us. But now that I know he doesn't know about me, I'm trying not to be so mad at him. It's just sometimes it feels like we're all alone."

"Isla—"

"It's true," she interrupts. "You can't even say it's not. Everyone else has family. Grandmas and grandpas, cousins and aunts, sisters and brothers. I don't even have a daddy." She chews at her lip for a moment. Then she looks up at me. "Today, at swim practice, I went to the bottom of the pool. And I guess I just… wondered what it would be like if I didn't come back up."

It takes every ounce of willpower I have to keep my jaw from dropping. I have no idea what to make of that. My fingers tremble so hard that I have to twine them together to keep Isla from seeing.

"That's really dangerous, baby."

"I know."

"It's a good thing Coach Gracie got you when she did."

"I know that, too."

"Sweetheart." I pull my hand out from under the table and offer it to her. She hesitates, but she slips her fingers into mine. "You can't ever do that again, okay?"

She nods, lower lip wobbling. "Okay."

"If you ever feel like life's too much, you need to come and tell me."

"You have enough to worry about, Mom."

"No, I don't," I say fervently. "The only thing—literally the *only* thing I need to worry about—is you. That is my full-time job. So please, if you need help, come to me. Okay?"

She nods. "Okay."

"I love you. How much do I love you?"

She smiles at the old question-and-answer we used to do every night before bed. After we brushed my hair and sang together, I'd ask, *How much do I love you?* And she'd croon back...

"*I'll tell you no lie.*"

Together, we finish the words, "*How deep is the ocean? How high is the sky?*"

When it's over, I look at my daughter, and my daughter looks at me, and for at least the length of a breath, all is right in the world.

28

DANIIL

Her eyes are hidden behind round glasses. She's got wild, curly hair. Thick braces. A dusting of freckles that are visible even from my distance.

At certain angles, she looks like Kinsley. At others, she looks like my mother. Very few things have shocked me in my life. But this…

Am I finding my undoing in the somber face of this little girl?

My phone vibrates in my pocket. I answer without taking my eyes off the two of them. They've been sitting at the ice cream parlor window for the last forty minutes now.

"What?"

"Hello to you, too," Petro says with his usual glee. "Where are you?"

"In front of Carino's."

"The don has a sweet tooth? Who woulda thought?"

"You know the place?"

"Do I know it? *Do I know it?* It only has the best Rocky Road in the whole damn city! I can't believe you went there without me. We could've shared a banana split."

I pinch the bridge of my nose. As usual, it takes Petro less than fifteen seconds to irritate the hell out of me. "Why are you calling, *sobrat?*"

"To remind you of the meeting. With the Greek don and his ragtag band of dick turds."

"You can handle that by yourself."

"You have to be there. You're the big boss. They don't want to shake on a deal with me."

"Well, today, they're going to have to make do."

"Okay, the jig is up: what's going on?" he demands. "You've never missed a business meeting before. And you've never handed me the reins without whining about it 'til the cows come home."

I grimace and check my reflection in the rearview mirror. "Something's come up."

"Something that's more important than the Bratva?" I don't reply. After a moment, Petro lets out a long, low whistle. "Does this something have something to do with the pretty brunette you can't seem to get off your mind?"

"It might."

"Oh Jesus, what's happened now?" he asks. "Crime of passion? How many bodies?"

"You need to stop talking."

"What I need is to—"

"What you need is to do a deep dive on Kinsley Whitlow," I order. "I want dates and details. I want a timeline of her life laid out in front of me. If she's ever gotten a parking ticket or had a cavity filled, I want to know about it."

"Okaaaay," he says, a frown in his voice. "That's a little vague, even by your usual less-than-helpful standards. Do I get to know what specifically I'm searching for? Or is this meant to be, like, a quirky game show challenge?"

"I'm watching her now."

"Not sure whether that's creepy or kinky, and it definitely doesn't answer—"

"She's got a child with her."

"Oh." The sound of his surprise is like air hissing out of a balloon. "A child? Like, a young person? We're talking a human being, right?"

"About nine years old. She looks like my mother."

The last of the remaining glee vanishes from his voice. I hear him swallow hard. "Are you telling me what I think you're telling me, Daniil?"

"That remains to be seen. I'll need confirmation first. Thus, the deep dive."

"What does your gut say?"

"That she's mine."

"Fuck."

I laugh grimly. *"Fuck"* doesn't even begin to cover it.

"What are you going to do?" Petro breathes.

"Find me the information first. Then I'll decide."

"Okay, I'll get on it immediately. Give me a little bit."

He hangs up. I turn my attention to Kinsley and—

Actually, I don't even know her name. My daughter. She has a name and I don't know it. For some reason, that's tearing me up inside.

They'd sat mostly in silence while they ate their ice cream. But now, they're talking. It doesn't look like the kind of conversation you'd expect to have with a nine-year-old. There aren't very many laughs or smiles. Kinsley's face is drawn tight with solemnity.

The child looks serious, too. There's something in her eyes. Sadness, maybe. Something else I don't like.

When they finish up and walk out of the ice cream parlor, I don't bother ducking down. If she sees, she sees me. Her expression will tell me everything I need to know.

Kinsley is too wrapped up in the girl, though. They get in the car and start driving. I follow along. I expect them to go straight home, but they make a detour and end up in a large park. I tail them surreptitiously. There are two other moms there with their children, a pair of happily giggling toddlers.

I park in the shadows and roll down my window. I'm close enough that I can hear them.

"… You used to love those swings," Kinsley is saying.

"I'm too old for them now."

"Coulda fooled me. It looks like you'd love to give it a try."

The girl—*my* girl, I fucking know she is, she's mine, goddammit— looks longingly over at the swings. "The other girls will make fun of me."

I clench up with an instinct for protectiveness I never knew I had. I don't know her name, but I'll go to war for her here and now without a second thought.

What is happening to me?

"I don't see them here," Kinsley assures her. "And I promise you, I won't tell. Mum's the word, lips are sealed, all that jazz. If you want to swing, honey, just swing."

The girl's eyes brighten, just a little, but she still looks unsure. "I want to get to the top of the monkey bars," she admits. "I've never been up there."

"I know. You were always too scared."

"I'm not scared anymore."

"Yeah? Prove it."

For the first time, I see her smile. It's got that shivery, quick-as-a-flash quality of someone who prefers to hide their joy before someone else can snatch it away from them.

She ambles off towards the monkey bars. I watch Kinsley watching her.

My phone rings. I roll the window back up for a moment.

"Okay," Petro says as soon as I pick up. "So, SparkNotes version: there is a record of a child being born to a Ms. Kinsley Jane Whitlow. November 11th at St. Michael's Hospital. Date on the birth certificate is nine years, three months, six days ago. Father unlisted."

Irrational anger surges through me. "She wasn't going to tell me."

"You never know," Petro tries to suggest. "She might have been, you know, just… waiting for the right moment."

"Surely there were one or two of those in the last ten years," I snarl.

"Well, everything else is pretty straightforward. She's changed addresses three times since the baby was born—"

"Name?"

"What?"

"The child's name," I growl. "What is it?"

"Oh. Isla Matilda Whitlow."

"Isla," I repeat in a reverent whisper. "Isla."

"Nice name. Pretty."

"I'll call you back."

"Wait. Where do you stand on the whole meeting tonight?"

"Same place I stood before. Take care of it yourself. I'll get there when I get there. *If* I get there."

"Okay, but—"

I hang up on him, drop my phone on the passenger seat, and step out of the car. There's only one other mother on the playground now. Her youngster is busy pushing sand around in the sandbox. As I watch, he tries to eat a fistful of the stuff. Not the brightest bulb, apparently.

Kinsley is sitting on the bench, watching Isla, who's now made it to the top of the monkey bars.

A strange, prideful thought flashes through my head like a shooting star: *That's my girl.*

I move closer, just as a guy in a Nike sleeveless hoodie walks by with his dog on a leash. He spots Kinsley, and his eyes turn predatory. He changes direction and sits down right beside her, his smile a little too wide to be innocent.

"Hope you don't mind," he says with a leery chuckle. I growl under my breath as he flashes Kinsley his pearly whites.

"No," Kinsley says uncertainly, looking around at the other half-dozen benches he could've chosen. "Of course not."

"Much appreciated. I'm Jason, by the way. And this right here is Barney." The bulldog looks annoyed that his walk has been cut short just so his owner can try to get his dick wet. Jason ignores his whimpers. "Are you here with a fur baby or a real one?"

"Are those the only two choices?"

"Well, you could just be here alone, I suppose."

She laughs, though it sounds forced to my ears. "I'm not. That's my daughter over there."

I already know as much. But hearing her admit it out loud, so casually, so damn *proudly*… It gets under my skin in a way I didn't expect.

"No way!" the man whistles. "That's your daughter?"

Kinsley's mouth slopes into a frown. "Why do you sound so surprised?"

"Because you look way too young to have a daughter that old," he says. The grin he's boasting says she walked right into that hapless little seduction line. "What is she, like, seven, eight? You must have been a teenager when you had her."

"Close enough," Kinsley mumbles.

"You still haven't told me your name. I'm not trying to pry or anything, but Barney's curious. He's got a thing for pretty women."

She laughs again. Every laugh she offers up to this stupid fuck sets my teeth on edge. "You must do this a lot, huh?" she asks suspiciously.

"Do what?"

"Use your dog to pick up women."

He shakes his head and sort of winces at the same time. It looks so practiced and polished to me. Motherfucker has his craft honed down.

"Not at all. I mean, don't get me wrong, it'd be nice to meet someone. But… I'm shy. And a little gun-shy, actually."

"I find that hard to believe."

"Scout's honor," he swears. "I'm just recovering from a tough heartbreak. So it takes a lot to get me to approach a woman. And by a lot, I mean, she needs to be really beautiful. The kind of woman you can't just walk by without spending the next week kicking yourself for not at least trying." He pauses, takes in a deep breath like he's working up the courage—which is complete and utter bullshit, I see right through his fucking shtick—then ventures to say, "Is it weird for you to say yes to a date with your daughter right over there?"

"No," Kinsley demurs. "It's weird for me to say yes to a date with a total stranger, though."

"Isn't everyone a stranger 'til you give them a chance?"

"Listen, Jacob…" she sighs.

"It's Jason."

"Shit. I'm sorry. Jason. You seem like a nice guy."

I laugh to myself. *Now, who's lying?*

"… But I don't see myself dating anyone right now."

Jason isn't fazed. "You don't want to disappoint Barney, now do you? He wants to see you again. How 'bout we just—"

"You heard what she said, fuckwad," I growl, stepping out of the darkness so that they can both see me. "Take a hike."

Kinsley's jaw plummets to the ground. Her eyes shimmer with undiluted fear, and before she can stop herself, she looks over at Isla.

Great. No need to spring for the paternity test. All the truth I need to know is written right there on her face.

The bulldog starts growling at me immediately, but I give it a look that silences the creature instantly. Haven't met a dog yet that I couldn't scare. It's all about establishing who's the alpha.

Dogs and men aren't so far apart in that regard.

"Who the hell are you?" Jason asks, springing to his feet like he'd stand a chance in a fight.

"Trust me—you don't want to know. She's not interested. Get the fuck out of my face."

But apparently, Jason is as dumb as the sand-eating toddler. He turns to Kinsley, as though she might be able to help him. "Do you know this guy?"

Her eyes are fixed on me. She's managed to swallow back the fear, but she's by no means relaxed.

"You should go, Jason," she says softly without ever peeling her eyes away.

The idiot looks back and forth between the both of us while his dog strains against his leash, trying to get away. The animal's smarter than the owner. No surprise there.

"Last chance," I warn him. "I'm not going to ask again."

And finally, he goes. Throwing a dirty glare over his shoulder at me and a regretful look at Kinsley. Of course, she misses both looks as she catapults to her feet. I don't miss the way her gaze slides past me towards the playground before it snaps back to my face.

"This is getting out of hand," she spits, full of bluster and forced bravado. "You're full-on stalking me now. You had no right to intrude on—"

"On what?" I demand. "Your scintillating conversation with the absolute nimrod?"

She tenses. She knows what's at stake here. If not consciously, then deep down in her bones, where the fear has lived in her for precisely nine years, three months, and six days. "How much did you hear?"

"Enough to know that you can do better."

"Like with who?" she asks, sparkling with feistiness. "You?"

"Only if you're aiming high."

"You need to leave, Daniil. Why are you even here? What do you possibly have to say to me?"

"I don't have anything to say to you," I tell her coolly. "But I do have something I want to ask you."

She might have stopped breathing; it's hard to say. One thing I know for certain is that she's trying very, very hard to keep her eyes from wandering. If I'm not mistaken, Isla is still on the monkey bars, blissfully unaware of the fact that her mother is locking horns with her father.

"You have some nerve trying to ask me questions when you've given me no answers."

"What would you like to know?"

She puffs a loose bang away from her forehead. "Why you seem to be obsessed with me. Why can't you just leave me alone. What the hell you *want* from me."

"You have something that's mine."

She goes pale and her eyelashes flutter back and forth. She's trying to determine how to play this: say nothing and hope to keep her secret hidden a little longer? Or just come out with the truth and admit it?

She just stares at me, waiting for the hammer to drop. She's been waiting ten years for this moment. She knew it was coming—she *had* to have known—but now that it's here, despite all that time to practice and prepare, she's borderline speechless.

So I do the dirty work for her.

"She's a cute kid, *sladkaya*. Who's the father?"

29

KINSLEY

I glance back at Isla. She's still on the monkey bars, but she's watching me now, wondering what's going on.

"Please, Daniil…" I whisper.

His voice comes out in a low growl, shot through with steel bars of warning. "Be specific. What are you asking me?"

"I'm asking you not to make a scene in front of—"

"I don't make scenes," he says, calm and stoic as ever. "I'm simply trying to have a conversation with you."

"Now's not the time."

"When would be the right time?"

"Never," I lash out. "Barring that, I'd say when Isla's asleep."

"You don't want her meeting me?"

He asks the question casually, but there's an underlying edge to this back-and-forth that's making me nervous. Which is probably what propels me to lie.

"I know what you're thinking," I breathe, "but you're wrong."

"Go on, *kiska*," he coaxes. "Tell me what I'm thinking."

"Her age checks out. You've probably done the math already. But she's not yours."

He arches an eyebrow, nothing more. He's so incredibly calm that it only rattles me. He's doing it on purpose; I'm sure of it. There's a menace to his composure that's ten times worse than if he'd been screaming and shouting.

"After… after you left me in the woods, I met someone else. We had a few dates and then I never saw him again. But I got pregnant."

"What was his name?"

"I wasn't interested in his name, okay?" I snap. "I just wanted to… forget."

"To forget me."

I nod like the world's stupidest bobblehead. "Yeah. Among other things."

"Let me make sure I understand," he murmurs. "You were supposed to get married. Instead, you ran from your wedding and slept with me. Then a week later—because you were so devastated about the way I left, presumably—you slept with some random fuck whose name you can't remember, and you got pregnant."

I grit my teeth together. "You have no right to suddenly appear in my life and start asking questions. You have no damn right."

"If that little girl is mine, then I have every right."

"She's not yours," I say as fiercely as I've ever said anything.

"Her eyes say differently."

That throws me for a loop. I blink in confusion. "What?"

"I recognize it, Kinsley. Try to hide it all you want, but I see myself in her."

"Then you're seeing what you want to see," I snap, still flailing to stave off the guilt and the obviousness of my lies. "Because she is not your daughter."

"Mom?" comes a timid voice.

My eyes go wide with urgency. "Please, Daniil," I hiss. "Not now. I'm begging you not to do this now."

He stands still for a moment that stretches on for eternity. His eyes are burning coals in the night. Just when I'm sure he's going to refuse my plea and blow my whole life up on the spot, he nods.

"I'll be in touch."

His eyes linger on Isla for a moment.

Then he turns and walks away.

When he's gone, Isla runs up to me. "Who was that?" she asks.

"Nobody," I answer automatically. "He was just… He needed directions."

"It seemed like he knew you."

"What makes you say that?"

"You said his name when you saw him. Daniel or something like that."

Shit. She was listening. "You must have heard wrong, honey."

Her mouth turns down, and I feel horrible. She knows I'm lying. Which is unfortunate timing, considering we'd just had a conversation that was pretty damn honest. It had gone a long way to restoring a relationship that needed a breath of life.

But I just don't know how to handle this situation. I never thought I'd have to. That sounds dumb, even to my own ears. I guess that as the years ticked past one after the other, I just managed to convince myself that the worst-case scenario would never come to pass.

Stupid of me. So, so stupid.

"Shall we go home?"

Isla nods and we walk over to the car together. I keep an eye out, waiting for Daniil to jump out at us unexpectedly. He's nowhere to be seen, but for some reason, I don't believe he's gone.

He's still here somewhere.

Watching me.

Watching us.

～

As we drive, I put on a bright, cheery tone in the hopes that we can simply gloss over the moment in the park. "So I was thinking we could go to the mall this weekend and—"

"Why?" blurts Isla.

"Well, I thought we could check out the dress store and pick out something for you to wear to the dance."

"I don't want anything."

"But I thought—"

"Actually, what I really want is for you to stop lying to me."

My hands tighten on the wheel. So much for glossing over the moment. "Honey—"

"I'm not a little baby, you know!" she huffs. "You can tell me stuff. You just told me about my grandparents. Or was that a lie, too?"

How had she transformed into a teenager in the last five minutes alone? It's too soon for this. One more thing I thought I wouldn't have to think about for a long time yet.

The moment I park the car at the house, she's out, flying towards the front door. Of course, she has to stand there and wait for me to arrive with the key, but she turns a cold shoulder to me the entire time. As soon as it's unlocked, she rushes through and into her room. The door slams shut.

"Great," I mutter to myself. "Just freaking great."

Ping.

DANIIL: *She did not seem happy with you.*

I type back furiously. ***Jesus Christ, are you stalking me?***

DANIIL: *If you won't tell me the truth, then I'll find it for myself.*

KINSLEY: *Like you even deserve the truth.*

DANIIL: *If I'm her father, that's exactly what I deserve.*

KINSLEY: *Too bad you aren't.*

DANIIL: *Swab her cheek and prove it.*

KINSLEY: *Leave me alone. You're crazy.*

DANIIL: *I will be standing outside your door at 8:30 tonight. If you don't answer, I'm coming in anyway.*

KINSLEY: *I'll call the cops, I swear I will.*

DANIIL: *Call them. I don't mind having this conversation with an audience.*

I scream at my phone and resist the urge to hurl it across the room. Then I let it fall from my slack fingers to the couch cushions. In the kitchen, I put on a pot of coffee, mostly just to do something with my hands. Caffeine is the last thing I need at the moment.

I'm starting to panic now. Big time.

I call Emma as the coffeemaker starts burbling. "Hey, hon," she greets. "What's up?"

"I have a problem. Daniil showed up."

"Jesus, Joseph, and Mary. Where?"

"In the park," I explain, leaning against the counter. "I took Isla. I was sitting there watching her play on the monkey bars when this guy came and sat beside me."

"Daniil?"

"No, no, it was this random guy, actually. Jack or Jacob or something like that. He had this bulldog. I can't remember what the dog's name was. Barry, maybe? No, that wasn't it. Bradley?"

"Good Lord, Kinz, who cares what the dog's name is?" Emma bleats. "Get to the good stuff!"

"Right. Yeah, you're right. Sorry. I got sidetracked."

"You were saying…"

"Barney!"

I can hear her frustration. "Are you having a stroke?"

"Sorry. I just remembered the dog's name. It was Barney."

"Focus, girl! When does Daniil show up in this story?"

"Oh. Right. A few minutes after whatever-his-name-was started hitting on me, Daniil showed up out of nowhere and basically told him to beat it."

"Bet homeboy got the hell out of there."

I almost laugh at the memory, but it dries up in my throat. "He was a little shook, I'd say."

"I would be, too, if I were faced with a sexy slice of man like Big Daddy D."

"You're really missing the point here, Em," I grumble.

"Because you're not getting to it!" she screeches back.

"Anyway, he left with Barney—"

"Wait, who?"

"The bulldog."

"For God's sake, enough about the bulldog. It's not an integral part of the story. What happened with Daniil?"

I sigh, the sound of escaping breath whistling through my teeth in a way that strikes me as weirdly mournful. "He asked me who Isla's father was. Well, he sort of said that he knew, actually. He doesn't really ask questions. He sort of just says things and dares you to disagree."

"Damn. That's heavy. Especially in a playground. How did he react?"

"To what?"

"This is like pulling teeth, I swear," she grimaces. Enunciating clearly, she says, "How did Daniil react to the confirmation that he is in fact Isla's father?"

"I obviously didn't tell him!"

"Um, why not? What's obvious about that? The only obvious part is that he knows already."

"But he doesn't have proof," I retort. "So I told him she wasn't his." I can practically hear her judgment and I wince. "Do you think… Did I make a mistake? I just thought it would… you know. Like, change everything."

Emma is quiet for a moment. "For better or for worse?" she asks eventually.

"I don't know." I switch hands on the phone. "Which is exactly why I want to keep things how they are."

"I think that's shot to hell now, honey," Emma says gently. "Time to work on Plan B."

"What would that involve?"

"Telling Daniil the truth, for one thing."

I shake my head fervently. "No. Out of the question. I can't expose Isla to him."

"Why not?"

"Because I still don't know anything about him or what he does! He's super cagey about his past and his life. And anyway, he disappeared on me once. What if he does it again to Isla?"

"I'm guessing he showed up because he wants to be a part of Isla's life," she suggests. "That's not exactly deadbeat dad behavior."

"For now, sure," I concede. "What about in six months, though? What about a year from now? Five years? Ten? I'm not that confident."

"You may be overthinking this, honeybuns."

"Why are you encouraging this?" I demand. "Why do you want—"

"Because he pulled you out of a river! Because he saved your life! Because he fixed and insured your car and expected nothing in return! He also gave you Isla, and that kid is the bomb."

"He had nothing to do with Isla," I snap.

"Um, pretty sure he needed to blow his load inside of you to make that happen in the first place."

"Ew. Ew on multiple levels."

"It's not 'ew' if it's science."

I sigh and slide down the cabinets until I'm sitting on the kitchen floor. "They should put that on a mug," I mutter.

"They really should. I'm full of great quotes like that. Should I try another one?"

"Please don't. I already have a headache."

Emma chuckles. "He seems legit, Kinz. Can you really afford to make this decision for Isla? She's old enough now to get a say."

"She's still only nine," I protest feebly.

There's a part of my little girl I'm just not willing to give up yet. But it feels like Daniil and Emma and the whole damn world are conspiring to rip it away from me.

"Physically, maybe," Emma says. "But mentally and emotionally, she's way older. Time to give her a little credit, Kinz. Trying to protect her might backfire on you."

"I just don't want him to hurt her," I breathe into the silent kitchen. "Fuck."

The word sounds pitifully insufficient in the silent room. I eye the toaster. Even it looks like it's judging me right now.

"Yeah," Emma says sympathetically. "Fuck, indeed. So finish your story. Where did you leave things with Daniil?"

"I asked him to leave. Told him we'd talk later. Then he texted me and said he'd be at my door at 8:30 tonight."

"Can I be there, too?"

"Why? And the answer better not be to ogle him."

"Oh. Well, then can it be a two-part answer?"

I roll my eyes. "Goodbye, Em."

"Fine. Party pooper."

"Thanks for the advice, though. I do appreciate it."

"Anytime, honey. Let me know what happens. I love you."

The coffeemaker dings to signal it's finished brewing. I pour a mug I don't really want, take it over to the kitchen table, and sit, sipping listlessly as I look over the years of our lives chronicled on the fridge photographs. Years that passed with neither sight nor sound nor thought of Daniil. Happy years, mostly. Hard, but happy.

Why does it feel like our little bubble is about to be popped?

I take a breath and go to Isla's room. I knock a few times, but when I get no answer, I push the door open and walk inside.

She's sitting at her desk, pouring over her sketchbook, completely lost in her own world. The concentration is admirable.

"Honey?"

She jumps about a foot out of her chair.

"I'm sorry. I did knock."

Isla just shrugs, shivers, and goes back to her drawing.

"Sweetheart, you're right. I wasn't being entirely truthful with you about the man I was talking to."

At that, she sets her pencils down. "So you do know him?"

I squat down in front of her. "I will explain things to you," I tell her. "I promise. But I just need you to give me a little time."

"Why?"

"Because I suppose… I'm still figuring things out," I admit.

She frowns. "What's there to figure out?"

"The right choice from the wrong one, for starters."

She turns back to her sketchpad. "I just want to draw right now."

"Okay. I'll go."

But as I get back to my feet, I notice the face she's drawn. It's not exact, but there is a resemblance. His strong jaw, his caved cheekbones, his intense eyes.

"You're… drawing him?" I ask softly, trying to filter the tense emotion from my voice.

She nods. "I liked his face."

I don't know how to feel about that. Happy? Scared? Jealous? Worried? I guess I'll just play it safe and juggle all the emotions. Because there's no denying it anymore.

Our bubble has already popped.

30

DANIIL

I'm outside the house with three minutes to spare.

The lights are on in the living room and the kitchen, but the windows are closed and the curtains are drawn. I can't help but smirk.

She's expecting me.

I didn't anticipate that I would need this time, this moment of calm before the storm. Not to compose myself—I've been composed since the day I stepped foot out of that godforsaken jail cell—but to soak in the moment. To let its weight settle on my shoulders.

It feels right.

When the clock strikes 8:30, I stride up to the door and knock. No answer. Annoyingly predictable. I walk around the house and hop the fence to get to the backyard.

It's claustrophobically small. A mound of boxes shoved up against one wall of the house bears a layer of dust that says they've been there for a while. In the window above, I see a curtain with a pattern of stars strewn across it.

My daughter's room. *My daughter.* What a fucking concept. I'm still wrapping my head around it.

The kitchen lights are on, but there's no movement. Then: "… Em, I'll call you back… Okay… Okay… Bye."

I watch through the window as Kinsley paces into view. She hangs up and puts the phone on the kitchen counter. Her eyes veer to a wall I can't see, where I'm sure a clock is telling her that it's now 8:36.

She sighs and turns back to face the window. At first, she's busy fussing with a coffee pot. But when she raises her eyes, she sees me standing there.

She screams immediately and claps her hands to her mouth. The coffee pot crashes to the floor.

"You'll wake Isla," I call softly through the grass, smirking.

"Goddammit!" she swears. She jerks away from the mess and stomps away.

A moment later, the back door bursts open. There's a chill in the air tonight, and she's wearing only a flimsy white t-shirt. It's just a little too big for her, so it falls off one shoulder. She's not wearing a bra, either. If the sight of her bare shoulder hadn't tipped me off, her hard nipples certainly would have.

"I did tell you I would come."

"I thought you were referring to the front door."

"I knocked. You didn't answer."

"Because I was… doing stuff."

"What stuff?"

"Mom stuff," she snaps. "Clearing up dinner, doing the laundry, cleaning up the living room. Not that you'd know anything about the single parent life."

"It seems like you chose it."

She narrows her eyes. "You're judging me. You really are. Incredible."

"I'm not judging anyone. I'm just trying to get the story straight."

"It's not a story," she retorts. "It's what happened."

"The whole truth and nothing but the truth?"

"That's rich, coming from you," she scoffs, her eyes flitting to the curtains in the corner of the house. "Since when have you ever given me the truth? You know what—never mind. I don't care about whatever bullshit you have in store for tonight. Isla is not your kid. I had a one-night-stand a week after you disappeared and—"

"A one-night-stand? That's funny. Because earlier, you said that you dated Isla's father a few times before you ended things with him."

She flushes hard. "I must have misspoken."

I take a cautious step toward her. She backs up to match me, like we're dancing. "I will of course need to do a paternity test to make sure I can rule her out as mine."

"Why?"

"Why?" I ask incredulously. "Do you really think I'm the type of man who would turn his back on his own child?"

"You turned your back on me. It's not such a leap to assume that you would turn your back on other things, too."

"You know what they say about assuming things, *sladkaya*."

We stare at each other for a moment. There are goosebumps on her arms and a shiver on her skin. She wraps her arms around her body, which presses her breasts up high over the neck of her t-shirt. It's obnoxiously distracting.

Focus, Daniil.

"If she's my child, then I deserve to know," I rasp. "And she does, too."

Maybe it's my words. Maybe it's my tone. But whichever the cause, Kinsley softens slightly, and the resolve drains from her face.

Beneath it is a confusing mélange of emotions. Hope, maybe. Fear, definitely.

Before I can fully suss it out, she turns abruptly and walks over to the balding, spindly tree looming in the corner of the yard. She hides herself in the shadows, but when she looks up at me her eyes are bright. Clear.

"You're right," she mumbles. "You both deserve that."

"She's mine, isn't she?"

"Yeah. She is."

I'm both relieved at the admission and infuriated by it. "You really weren't going to tell me."

She sighs and leans against the trunk. "You disappeared. I didn't see you for ten whole years. And when you miraculously reappeared, you were a different man. How could I trust you with my child? I don't actually know you. And let's face it: even back then, you didn't have the greatest track record."

"You know why I was imprisoned in the first place."

"Do I?" she demands. "Do I really, Daniil? I only know what you told me. You could have concocted some story to make yourself look like the hero."

"I'm not in the business of making myself look like anything."

"Right, because you don't care what people think. You've made that abundantly clear. But the thing is, you needed an alibi back then, and I showed up in my stupid wedding dress and gave you the perfect one. Who's to say you weren't willing to lie to get what you needed?"

"It wasn't a lie," I intone into the still night.

"So you were put in jail by your powerful boss because you stopped him from beating up his wife?" she asks. "That's the story? C'mon. Get real."

"It's the truth."

"You know what's the crazy part? I believed it then," she says softly. "Because I was naïve enough to believe anything if it was told convincingly enough. But I expect more now."

She has changed. I can see that in the confidence in her stance, the way she takes up space like she's entitled to it. Between that and her hard nipples, my cock has no chance of staying asleep.

"You could have been in prison for murder, for all I know," she finishes.

"I never denied that I've killed men."

"Jesus," she says with a horrified shudder. "You can't just say things like that so casually."

"That's not what I was put in jail for, though."

"Fine. Arson? Burglary? Did you jaywalk too many times in front of the wrong cop?"

"Don't be a fool, Kinsley." She jerks slightly at the harsh lash of my voice. "You have instincts. You have intelligence. Tell me, do you really believe I'm lying to you?"

She knows what I'm asking. "No," she says. "I don't."

"Then stop trying to convince yourself of nonsense. Look at the facts. They're right in front of your face."

"Fine," she says, her eyes blazing brightly. "I don't even care, honestly. That's irrelevant. The important fact is that you weren't around. You left. Without a word. I didn't even know your last name. If I did, maybe I would have tried to contact you."

"Somehow, I doubt that."

She stares at me for a long time, fumbling with what and how much to say. I don't even think she's lying to me at this point. I think she genuinely doesn't know where the fairytale ends and real life begins.

"You wanna know something embarrassing?" she murmurs. "I used to go back to that spot every now and then. I guess a part of me used to hope you'd be there one day."

"You were looking for me."

"Yeah," she says with a timid nod. "I guess I was."

"Because of Isla."

She hesitates. "Yes, because of Isla. You think I wanted to be a single mother? You think I wanted to raise a baby on my own? At twenty? I was fucking terrified, Daniil. And I thought that maybe if you were around, I'd be less terrified. But every time I went back to that spot, it was empty. You weren't there and it brought back that… that horrible feeling."

"What feeling?"

"Being left behind."

It's not hard to see the pattern. Her father. Her mother. Her fiancé. Me. Everyone she's ever loved or tried to love has left her in the lurch, frantically grasping out as cold waters closed over her head.

I'm the only one who ever pulled her out of that dark river.

Maybe that's why my betrayal hurt her the worst of them all.

"I know that we were strangers," she continues. "You owed me nothing and you didn't trick me into anything I wasn't willing to do. I slept with you that night because I wanted to, and I don't regret that.

But as the years went on, I started to realize that it was better this way. I was better off on my own, raising Isla the way I thought was best."

I grit my teeth. "And it's 'best' for her to live in this crappy neighborhood, in this hovel, with no father, while you struggle to put food on the table. Is that what you're telling me?"

She bristles upright, as proud and fierce as ever. "Excuse me?"

I press in closer, hemming her against the tree. "I can look after her, Kinsley. I can look after both of you. I can buy you a proper house. A proper *home*."

"There's nothing wrong with this place. We may not be rich, but at least we're happy."

"Bullshit."

The word twists and contorts to mean so many things at once. She blinks at me, her expression complex and confused. "What do you mean?"

"I watched you and Isla at the ice cream parlor today," I explain. "She doesn't look like a normal nine-year-old girl."

Kinsley's eyes flash with anger and she lunges towards me with a finger in my face. "How dare you? You think you can just show up, disrupt our lives, and think you know what's best for my daughter? How dare you? How fucking *dare* you? You don't know anything about us. *Either* of us."

I'm unmoved by her rage. "I intend to find out."

"Here's an idea: how about you get back to living your miserable life so we can get on with ours?"

"Do you really think that's in Isla's best interests?" I ask. "Preventing her from getting to know her father. Do you think she'll be better off?"

The argument is living and dying on her tongue without ever coming out. It's easy to see how half the work has been done for me. I was right about the sadness in Isla's eyes. I was right about the strain in Kinsley's shoulders.

They need me more than she will ever admit.

Both of them.

"Stop trying to push me away, Kinsley," I tell her. "Stop trying to punish me for leaving you."

She narrows her eyes. "Of course you'd make it all about you."

"You're still mad about what happened between—"

"That's what you really think, isn't it?" She laughs crazily. "You think that night was so orgasmically transformative for me that it ruined me for other men forever? And I've spent the last decade pining over you?"

"If the shoe fits."

She gets right up in my face. Her scent fills my nose, intoxicating and delicious. "I trusted you that night. You spat in my face. So yeah, I'm a little salty about it. My daughter doesn't need to know what it feels like to be left behind."

"I never made you any promises, *sladkaya*."

Kinsley's anger seems to shrivel up just a little. Like she's been bearing it for so long that she's just tired of the burden. She glances back at Isla's window and then towards me.

"I wasn't asking for anything but a goodbye," she says softly. "Was that really too much to ask?"

No, I say in my head.

Out loud, I say, "I don't do goodbyes."

"What do you do then, Daniil?" she asks. "Because it seems like you don't do relationships, or answers, or explanations. So what *do* you do?"

In answer, I grab her around the waist and walk her back into the shadows. She bumps her back against the tree trunk and yelps softly.

"Stop it," she demands. But it's weak, uncertain. Unconvincing.

"I could do *you*," I whisper to her. "I could fuck some of the resentment right out of you."

"That's some ego you've got. Ten years hasn't put a dent in it." She wriggles in my grasp. "Let me go."

"Make me."

"You're a freaking giant. You really expect me to push you off me?"

"So you're not even going to try?" I taunt. "Sounds more like an excuse to me."

She pushes against me with her whole body, but that only succeeds in making me harder. God, this woman feels so damn good. You'd think I just got out of jail again by how deliriously hungry she makes me. I want to taste every inch of her until she's quivering on my tongue, on my fingers, on my cock.

"You're the one with all the excuses, Daniil," she snaps at me.

"No excuses anymore," I say. "For either one of us. I want to meet my daughter."

Her eyes go flat and cloudy.

"I'm not asking, *sladkaya*."

Then I bend my lips down to her neck. She gasps and shivers when my kiss brushes over her skin, but she stops struggling.

I pull back and stare at her pretty green eyes. There's longing in them. There's lust. There's need.

And I could satisfy every single one of those desires. My cock is desperate to give her everything she's refusing to ask for.

But I can't. Not yet.

"I'll be back," I murmur to her. "You know what I'm expecting when I return."

31

KINSLEY

I stand in front of the mirror to check the spot on my throat where he kissed me. It still feels hot, like he's branded me somehow. There's no actual trace of him—no visible trace, at least—but his scent still clings to me and the head-to-toe shiver he left behind isn't leaving anytime soon.

When the doorbell rings, I rush to answer it. The tingling at the nape of my neck stays exactly where it is, a constant reminder of what and who was just here.

"Em!" I croak.

"Hey," she says, breezing into the house and looking around in the corners as though Daniil might still be there. "Where's Isla?"

"Sleeping."

"So she didn't see him?"

"Not while he was here, no."

"Okay, that's… good? Would we call that good?"

I throw my hands up in the air. "I don't even know anymore," I groan. "I'm sorry I called. I know you have an early morning tomorrow."

"Oh, please," Emma says, waving the apology away. "It's barely ten o'clock, you grandma. Come on."

We move into the living room, where I have a tray of cookies, coffee, and gummy worms laid out. Emma takes one look at the setup and turns to me with a touched smile.

"Did it hurt when you fell from heaven?" she sighs dreamily. She grabs the bag of gummies and plunges herself onto the sofa. "If only we were lesbians. I'd just marry you and live happily ever after."

"That actually sounds pretty good right now."

I sit down next to her and touch my neck instinctively. I can still smell his oaky, woodsy scent. So primal. So masculine.

"Really, though, you didn't have to do all this," Emma says, glancing at the tray. "It feels a little extreme, actually. Even for you. Are you fattening me up to eat me?"

I grab a cookie and lean against the sofa while I nibble around the edges. "I had a lot of nervous energy I needed to work off. I also have a cheese plate in the fridge if you're interested."

"The day I say no to cheese is the day you push me off a cliff, lover girl."

I laugh, go fetch the cheese plate, and rejoin Emma on the sofa. We face each other and cross our legs with the cheese plate arranged prettily between us.

"We should do this more often," Emma says, reaching for a piece of gouda.

"Actually, this is something I'd rather avoid."

"Right. I forgot for a second that you have some major drama going on."

"Unfortunately, I don't have the luxury of forgetting."

She makes a grossed-out face. "For the record, I don't recommend gummy worms and gouda. Great for alliteration. Not so much for flavor." She takes a sip of coffee to rinse the taste away, then fixes me with a stern glare. "So. Tell me everything. What happened?"

I sigh, my shoulders slumping forward. "He showed up exactly when he said he would. I pretended like I didn't hear the knock."

Emma raises her eyebrows. "You really thought that was going to work? Like, ostrich-with-its-head-in-the-sand-type deal?"

"I was desperate," I snap.

"Let me guess: he got in anyway."

"Snuck around back and scared the shit out of me. He was standing outside in the garden. Just, like, *brooding*."

"Like a sexy vampire, huh?"

I narrow my eyes at her. "Em. Focus. I need your serious face on."

She winces. "Sorry. I've been listening to *Twilight* on audiobook on the commute to work. It's top of mind. Anyway, go on."

"Well," I say, "I had to admit it."

Her eyes bulge. "Wait! You confirmed that Isla was his? I thought you were going with hard denial, no matter what."

"I thought so, too," I say miserably.

"But...?"

"He... he has really intense eyes."

Emma smiles and does a little squeal-and-shimmy. "Oh em gee, you want him! You totally want him!"

The slump in my shoulders gets a little more pronounced. "I'm trying really hard not to. He's bad news, Em. I don't know exactly how. But I do know that."

"He's the only guy who's ever made you feel anything," she retorts, munching happily on a cracker spread thick with brie.

"That's not true."

"She said defensively."

I narrow my eyes at her. "You know I hate it when you do that."

"She said in frustration."

"Em!"

"Sorry," she says, swallowing the cracker and reaching for the grapes. "I'm just excited for you."

"Which part exactly are you excited about?" I demand. "This is serious, Em. He wants to get to know Isla. He wants to be a part of her life."

"So what? *That's* the part I'm excited about!"

"So that means he's going to be part of my life!"

"Ah," she muses wisely. "So that's what this is really about."

I stop short. "Um… care to clarify?"

Emma waggles a scolding finger in my face. "You're scared that once he's always around, your feelings for him are just going to get worse and worse and worse. Until you cave and bang the living shit out of him."

If only it were that simple. "That's not it," I say out loud.

"Mhmm. Well, then what are you worried about?"

"It's not that I'm *not* worried about exactly that situation," I admit, blushing. "But if he's just looming in the background like a… like a…"

"Sexy vampire," she chimes in, extremely unhelpfully.

"Like a freaking *boogeyman*," I spit, "then how can I move on with my life? And what if he moves on with his life after a little while? What if he—shit, this is all coming out twisted. If you saw Charlize, you'd understand. If he wasn't willing to commit to that woman, then I don't have a chance in hell. Not that I, you know, like, want one…"

I try to save face, but Emma is already looking at me with a one-quarter sympathetic and three-quarters excited grin. Which just makes me want to shove my foot in my mouth.

"Honey, are you forgetting who you're talking to?" she asks, then barrels ahead without letting me speak. "You don't have to pretend with me. I already know where you stand with Daniil. You've been in love with him for ten years. What makes you think that's going to just go away now that he's actually here?"

You've been in love with him for ten years. It's not so easy to deny in my head. Which means it's not easy to deny at all. Because the fact is, it doesn't sound wrong. Not even a little bit.

It hurts the way only true things can.

"It may not be… you know, that word you just used."

"Love?"

I cringe. "Right. It might not be that."

"Do you have another explanation?"

"Lack of closure," I say with false confidence. I sigh and grab a cracker and some nuts. "How did my life become so damn complicated?"

"I think it started around the time you decided to get frisky with a felon in the middle of the woods."

"We were in a car."

"What?"

I blush fiercely. "We weren't rolling around in the dirt and leaves. We were in a car."

"Oh. Right, much classier."

I glare at her and she chuckles. "You don't understand, Em. He... he takes up space."

She frowns. "What does that mean?"

"I mean he's just a presence. He's… larger than life." That glee on her face ticks up another notch, and I shake my head. "This is coming out wrong."

"Or maybe it's coming out exactly right. When was the last time a man made you feel like he did?" she ponders.

"Doesn't matter. Irrelevant."

"Like hell it is! Look, babe, if there's one thing I've learned from Queen Stephenie Meyer, it's that the whole purpose of life is to find that person who makes you feel everything. Butterflies and other assorted insects in the pit of your stomach. I've been searching for that feeling since I was fourteen years old. Still haven't found it."

I smile and bite back a laugh. "He scares me, Em."

"As in, you feel physically threatened?"

"No, no. Not like that."

"Then I think it's safe to say that he's giving you the type of fear that's healthy."

"I wouldn't call what I'm feeling 'healthy' in any sense of the word."

"Only because you're scared of the consequences of this feeling," she proclaims. "Which is a roundabout way of saying you're scared to get hurt."

"It's not just me anymore," I point out. "I have Isla to think about, too."

Then I hear a sound and I stop talking.

Emma goes still. "What's going on?" she whispers. "Is he here?"

I don't answer her. "Isla?"

For a few seconds, there's no sound. No response, either. Then, from around the corner, Isla appears in her cotton pinstriped pajamas.

"Hey, kiddo," I rasp through a voice that's suddenly thick with emotion.

"I couldn't sleep," she mumbles blearily.

Emma twists herself around on the sofa. "Hello, little miss! How long have you been hiding back there?"

"Just a minute."

Emma fake gasps. "A whole minute, and no love for Aunt Emma?" She raises her arms and Isla runs into them. She curls up against Emma's chest and looks at me. I see that gleam in her eyes and I know: she's overheard more than she should have.

"Are you still mad at me?" I ask my daughter.

She shakes her head. "No."

"Did you have a nightmare?"

"No. I just couldn't sleep."

Emma and I exchange a glance over her head. Isla's curls fly loose in every direction. She does look as though she's spent the last hour tossing and turning in her bed.

Did she see Daniil and me outside in the backyard?

Did she see him kiss my neck?

What did she overhear?

I take a deep breath, realizing that I'm trying to retain control of a situation that I've already lost control over. Maybe I just need a change of perspective. Maybe I just need to… let go.

"Honey," I say as she settles down beside Emma and reaches for a wedge of cheese. "I have something I need to tell you."

Emma tenses up immediately and her eyes find mine in a panic. *Are you sure?* she mouths to me. The answer to that is hell no, I'm not sure. I'm not sure I have enough emotive resources to convey what I'm feeling now. I'm not sure I can—

No. I have to do this now or risk losing my daughter's trust.

"This thing is a little difficult for me to talk about, but I think you should know anyway."

Isla nods like someone twice her age. "I can take it."

I smile. She makes me proud, even when it breaks my heart simultaneously. Emma squeezes Isla's shoulders. "Remember the story about how I met your father?" I say.

She nods.

"Well, all that was true. We were together that one night and then he went off to live his life and I went off to live mine. But recently, by chance, we ran into each other again."

Isla's eyes go wide. "Really? Was it that man in the park today?" she asks. "The really tall one?"

I wince. I'm glad it's coming out sooner rather than later, though. Some secrets can rot you from the inside out. "Yes, sweetheart. That was him."

"I knew it!" she says proudly, as though she's cracked some kind of secret code. "I knew that he was someone important. Someone special."

Emma glances at me and smiles. "Well, you were right."

"I'm sorry I lied to you before," I continue. "I just wasn't prepared to see him, and the truth is, at the time, he didn't know about you."

"You mean, you didn't tell him?"

"Well, I wanted to make sure I could trust him."

"But… he's my daddy."

"I know, sweetheart. But it's not as simple as that. He may be your dad, but he may be… a lot of other things, too."

"What do you mean?"

"I guess I just mean that I was scared when I saw him again. I was worried about how his presence might affect you."

"But I want to get to know him," she insists. "Does he want to know me?"

As boldly as she asks the question, I can sense the tenuous vulnerability there. She's scared of being rejected. Scared of proving her bullies right.

My heart breaks all over again.

"He does," I say. "In fact, he can't wait to meet you."

She smiles widely. It's the most outward happiness I've seen from her in a long time. I'm ashamed of how jealous I am to know that Daniil managed to elicit that smile when I've failed again and again over the last few months.

And he hasn't even met her yet.

"Okay. Wow. When do I get to meet him?"

"Soon," I promise. "He said he'd contact me in the next few days, so I'm sure you'll have the opportunity to meet him face to face."

Isla glances at Emma. "Have you met him, Aunt Em?"

"Unfortunately not," Emma confesses. "But I'm looking forward to it."

"He's really handsome," Isla informs her proudly.

Emma gives her a wink. "So I hear."

Isla looks suddenly worried, though. "Mom, what do I wear when I meet him for the first time?"

"Whatever you're comfortable with, love. It won't matter what you wear. He's going to love you either way."

But I can see that Isla's already starting to spin out a little. She's pulling at her fingernails and snapping her tongue against her braces. Both nervous tics she developed a few years ago.

I lean forward and grab her hands, kiss them both, and look her in the eye. "You have absolutely nothing to worry about, okay? He's going to love you."

"But… what if he doesn't?" she asks softly. "I saw him today. He's really handsome. So how come… how come I look like this?"

"Come on, cutie," Emma interjects dismissively. "You're a freaking babe!"

I force a smile onto my face. "What Aunt Em means to say is that you're beautiful, sweetheart. Not that love and beauty are intrinsically linked in any way. If someone loves you purely because you're beautiful, then it's not real love."

Isla considers that for a moment. "Will you tell me when I can see him?" she asks nervously.

"Of course."

She nods. "Okay. Then I'm going to go to bed. Goodnight, Mom. Good night, Auntie E."

I'm pretty sure she's going to be up sketching until the wee hours of the morning, but I'm in no mood to pick a fight. Her door clicks shut, and Emma and I let out simultaneous weary exhales.

Emma exhales deeply. "Wow. That was a roller coaster. I think it went pretty well, though?"

"I hope so," I mutter. "The next part won't be any easier."

Emma pokes me in the shoulder playfully. "I wanna meet him, too, you know."

"Urgh."

She laughs. "It's not gonna be that bad."

"How do you know?"

"Faith," she says proudly. One word. Like that's the answer to everything.

Faith.

Too bad I left all of mine at the bottom of a river.

32

DANIIL

The last place I want to be right now is Cirque.

Petro is lucky I even showed up, because I'm not in the mood for this obnoxious, ostentatious nightclub. Especially not now. Not with Isla on my mind and Kinsley on my lips.

The VIP section is cordoned off. The lights have been dimmed and emit a mercurial glow that resonates through to the bar at the end of the carpeted area reserved for only the richest and most influential.

"Hey, handsome."

One of the waitresses sashays over to me. She's wearing a black bra that just barely conceals her nipples. Her skirt is hemmed short and riding low on her hips, low enough to reveal the straps of a matching black thong. As if that wasn't enough, she's also wearing a body chain that hooks around her neck like a thin collar, dips between her breasts, then down to her stomach and loops around her waist.

She's the epitome of sex in every sense of the word.

And yet I can't seem to generate the slightest bit of interest.

"Your boys are right over there. How about I escort you over?"

"I can find my own way." I leave her behind without so much as looking at her face.

The Bratva men are spread out over three sofas. Petro sits in the middle, with soldiers sprawled on either side and women propped up on their laps like shimmering ornaments.

"Is this a business meeting or a party?" I demand.

Petro's eyes veer to mine and he smiles. "Hey, the boss is here."

The men seem pretty far gone at this point. The smell of smoke, alcohol, and sex taints the air. I notice two couples fucking in the corner of the space. Technically, they're in private rooms, but neither one has seen fit to draw the gauzy curtains.

"Come and join us," Petro says, waving me over. "Sit beside me. You want either Nessa or Constance, for sure. They're both hot as shit. Full disclosure, though, I fucked Constance earlier tonight."

I stay standing where I am. "Petro, I asked you to handle business. Not make a mockery of it."

He scowls at me. "Everything is done and dusted."

"Then show me the contracts."

"Uh… contracts?"

"Jesus Christ, you fucking idiot," I growl. Then I turn around and head into one of the unoccupied private rooms to escape the stink and debauchery.

It doesn't take long for Petro to follow me. Before he can close the curtain, another one of the hostesses appears at the threshold. This one is wearing a dress, with a side slit that almost reaches her pussy and a neckline that swoops down to her navel.

"You boys want privacy?" she asks with a little wink. "Or you want me to slide between the two of you?"

Petro takes one look at her long ginger hair and turns to me. "Heads or tails?"

I sit down in the center of the sofa and close my eyes. "Leave us."

She huffs in disappointment, but she leaves without a fuss. The moment she's gone, Petro turns on me. "Why'd you send her away? Now, she's going to think we're the ones fucking in here. I'm keeping the damn curtain open."

He's about to drop down on the couch when I hold up my hand. "No."

He hesitates. "No?"

"You will remain standing until I say otherwise."

"Oh, fuck," he says, sobering up fast. He knows I'm pissed.

"I left you in charge tonight." I make sure to look him dead in the eyes so he can see just how serious I am.

"To be fair, I told you that wasn't a good idea."

"You're supposed to be my right-hand man. My closest Vor. If I can't trust you to handle shit when I can't, who the hell am I supposed to trust?"

"Daniil—"

"Don," I snap. "Right now, I'm not your friend. I'm your boss and master. *Ponyal?*"

He bows his head. "*Da, Don. Prostite menya.*"

I snort. "My forgiveness doesn't come that easy."

Petro looks at me cautiously. "I didn't get the contract signed. I fucked up. But they agreed—"

"What they agreed to tonight means nothing if they can't remember it in the morning. We will need to do this all over again."

"I'll take care of it, sir."

"Can you? Can you take care of it?"

"I will," he says with determination. "I just got… sidetracked tonight."

"Pussy and booze," I growl. "They'll be the death of you."

"And what a way to go," he says with a tentative smirk.

I roll my eyes. "Sit down and shut up."

A grin flashes across his face as he drops down on the far end of the sofa. "How did things go?"

I shrug. "I've got things in hand. I'm just giving her a little time to process. Before I pounce."

Petro's eyes narrow immediately. "You've never given any other woman—scratch that, any other *person*—that opportunity before."

"She's… different," I reply evasively. "She's the mother of my child."

"Fuck," Petro breathes. "Gives me chills when you say it like that. I'm practically stone-cold sober again."

"Highly doubt that."

"You have a child," he murmurs like he's testing out the concept. "You have a daughter." He shakes his head and meets me with a stunned gaze. "The hell do you know about girls, *sobrat?*"

"Not a damn thing."

"You are so fucked. Mega-fucked."

"I broke out of jail," I remind him. "I can handle a nine-year-old."

Just then, the girl from before circulates back through and sticks her head in the room. "You boys change your mind on some company?" she asks, making sure to bare a slice of thigh for us to see.

"No," I growl. "But you can get us some drinks. Gin. And whiskey."

"Right away, handsome."

"Jesus Christ," he groans when she's gone. "Turning down easy pussy? You're already whipped. This is gonna change everything."

"It changes nothing," I retort. "Kinsley is the mother of my child. That's all."

"And you don't want to make her anything more? Like, oh, let's say… your wife?"

I scoff. "Don't be ridiculous."

"It's a fair question. You've already seen her in a wedding dress. Maybe you liked what you saw."

"You're very close to getting punched in the face, my friend."

"Have you thought about it?" he persists.

"Punching you in the face? Every fucking day of my life."

"Have you thought about marriage, I'm asking."

"Jesus Christ. You're a child."

"Exactly!" Petro crows. "Why do you need another one?" I turn to him and he falters a little under my glare. "I don't know how to deal with relationships, okay?" he admits. "Or kids. And now, it looks like you've got both."

"Buck the fuck up, man," I snap. "This changes nothing."

He sighs. "I wouldn't be so sure. Have you thought about the consequences of this information getting out there? Consequences that go by the name of Gregor Semenov?"

"Pah! That old fuck is scared shitless of me. He won't try anything, even if he does find out."

"'Even if he does find out'?" Petro echoes. "Come on, Daniil. He's definitely going to find out. It's only a matter of time. Especially if you plan on playing an active role in this girl's life."

"She's my daughter. Of course I'm going to play an active role in her life."

"My point exactly. So he can use her to get back at you."

"For doing what exactly?" I demand. "Getting out from under his thumb? Doing things my own way?"

"Both," Petro says. "You took his secrets and—"

"*His* secrets?" I explode. "I did whatever the fuck he asked of me, whenever he fucking asked it. He wanted a stooge? I was that for him. He wanted a killer? I was that, too. But there were certain lines he shouldn't have crossed."

"I agree. Clearly. It's why I jumped ship with you."

I let my fists unclench. "I remember."

"I did that because I always knew he was half the don you were. And not even a fraction of the don you would become."

I eye him suspiciously. "Is there a reason you're trying to butter me up?"

"Just got sentimental for a second," he muses. "About old times. Makes sense, considering life's about to change in a big way. I mean, I always knew you'd have a kid. Someone's gotta carry on the family legacy. But this way? Can't say I ever saw that coming."

Sighing, I slump back in my seat. "It's not your job to worry about this shit."

He shrugs. "It's my job to watch your back. That's what I'm doing. I don't want this new development to cloud your judgment."

"Nothing's clouded. I can see things clearer than ever. I have a higher responsibility now."

Petro looks nervous. "Have you thought about the transition for *them*, Daniil?" he asks. "They're civilians. Do they even know who you really are? What you really do?"

"They'll figure it out when it matters."

"Hoo boy. Shit's gonna hit the fan."

"I can handle Kinsley."

"And what about Gregor?" Petro asks bluntly. "Are you prepared for his move when he discovers this?"

"Let him move. I won't hide. The old bastard wants to come at me? So be it. He better shoot for the head."

Petro grumbles. "I wouldn't put it past him. Jesus, you've got some balls on you. I really hope you know what you're doing, brother."

I smile. "Don't worry. I always do."

33

KINSLEY

DANIIL [2:14 AM]: I'll stop by at three tomorrow afternoon to see Isla.

That was it.

I've been pulling up that text throughout the day just to look at it again and again. It's not doing much in the way of calming my nerves, though.

"Miz Whitlow? My nose itches."

I look up at Avery, one of my pint-sized pupils. He's sitting at his little round table with hands absolutely covered in blue glue and sparkles.

Arts and crafts day always goes a little wrong when there's a whole brood of six- and seven-year-olds causing mayhem. Glue gets eaten, thrown, and stuck in every orifice. The day I allowed them to use glitter remains one of the most haunting days of my entire life.

"Oh, Avery, honey. Hold on. Let's go get you fixed up."

I come to his rescue and lead him to the bathroom to clean him up while Kendall, my assistant teacher, supervises the classroom in my absence.

When I get back, Kendall is ordering everyone to put away their supplies. "Pack up your things, kids," she says. "The bell's about to go off."

I offer up a silent *Thank God*. It's been a doozy of a day.

We take the kids to their pickup spots so their parents can scoop them up. One by one, they're dispatched, until at last we're mercifully off-duty.

When we get back into the room, Kendall is eyeing me strangely. "You alright?" she asks in a concerned tone, toying with the ends of her long blond braid.

"Sure. Why do you ask?"

"You seem really distracted today."

"Do I?"

"And you checked your phone like five hundred times. You never touch your phone during school hours."

Damn it. "I'm just… waiting on a call," I lie.

How am I supposed to explain that I've been staring at a text from the felonious long-lost father of my child? I almost laugh out loud as I think of starting that whole story from the very beginning. *So I was supposed to get married…*

"Oh," she says. "I thought you'd met someone."

I laugh. "No, no, nothing like that."

"You know, if you're interested, I know this really great guy I could set you up with…?"

I smile as pleasantly as I can. "Thanks, Kendall. That's sweet of you. But I'm not really dating right now."

"I've been working here for over a year now. That's been your standard response the entire time."

"Has it?"

"Definitely. When that sub asked you out, you turned him down cold."

I frown. I don't even remember that. "Sub? What sub?"

"Oh my God, you're joking! Connor Reynolds. Six foot-one, broad shoulders…" She lowers her voice a little and adds, "Really cute butt."

I blush and turn back to whatever I can do to keep my hands occupied. "Doesn't ring a bell."

"Okay, if you don't remember Mr. Reynolds, it's because you've clearly got the hots for someone else. So spill. Who's the guy?"

"There's no guy," I insist weakly. "Just a lot of drama in my life. I'm just… I'm really worried about Isla, actually."

Kendall frowns. "Is she still having problems? I thought that was sorted."

I sink to a seat on the edge of my desk. "I thought so, too. It turns out the girls who are bullying her just got smarter about how they do it."

"Urgh. Nine-year-olds are the worst. Except for Isla, of course."

I smile, but it falters after a moment. "She doesn't want to stay at this school anymore," I confide. "She wants a change, and honestly, I think she deserves one."

"But… what would that mean for you?" Kendall asks. "Would you still work here?"

"I don't think that would make sense. I'd try to get a job at whatever school Isla gets into."

"Nooo! You can't leave me here."

"Don't worry," I assure her. "If I do leave, we'll still keep in touch. We'll do drinks after work every week or something."

Kendall smiles. "Yeah? Sounds fun." She very kindly neglects to mention that I've turned down every happy hour invitation I've gotten since I started working here.

"But in the meantime, I think I need to talk to Heather about Isla again."

Kendall scrunches up her nose. "You think?" she asks. "I mean, I don't know Heather very well, but she seems… cold."

"That's a lot nicer than the word I'd use." We laugh together for a moment. Then I sigh. "Go ahead, get outta here. I'll finish cleaning up."

"You sure?" asks Kendall.

"Positive. Scram. Live your life. I gotta go grab Isla anyway."

"Thanks, hon," she says. She touches me once on the elbow and lets her gaze linger for a little too long, her eyebrows a little too furrowed with concern.

I don't like people being concerned for me. It feels dangerously close to pity.

Then the moment ends and she gathers her things and walks out the door. I tidy up the classroom and get stuff ready for the morning, then I pull open my computer. The fifth graders get dismissed last, so I use the time until the final bell to start researching other schools in the area.

I end up with an avalanche of information and a burgeoning headache. All the public schools here are cesspools and any of the private schools worth a salt are obscenely expensive, outrageously selective, or both. How am I going to tell my daughter that her mental health isn't really conducive to my bank account balance?

A nasty, cynical voice in my head chimes in. *Worst comes to worst, you could always bite your pride and ask Daniil for help.*

But the very thought makes me cringe.

Especially with his words still thrumming through my veins. *I can look after her, Kinsley. I can look after both of you.*

I slam the computer closed and make my way down to Isla's classroom. She's sitting on the floor in the hall, doodling so intently that she doesn't notice me approaching until I'm practically right on top of her.

"Hi, honey," I say softly.

She nearly jumps out of her skin. "Oh! Hi, Mom."

"Would you mind sitting out here for a few minutes?" I ask. "I just wanted to have a quick word with Ms. Roe."

Isla looks immediately nervous. "Why?"

"Just boring work stuff," I tell her, getting increasingly concerned about the rate at which I'm lying to my nine-year-old. In the grand scheme of things, though, one small white lie won't stunt her growth or anything. At least, I don't think it will. "I won't be long, okay?"

She nods uncertainly and goes back to her drawing.

When I enter her classroom, Heather is sitting in her chair with her feet propped up on the table. "Oh!" she exclaims when she sees me. "Kinsley."

"I'm sorry to disturb you, but I wanted to talk to you about something."

Her eyebrows rise and I can already see her reluctance. "Okay?"

"It's about Isla. The thing is, she told me that she's still being bullied."

Heather's eyes flatten. "Did she now?"

"The girls who're bullying her are just being more subtle about it. But it's definitely still going on. I was just hoping—"

"I can't babysit your daughter, Kinsley," Heather says abruptly. "She doesn't get special treatment. I have twenty-eight students in this class and I can't keep my eye on every single one at all times. It's not humanly possible."

"I understand that, but—"

"Isla just has to be more assertive. She's a good kid, but she's quiet and asocial. It rubs the other students the wrong way."

"So this is *her* fault?" I demand, getting on the defensive instantly. "Is that what you're trying to say?"

"No, of course not—"

"Because Isla's just being herself. She shouldn't be punished for being who she is."

"That's not what I'm saying—"

"She's 'quiet and asocial.' Isn't that what you just said? 'It rubs the other kids the wrong way.' What the hell am I supposed to take from that?"

She's seated upright, hackles raised now. "Ms. Whitlow, you need to calm down."

"Like hell I do!" I rage. "How dare you blame my kid for getting bullied? Blame the victim—is that how you do it in your classroom, Heather?"

"You're twisting my words."

"You call yourself a teacher?" I hiss, completely undeterred by her protests. "You're supposed to be looking out for these kids. Not throwing them under the bus when they need you the most."

Her eyes flash menacingly. "Okay, now, you listen to me—"

"No, I don't think so," I snarl, taking a step towards her. "I think it's time that you listen to me. My daughter wants to change schools because of all of this. She's not happy here, Heather. And that's on you."

"I will not be blamed for your daughter's failings. It might be her fault or it might be yours, but it sure as hell isn't mine."

Don't say it. Don't say it. Don't say it.

"Oh, you fucking bitch."

Whoops. I said it.

Any hope of a professional conversation between colleagues goes out the window. Heather leaps out of her seat so fast that her rolling chair goes slamming into the wall behind her, sending half a dozen pinned-up science projects fluttering to the ground.

"Excuse me?!"

Stop now, you dummy! Stop while you still can!

"Bitch. B-I-T-C-H. Want me to write that down on your fucking whiteboard?"

Heather just stares at me in shock. Somewhere between the strains of silence, I realize that I've just crossed a line. Partly because I've been tightly wound the entire day, and partly because I am genuinely frustrated with this woman.

Yes, she is a fucking bitch. But she's still Isla's teacher and my colleague, and I shouldn't have said as much to her face.

It's too late to walk my words back now, though. Any apology will seem insincere, especially because the sentiment still remains, even if my word choice wasn't quite up to snuff. So I do the only thing I can do: turn and walk out.

"Come on, honey," I tell Isla brusquely as I slam the door closed behind me. "Let's go home."

I'm aware I'm walking fast towards the car and she can barely keep up, but I just want to be away from this damn school. Isla waits until we're both buckled in to ask, "What happened?"

"Nothing," I say quickly. "Like I said, just some work stuff I wanted to talk to Ms. Roe about."

I pull us out of the parking lot. I've noticed recently that my anxiety is cranked up to a ten whenever I'm behind the wheel. I tell myself I'm just being cautious after some bad luck driving lately, but I know the truth: it's Daniil's mocking voice in my head that has me on pins and needles.

"Mom?" pipes up Isla from the back. "Is… is he coming to see me today?"

I plaster a fake smile on my face. "Yes, baby. He's coming. He'll be at the house at three o'clock."

Her eyes go wide, but she says nothing. She's quiet for the longest time after that. It's only when we're parked in front of the house that I can really look at her and study her expression.

She's chewing at the inside of her cheek for a long time as we idle in the driveway. Then she looks up. "Mom, what if he doesn't like me?"

I do a double-take. "What do you mean? You're awesome!"

"You and Aunt Em are the only ones that think so."

"Because we're the smartest people out there. Trust me, honey: he's going to love you." Her little cheeks wobble a little and for the first time in a while, she looks younger than her age. I grab her hand and hold it to my chest. "My darling girl, you have no idea how special you are. Or how beautiful."

"I'm not any of those things, Mom," she mumbles.

"Of course you are. You're—"

She rips her hand from mine. "No, I'm not. I got a C and a D+ on my last two tests. And I'm not beautiful. I have eyes. I can see for myself."

"Then you're not looking hard enough," I say firmly.

She looks down at her lap. "I wish I looked more like you."

"You do look a lot like me," I tell her. "You have my nose and my ears. You have my hair color and my knobby knees. You have a birthmark on your stomach that's a carbon copy of mine. And you have my smile. Even though I don't get to see it often anymore."

That elicits the tiniest of grins.

"I wish you'd see yourself the way I saw you," I add. "I'm your momma. I know you best."

"But he doesn't," she points out. "He may be my dad, but he's a stranger."

"For now." I sigh and resist the urge to touch her again. "How about we go inside and make some sandwiches?"

She nods distractedly and we head inside. I put on a pot of coffee and hand Isla a juice box while we get to work on the sandwiches for lunch.

It's already 2:20 PM. If he's prompt, that means we have less than an hour before Daniil is knocking on our front door.

"What's he like?" Isla asks abruptly as we continue our little production line. I spread mustard and mayo. Isla stacks up the cheese and meat.

I wince. *Jesus, that's a loaded question,* I think to myself.

"He's... a very interesting man," I say aloud. "Mysterious. Like a spy."

Isla looks giddy. "He's a *spy*?"

"No, I said he's *like* a spy. Truthfully, I have no idea what he really does."

"Oh. It'd be kinda cool if he was, though." She ponders that for a little while, then asks, "Do you think that if he were a spy, he'd tell us?"

"I don't think so. That'd kinda defeat the whole purpose of being a spy, right?"

"I think he would," Isla replies confidently. "Just not yet. He'd wait to make sure he could trust us and then he'd tell us. And we could help him."

"Help him?"

"Yeah, help him do his spy work."

I laugh. "Pretty sure he'd be the kind of spy who works alone."

DING. The doorbell feels to me like an icepick in the eardrum. To Isla, however, it's more like Fourth of July fireworks. She drops a slice of ham on the floor and races around the corner to check the clock on the living room wall.

"Mom!" she screeches. "Mom, it's three o'clock!"

"That's him then," I say, feeling goosebumps erupt across my body. "Shall we go get the door together?"

"No, you do it," she says, suddenly shy.

Then she proceeds to run straight to her room. I take a deep breath and make for the front door, praying that I haven't made a huge mistake by agreeing to this.

I've made enough mistakes as it is.

34

DANIIL

"Hello, *sladkaya*."

Kinsley is stiff as a post, regarding me with a wary expression and rangy eyes. "Did you come alone?" she asks, as though I'm here for some shady drug deal.

"Who else would I be here with?"

She doesn't respond to that. Her eyes are on my face, but it's obvious that she's distracted. "Come in."

The house is small, though Kinsley has done her best to make it a home. Isla's things are littered all over the place, her drawings framed on nearly every wall.

"She's an artist," I observe.

Kinsley's entire face and posture softens. "Yeah, she is. She started drawing when she was a year old and she's never stopped."

I stop in front of a framed watercolor painting of a dragon with outstretched wings. "She's good."

"I know. Lately, all her drawings have been really, like, fantastical. I think it's her escape."

"Does she need an escape?"

Kinsley shrugs. "Don't we all?"

It's a far cry from my home. There's much more color here. Color in the curtains, the carpets, the sofa, the walls. I spy a dreamcatcher hanging from one corner and a toy mobile hanging from the other.

Nothing matches. And maybe for that reason, it all fits together. A jumble of chaos and brightness, with no reason behind any of it other than that it made one or the other or both of them smile.

I like that.

"Admiring my decorating skills?" she asks with a nervous laugh.

"It's… cute."

She rolls her eyes. "Tell me what you really think, why don't you?"

"I said it's cute."

"Sounds like code for 'tacky.'"

"If it was tacky, I would have said so."

She almost smiles at that. "You know, I actually believe you would."

I meander along to the refrigerator, which is wallpapered in photographs. Lots of Isla. A few of Isla and Kinsley together. Some include Emma as well.

But apart from the three of them, no one else graces the pictures. Looks like it's a closed society.

"Where is she?"

"In her room," Kinsley explains. "She heard the doorbell ring and bolted."

"She knows who I am?"

"I told her."

I didn't expect that. I turn to her in surprise.

"I had to," Kinsley says nervously. "She's a smart girl, Daniil. She figured it out."

"She figured out that I was her father from one glance in a park?"

"Well, to be fair, I've told her the story before."

I frown. "A version of it or the real thing?"

"The real thing," she says softly. "I felt like I owed her the truth, so I told her the truth. I ran from my own wedding, I got into a car accident, lost my bearings, and fell into a river. You fished me out."

"And the part that follows?"

"I told her we talked and we… spent the night together. Then you were gone the next morning."

I have some issues with her delivery, but the facts are in order, more or less. "What about the part where I was running from the cops?"

"Obviously, I left that part out."

"Why?"

She looks at me incredulously. *"Why?"*

I nod. "Why didn't you tell her about that part?"

Her eyes go misty for a moment and she turns away from me. "Maybe I felt she had enough to process. And—"

She cuts off suddenly, piquing my curiosity. "And?"

"Never mind."

"Sladkaya."

"Do you really have to call me that all the time?"

"Finish your thought."

She sighs, but she knows some battles aren't worth fighting. "The 'and' part is that she really needs to believe that her father was—*is*—a good guy."

"Who says I'm not?"

She looks me dead in the eye and snorts. "Right."

"Are we still stuck on the whole disappearing-the-morning-after thing?" I ask. "Because you've got to let that go."

She narrows her eyes at me. "You don't know me very well. But in time, you'll come to realize: I hold grudges."

I roll my eyes. "And here I was thinking you were different from all the other women I've dated before."

She snorts again. "I think the word 'dated' is doing an awful lot of work in that sentence, pal."

I fold my arms and lean against the kitchen counter. "What would be the more appropriate term?"

"'Fucked,' probably," she says bluntly. "Let's face it. You don't date women. You sleep with them. Then you forget them right after." She looks down where she's wringing her hands in front of her lap. Then she looks back up at me and says, "She has to be different, Daniil. You can't forget about her. I won't let you."

Her eyes burn with a fierce sense of protectiveness. And I know she means it. This is one grudge she will not ever let go.

"I don't intend to forget her at any point, *sladkaya*. Either of you."

"Good," she says. "Because if you do… I'll kill you."

Promising to kill me out of love? She really is a woman after my own heart.

I give her a grin. "I believe you."

"Good. Because I mean it."

"I know you do. Now, are we going to continue to banter in your kitchen, or can I meet my daughter?"

She glares at me. "Just so we're clear," she says, stepping towards me, her finger jabbing into my chest, "she was *my* daughter first."

"And you'll kill me if I hurt her, I'm sure."

"Damn right I will. Without fucking blinking."

She's so deadly serious that I can't help but start laughing. Right in her face.

She gnashes her teeth at me. "This is not a joke, goddammit!"

"Then stop making me laugh. Tell you what: I'll just go find her myself." Without waiting for an answer, I walk out of the kitchen and start down the hallway. I stop at the whitewashed door to the left and knock twice.

I hear the scurry of feet. Then it opens and I find myself staring at a little girl with big eyes and a face full of freckles.

She's the most beautiful thing I've ever seen.

She looks stunned to see me. "Hi, Isla," I say as gently as a man like me possibly can. "I'm Daniil."

Her eyes go wide behind her round grandma glasses. "H… hi."

She glances behind me, searching for her mother. But I'm not about to call for Kinsley now. This moment is about the two of us. "Your mom is hanging out in the kitchen. I was hoping you and I could talk."

She still doesn't say anything. Her hands are shaking at her sides, though I can tell from her measured breathing that she's trying hard to control herself.

"I saw your pictures," I add. "They're amazing."

That's what finally does it. Her face ripples with pleasure. "You liked them?"

"They're perfect."

She smiles. It's slight, still nervous, and very, very shy. But it transforms her entire face. She looks like a child now, rather than the dour miniature adult who opened the door for me.

"Can I come in?"

She nods and moves aside to allow me to enter. The door clicks behind me and I look around her tiny room. It's only large enough for a single bed, a small green cabinet, and a desk littered with pens, papers, and half a dozen open notebooks. Like the rest of the house, her art is tacked up over every available inch of wall space.

"This is a pretty cool room."

She doesn't seem to know where to go. I don't exactly blame her. The moment I entered, the air in here became considerably thinner.

In the end, she walks around me and sits at the chair in front of her desk. There's no other place to sit, so I go for her little single bed with the pink cotton candy sheets.

"You drew all these pictures?" I ask, gesturing to the wall just behind her.

"Most of them," she mumbles.

"Is this what you want to do when you grow up?" I ask. "Draw, I mean."

"I want to be a cartoonist for the movies," she recites at once.

I grin. The seriousness of her ambition is like looking into a mirror. "Then I'm sure that's exactly what you'll do."

She's tall and proud for a second. Then her shoulders fall forward. "You're the first person besides my mom and Aunt Em who's ever said that," she whispers. "Everyone else says it's not realistic."

It's hard not to study her melancholy. She's a child, and her face and body suggest exactly that. But her manner, her tone, her words—they all convey the depth and maturity of someone much older. Someone who's seen far too much.

"Forget what other people say. Nothing ever seems very realistic until it happens. But I'd cling to the unrealistic dreams. They're the only ones worth doing."

She smiles and another little knot of tension in her face dissipates. I like doing that—making her breathe, making her relax, making her unclench, even if it's only a fraction at a time.

"Are you a spy?" she blurts out suddenly. As soon as the words are out of her mouth, she blushes again. "If you can't tell me, I'll understand."

I suppress a grin. Making a big show of glancing out the window and towards the door, I then lean towards her, cup my hand over my mouth, and whisper, "Yes. But you can't tell anybody."

"Really?" she gasps, her eyes going wide with wonder. Not so good at secret-keeping, this one. That makes me laugh, too. "Who do you spy on?"

"Men who are up to no good."

"Is that why you left my mom that morning?" she asks. "You were undercover on a mission and you had to get back to it?"

I bite back a wince. It's sweet how she's willing to give me a pass for my past sins. Her hope is contagious. It swallows me up in the revisionist history she's creating for me.

She isn't just an artist; she's a storyteller. She sees a better world.

I want to make it come to life for her.

"That's exactly right. I did have a mission," I tell her. "And I did have to get back to it."

"Did you succeed?"

I glance down at my navy-blue Armani suit. "As a matter of fact, I did. It's why I can dress the part now."

She giggles. "Is it exciting? I bet it's so exciting. I think... I think I want to be a spy one day, too."

"A cartoonist by day and a spy by night. I can see it."

She twists her fingers together, trying to wring out her nerves. Neither one of us has addressed the elephant in the room. I'm not about to leave it up to the nine-year-old.

"I'm very happy to meet you, Isla."

She smiles again, back to being a little more shy. "I've been wanting to meet you my whole life."

"I'm sorry I didn't show up before now."

"You didn't know about me before."

"True. But I still should have looked."

She's confused by that, but she doesn't press me on it. She just sits there, trying to figure out what she should say next. "Can I ask you a question?" she says once she's worked up enough courage.

I nod solemnly. "You can ask me anything."

"How did you feel when you found out about me?"

I lean back on one elbow. What a damn question. "I felt shock at first," I tell her honestly. "And then I felt... excitement."

Another blush. As sweet and innocent as her mother's—back in the moonlit moments before I'd jaded the hope right out of her.

"You were happy?"

"Happier than I've ever been in my life, Isla." I tilt my head to the side to look at her from a new angle. "How about you? How did you feel?"

"Like it was the right time," she answers promptly. "I've always wondered about you. But Mom didn't really talk about you much. Then, finally, she did. She told me you saved her from a river."

I laugh. "That's true. I did."

Isla scoots a little closer to me. "What did you think about Mom when you first saw her?" Isla asks. "When you first saw her face."

I smile. "If being a cartoonist doesn't work, I think you have a promising future as a journalist. You ask the hard-hitting questions."

"I just want to know how I got here."

"That's a very wise thing to think about, *malyshka*. I saw your mother and thought: now, there's a train wreck."

Isla blinks slowly. "A... a train wreck?"

"She was a mess. She looked like white cotton candy with a face full of streaked makeup. She looked miserable and terrified. I had to jump in after her. I knew I couldn't let her die looking like that."

Isla stares at me for a moment longer, and then bursts out laughing. "I thought you were gonna say something different!"

"The truth is always far more entertaining than fiction," I tell her. "You'll learn that soon enough."

"Did you think she was beautiful?" Isla presses.

I smile. "Once I'd cleared all that gunk off her face, yes, she was beautiful. Still is."

For some reason, that makes Isla's face drop. "I used to think I looked like my daddy," she admits. "Because Mom has always been so pretty. But now that I've met you, I don't know who I look like."

"You look like both of us. The best of both of us."

She thinks about that for a little while. Her eyes flit from me to her walls and then back to me.

She's thinking hard; I just don't know what's on her mind. Finally, her gaze lands on me and stays on me. Another blush creeps up her cheeks, and she keeps pulling at her fingers.

"I like you," she admits, baring her soul the way only a nine-year-old can.

I can only grin. It's the best compliment I've ever gotten in my life.

35

KINSLEY

I'm making pasta for one reason and one reason only: it's damn near impossible to screw up. Given how scattered my thoughts are right now, that's exactly what I need.

I recite the old mantra that Emma and I used to sing back when we lived together: "When in doubt… add cheese."

So on goes globs of white sauce and a thick layer of parmesan, then one more layer just for good measure. I pop the dish into the preheated oven and glance for perhaps the hundredth time in the direction of Isla's room.

They've been in there for almost an hour now. I can't make out individual words, just the rumble of Daniil's bass voice and Isla's chatter skittering around on top of it. I even hear laughter—from both of them. I'm not sure which one laughing is more of a miracle.

I creep down the hall to listen closer, but their laughs are still frustratingly muffled. So I tiptoe closer, and closer, and just when I can take it anymore and I'm about to go burst in to see what's so funny, my phone rings.

I high-tail it back to the kitchen and press Answer without looking at the caller. "What?"

"Oops, bad time?"

"Oh. Em. Hi. Yeah, you can say that again. You almost gave me away."

Emma giggles. "Were you spying on them?"

"I was trying to."

"Step one of eavesdropping is to put your phone on silent, goober. Haven't you ever seen, oh, I dunno—every movie ever?"

"Shut up."

She giggles some more. "How's it going, though, for real?"

"Swimmingly."

Whoa. That sounded bitter. Wait. Am I bitter?

"Easy there," Emma says, snatching the thought right from my head. "You doing okay?"

"Sorry. Don't know where that came from."

"It's perfectly natural to be a little insecure."

"I am *not* insecure."

"Defensiveness is perfectly understandable, too. I was almost a therapist, you know."

"Can you stop trying to psychoanalyze me? Barely passing two psych classes in college does not make you a therapist."

"No, it *almost* does. Like I said."

I roll my eyes. "Lucky me."

"Just breathe, okay? Where are they right now?"

"In her room. They've been in there for an hour."

"And where have you been all that time?"

"In the kitchen, cooking dinner."

"He's staying for dinner? Oh my, the plot thickens." She must be able to hear me pacing in a tight circle around the kitchen island, because she adds, "It's cute, you know. How nervous you are. Like a teenager on her very first date."

"This is *not* a date."

"It was a joke, Kinsley Jane." I can practically see Emma grinning from ear to ear while she toes the line between distracting me from my anxieties and infuriating the shit out of me. "I'm just here to let you know that whatever you're feeling is completely and totally acceptable."

I take a deep breath, but cling stubbornly to denial. "I'm fine."

"And Isla? How's she?"

"She's having the time of her life, if the laughter I'm hearing from her room is any indication."

"Laughter, huh?" Emma asks in disbelief. "No way. That's great. She needed that."

"Shit. You're right." I stop pacing and rest my forehead on the cool countertop. "Oh God, what's wrong with me? I want this to go well for her, I really do. But why do I feel so… inadequate? Hearing her laugh just makes me seem like such a failure. She's so heartbroken all the time when it's just me and her. Then he comes in and boom, she's a laugh a minute."

Emma sighs. "He's her father. And let's face it, Kinsley: she's been waiting for him a long time."

I sigh. "I know."

So have I.

"I should get going," I say. "I'll call you later and let you know how it goes."

"Love you, Kinz."

"Love you, Em."

I hang up, put my phone on silent per Emma's instructions, and leave it on the kitchen table this time. Tiptoeing down the hall, I stand close enough to the door to listen without needing to lean on it.

Isla is talking. "… I really look like her?"

"You do. The spitting image. I'll have to dig up some pictures for you."

"What was she like?" Isla asks.

"Quiet. Proud. Very introspective. You like to draw and she liked to knit. She knitted cushions, sweaters, scarfs… The list goes on and on."

"Do you have anything she made?"

"Not anymore, no."

"Why not?"

"I'm not a sentimental person," Daniil admits. "What I keep are memories."

"That's really pretty."

"Your mother accused me of being a poet once."

I can practically hear Isla frown. "I don't think she likes poets very much."

"Why do you say that?"

"She always says that poets are people who spend so much time feeling that they never actually experience anything in life."

I bite my lip hard, thinking about the way Daniil looked when he'd first said those words to me. I'm hoping he doesn't remember it, even as I'm absolutely certain that he does.

"Well," he muses, "a very wise person must have told her that."

Yeah, so much for not remembering.

"Are you and my mom friends?" she asks suddenly.

I have to strain to hear the sentence because she speaks so softly. I press my ear to the door because I do not want to miss Daniil's answer.

"I think we are," he says. "Your mom just doesn't know it yet."

Isla giggles. A laugh that sounds like it actually belongs to a nine-year-old. Then I hear the creak of bedsprings, and it takes me all of three seconds to realize that they're heading for the door that I've got my ear pressed up against.

I dart back and try to make a run for it, but the door's already swinging open by then and Daniil is looking me right in the face.

"Lurking in the hall, I see," he notes with amusement.

I try to keep my attitude at a minimum, considering we have an audience today. "I was just passing by. Did you two have a good chat?"

Isla is standing right behind Daniil, looking curiously back and forth between us. Then she sniffs the air, momentarily distracted. "Are we having pasta for dinner?"

"Yes, ma'am," I confirm.

"Yay! I'm hungry."

I nod, trying not to shed a pathetic tear at how good it is just to see her happy about something so small and simple. "Good. Why don't you go set the table for dinner?"

"Daniil," she says, glancing up at him. She has to crane her neck pretty far. "You're staying for dinner, right?"

He doesn't even bother to glance at me. "I'd be honored."

Isla's grin makes her whole face glow. She skips off towards the kitchen, but Daniil just stands there, looking at me. His intense eyes are a deep blue, almost gray, under the muted light of the narrow hallway.

"You're too big for this house," I observe.

He smiles and steps the rest of the way into the hall, forcing me back against the opposite wall. His breath is warm and minty in my nostrils and there's maybe an inch of space between my body and his. I'm overwhelmingly aware of that lone little inch.

"So, uh..." I stumble, "how'd it go?"

Just act casual. Don't let him have the upper hand.

But it's obvious that I'm fighting a losing battle. A battle against his height, the width of his shoulders. Against the depth of those eyes and the fullness of those lips.

"It went well," Daniil murmurs. "I'm sure you heard as much when you were eavesdropping." He sees me wince and open my mouth to lie. Before I can, he says, "Don't bother, *sladkaya*. I saw you jump back when I opened the door."

"Are you trying to make a point or something?" I demand, trying to infuse some sorely needed confidence into my voice. "Or is there a reason you're not respecting my personal space?"

He smirks and arches an eyebrow as he gives me a skewering once-over. It's a devastating combo. "That's a nice dress," he remarks.

I look down at the white cotton sundress I'm wearing. The straps are thin, the bodice is fitting, and the sweetheart neckline is deep without abandoning all modesty.

I frown. "What are you trying to accomplish with a line like that?"

"I'm trying to give you a compliment."

"If you were standing a little farther away from me, I'd believe you," I say slowly. "But given the proximity between us, it feels more like... more like a... a..." *What's the word?* "A threat."

He looks at me a little while longer, still not saying anything. I gasp when his fingers brush against the side of my dress. He hasn't even really touched me, and still, heat spreads down my legs.

"What are you doing?" I stammer.

"I've been having an internal conflict since I got here."

"Which is...?"

"Which part of you I want to taste first."

Oh, for the love of God.

More heat. More palpitations. More tingling nerves that make me feel like a damn teenager. I open my mouth to say something, but nothing comes out.

He grabs a fistful of my dress and starts lifting it up to my waist. And I just stand there, unable— no, unwilling—no, both—to ask him to stop.

His fingers slide along the bare skin of my thigh, close enough to my hip that he can feel the waist strap of my cotton panties.

"Here, maybe," he ponders. "This is a good spot."

The weight of his fingertips is both feather-light and also the only thing I can possibly focus on. He's just touching the outside of my leg, and it's already leaping to the top of the list of the hottest things that have happened to me in the last ten years.

My body feels like it's on fire. My center feels like it's on fire. Another inch higher and I might start to actually melt.

"Mom!" calls a voice from the kitchen. "Mom!"

I gasp and jerk away from him. My skirt falls back into place like nothing was ever wrong to begin with.

"Mom?" Isla says again, peeking around the corner. "The table's set."

"We're coming, honey."

I can't even look at Daniil in case I give myself away and blush. I just follow Isla into the kitchen, where the table has been set for dinner neater than she has ever done it before.

I put on my oven mitts and grab the lasagna dish from the oven. By the time I set it down on the table, Daniil and Isla are both sitting.

"Dig in," I mumble, slipping into the empty chair across from Daniil.

I don't make eye contact, but I can feel his eyes on me. The man is as cool as a glacier. Completely freaking unflappable. I, on the other hand, am barely holding it together.

I take a back seat in the conversation and listen to Daniil and Isla chit-chat. It's mostly little things: what she likes to draw, how she taught herself. What movies she likes watching. What are her favorite ice cream flavors.

He never once looks bored. She never once looks sad. Even when the food is long gone, they're smiling at each other like I've never seen either one do before.

When Isla excuses herself to go to the bathroom, I realize I can't avoid his gaze any longer. I look up, only to find that he's looking right back at me.

The silence is dangerous. Anything can happen in silence.

"You're good with her," I croak through a weirdly choked throat.

"You doubted I would be."

"Maybe a little."

"Why?"

I shrug. "You don't strike me as the type of man who's very kid-friendly."

"This is different. She's mine."

So possessive already. It should terrify me. But it has another, more curious, more worrying effect instead: the tingle in my legs spreads upwards.

"You've done a great job with her, Kinsley. You should be proud."

I swallow hard. I was wrong: conversation is way more dangerous than silence.

36

DANIIL

"Can I stay up ten more minutes?" Isla begs.

"I already gave you ten. And it's…" Kinsley checks her watch. "… an hour past your bedtime. Request denied, little missy."

"But we're almost done with the west wing of the castle!"

Kinsley turns to the massive Lego castle that takes up most of her coffee table and grimaces. "Urgh, why did I agree to let you guys use the coffee table?"

"Because it needed a centerpiece," Isla offers helpfully.

Kinsley throws her a wry look. "A centerpiece isn't supposed to take up the entire table. It's supposed to be just in the center."

"Well, when we started, it was gonna be a house. Then it turned into a castle. And castles are big."

"Right. Big. Kinda like the mistake I made when I said yes to this."

Isla giggles. I can see Kinsley's face soften at the sound. "Ten more minutes," she concedes. "Not a second more."

"Yay!" Isla turns to me excitedly. "We can finish the tower."

"And then bedtime," I warn. "Your mother's right."

Isla's little button nose wrinkles up adorably. "Are you two gonna be ganging up on me now?" she asks, reaching for a blue block.

"Agreeing with each other doesn't mean we're ganging up on you," Kinsley retorts as she stretches on the couch across from me.

Her bare feet are pressed against the soft cushions and her body reclines back as she watches our progress. Every few seconds, her eyes flit to me and then away again. It's cute how she thinks I don't notice it.

"Is this the first Lego castle you've ever made?" Kinsley asks me.

"Yes."

"Really?" Isla gasps in abject horror at the mere thought.

"Really. I had a different set of toys when I was your age."

"Like what?"

"Guns, mostly."

Isla doesn't really react, but Kinsley's eyes go wide with alarm. "You mean toy guns, right?" she asks. *"Right?"*

I smile placidly. "Sure. Toy guns."

I resist the urge to wink at her. She looks extremely good in that white dress. The fabric is just see-through enough that I can make out the faint outline of legs, the swell of her breasts. I wasn't lying earlier in the hallway: I'm really having the hardest fucking time deciding which part of her I'd like to taste the most.

"Do you have any brothers or sisters?" Isla inquires.

"No," I reply, wrenching my attention back to my daughter. "It's just me."

"Like me," Isla says. "And Mom. We're all only children."

"There's still time for you," I murmur. I lift my eyes to Kinsley's a second later, but she averts her gaze instantly. I recognize that move now: she's fighting a blush.

"What else did you like to do when you were my age?" Isla asks.

"Mostly, I observed."

It's an odd answer, but Isla doesn't bat an eyelid. Instead, she beams at me. "Hey, I do the same thing! That's why the kids call me a freak at school."

Kinsley's reaction is more pronounced than Isla's. She stiffens from head to toe, and her gaze teeters over to Isla. She doesn't say a word, just holds her breath so hard it starts to look painful.

Isla picks up on the tension and shrugs. She's trying to act nonchalant about it, probably to impress me, but the depth of her pain is obvious.

"And are you?" I ask quietly.

She blinks up at me, like the concept of that question has never occurred to her before.

"Of course she's not a freak," Kinsley cuts in right away. Ever the lioness prowling around her cub. I hold her gaze for a moment, enough to make it clear I'm waiting on an answer from Isla, not from her mother.

"I… I don't think I am," Isla says finally. "I mean, sometimes I feel like one because of the things they say to me. But when I'm drawing, I don't feel like one."

"Good. Trust your own instincts, Isla," I tell her. "They'll never fail you if you listen close enough."

She frowns. "That's not as easy as it sounds."

I laugh. "Very true. If it were, everyone would be confident all the time."

She ponders that for a moment. "Did you ever get bullied?"

I hate that she's been forced to endure this. I hate that she's had to stare at herself in the mirror and wonder what makes her the odd one out. Why she was the one they chose.

"No," I answer succinctly. "I didn't."

She nods as though she expected the answer. "Yeah, neither did Mom. Because she's beautiful and you're handsome."

"There's more to life than looking a certain way, Isla. In time, you'll come to see it's actually very boring to look like everyone else."

"I don't mind being boring if I'm left alone."

"That's not a lot to ask for."

"I dunno. Some days, it feels like a lot," she whispers.

I can feel Kinsley's nerves radiating from across the coffee table. Her leg keeps bouncing up and down, upending the throw pillow she's placed against her knee.

"Well, you'll look better than everyone else at the dance," Kinsley says. "I promise you that."

Isla's eyes flatten. "I told you, Mom, I'm not going to that. You promised me that I could switch schools."

"We agreed on the end of the semester, honey."

"I know. But it doesn't make sense to go to the stupid dance if I'm leaving anyway."

Kinsley sighs. "I thought of it differently. If you're leaving anyway, why not go and have fun?" she suggests. "Who cares what those little snots think?"

Isla looks down at her lap for a moment. She might as well scream, *I do. I care what they think.* Kinsley seems to realize the same thing, because she exhales silently.

"I'll get you any dress you want," she says. "We can pick it out together."

"It won't matter what I wear. I'll still be me."

I can practically hear Kinsley's molars grinding together. "We'll talk about this later, okay?" she says.

"There's nothing to talk about," Isla retorts. "I don't want to go." Then she stands up, announces she's thirsty, and disappears into the kitchen to get a glass of water.

I reach out and put my hand on Kinsley's leg. She stops short, her eyes going wide at the unexpected contact. She's forced to look at me.

"Don't push her," I say softly, so that only she can hear me.

She pulls her leg away angrily, but before she can retort, Isla comes back into the room. "Honey," says Kinsley, "I think it's time to say goodnight."

Isla nods. "It was nice meeting you, Daniil," she says to me, suddenly shy.

"It was my pleasure, Isla."

She walks right into my arms and I hug her, staring down at her dark curls. It feels so natural, so fucking *right*. I'm floored by the warmth coursing through me.

"Can I see you again?" she asks as she pulls back.

"Whenever you want."

She smiles. "Yay. Goodnight."

"Goodnight, Isla."

"Goodnight, Mom."

"Goodnight, sweetheart."

Isla heads to her room. Kinsley springs to her feet automatically. But before she can follow Isla into her room, I put my hand on her shoulder.

"Let her breathe, Kinsley."

She's already on the cusp of anger. That just pushes her right over the edge. "Who do you think you are?" she demands. "Telling me how to parent my child after being here one damn afternoon?"

"I was a lot like her when I was that age."

"So?"

"So maybe I understand her a little better than you do."

She rails back as though I've struck her. "Yeah? Did you know that she's allergic to peanuts? Or that she hates clowns? Did you know her favorite movie is *E.T.*? Did you know she had a full head of hair when she was born?"

I'm silent, watchful. Letting her breathe.

"Yeah," Kinsley presses. "I didn't think so. You don't know anything about that little girl. You left before I could tell you she existed. You left before even *I* knew she existed."

"I'm aware of the timeline, Kinsley."

"Are you, though? Because you're acting as though you've been here this whole time. You're acting as though you were there for us from the beginning." Her eyes flash brightly. They're a haunting, ominous green tonight. "You're acting as though you have the right to tell me how to parent my kid. Newsflash: you don't."

Her cheeks are flushed pink. So's the spot between her breasts.

"It must have been difficult for you," I muse somberly. "Being a single mother. Suffering in silence."

That takes her off-guard. She's so used to our crackling, combative energy that this pivot is throwing her for a loop. The anger battles for superiority for a moment, and then it dies.

"Yeah," she says, slumping forward. "It was."

She sinks back into the sofa, completely forgetting that she was supposed to follow Isla into her bedroom.

"Were you alone for the birth?"

She looks up at me. "Do you actually care?"

I sweep aside some of the building blocks that litter the coffee table and sit down on it so that I'm right in front of her. Close enough for our knees to graze.

"If I didn't, I wouldn't ask."

I watch her throat ride up and down as she swallows. "Emma was with me," she whispers. "They let her into the delivery room because… well, I had no one else. She held my hand the entire time. She told me I could do it. She was great through the whole thing."

"But she's not the one you wanted with you in there, was she?"

She looks away. "It doesn't matter who I wanted. I had Emma. And everything went fine. Or at least, as fine as that kind of thing can go when you refuse the epidurals."

"Jesus. Masochist?"

She laughs bitterly. "I wanted to be aware of everything. I wanted to be present so that when Isla asked me the story years later, I'd be able to tell her exactly what happened. She hasn't asked me yet."

"Maybe you remembered for my sake then."

Kinsley winces and blushes and glares at me, all at the same time. It's actually impressive. Then she sighs and floats off into the memories again. "She was a fussy little baby. She cried for everything. But she also laughed a lot. Loudly. Which is why I never expected her to turn into this sad, melancholy kid."

"Have you addressed the bullying?"

"Of course," she snaps. "I mean, I've tried. I've spoken to the principal and her teacher multiple times."

"And?"

"They claim to have dealt with it. But according to Isla, her bullies have just gotten sneakier. Little bitches."

"And the teacher's not catching any of this?"

"I honestly don't think she cares to," Kinsley admits. "The woman's a total bitch."

"I believe you."

"I promised Isla that I would look for another school for her. A better school. But I'm nowhere close to deciding where. And in the meantime, I don't know what the hell to do."

Her worry is palpable. It makes my skin crawl in the strangest way. Like her feeling that way is a personal affront to me. Something that is crying out for me to fix it, to shield her from that pain.

I set that aside for now. "Tell me about this dance."

She smiles. "It's a father-daughter dance."

"Ah. Well, my timing has always been on point."

"You heard her. She doesn't want to go."

"That's because I haven't asked her yet."

"What makes you think that will make a difference?" I just raise my eyebrows, and she rolls her eyes. "Does that well of confidence ever run dry?"

"Not since the day I was born."

"You could have passed along those genes to Isla," she says wryly.

I smirk. "She's got them in her; don't worry. It'll just take some time until she realizes what you and I already know."

"Which is what exactly?"

"That's she's extraordinary."

Kinsley looks at me with new appreciation, and perhaps a tenderness that she's been trying hard to deny or conceal. "She really is, isn't she?"

I nod. "Leave the dance to me. I'll take her. And I'll put those bullies in their place while I'm at it."

She shivers. "I hope that's just a lot of talk. Any other guy makes that kind of statement and you know they're joking. But you… I'm never sure."

"Good. I like it that way."

She white-knuckles the pillow in her lap. "No, it is not 'good,' Daniil. This is still Isla's school."

"That she's apparently leaving soon enough. I say we burn the bridges."

Kinsley contemplates that in silence for a while. Then she looks up at me. "Did you really play with guns when you were her age?"

"My parents were, shall we say, less than orthodox."

"I still don't know anything about them," she reminds me. "But you know all about mine."

"I know only that your father was an abusive bastard and your mother died."

"Committed suicide," she corrects firmly, as though acknowledging it has been a big step in her healing process. "I actually… I admitted as much to Isla the other night. I still wonder if that was the right thing to do."

"I don't believe in shielding children from harsh realities. The sooner you realize the world is an ugly place, the sooner you can prepare yourself to fight for your way in it."

She nods, like she sees the wisdom in that but wishes it were any other way. I've never seen the point in wishing for something like that, though. Life is what it is. You either shape it how you want, or you let the weight crush you. There are no other choices.

"I fibbed a bit, though," she confesses. "I told her it was an OD on sleeping pills."

"Which part was the lie?"

"She slit her wrists." Her face visibly pales when she speaks about it, probably imagining the exact moment when she had walked in on that scene. I imagine that it's not something you can forget easily. The devil knows I have plenty of blood-soaked memories seared into my brain.

One in particular that's haunted me for twelve endless years.

Kinsley's eyes go misty. "It felt like nothing I've ever experienced before. Like I was stuck in some horrible nightmare that I couldn't wake up from. I probably stood there for minutes, just… staring."

She blinks and a tear rolls down her cheek. She catches it before it reaches the bottom of her chin and wipes it away, embarrassed.

"It was a long time ago. I don't know why I'm even bringing it up." Her green eyes soften for a moment, and I catch sight of that keen vulnerability that she tries so hard to hide. She sits up like that'll right her frame of mind, but the movement just puts her right in the V of my legs. She seems to realize that a second too late.

"Anyway, it's late. You should go. You came to see Isla, and she's gone to bed. So…"

She gets caught up in my lips. Her eyes go unfocused as she stares.

"You seem stressed," I observe with an undercurrent of laughter.

"I wonder why."

"I imagine it's because no one has made you come in a long time."

It takes a second for that statement to register. When it does, her eyes go wide with shock, then indignation. "I… That is… You—" Her eyes harden. "I take care of myself, thank you very much."

"You need to relax, *sladkaya*."

"You need to leave."

"I will," I tell her. "But first, you'll have to come for me."

I don't waste any time waiting for that sentence to sink in. I just grab a hold of her and push her lengthwise along the couch. Her thin white dress slips up of its own accord.

"Isla—"

"Is sleeping," I reply as my hand slides up her skirt to the soft smoothness between her thighs.

She shudders underneath me, her hands gripping at my biceps. She's barely concentrating on my words anymore. My fingers brush over her panties. Soft and smooth. Just like her dress. Just like her skin.

"That's only… oh God…"

Her eyes pinwheel in their sockets. Her clamp on my arms is hard, as if to make sure I'm real. I shove aside her underwear, run my fingers down her slit, and catch wetness.

"I think you're ready for me," I rumble.

"I'm thinking of someone else."

I laugh and dance a finger half an inch inside of her. She writhes around until I pin her down with my weight on top of her "Breathe, *sladkaya*," I advise, "or you're going to come way too quickly."

"Fuck, I hate when you call me that."

"Why?"

"Probably because I like it too much."

I chuckle and bend my lips down to her neck. The same exact spot I'd kissed the last time we were under the tree in her sorry excuse for a backyard. Her body arches towards me and I can feel her pushing her hips up against my fingers. She smells so sweet. Like honeysuckle and fresh-baked cookies.

With two fingers inside her, I press my thumb to her clit and start swirling. Her eyes roll back in her head. "Oh God… oh God… oh God…"

"You can call me Daniil."

She chokes on laughter and lust. I redouble pressure, lock her lips in mine, and capture the first exhale of her orgasm. She comes almost instantly, with a gasp and a cry and a moan that makes my dick throb painfully in my pants.

But this isn't about me. Not tonight.

This is about her.

I apply pressure with the heel of my hand to help her coast back down to earth. I allow myself to give her another kiss, right at the nape of her neck, so that her sweetness stays buzzing on my lips for long after I leave.

Then I withdraw my fingers and stand up, barely a hair out of place.

In comparison, Kinsley looks like a woman ruined. Her dress is bunched up around her waist and her panties, which stayed on the entire time, are stained with her juices. The thin straps of her dress have fallen off her shoulders.

She stares up at me like I'm some mirage she can't make sense of.

I look back down at her like she's the exact same thing.

37

KINSLEY

I stare up at him, cushioned in the glorious, delirious aftermath, as the last remnants of pleasure crackle through me like heat lightning.

Then a screeching ring slices through my daze.

I jerk upright and all that warm, tingly goodness vanishes. Daniil looks pissed as he grabs his phone and answers it.

As he turns from me, I notice the bulge in his crotch. I'm so preoccupied with that that I miss the first bit of the conversation. It's not until Daniil's tone twists with anger that I start to pay attention.

"… don't fucking care… You know where I stand."

His back is to me, but I can see the indentations of his muscles from underneath his shirt.

"He wants what he can't have… Yes, I'm aware…"

He stops short as the person on the other line starts talking rapid-fire. The words are a blur, but the panic is obvious.

And, not for the first time, I wonder…

Who the hell are you, Daniil Vlasov?

"Petro," Daniil cuts in harshly. *"On khochet svoyego naslednika. On umret razocharaovannym. Ne bespokoy menya snova."* He hangs up right after that. My Russian isn't good enough to puzzle out what he said.

"Everything okay?" I ask. His eyes flicker to my shoulders, where the straps of my dress have fallen.

"Fine. Just business."

"Right. Of course. Let me guess—you can't tell me what it's about."

He sighs. "I was hoping I'd get a good snark-free hour before the after-effects of the orgasm wore off."

I narrow my eyes at him. "The call accelerated the timeline prematurely."

"Fucking Petro," he mutters.

"Petro," I repeat. "Who's that? Your lap dog?"

He snorts with laughter. "I like that. I'll be sure to tell him he has a new title." He runs a hand through his perfectly tousled hair. "He's a friend," he says. "And he works for me as well."

"A colleague."

"No. That implies we're equals."

The cocky smirk is back on his face. Meanwhile, I'm no closer to understanding who he is or what he does. It's starting to really get to me.

"Why are you so secretive?" I demand. "Are you, like, a mobster or something?"

His silence is telling in the weirdest way.

I bolt upright. "Wait," I gasp. "Are you really?"

"I'm Russian."

I frown. "You're a Russian... mobster? I'm confused. Is this like a Mad Libs thing?"

He smiles at me like you'd smile at a little kid who doesn't understand the situation. "There's Italian mafia. There's Russian Bratva. I'm the latter."

"Oh my God," I murmur. "I was joking. You're not."

I feel like an idiot now for not seeing it before. The way he handled the cops ten years ago. The way he saved me from Liam. The aura of untouchability. It's not an act—he really is untouchable.

"Those guns you played with as a child," I say. "They weren't water guns, were they?"

He shakes his head. "No. They were not."

"Jesus Christ." I leap to my feet. He regards me calmly from where he's seated, but he doesn't say a word. "You're a criminal. You're a criminal. You're actually a literal, real life criminal."

"You keep saying that."

"Because I'm trying to process it. I always knew you were shady, but this... You mentioned you'd killed men, back when we first met. You told me that the men you killed deserved to die," I say, recalling faint snippets of the conversation.

"The life expectancy for men in my line of work is rather short."

"Oh my God," I gasp for the dozenth time as I start pacing around the room.

I just came on the hand of a murderer.

I just came on the hand of a murderer.

My lips and feet are working faster than my brain right now. All I can do is vomit up bits of half-remembered memories, trying to stitch them all together into a complete picture.

"So the man you worked for…"

"Don Gregor Semenov," Daniil fills in. "I served him faithfully most of my life. I was trained to obey. And when I stopped, he decided to teach me a lesson."

"By putting you in jail. Jesus Christ." I tug nervously at the roots of my hair. "Should I be worried, Daniil?" It's the one thing that's burning at the forefront of my mind now that I'm calm enough to think about the right questions.

He, on the other hand, looks utterly relaxed. "You and Isla are under my protection now. No harm will come to either one of you. Not while I breathe."

That *should* terrify me. It should *not* comfort me.

But guess which option my screwed-up brain chemistry goes with?

"But is there a possibility of harm coming to us?" I press anyway. "Do you have, like… enemies?"

"A don always has enemies."

"This Semenov guy, your former boss," I say. "Is he one of them?"

Daniil smiles inwardly. "I wouldn't call him an enemy."

"He put you in jail. Doesn't sound like he's a pal."

"Believe me, I remember. But his intention was never to alienate me."

I look at him incredulously. "What was his intention then?"

"He wanted to put me back in my place. Remind me that, while he was living, he was the don and he wouldn't tolerate insubordination from anyone. Even those closest to him."

"Yeah, well, that worked out really great for him, didn't it?"

He laughs, still at ease like we're having a normal chit-chat. "I was never very good at taking orders anyway. It was only a matter of time before I snapped."

"You told me that you broke up an argument between him and his wife."

"It wasn't a fight," he corrects with disgust. "A fight implies that she was fighting back. She was lying on the floor with a bruised, bloodied face while he kept kicking her."

I wince at the image it conjures up. It's so hauntingly vivid—and that's because I've lived through that exact scene before.

Except when I see the woman lying in a fetal position on the floor, she has my mother's face. And the man standing over her, kicking the shit out of her, has my father's.

"I... I never asked you what happened."

"What happened is I stepped in between them. I pushed him back so hard that he stumbled and fell. I still remember the way he fell. Now that I think about it, actually, that was a pivotal point in my life."

"How so?"

Daniil's eyes are hazy with memory. "I realized he *could* fall. He wasn't invincible. He was just a man, same as any other. And if you pushed him, he would fall."

His words hang heavy in the air. "He put you in jail for that?"

"No, he put me in jail for breaking his jaw."

My eyes nearly pop out of their sockets. "You did *what?*"

He smiles. "You would have done the same."

I laugh, ironically enough. "No," I say with grim certainty, "I wouldn't have."

All the shame and guilt that I haven't allowed to surface for the past several years comes bubbling up. It gets easier to bury when enough years have passed. At least, it feels that way. But then it comes bursting free when you least expect.

Daniil rises to his feet and steps closer to me. I lift my eyes to his reluctantly. "I know I wouldn't because I didn't. I watched my father hit my mother, but I didn't intervene. I just hid at the top of the staircase and waited for it to stop."

"You were a child."

"Sure—the first time. But I grew up, and it didn't stop. The most I would do is go down and beg him to leave her alone. I never got between them. And I certainly never punched him in the face."

"You were scared."

I nod, blinking back tears of shame. "Yes. I was terrified."

"I was never allowed to be scared, *sladkaya*," he explains softly. "I lived in a world where fear in a boy was not tolerated. If I was scared, I killed that fear and got on with things."

I laugh again, though it's choked with a sob this time. "You can't kill your feelings. Believe me, I've tried."

"I got close enough," he says. "Until…"

He's quiet for a long, long time. It feels like seasons pass outside of the window as his silver-blue eyes flash with a dozen different sources of light, each more ethereal than the last. I couldn't look away if I wanted to. And for most of that time, I can't speak, either.

"Until what?" I croak finally.

He doesn't blink, not even once. "Until you."

He smiles at me then. It's tight and almost melancholy, in a way I can't quite explain. His eyes ripple one more time with the strangest light yet.

Then he nods once, brushes my cheek with his thumb, and says, "I'll be seeing you, *sladkaya*."

His hand falls from my face and he leaves.

I just stand there for minutes after the door closes behind him, caught in a moment that's already abandoned me. Tethered in place by the lingering heat of his touch.

I might've stood there all night long if my phone hadn't started to vibrate from where it fell in between the couch cushions. I fish it out to find a long string of unanswered texts from Emma.

10:00 PM: How'd it go? Has he left yet?

10:30 PM: I'm assuming Isla is in bed by now. So either you're asleep too or you're entertaining the black knight.

10:53 PM: Are you asleep? I'm exercising maximum self-restraint by not sprinting over to your house right now. I deserve a medal.

11:31 PM: Hoping everything went well.

11:44 PM: Jesus, Kinsley!!!!!

I call her before she has an aneurysm. She picks up immediately. "Oh, thank God! I was low-key worried that you and Isla had been murdered or something."

"Your texts didn't sound so low-key," I drawl.

"Yeah, well, I'm not really a low-key kind of person. How'd it go?" she asks eagerly.

"Good," I say in a voice that doesn't really feel like mine. "Fine."

"Ooh boy. I know that tone."

I frown. "There's no tone."

"There is abso-freaking-lutely a tone. Something happened. I can feel it."

"Nothing happened. It actually went so much smoother than I ever thought possible."

"He was good with her?"

"He was great with her. To the point where I felt sort of… jealous."

Emma squeals in delighted surprise. "No way."

"They seem to understand each other. She even told him that she gets bullied in school."

"Wow, really? She didn't even tell you for the longest time."

"Gee, thanks for pointing that out."

"My bad," Emma says, clearly not sorry at all. "But this is a really good thing, right? I mean, best-case scenario and all?"

"Yeah. Maybe."

"You sound… unsure?"

"As usual, it's complicated." I toy with the ends of my hair. "He… opened up to me a little tonight."

"Oh yeah, that's the good stuff. Did you, ya know, *open up to him?*" she says with a suggestive cackle.

"Not like that, Em."

"Meh. Buzzkill."

I lean back on the couch and keep combing my fingers through my hair, thinking of my mother as I do. "He told me he's a… Or he's in, maybe… like, a Bratva. A mafia, but Russian. He was in another one but now, he runs this one, or something like that, and so there's this guy he used to work for who… who… Shit, I don't even know. It's a lot."

There's a whole lot of silence and breathing on the other line. Then… "*What?!*"

I nod. "Yeah. I know."

"Okay, don't judge me, but this guy just got a whole lot sexier."

"Emma!"

"I told you not to judge me! You're not in the slightest bit turned on that he's a sexy, certified bad boy?"

"No. Not at all. I'm terrified, actually."

"Kinz. C'mon. He's hot, he's good with Isla, he's great in bed—"

"Great with his fingers," I correct. Then I wince immediately, knowing that Emma will never pass up that kind of bait.

Sure enough, she screams so loud I have to hold the phone away from my ear. When I put it back, she's saying, "… I knew it! I knew it, I knew it, I knew it. You little tramp, God, I love you."

I can't help but laugh with her. It's the only way to approach this whole situation, really. If I don't laugh, I might just break down in tears. "You're ridiculous."

"Guilty. But I also happen to be right in this case. Okay, glad we got that out in the air. But onto more important things. Forget the orgasm. You have feelings for this guy, don't you?"

I'm quiet, chewing at my lip.

"I know the sound of that silence, Kinz. Don't worry, I won't make you say anything out loud. But my advice? Explore this. See what it could be."

"It could be a lot of heartbreak. That's what it could be."

"Anything worth doing is a risk, Kinz. Time to stop wasting your life on old memories and make some new ones."

"But Isla…"

"Give Isla some credit. That kid is a badass. Just like her momma. Just like her dad, too, it seems." She exhales. "Just… just think about it, okay?"

"Okay."

I can hear her grin through the phone. "He sounds like a real heartbreaker."

"Yeah," I mutter back. "That's precisely what I'm worried about."

38

DANIIL

"Don Vlasov."

Ribisi stands to the side, waiting for me to invite him to sit down. I give him only a casual glance and reach for my whiskey.

"I take it you're here because you have news for me."

"Yes, sir. Don Semenov is desperate to meet with you."

"That is not news," I say, glaring up at him. "It's common knowledge. Are you trying to trick me into believing you're loyal to me?"

"No, my don."

"I am not your don yet," I remind him harshly. "I'm still deciding what to do with you. You were his creature for a long time."

"And I still would be," Ribisi agrees, "if he hadn't spat in my face."

Petro rolls his eyes. "I'm gonna spit in your face, too, amigo, if you keep boring the shit out of me with the same old sob story. And not in the 'pay extra because that's what you like' kind of way."

Ribisi's face sours, but he stands his ground. I wonder how long it'll take before he snaps under Petro's humiliations. If he takes the insult on the chest, then I'm willing to explore his potential in my Bratva. But if he snaps like I suspect he might, I'm not going to take the risk on someone so reactionary.

If he can defect to me, he can defect back to the old fuck just as easily.

"I do have additional news that isn't common knowledge," Ribisi adds.

"Well, what the hell are you waiting for then?" Petro asks, flagging down one of the Cirque serving girls. He's had his eyes on this particular specimen the whole night. Blonde hair. Blue eyes. Big tits. The Petro Special, as we call it.

"He has his spies on you," Ribisi confides, inching closer. "They're watching your every move. What's more, he'll be arriving here soon, hoping to trap you into a conversation."

I arch an eyebrow. "He's coming here? Tonight?"

That is news to me. It's also surprising. Gregor Semenov used to think he was above making house calls. Times have changed, it seems.

Petro gives me an intrigued glance from behind Ribisi. He knows as well as I do that this is an interesting turn of events.

"As I said, he's determined to talk to you."

"I've managed to evade that conversation for ten years," I point out. "I can do it for another ten if I have to." I sip my drink again. "I'll call you again if I need you. Leave us."

Ribisi bows his head and disappears as surreptitiously as he appeared.

Petro removes the blonde's arms from around his waist and dismisses her with a wave of his hand. Her face twists with annoyance, but she leaves. He pours another drink and drops down next to me, spilling half of it in the process.

"That bastard gives me the willies."

"Semenov or Ribisi?"

"A little Column A, a little Column B," he admits.

I chuckle. "Aw, is poor little Petro feeling frightened?"

He makes a sour face. "He was my don. And I betrayed him for you. That's the kind of choice that demands retaliation, if he ever gets close enough to do it."

"It wasn't a betrayal. And he was a shitty don."

"He was a decent don," Petro says carefully. "He was a shitty person. There's a difference."

He's not wrong, much as I hate to admit it. I nod and lean back against the sofa. "By the way, before you can ask: we're not leaving."

Petro pales. "Are you serious? You heard Ribisi. He's coming here tonight! He ain't exactly bringing party favors, *sobrat*."

"I heard. I think it's time we had that conversation."

"What happened to *'I've avoided it for ten years'*?"

I shrug. "Changed my mind."

Petro scowls and crosses his arms over his chest as he nurses his drink. More hostesses flit past at the edge of our VIP area, just begging to be called over, but for a change, he ignores them altogether.

"Can I ask you a weird question?" he blurts suddenly.

"That's all you ever ask me."

He scowls. "Do you miss it?"

"Miss what, exactly?"

"Being the one in the passenger's seat, as opposed to the man making all the decisions. Not having to deal with all the bullshit."

It takes me no time at all to settle on an answer. "No," I snort. "I don't miss that at all."

Petro sighs. "Yeah, I didn't think so." He strokes his three-day beard, deep in thought. "He really should have seen it coming."

"The jailbreak or the disobedience?"

"Both," he replies. "It was ballsy as hell."

"So was leaving his Bratva to join mine," I point out. "Which means you're complicit right along with me, my friend."

Petro's scowl deepens. "Yeah, well, that's what I'm afraid of. You realize we haven't come face to face with the man in ten years?"

"I've been painfully aware of every second that's passed since that day, Petro. So yes, safe to say I realize."

"And you really think meeting him is a good idea? Even with your… new situation?"

I raise an eyebrow. "Are you actually worried about my 'new situation' or are you just trying to find a way out of this because you're chickenshit?"

"Can't it be both?" He clutches his glass in both hands and leans closer toward me. "He's the kind of man who holds a grudge, Dan."

"Yeah? Funny. So am I."

"Don't I know it," he mutters under his breath. "My question stands, though."

"No one knows about Kinsey and Isla except you and me," I say. "It's going to stay that way."

"Right, but you heard Ribisi. Ol' Greggy's got his spies scoping you out. What if they stumbled across your new family?"

"That wrinkly motherfucker won't have the guts to do anything about it."

"You're taking a risk," he warns. "A big one."

"My entire life has been a risk, Petro," I point out. "Why stop now?"

Ping. I look down and catch a text from Kinsley.

KINSLEY: *Thought you'd like to see these.*

Ping. Ping. Ping.

"Who is that?" Petro asks.

I ignore him and open up our text thread. She's sent me three pictures of Isla. The first is her as a newborn, all pink-faced and wrinkly, swaddled tight in a yellow blanket that reveals only her round face and a single lock of curly hair fallen over her forehead.

In the second picture, she's at least six months old. She's wearing corduroy overalls and a face smeared full of cake frosting. The freckles shine through like a constellation of stars.

The last shows a young Isla toddling through what have to be some of her very first steps. Her dress is blue and cotton, flared out around chubby, biscuit-dough thighs. That smile is undeniable.

"… Hello? Earth to Daniil?"

"Eh?" I ask, looking up.

"Something more important than the fate of our lives going on over there?" He snatches my phone and gawks at the screen. Then he looks up at me in shock. "These are… baby pictures."

"You're a smart one, my friend." I tap my chin in thought. "It's Isla."

"Oh," Petro says, looking back down at the phone. "*Oh.*"

"Sometimes, you can be so thick I question my decision to keep you around. Give me back my phone."

"Gimme a second," Petro argues, leaning away from my reach and scrolling through the pictures. "Gotta say, she's cute. Takes after her momma, fortunately."

"The only fortunate thing here is that I'm not rearranging your face with my fist."

He laughs good-naturedly and hands my phone back. "I take it things are going well then?"

"Time will tell. For the moment, we're both trying."

She certainly tried last night when she'd come around my fingers like a good little *kiska.*

"Does that mean you banged her?" I narrow my eyes and he gives me a knowing smile. "Was the second time as good as the first?"

"Nothing happened."

He frowns. "I would have thought she'd stop playing hard to get by now." Something occurs to him and his frown sours more. "Is that why you're so distracted by the broad? She won't let you get between her legs so you want her more?"

"I've already been between her legs," I remind him coldly. "That's how children are made."

"Sure, when she was young and vulnerable," Petro replies. "She's a capital-W *Woman* now. Not as likely to fall for your bullshit."

"Bullshit is your department, not mine."

Motion off to the side catches my eye. I glance over and see him coming. Petro notices my stance change instantly. Hackles rising, fists clenching, jaw going taut with tension.

"Oh fuck, fuck, fuck. Is he here?"

I don't bother answering. This moment has been ten years coming. Now that it's here, I'm noticing every tiny, inconsequential detail of it, like time itself is slowing down.

The way the lights seem to dim and sharpen and blur, all at the same time.

The way the music drops low and bass-heavy, enough thump to rattle my bones.

The way men tighten up all around me before they even know what's happening. The scared ones cower. The smart ones disappear.

I haven't seen the old bastard in ten years. Before that, I saw him every day for decades. It seems that our relationship only exists in the extremes.

Then Gregor Semenov steps into a beam of light, and I see the don I left behind.

He's aged well. Completely bald now, but it works in his favor. The strobes from the dance floor bounce off his skull. He's wearing a suit, of course—dark and double-breasted, with diamond cufflinks that catch the lights. His diamond-studded watch does the same.

His rangy eyes land on me seconds after he enters the VIP section, flanked by an entourage at least a dozen men strong.

"Has he seen us yet?" Petro hisses. "Should I go?"

"If you wanted to leave, you should've left ten years ago, brother," I tell him coolly. "He's here."

"Good evening, Daniil."

Petro swallows and then composes himself. He talks like a coward, but I know him better than that—deep down, he's a warrior. It's the only reason I tolerate his bullshit.

He gets to his feet, and the nerves vanish from his features just before he turns to Gregor.

"It's Don Vlasov to you," he corrects his former don. "Pay him the respect he deserves."

"Petro fucking Maximov," Gregor growls. "You have some balls to stand there and look me in the eye."

"I've avoided it as much as possible, I assure you," Petro retorts.

Gregor's teeth grind angrily, matching the furious but controlled flare in his eyes. He sits down, ignoring Petro, while his men slither around him, fanning out on either side. A few of them I recognize. Most are new to me.

"You brought all these friends to see me?" I ask. "I'm not sure if I should be scared or flattered."

"A wise man would be scared," Gregor replies. "But you've never been all that wise."

He's got a twitch in his left eye. It gets more pronounced the more we talk. I wonder if that's a nervous habit he developed over the years, and I chuckle inwardly at the thought that perhaps I'm the one who caused it. Whatever it is, it makes him seem human. A part of me always doubted whether he was or not.

Until I pushed him and he fell. That part I will never forget.

"That's an interesting way to segue into what you've come here to discuss with me," I say.

His brow furrows. "How do you know what I've come to discuss?"

"Intuition. Intelligence. Lucky guess. Take your pick."

He crosses one leg over the other and leans back in his seat to regard me. His men bristle on all sides around him, a forest of idiots in cheap suits.

"An alliance," he says, so quietly I almost miss it. "Both of us need a line of succession. This allays that need for the time being. You'd be a fool to pass this up."

"I believe you just finished calling me a fool, funny enough."

"Daniil," he growls, his anger besting him for a moment, "this is not a fucking joke."

"I'm not laughing."

We stare at each and the years compress down into nothing. He's still the man who wants complete control and complete obedience. I'm still the man who refuses to give him either.

"You wasted your time coming here today," I tell him succinctly. "Keep your Bratva and your legacy; I don't want it. I've built my own."

"I could destroy it, if I wanted to," he warns.

"Have we moved onto the part of the night where threats are exchanged already?" I ask casually. "I suppose it has been ten years. No point in beating around the bush anymore."

"Exactly. Ten years. Ten fucking years, Daniil."

I raise my eyebrows. "You say that as though it's my fault. That's not how I remember it."

"Your damn pride and stubbornness is what led to this," he says with a vicious scowl. "She was not yours to protect. She was mine to do with as I fucking pleased."

"That's not how I remember that part, either."

He grimaces and rubs at his twitching left eye like it's irritating him. "I should have sent you to burn in hell."

"You tried. I'd have broken out of there, too."

With that, I'm done exchanging words with this dinosaur. I stand, straighten my cuffs, and walk away.

39

KINSLEY

"Did you call her a B-I-T-C-H?" Principal Bridges asks me.

He's hesitant to even spell the word out. I'm torn between cringing in shame and laughing out loud. If not answering were an option, I'd plead the fifth all day long. But Heather is brewing up a storm right outside the office, and I know there's no way she's letting me get off the hook that easily.

"Would it... would it make a difference if I said she deserved it?" I venture.

"Ms. Whitlow."

I sigh and let my shoulders slump forward. "I know I behaved terribly. I should never have confronted Heather that way. I should have... Honestly, I'm not even sure what I should have done."

"She claimed that you called her an 'F-ing B-word,'" he says dourly. "And that you..." He checks his notes on the yellow legal pad he totes around everywhere. "That you asked her if you should 'spell it out on her whiteboard for her.'"

"I wanted to make sure she understood," I mumble.

He laughs—at least, I think he does—though it quickly morphs into a wheezy cough. He clears his throat and folds his hands in front of him. "Kinsley, this is serious."

I compose myself and nod. "I know."

"I understand you were upset about Isla and you wanted to protect her. But picking a fight with her teacher is not the way to do that."

"No, it's not. I completely agree."

"Ms. Roe is asking that you be fired in the face of the verbal abuse she was dealt."

I blanche immediately. "Principal Bridges, I—"

"I'm not going to do that," he interrupts with a tight smile. "You're an excellent teacher, Kinsley. And you're a good mother. I don't want to punish you too harshly for trying to protect your daughter. But I do have to make a statement here. Which is why I'm suspending you without pay for the next two weeks."

I take a deep breath—the latest of many since he called me into this overcrowded, mildewy office—and arrange my next words in my head. He's being generous and I'm fully aware of that. Which is why I feel doubly bad that I have to tell him what I'm about to tell him.

"Colin, I'm resigning."

His eyes go wide. "What? Ms. Whit—Kinsley, that's not necessary."

I shake my head. "It's not because of this. That is—well, it is because of this, but not in the way you think."

"What do you mean?"

"Isla told me that she's really not happy here. She wants to change schools at the end of this semester. With this stuff piled on top, it'll be easier on everyone if I leave with Isla. For practical reasons as much as personal ones. So here I am, giving you my resignation, four months in advance."

His face drops. "That makes me very upset to hear that. Louisa would be upset, too, you know."

I grimace at the mention of Louisa's name. All these years later, it still hurts. The space in my heart where she should be is raw and ragged and bleeding.

Colin has a hole in his own heart that matches; I know that. But it's hard to recognize the common ground right now. The desk between us is too big, too self-serious.

"You did what you could for her," I rasp. "And for me. But I think she's hit a limit. She wouldn't have asked me to leave if she hadn't."

He sighs. "And there's nothing I can do or say to change your mind?"

"Not really, no." He looks defeated. I feel bad that I've put him in this position. "You really have been a wonderful boss, Colin."

He smiles sadly. "I'm glad to hear you say that. But I feel as though I've failed Isla."

"That just proves you're a dedicated educator. Unlike the woman sitting outside right now."

"Alright," he says, his eyes sparking with determination. "This is how we're gonna spin it."

I frown. "Spin what?"

"Heather doesn't have to know the particulars. I will tell her that you've been fired, effective from the end of this term. That ought to quiet her down for a while."

"You don't have to do that."

"I want to," he insists. "I'll give you an excellent reference when you leave. You'll have no problem finding another job."

"You're a gem. Thank you, Colin," I say as we both get to our feet.

He returns a grateful smile, rounds his desk, and takes my hand in his. "She would be proud of the woman you've become, Kinsley. I know that to be true."

I smile back and nod, not trusting myself to speak right now.

He nods in return. "Then I think we're done here. Send Heather in on your way out, please."

I slip out of Colin's office. Heather lurches to her feet immediately. She tries to move past me without making eye contact, but I block her. "Heather, before you go in, can I have a minute?"

She sniffs, nose held high in the air. "I suppose so."

"I just wanted to apologize to you. Sincerely."

"For yelling at me and calling me a fucking bitch, you mean?"

I still mean it, says the petty voice in my head.

"Yes. I was way out of line and I should never have said those things to you."

Out loud, at least.

She considers my apology for a moment and nods with another indignant sniffle. "I'm just doing my best here, you know. It's hard enough dealing with the kids, much less their parents. You should understand that better than anyone."

"Well, I would never allow bullying to take place in my classroom," I say, unable to bite my tongue on this one.

"Neither would I. There has been no bullying in my classroom," she says defensively.

"So what you're saying is that Isla is making it up?"

Her eyes narrow. "Some kids just like the attention."

The voice in my head goes apeshit. *You absolute fucking BITCH! You snobby, arrogant, inadequate little—*

But I manage to rein myself in. Instead, I give Heather a tight smile. "You call it attention; I call it a cry for help. But I suppose our teaching styles are just very different."

Then, before she can say anything else, I walk away.

I find Isla waiting for me in the courtyard outside. She's hunched over her sketchpad with a one-hundred-and-eighty-degree crick in her neck that is probably making every chiropractor in the county start to drool.

"Hey, kiddo. Is that even comfortable?"

She shrugs. "Just doodling. What did Principal Bridges say?"

"Nothing terribly interesting."

"Just administrative work?" she asks pointedly.

I smile. She's so perceptive. "Okay, you want the truth? I was asked to apologize to Ms. Roe."

"Why?"

"Um, I may have called her a not-so-nice word."

Isla's eyes bug out and her jaw drops to the ground, full-on *Looney Tunes* style. "You did?!"

"I'm not proud of it," I insist, hoping that Isla won't see through the lie, because in truth, I'm pretty damn proud of defending my daughter. "I was running high on emotion and she was rubbing me the wrong way."

"It was about me, wasn't it?"

"Maybe."

She seems happy about the fact that I'm not lying to her. "Jeez. I can't believe you called my teacher a bitch, Mom."

"Language! Just because I said it doesn't mean you can. Anyway, it was a lapse in judgment. I was just worried about you."

"You won't have to worry at the end of the semester."

I nod and wrap my arm around her shoulders as we head to the car. "So I have a little surprise for you."

"For me?" she asks. "Really?"

I nod. "We'll go home to drop off the car, and then we're heading over to the mall. For burgers and milkshakes and a little shopping."

"Can we go to the stationery store and the art supply store?"

I laugh. Whenever we go to the mall, those are the two spots that we have to visit every single time. It's become routine at this point.

"We can stop there, too, if you want. But I was thinking that you and I can pick out a dress for the dance."

She buckles on her seatbelt and turns to me warily. "Mom! I told you I didn't want to go to the stupid dance."

"But you have someone to take now."

"I told you, it's weird if I go with you."

"I'm not talking about me," I say. "I'm talking about—"

"Daniil?" Isla gasps. "He actually wants to take me?"

"Of course. It was his suggestion."

She looks shell-shocked and very excited all at the same time. "Oh..." She glances towards me, her beautiful eyes magnified by the strength of her prescription lenses. "We can just look at some dresses," she concedes.

I grin happily. "I'll take it."

Daniil is already parked out front when Isla and I pull up in front of the house. He's leaning against his car, looking like a model in an ad campaign. I'm not even sure what he would be modeling. The stupidly expensive car? The effortlessly cool jacket he's got on? Himself?

Isla unbuckles and jumps out of the car. She flies towards Daniil, who straightens up and gives her a hug. They look so easy together, so natural. It makes my heart do funny wiggles in my chest.

I get out and walk over to the two of them. "Ready to hit the mall?" I ask, feeling a little like I'm intruding on their moment.

"The mall?" Daniil scoffs, wrinkling his brow in disgust.

I shoot him a glare over Isla's head. "Honey," I tell her, "here's the door key. Why don't you put your backpack inside, change, and meet us out here in five?"

The moment she's in the house, I turn to Daniil. "Don't want to mix with the rabble, huh?" I mock.

He glowers. "Isla deserves better than a mall dress."

I narrow my eyes. "The so-called 'mall dress' that I have in mind costs two hundred dollars. Which is way more than I can afford."

"Don't worry about cost today. I've got it."

"You don't have to—"

"No, Kinsley, you're right," he sneers. "I don't have to. Matter of fact, I don't have to do anything." Then his voice drops in register and becomes less aggressive, more tender. "But I want to. You've shouldered the financial burden all these years all by yourself. So now, let me take some of the weight. I won't think less of you for it."

I open my mouth to respond, then let it fall closed again. Meanwhile, I pull at my nails, wondering if letting him have this would be admitting defeat in some way.

Stop it. This is not about pride. This is about Isla. What's best for Isla.

"Okay, fine. But Isla gets final say."

"I wouldn't have it any other way."

"Ready!" Isla calls from the stoop as she locks the house back up and skips over towards the two of us in a fresh t-shirt and shorts. Daniil opens the door for her and she glides right into the back seat.

Then he walks around to the passenger's side door so that he can open it for me. I hesitate, looking up at him. That scowl, that flash in his eyes, even the ink peeking up over his collar—it all screams *Danger.* Suddenly, I'm consumed by a bizarre urge to grab my daughter and run screaming for the hills.

Then his lip tilts up in a wry smirk. "Would you prefer to handle the doors yourself, *sladkaya?*" he teases.

I grimace and get in. Chuckling, he shuts the door behind me.

We end up driving for almost thirty-five minutes before Daniil comes to a stop in front of a huge glass-front store called… Actually, there's no signage out front. No signage anywhere I can see, actually. It's just an ocean of one-way mirrors around the exterior of the building, reflecting the smooth contours of the car right back at us.

"This is not a mall," I observe.

He sighs. "Nothing gets past you, does it?"

"There's no name, either."

"No," he agrees. "There's not." He gets out of the car and waltzes up to the front without waiting to see if we're following.

I take Isla's hand in mine and we reluctantly go up to where Daniil is typing some number combo into a subtly placed keypad. There's a dial tone, and he says his name in a deep, rumbling baritone. Then a soft bell chimes and the door swoops inward silently.

Creepy.

"Coming?" he calls over his shoulder. Once again, he doesn't stop to make sure.

The first twenty feet is a narrow hallway lined with alternating crimson and gold lights and strange, futuristic-looking arrangements of barren branches. The scent of flowers is intoxicating.

Daniil disappears around the left-hand corner. We trace his footsteps, and then—

Just like that, the store opens up. Suddenly, it's not chill-inducing red lighting—it's gleaming white everywhere, gilded edges, lilies in hand-blown glass vases that look too delicate to be real. A small army of stunning blonde women in matching white dresses floats around the perimeter, all displaying the same dazzling white smile.

Isla sidles a little closer to my side.

"Daniil," I hiss. "We're underdressed."

His eyes scan over me and linger on my legs for a moment. "Hm. I suppose you are. That can be easily remedied."

He turns and strides away before I can ask what the hell he means by that. Isla looks up at me, equal parts nervous and intrigued.

"Mr. Vlasov! How lovely to see you," croons an angelic voice. The woman speaking is thin and tall. Like the others, she's blonde, Botoxed, and veneered, though no less beautiful for it.

Posh Barbie diverts her gaze towards Isla and me. "And who do we have here?" she asks pleasantly.

"Juliette, this is Kinsley," Daniil introduces. "And this is Isla."

I frown, weirdly perturbed by how casual he says that. Somehow, just offering up her name doesn't feel like sufficient enough of an introduction. My daughter is not an inconvenience to be swept under the rug.

But if Daniil notices my irritation, he completely ignores it. "We need to find Isla a dress for her school dance," he explains to the Barbie doll. "And while we're here, let's get both of them some new clothes. Out with the old wardrobe, in with the new."

"How lovely!" she says, clapping her hands together. "I'll go and gather some choices that I think will suit you perfectly," she says. She beams down at Isla.

"Why don't you go with her, honey?" I urge Isla. "So you can tell her what you like and what you don't."

Isla looks hesitant, but I give her an encouraging nod and Posh Barbie offers her hand for Isla to take. "Come on, princess. It'll be fun."

The moment the two of them move into another room in the store, I turn to Daniil, who has slumped on a nearby couch. "What the hell do you think you're doing?"

"I have a feeling you're about to tell me."

As always, Daniil is infuriatingly unflappable. Maybe that's why I'm as flappable as I am. Yin and yang, or something annoying like that.

My brow furrows. "Is there ever a moment when you're not glacially calm?"

"Would you prefer I not be?"

"Yes! It would reassure me that you are in fact human."

His smile only gets wider. "I assure you, I am in fact human. But if you need to be sure, you can always come over here and explore me."

I'm blushing hard, and simultaneously wishing society would return to Victorian-era beauty standards of thick white foundation so he wouldn't be able to see the flame on my cheeks.

I force myself to take a deep breath. I have a point to make here. I just need to concentrate long enough to make it.

"This trip was meant to be about finding Isla a dress to wear to the dance."

"Right."

"Not buying either of us a 'new wardrobe.'"

He shrugs. "You mentioned you were underdressed."

"It was an offhand comment, in response to this… this… *place* you've brought us to. I didn't expect something so fancy. And I sure as hell didn't ask you to dress me up like you're playing with dolls."

"I'm not trying to dress you up, *sladkaya*."

"Then what are you trying to do? Go ahead—I'm all ears."

"I'm trying to buy you clothes," he explains with more patience than I knew he possessed. "If you don't want to try anything on, you don't have to. I just thought it might be something you and Isla would enjoy. Together."

I cringe. Of all times for him to start being reasonable and sweet—well, sort of sweet; what passes for sweetness from him, if nothing else—why now?

I take back what I said about his unflappability being the most irritating thing about him.

No, the most irritating thing about Daniil Vlasov is that he knows exactly what to be at any given moment to drive me up the wall.

I look around self-consciously, wondering if any of the Amazonian angels shimmying through the store can see the smoke coming out of my ears. But we're still alone, more or less. The few employees who accidentally venture into this little alcove avert their eyes and venture right back out.

Finally, my gaze settles back on Daniil. That half-smirk still dances on his face. Infuriating, of course—but also infuriatingly tempting.

"Do you always spit in the face of a gift?" he asks.

"I can buy my own clothes."

"That wasn't the question."

I look around again nervously. Isla and Posh Barbie are nowhere to be seen, though. And I'm starting to think that being alone with Daniil is not a good idea.

"You… you don't have to give me anything," I tell him, tripping awkwardly over my words. "The insurance is enough."

"So you are accepting it then?"

"Under duress."

He nods. "Noted."

A moment of tense silence swallows us up. Well, it's tense for me, at least. Daniil looks like he could close his eyes and take a peaceful nap right now if he wanted to.

"Daniil?" I say. "About what happened the other night—"

"Mom!"

I jerk away from him as though I'm guilty of something heinous when Isla rounds the corner. Posh Barbie follows behind with a rolling rack filled with a rainbow's worth of dresses.

"This place has the most amazing dresses, Mom. You should see them. I picked some out for you, too. Juliette helped me."

"That was very nice of her, but I won't be trying anything on today."

"Aw, why not?"

The words feel thorny on my lips as I look down at my daughter. She's so animated today, so sparkling with life. This is the first time in a long time that she's acted like a child.

"Honey, I have plenty of dresses already."

"Not like these ones," Isla points out. "Come on! Daniil said you could choose one, too."

"How about we find you a dress first?" I suggest, sensing the heat of Daniil's smirk out of the corner of my eye.

Isla nods excitedly and pulls out a smoky blue dress with a layer of tulle over the skirt. A pattern of swans swims around the hem. It's every bit the fairytale dress a nine-year-old would fall in love with.

"This is it. This is the one," she says, so solemnly that it takes everything in me not to laugh out loud.

I think adults forget sometimes how serious parts of the world can be when you're young. Things that don't matter seem to matter more than anything, and things that do matter don't matter at all.

Dresses are life. Absentee fathers and broken-hearted mothers? Eh, that's just par for the course.

"You've already chosen?" I ask.

"Yup. I don't need to try on anything else. Those dresses are for you."

Oh boy. "Why don't you go try yours on first?" I offer. "I want to see you in it."

She nods and Posh Barbie leads Isla to one of the dressing rooms. I move to the sleek white sofa that Daniil is lounging on, though I carefully lower myself to a seat at the very far end away from him.

"You don't have to be so suspicious, *sladkaya*. The world is not out to get you. Nor your daughter."

"I'm not a pet or a doll," I snap. "More importantly, neither is she. It's not just about dressing her up and buying her pretty things. Being a father is about much more than that."

"I have a feeling you're trying to tell me something," he drawls. I notice there's an edge to his tone. Not quite defensiveness, but bordering on it.

"When we first walked in here, you didn't introduce Isla as your daughter."

He nods. "And you think I'm trying to hide that fact." It's not a question.

"Well, are you?"

"If I am, I have a good reason for it."

My frown furrows deeper. "That's not a denial."

"Because I'm not denying anything. You're right—I didn't introduce Isla as my daughter. That was intentional."

"Because you're ashamed of her?" I demand. "Or me?"

"That's quite the assumption."

"Answer the damn question."

"Ask the right one and maybe I will." He's sitting up now, vibrating with intensity. His eyebrows are pulled together and his jaw is made of sharp, unforgiving lines.

"What do you think?" Isla chirps as she steps out of the dressing room in her fairy blue dress.

"Honey!" I say, clapping my hands together. "You look gorgeous."

She really does. I have a feeling this is the first time in a while that Isla herself feels good. The smile on her face tells me as much—it's blinding if I look at it too close. But I can't bring myself to look away.

"You're a knockout, Isla," Daniil says with an easy smile.

She twirls around a little, giggling as the skirt flows out around her. "Are you sure you don't want to try on any others?" I ask.

"A hundred percent sure."

Daniil nods. "I like a girl who knows what she wants."

I'm not sure if it's my imagination or not, but I feel his eyes slide to me when he says that. Isla gives us another twirl and then she goes back towards the dressing rooms to change back into her street clothes.

"Listen, Daniil, I just—"

"You know who I am now, Kinsley," he says coldly. The way he says my name sets my teeth on edge. It feels so formal, so distant. "You know I have enemies. For the moment, none of them know that Isla exists, and the reason I want to keep it that way is to protect her. And you, if you'll let me. So it would be nice if you could give me the benefit of the doubt. Just once."

Gotta admit—I feel real shitty all the sudden. His intense eyes darken when they land on me, making me feel guiltier and smaller and that much shittier.

"I… I'm sorry," I whisper.

He glances at me. "What was that?"

"I said I'm sorry."

"One more time."

I narrow my eyes at him. "You heard me perfectly the first time."

The coldness melts away suddenly and he gives me a half-smile. "I figured it would be a while before I got another apology from you. Might as well stretch this one out."

"Ass."

"And just like that, we're back to the status quo."

I suppress a smile and give Isla a wave as she bounds over to us. Posh Barbie follows her with the blue dress thrown over her arm.

"Ms. Kinsley, I think it's your turn."

"Oh no—" I start to protest.

"Aw, come on, Mom! I've seen all your party dresses soooo many times. You should get a new one, too."

She's buzzing with joy. I meant what I said to Daniil—it's my job to protect that. To keep her innocence unstained for as long as the world will let me.

So if trying on some dresses that cost more than my house will do that, fine. I'll try on every damn dress in the store.

40

DANIIL

Isla is the one who opens the door when I arrive a few days later to pick them up for the big dance. She's already wearing her blue dress, and her hair has been brushed back in an effort to tame some of her more unruly curls.

"Whoa!" she says, the moment she sees me in my suit. "You look like James Bond."

I laugh. "You look wonderful, *printsessa*."

"Mom let me put on a little lipstick," she admits with a shy blush. "But only the nude kind." Her blush deepens in a way that looks almost exactly like her mother's. Kinsley just hides her fears somewhere deeper.

"Where is your mom?" I ask.

"In her room, putting her shoes on. She'll be out soon."

I follow her into the living room, which looks like the scene of a crime. "What happened here?"

Isla giggles. "Mom and I made a fort in the living room with our old scarves and blankets."

"Might need some architecture lessons," I drawl under my breath.

Isla doesn't hear me. "This is my old baby blanket," she announces, picking up a faded green blanket from the sofa. "I carried it around 'til I was six."

"Your mom kept it?"

"She keeps everything."

"What do I keep?"

I turn around to find Kinsley standing at the threshold between the living room and the front door—and my fucking breath catches hard in my chest.

She's wearing the dress I forcibly bought for her on our little shopping trip. It's the first time I'm seeing it on her, though. The garment is an off-the-shoulder midi, with an A-line skirt and intricate beadwork through the entire length of it. The material is a soft silk in a deep, rich green. Her eyes shine out like something otherworldly.

She's wearing her dark hair down, and it's scooped over her one bare shoulder, tousling down to her right breast. She's not wearing any jewelry, but it suits her—it would only distract from the glow.

"You look ravishing, *sladkaya*," I murmur in the same voice I'd use to pray, if that was something I'd ever done in my life.

Cue the blush.

"Thank you," Kinsley mumbles back. "You look... very nice yourself."

I incline my head in a subtle bow. "Are we all ready to go?"

"Mom, can I use some of your perfume before we leave?"

"Sure, honey. You know where it is."

Isla runs into her mother's room as Kinsley tries her best to avoid my gaze. She lasts about ten seconds of fidgeting with the hem of her skirt before she glances up at me.

"Nice suit."

"I got all dressed up for you."

She smiles shyly. "Thanks for doing this. She's been really excited all week."

"You don't have to thank me. I wanted to do it."

"I know. But still. I didn't think she would ever agree to go. I'm glad she's finally excited about it. She deserves to be."

"She deserves the world. Speaking of which, if you point out the little shits who're giving her a hard time, I'll give them what they deserve, too."

"That has a new meaning now that I know who and what you are," she says with a choked giggle and a simultaneous frown.

Her eyes keep flickering over me, like she doesn't want to stare too long, but she can't help herself. I'm much less skittish about my gawking.

Mostly because it would take a team of wild horses to rip my eyes off of her.

She's not just gorgeous, and even "ravishing" doesn't do her justice. She's a dream inside of a vision inside of a mirage. She's beautiful. She's radiating. I want to rip that dress to pieces and then kiss every inch of skin I expose.

It's not just the dress or the hair, either. It's the light in her eyes. The flush in her cheeks—not a blush of shame, but a gleam of pride. Of hope. Of, dare I say… happiness.

It looks good on her.

We both turn at the pitter-patter of footsteps returning down the hall. I expect a bright-eyed and bushy-tailed Isla, but by the time she reaches us, she lingers uncertainly at the threshold. She's wringing her hands in front of her over and over again.

"Honey?" Kinsley says. "Are you okay?"

Isla nods and swallows. "I'm just a little nervous all of a sudden."

I step forward and kneel in front of Isla before Kinsley can. I take my daughter's hands in both of mine and look her right in the eye. "Listen to me," I growl. "Fear is just another thing we notice in ourselves. You're too strong to let it drive you, *printsessa*."

She shakes her head. "I don't know about that."

"I do. You're my daughter."

She chews on her bottom lip. "I'm not like you, though," she says quietly. "You're James Bond. And I'm... I'm just me."

I smile and put as much force as I can into my words without scaring her. "That's the best person to be, Isla. If you do get scared tonight, that's okay. Just remember that I'm with you. I'll always be with you."

It takes a moment for that to sink in. I watch her face, but can you ever really know the mind of a child? The world takes on strange shapes from their perspective. The shadows seem darker. The boogeymen are real.

But when I stand and offer her my hand, she takes it.

That's bravery.

I straighten up and keep her hand clasped in mine. We head towards the door with Kinsley trailing us, still saying nothing. I can feel her eyes on my back, watching my every move.

Outside, I turn to Kinsley after I help Isla into the back seat. Her expression is careful and composed.

"As pep talks go, that wasn't bad," she murmurs.

"Such high praise. It's all going to go straight to my head, you know."

She gives me a meager smile and slips into the passenger seat. I shut the door behind her and go take my place behind the wheel.

The drive is mostly quiet. The radio and the wind trickle through the car and Isla sings along under her breath. Kinsley fidgets with bracelets she isn't wearing, no doubt wishing she had something to occupy her hands.

When we reach the school, I park my convertible and roll up the top, and the three of us head inside. The way is marked with luminescent signs and dozens of pink and blue balloons. A pair of teachers flank the front doors of the auditorium. Kinsley offers them a wave, but Isla stops a few feet from the door.

"Isla?" Kinsley says softly.

She glances up at the both of us. I see tears budding in her eyes like fresh dew. "I don't want to go in," she whispers.

"Oh, honey—"

I take Isla's hand. "You're not going in alone," I remind. "Come on, princess. I can't enjoy this father-daughter dance without you. You're one half of the team."

She gives me a tenuous smile and glances towards Kinsley. "Mom, you'll be around, too?"

"Of course. Don't worry about me. I'll be right behind you guys."

Isla nods and squeezes my hand tight enough for her nails to dig into my palm. Then we step into the gym. I hear whispering behind me, but I concentrate only on Isla. No one else matters.

The auditorium is a swirling mass of sweaty, awkward dads and their girls dressed in acres of tulle. The music thumps pleasantly from speakers arranged around the edge of the room.

I turn and face my daughter. "May I have the first dance?" I ask formally.

Isla giggles and nods. More eyes follow us as we glide towards the dance floor. I take her little hands in mine and we start to sway in time to the beat.

The craziest part of all this—a don at a school dance, a frightened little girl in a ten thousand dollar dress, gaggles of civilians staring at me like Bigfoot just wandered into their auditorium—is that I *want* to be here. There isn't another damn place on Earth I want to be, in fact. Give me money, threaten me with death—I don't give a fuck.

This is where I should be.

This is where I belong.

"I think I need to have some punch," Isla decides once the song ends.

"Good call. Dancing is thirsty business."

I look around for Kinsley as we go to the refreshments table, but she's nowhere to be seen. The woman working the punch bowl hands us both cups. A few kids pass by with their fathers. A number of them say hi to Isla. The shyer ones wave.

"Friends of yours?" I ask.

She shakes her head. "Connor and Malcolm aren't really my friends, but they're not mean to me. Same with Jess and Reese. But Lucy and Rachel are… not so nice to me all the time."

Ah. The little shits I was looking for.

I clock the two girls she's talking about. Both look sweet as angels as they cling to their fathers' arms. What I wouldn't give to walk over there right now and scare the bejeezus out of them so they won't even think about bullying my daughter ever again.

When I look back down at Isla, I notice she's staring at a girl who's sitting on the benches by herself. She's got stringy brown hair and she's wearing a dress that's too big for her in an unfortunate shade of bubble-gum pink.

"Is that another one of the not-so-nice ones?" I ask, hackles rising.

She shakes her head. "No. That's Molly. She's in my grade, but she's in a different class. I heard some of the kids being mean to her, too."

I frown, taking in her expression. "You look guilty, Isla."

"I… I should have stopped them," she says softly. "But I didn't. I just walked away because I was scared that if I said something—"

"They'd turn on you."

She nods. "But now, I wish I'd stood up for her."

"You know, there's a way you can correct that," I point out.

"How?"

"Go over to her now," I advise. "Say hi. Make friends."

Her eyes go wide. "Right now?"

"Why not?"

She looks over at the girl and then back at me uncertainly. "What if she doesn't want to talk to me?"

"You won't know until you try."

She shifts from one foot to the other. Automatically, her hand slips into mine. It's such a sweet, vulnerable gesture. I feel it in my chest, like she reached into my rib cage and squeezed my heart.

"Okay," she decides. "I'll try."

I give her an encouraging wink. She drains her punch and tiptoes up to the girl. Isla is awkward about the introduction, but the girl seems to appreciate the effort. Within seconds, they're talking. Soon after that, they're smiling.

"Hello there! Are you Isla's father?"

The woman from behind the punch bowl is the one who spoke. She's blonde, petite, with far too much makeup daubed around her eyes. I'm assuming she's one of the moms.

"I am."

"How wonderful to meet you. It's strange to think I've had Isla in my class for almost a whole semester now and never met you."

"You're her teacher?"

"Heather Roe," she says, offering me her hand.

My teeth clench automatically. *Heather fucking Roe.* I know that name.

"I'm glad you were able to make it tonight," she continues, oblivious to the storm clouds gathering behind my eyes.

"It took some convincing," I tell her. "Isla wasn't inclined to come tonight because of everything she goes through in school."

Her smile falters. "Well, on that front, you can be rest assured that I do everything I can to make sure Isla feels safe and comfortable."

"Is that right?"

"Of course. I take teaching very seriously."

The effect is lost when she giggles right after that statement, however. She leans in a little for effect, making sure I can see her cleavage under the spotlights.

"Would you like to dance?" she asks. "They've opened up the dance floor to everyone now."

I turn the full force of my gaze on her and make sure to deliver my words with excessive calm. "I'd rather not dance with the cowardly teacher who refuses to do her fucking job."

It takes a moment for the words to hit, but the moment they do, her eyes go wide with shock and her mouth falls open.

"Now," I add, "if you'll excuse me, I have to go find my other date for tonight."

As it turns out, I don't have to look too far, because Kinsley is standing a few feet behind me. By the expression on her face, I'm pretty sure she's heard my exchange with Ms. Roe.

"Dance, *sladkaya?*"

She doesn't even try to decline. She just takes my hand and we walk onto the dance floor together.

"That was…"

"Sexy as fuck," I suggest.

She smiles. "Okay, we can go with that. Where's Isla?"

"Over there," I say, spinning Kinsley in Isla's direction. "She made a new friend tonight."

"Oh, wow, that's… that's great. Did you have something to do with that?"

"A magician never reveals his secrets."

She laughs, and for the first time since I came careening back into her life, it doesn't sound so burdened. It sounds free.

"They're laughing now," she observes, peeking around my shoulder. "It looks like it's going well."

I spin Kinsley back around to face me again. "Stop stressing. She'll find her way." I take her hands and we start to revolve slowly as a soft song croons from the speakers.

"You're really good with her," she whispers.

"I seem to have a knack with the Whitlow women."

She blushes and hides her face for a moment. "So what did you think of Ms. Roe?" she asks once she's composed herself, in an obvious attempt to change the subject.

"Predictably annoying. Brown-noser. Too much makeup."

She raises her eyebrows, impressed. "I'd say you hit all the highlights pretty succinctly."

"I'm nothing if not straightforward."

"She was practically drooling when she saw you. Did she ask you to dance?"

"She did."

"And you told her to stick it where the sun don't shine?"

I smile. "Something like that."

Kinsley's eyes float over the crowd. "No wonder she's pouting in the corner now," she observes with a satisfied smile. She looks back up at me with bright eyes. Hopeful eyes. Open eyes.

And when I pull her closer against my body, she lets me.

41

KINSLEY

Who would have thought, when we met on that frigid river bank under that godforsaken bridge in the middle of nowhere, that ten years' time would find us in a school gym, slow-dancing to Michael Bublé and sneaking glances at our daughter, who's still sitting on the benches, laughing at something her new friend just said?

Daniil catches me staring. "Are you always this nervous?" he asks with amusement.

"When it comes to Isla, yes. One thousand percent."

"Give the girl more credit. She's smart. She'll get by."

"She didn't all this time. Until…" I sigh and meet his eyes. "Until you came into the picture."

Daniil's lips pull into a smirk. "How will you ever thank me?" he murmurs, pulling me closer to him.

I press a hand on his chest and laugh. "This is a family dance, you perv."

"We've got to give them something to stare at, don't we?"

I scoff as I look around, catching a dozen sneaky glances in the act of gawking. "They're already staring pretty hard, I'd say."

"It's your fault. Your dress's fault, to be more specific."

"Hardly," I say, trying to suppress the blush. "You're the one they're staring at, Mr. Bond."

He grins—a sexy, lopsided smirk that sends a bolt of excitement from my heart all the way down to where my thighs meet. "Your arch-nemesis is staring, too."

I roll my eyes. "Watching us dance is probably eating her up inside."

"Imagine how she'd suffer if I kissed you right now."

The knot in my throat suddenly feels huge. "A lot, probably," I say, hoping to sound casual about it. "But you'd never be that cruel."

He raises his eyebrows. "You clearly don't know me very well."

"Coulda fooled me. You're cruel?"

"I can be. When the situation demands it," he muses. "And in this case, I think the situation definitely demands it."

"Daniil…"

I don't even get as far as framing my thought before his lips brush against mine and my mind goes blank.

Holy hell.

As far as kisses go, it's a chaste one. The softest of brushes, slight pressure, and the hint of more lingering just out of reach. Then he pulls back, his eyes intensely bright under the cheap lights.

"Do you want a tour of the school?" I blurt out. "I could show you my classroom."

He nods. "Lead the way."

He drops his touch from my waist, but keeps hold of my hand as we glide through the gymnasium towards the exit. I steal a quick glance over my shoulder at Isla. But she's absorbed in conversation with her new friend. She doesn't even notice us leave.

"You think she'll be okay?" I ask anxiously as we step into the dark, silent hallway.

"Of course she will. She's half you and half me."

Eyes follow us out of the gym, but I realize suddenly I don't care. I'm not worrying and stressing about tonight. I've just crossed over into "I don't give a fuck" territory. And it feels absurdly freeing.

I lead him down the hall and take a right. My heartbeat picks up with every corner we turn, with every step of distance between the gym and us. The silence is pressing in on me from all sides, but in a good way, like being swaddled up tight in blankets on a cold night. I'm intensely aware of Daniil's presence next to me. His warmth, his smell.

"So," he says, his voice echoing down the empty hallways, "this is you in your element."

I laugh. "Something like that. It's a hellacious profession. But the heart wants what it wants, I guess."

"And your heart wanted to teach?"

"Sort of. Really, I wanted to be Louisa."

His brow wrinkles. "Who is that?"

"She's the whole reason I wanted to become a teacher in the first place," I explain. "Mrs. Louisa Horton, Crestmore's social studies teacher from when I was a kid. I loved her like—like in that way that only kids can love someone who shows them the best of themselves. 'Learn from history, lest ye be doomed to repeat it.' That's how she ended every class, in this goofy, baritone, dramatic voice that always made me laugh. She was always pretty dramatic, actually. She just loved what she did. It was infectious. And then..."

He's quiet and contemplative, waiting for me to pick up the thread of the story again.

"And then she was there for me after my mother's suicide. She was the only teacher who really understood. Or tried to understand, anyway."

Daniil's silent solemnity is comforting in the strange way. Maybe it's because people usually fall all over themselves to tell me how sorry they are about my mother. But it's always fake, because they don't actually care about comforting me—they just want me to think that they're good people.

But Daniil couldn't care less what I think of him. He knows precisely what he is, and he's offering me strength, not pity. That feels so much better than forced well wishes.

"Do you still keep in touch with her?" he rumbles.

I shake my head. "No. She died two years after my mother."

He nods. Again, he's not sympathetic or gushing. He just takes it quietly. I like that more and more.

"Breast cancer," I say. "She was in remission for a while, and we thought she'd beaten it, and then it came back stronger than ever. Even after she resigned from school, I used to go and visit her at home. Her husband was really nice. Toward the end, he barely let her walk anywhere. He carried her up and down their two flights of stairs."

I look at him out of the corner of my eyes. We're wandering aimlessly now, which is fine by me. I just want to be alone with him. Between the quiet and the dark and the solitude, it feels like I can finally say things I've been waiting a long time to say.

"Sometimes, it feels like life is so unfair. The bad get away with everything and the good live tragic lives and have tragic deaths. How is that right?"

"It's not right," Daniil agrees. "But the world doesn't care what we think of it."

We stop outside the biology lab. A draft of cool, soothing air flows out from beneath the door. I slip inside, Daniil behind me.

"I hated biology in school," I admit as I roam slowly between the tables. "I don't know exactly why. I guess it just felt so intrusive. Cutting open frogs and things. Shouldn't every living being be entitled to peace after death? Life is hard enough. Death shouldn't be harder."

He tilts his head to the side and considers that. "I liked biology. It taught me how vulnerable we all are. All it takes is one pinched artery, one severed nerve, and everything you knew comes to a screeching halt."

I shudder. "That's an extremely disturbing take on the subject. I guess I should've expected it from you."

He laughs softly. "My education was probably very different than yours."

"I never asked you how you ended up in a Bratva in the first place," I say. "Or anything about your past, really. What were your parents like?"

He's quiet for a long while, stroking his finger in swirling patterns through the dust gathered on the lab tables. "My mother was a broken woman," he says at last. "Sad and lost and lonely. My father was the one who made her that way."

"It sounds like you're describing my parents," I mutter bitterly.

Moonbeams slant in through the windows. The smudge of the double-paned glass gives everything a smoky, ethereal tone. Everything is soft and murky in a way that feels like a dream.

"They should never have had me," he says. Despite his words, his tone and his expression aren't harsh. He says it simply, a matter of fact rather than resentment.

I wince. "I'm sorry," I say, then hate myself for it. Daniil took my tragedies in stride, but he says one slightly sad thing about his own life and I'm immediately doing all the things I hated when other people did them to me.

He doesn't seem to notice, though. "Don't be sorry. It made me stronger."

"Guess that's another thing we have in common," I say. "Parents who weren't ready to take on the responsibility of a child."

He meanders toward me, keeping a lab table between us, which feels like a strange mercy he's doing for my benefit. The moonbeam falls across his face, casting half in shadow and half in light.

"You've done better than your parents did," he says softly. "You've done right by her."

I smile humorlessly. "It was a really low bar." I lift my eyes to him and I'm pretty sure he can see the tears swimming inside them. "I feel like I've failed her, Daniil. I've tried so hard and I... I just can't seem to get my head above water. Every day, it feels like she's slipping farther and farther away from me."

"You can't protect your kids from everything," he says.

"So why do I get the feeling you would have?"

"Kinsley, you—"

I don't let him finish the sentence. I round the corner of the table and jump right into his arms before I pull his lips to mine.

I might've taken him by surprise for a change, because it takes him a few seconds before his body relaxes against mine. He lets out a low growl when his hands slip under my ass. My legs feel like they've turned to jelly. The cool, close silence suddenly feels molten and alive as our breath mingles in the tiny sliver of space between our faces.

"Raise your hands," he commands as he sets me down on the closest table.

"Huh?"

"Raise. Your. Hands."

I'm in no position to argue when my brain feels like it's short-circuiting, so I do as he says. He rips the dress up over my head and tosses it aside in one smooth motion. I shiver at the onrush of cold air, but then his mouth is on my bare nipples and the gasp turns into a moan.

He plucks me off of the table, spins me around, and plants one huge hand between my shoulder blades. I fold easily in half, my cheek pressing against the countertop, as he tears my panties down around my ankles.

"You're beautiful like this, *sladkaya*," he murmurs. His bulk is pressing down on me from above. I'm swallowed up by him in every way possible. He strokes my hair away from my face as, between my legs, he rubs the tip of his cock against my dripping wet opening. "You're a fucking vision bathed in moonlight. Now, I want to hear you make sounds that are as beautiful as you are."

I bite my bottom lip and brace myself for the thing I've been waiting ten years to feel again. My eyes are scrunched closed and I'm ready for it, I'm waiting for it—

Then, instead of filling me, Daniil drops to one knee behind me and runs his tongue over my pussy.

"Oh God!" I gasp. I'd have buckled to the floor if his strong hands weren't supporting my thighs. My vision darkens at the edges as he laps away at me. When he adds two fingers, my breath catches in my chest.

I'm spluttering and thanking God he can't see my face right now, because I'm a mess. I'm a complete and utter mess. I can't breathe and I can't think and I can't move; all I can do is try to survive what he's doing to me.

"Fuck, you have a sweet little pussy," he growls.

Then I feel his tongue on my clit and I completely lose it. My body rolls with pleasure and I jerk backwards, right into his face.

I come like that, bent over a table while the man I thought I lost forever eats me out from behind.

Something clatters to the floor with the last of my writhing, but I couldn't care less what it is. I'm vaguely aware of Daniil pulling away. Standing up. Lining himself against me and then, "Oh fucking Christ," he slides all the way home.

It's deeper than anyone's ever been before. It feels like he's fucking my soul, and I didn't know until now just how badly I needed that.

Any tenderness from before vanishes quickly. The moonlight catches drops of my sweat staining the tabletop as he delves into me again and again.

His thrusts are hard, furious. His breathing comes in short, determined bursts. His fingers dig into my hips, spearing me on him viciously.

He collects my hair into a loose ponytail and pulls like reins as he increases the speed of his thrusts. It's only slightly painful, in the way that makes the pleasure so much more heightened by contrast.

I know I'm going to come again when his hand slides around my torso to palms my breasts. One light graze of my nipple and I explode once more.

This time, I do collapse. He grabs me and we tumble onto the tile floor together in a mess of sweaty limbs. My heart is hammering hard against my chest. So is his. And for a long time, it's the only thing I can hear.

It's good enough for me.

42

DANIIL

I'm lying on the floor with my hand hooked behind my head. Kinsley is resting beside me on her side, propped up on her elbow. She looks down at my chest as she traces patterns on my muscles.

"I like your tattoos. This one is a little violent, though," she observes, pressing her finger against the sword splitting a bull's head in half. "What did the poor bull do to you?"

"The bull was the symbol of the Semenov Bratva," I explain. "The sword is the symbol I chose for mine."

She's still naked, but she's pulled her dress over her body like a bedsheet. It's annoying the hell out of me, so I reach over and pluck it away. Why would anyone want to cover up that body? She's a work of art. I want to memorize every goddamn inch of her.

Kinsley shivers, but she lets me do it without protest. "Sometimes, Daniil, you scare the hell out of me."

I stroke her bare hip. Goosebumps erupt in the wake of my touch. "You don't have to be afraid of me, *sladkaya*. There's not many people I've said that to."

"You said something similar to me back then. When we met."

"See? It's a promise sealed over a decade."

"Is that what it is?" she asks. "A promise?"

"What's wrong with that?"

"Promises can be dangerous," she says with a shrug of one shoulder. "They're easy to make and easier to break."

I frown as her green eyes go hazy with memory. "Who told you that?" I ask, pulling her closer against my body.

"My mother," Kinsley admits. "Most everything else she ever told me is a blur, but I do remember that. She said it often."

"Was she referring to your father?"

"I assume. She never bothered to clarify, not even when I asked. She would just say something nutty and disappear on me. When I was younger, I truly expected her not to come back one day. I thought she'd disappear forever and we'd never see her again. But she always came back."

"Maybe she came back for you."

Kinsley frowns. "I doubt it. God knows I wish that were true. I… I loved her so much, Daniil. There were days when she seemed like the perfect mother. She'd laugh and dance around the kitchen while she baked cookies and made ice cream floats. We'd stay up late watching old movies, and build pillow forts in the living room…"

I think about the pillow fort I'd seen in Kinsley's living room. Maybe we really are doomed to repeat our own histories, like her teacher said. Maybe it's coded into our DNA. Maybe fighting against it just guarantees that everything will happen the way it was always meant to.

But this shit—her shit, my shit, our shit—won't repeat itself. I won't let it.

"Then she and my dad would start fighting and it would end in a punch or a kick or a fall. And she would go silent for days, weeks. She would leave the house and when she returned, she'd be her old self again. Or closer to her old self, at least."

"That must've been confusing."

"It wasn't confusing—it was enraging. But you know what's the craziest part?" she muses. "It wasn't him I was so angry at, even when he was the one doing the hurting. I was angry with my mother. I hated her."

"Why?"

"She never left," Kinsley says softly. "I mean, she had a child. Shouldn't she have left him? Shouldn't she have taken me and run?"

I trace circles around her back. "Some things are more frightening than pain, Kinsley."

"Like what?"

"Loneliness."

She considers that for a moment. Her eyes grow misty with memory and sadness. Then she turns to me and the haze clears. She gives me a small, tight smile that lacks all warmth. "You know, I think that's the whole reason I agreed to marry Tom in the first place. I was already alone. I guess I didn't want to have to face that for the rest of my life."

"You had Emma."

"Yes," she says softly, a lilt of self-disappointment in her tone. "But I was too young and too stupid to realize that friendship would be enough. I clung to the idea of true love. I clung to the idea of a man who would protect me. Even when all the evidence to the contrary was screaming in my face."

There's a strange restlessness stirring in my chest when she says that. The need to reassure her. To hold her close and convey exactly how fiercely I'm going to protect her.

"Do you believe in love?" she whispers into my neck, as her body sidles a little closer.

"I've never thought about it."

"Well, what about now?" I glance at her, wondering what she's expecting from me. She seems to realize how her question has landed and hastens to rephrase. "I—I don't mean—I'm not asking about you and me. I was just… curious." When I still don't say anything, she looks away, cheeks burning. "Probably not, right? A man like you probably doesn't believe in love at all."

"What is 'a man like me'?"

She shrugs. "Someone whose life revolves around power and violence and control. Love is the one currency that isn't transactional. It's completely sincere and completely selfless."

"Sounds like I should count you as a believer then."

Kinsley gives me an embarrassed little chuckle. "I'm afraid so. Maybe I'm still the same naïve girl you pulled out of that river." She sighs and places her head on my chest. "Can I ask you a question?"

"You can ask me anything. I can't always promise an answer."

She rolls her eyes at my crypticness, but charges forward anyway. "The day we met, what was your plan?"

I sigh and think back, though I don't have to think hard—that day has been seared somewhere permanent in my brain. "I didn't really have one. I was winging it. I needed to get to the pick-up spot that Petro had arranged. But since the cops were on high alert, I needed to lie low for a while. My only other option was—"

"An alibi."

I nod.

"So I was just in the wrong place at the wrong time."

I shrug and stroke a fallen lock of hair out of her face. "I prefer to think you were in the right place at the right time."

Kinsley purses her lips as she thinks about that. "One more question," she says after a while of just breathing and thinking. "The next morning… did you even consider saying goodbye?"

I don't have to think hard about that one, either. "I don't do goodbyes."

She nods again, sort of curtly and professionally, like it still stings but she was expecting it this time. "I never said goodbye to my father. Before I left, I mean."

I raise my eyebrows. "Your father's still alive?" I ask. "I assumed he died."

"No, Dad's still tottering along. Living in the same house, working at the same job. He's semi-retired now."

"You keep tabs on him."

"I don't know why I do," she admits. "I guess a part of me still feels guilty for leaving the way I did."

"He didn't feel bad about beating the shit out of your mother while you watched," I point out. "Why should you feel bad about leaving him without a second glance?"

"I know. Which is why, every time I feel guilty about leaving, I end up feeling guilty about feeling guilty. Does that make sense?"

"No. But I get it."

She smiles. Then, slowly, the smile slips off her face. "In a way, leaving like that was my only way of letting him know how deeply I hated what he did to her," she says. "I didn't have the guts to fight him like I wanted to. I could have…" She meets my eyes, desperate for absolution that I cannot give her. "I just felt so helpless in that house. Sometimes, I still get that feeling. Mostly with Isla."

"Isla will make her own happiness. She just doesn't know it yet."

Kinsley's eyes flash fiercely. "I'm her mother. I should be able to keep my own daughter happy. I wanted to do so much better than my parents. I didn't want to repeat old mistakes."

"You won't."

"How do you know?"

"Because you're so worried about it." I prop myself up on my elbow and gaze down at her. "I'm speaking from experience, Kinsley. I have my own demons. Some I've slayed and some I've yet to."

I should tell her more. Hell, a part of me wants to tell her, if only out of some bizarre sense of fairness. She's given me her whole life story in a nutshell, and I've given her crumbs in return.

She leans in and kisses the side of my neck, still gloriously naked and growing more and more comfortable with that fact.

"If you don't want to tell—"

RIIIING!

Kinsley jerks away with a gasp. "My phone!" she exclaims. "Shit, my phone…"

"In your bag," I say, pointing to the discarded purse just underneath her dress.

She grabs at it and pulls out the ringing phone. "Hello?" she says breathlessly. "Yes? What do you mean…? No, she's not with us… No… I'll be right there."

She hangs up, her eyes stricken with panic.

And just like that, my heart cracks in two.

"Isla's gone," she whispers. "Her friend… the girl she was with… they're saying… they're saying—" She breaks down in a panicked sob.

I grab hold of her. "Breathe. We'll find her. Put on your clothes and we'll go get our daughter."

She gets shakily to her feet, but I'm the one who has to put her dress back on. She's in no position to do anything but shake.

"Come on," I say when she's clothed, grabbing her hand and pulling her out of the laboratory.

We run through the hallways, back to the gymnasium on the other side of the building. Kinsley doesn't say a word, but I can feel her fear. It's pounding like a drumbeat in my head, drowning out every other thought.

This could be a simple misunderstanding.

Or it could be the one demon that's escaped my bullet.

We burst into the gymnasium, but the scene has changed significantly. Most of the volunteers and the staff are congregated in the left side of the space, their expressions grave. Kinsley shakes off my hand and flies towards an older man in the center of the throng.

"Colin!" Kinsley cries out. "Isla… where is she?"

That's when I notice the girl Isla had been talking to when Kinsley and I left the gymnasium. While Kinsley talks to the principal, I walk over to the little girl, who's sobbing silently into her palms. Her somber-faced parents are sitting on either side of her, trying their best to comfort their daughter.

I crouch down on one knee. "I'm Isla's dad. What's your name?"

"M-M-Molly," she stammers tearfully.

"She's in no fit state to explain this again," Molly's mother says adamantly.

I look right at the woman. "I just need to hear Molly's account of what happened. It'll take only a minute."

The parents exchange a glance, and then the mother nods. "Molly, sweetheart, will you tell Isla's dad what happened?"

"I don't really know," Molly sobs. "We went to the bathroom together. I heard Isla leave her stall and start to wash her hands. And then… I heard her scream."

I wince and close my eyes. I already know where this story is going. History repeating itself. The echo of a pain I've felt before, twelve long years ago.

Molly shudders and continues. "I heard a door slam and then… I was scared. So I didn't come out of my stall for a long time. When I came out, Isla was gone."

I rise to my feet, fists trembling with pent-up emotion. "Thank you, Molly," I growl. Then I turn and stride away.

As I go, I pull my phone out of my pocket. My fingers find what I'm looking for instinctively, automatically, though it's been a long, long time since I called this number. A part of me always knew I would need it one day.

Ring. Ring. Ring. Ring.

"Come on," I growl at the phone. "Pick up, motherfucker."

"Daniil, who are you calling?" Kinsley asks from behind me. I ignore her.

Ring. Ring… Click.

"Daniil."

"Do you have her, you bastard?" I growl as soon as I hear his rattled breathing.

Gregor Semenov just chuckles. "Mistakes were made, son. Mostly by you."

Then the line goes dead.

TO BE CONTINUED

Daniil and Kinsley's story continues in Book 2 of the Vlasov Bratva duet, Arrogant Mistake. Click here to keep reading!